"I had a heck of a time putting it dow[...] getting blurry."

—*Flint (MI) Journal*

"Spun like poetry . . . the masterful writing of this book stands as a symbol, a testimony, to that most precious of relationships. It is a treasure, . . . one no self-respecting sporting library should be without."

—*American Hunter*

"It is destined to become one of the classics of modern literature."

—*GoUpstate.com*

"Every bird dog owner loves a good dog story, or at least they should. . . . This fast reading tome put me immediately in mind of many of the themes found in Norm McClean's *A River Runs Through It.*"

—*TheCheckcord.com*

"One of the top twenty-five dog books of the last quarter century."

—*The American Field*

"Gaddis stands up and looks both life and death straight in the face. An excellent story and excellent literature, a must-read."

—*Field Trial Magazine*

"This is a heartwarming story that will have you laughing and crying . . . A story of strength, character and bonds among friends, human and canine. I highly recommend this book to everyone."

—*The Boykin Spaniel Society Newsletter*

"The only problem with this book is one encountered before, the inability to put it down for a moment before reaching the satisfying conclusion."

—*The Discriminating Shooter*

"A commendable story, one that may even make you look forward to growing old."

—*All Things Quail*

"A wonderful novel and moving tale . . . a Signature Series Selection."

—*Sporting Tales*

"A dog able to touch the hearts of those around her. But JENNY WILLOW is not just a 'dog story.'"

—*Asheboro Courier Tribune*

MIKE GADDIS

JENNY
WILLOW

A NOVEL

THE LYONS PRESS

GUILFORD, CT

AN IMPRINT OF THE GLOBE PEQUOT PRESS

The Lyons Press is an imprint of The Globe Pequot Press

10 9 8 7 6 5 4 3 2 1

Printed in the United States of America

Frontispiece *Steadying the Pup* by Bob Abbett

ISBN 1-59228-492-2

Library of Congress Cataloging-in-Publication Data is available on file.

· 1 ·

BB en Willow stood at the window, gazing absently across rolling green
pastures to the mountain.

"I ought to let it go, Libby," he declared.

There was no answer. The room was empty save the murmur of a
clock.

"It shouldn't be," he vowed to the silence.

The soft yellow arms of the new sun were gently lifting the veil of mist
from the hillsides. Along the lower slopes, poplar and maple were beginning to color. In the orchard on the toe of McCathern's Knob, he could
make out faint clots of red where clustered apples burdened the limbs of
the gnarled old trees. The grouse would find them soon. Once the frosts
mellowed the fruit on the stems, they would come.

He made his way to the kitchen, poured a cup of coffee from the per-
colator, and stepped onto the back porch. The air was bracing. Crows
were about.

"It isn't morbid," he argued to himself. "Just honest."

He found the rocking chair, studied the play of morning light on the
banister, considered the feeble shadows.

They had been the breath and being of him, his dogs. They drove his sun and set his moon. From their fire and tenacity came his grit for living, from their heart and fearlessness would come his courage for dying.

But it was just too late. He was far less than a young man anymore, and he simply shouldn't.

There was a stumble to his step now, a poverty about his frame. There was a flutter in his speech, and a sag to his jowls. Furrows creased the wrinkled slopes of his cheeks, and the skin purled flaccidly about the hollow at his throat. Within the pale stubble of his whiskers only the slightest working of color persisted.

"Where has it all gone, Libby?" he asked emptily.

He looked at the spindly legs diminished by the baggy folds of his pants. How many good years were left in those pitiful old stilts anyhow? Five? Ten *maybe?*

Legs were always first to go. He had weathered seven generations of setters. Whelp to wilt, it was always the same. If they lived to old age, it wasn't the gray on their muzzle that brought them to doom, nor the droop of their shoulders. It was the creeping, evil waste of their hindquarters. It refused to be reversed or tempered after a point, withering the knotted muscles flat and gaunt, until ultimately they were useless.

It was at work already in his own haunches. He could see it and he could feel it.

He knew he should not allow himself to pursue the matter further.

Time had inverted the hourglass. Ever before, it had run against the dogs, the keenest injustice conceivable, that each must be taken from him within his own lifetime. That upon each occasion he must place an essential part of himself in a hole in the ground, bury it forever under a cold hump of earth, and be expected to go on living with what was left. He knew the abysmal pain in that, sixteen times over.

But bitter as it was, at least he had been there to care for them, to see them away, to ease the passing, to whisper over their graves. There was comfort in that. Now the glass ran against him, and the hours were low.

And now it was unlikely that he would last the dozen or so years that measure a canine life span, and even if he should, the probability of remaining sound was slight. The thought of infirmity was more disconcerting than death. And in either case, who would there be to *truly* care, to caress away the loneliness from a silky forehead, to salve the hurt in bewildered hazel eyes? There was no one left. Libby had been gone six years now. No day could ever again be complete without her. He had wanted to live one day beyond Libby, one day and one only.

His brother Asa and his sister Geneva, both taken before their time. His daughter Andrea was in Germany with Steve. Andrea had been in for a week recently, all the harder, for he still suffered the depression of her parting. Cancer had taken Clayson, after all the years and all the seasons. Sixty years they hunted and fished these mountains . . . since they were sixth-graders and both sweet on Barbara Mason. Bill Waiman was on his back with pneumonia — likely where he would stay — failing painfully. All gone, but him.

The honor and loyalty of a dog had no equivalent with humankind. It was the difference between diamonds and cut glass. Hard and long ago he had learned that, and its value. There could be only one acceptable exchange. When you accepted the trust in canine eyes, it must be for their lifetime. Anything less was a betrayal. A betrayal he could not abide. Particularly with a dog bred for the gun.

Grab up a vest and a gun on a mellow November afternoon when birds are about. Ply the tawny fields, walk the fragrant bottoms, climb the painted hills. Give these things to a gun dog even once, and to take them from him is to destroy the first of his two reasons for living. Desert him also, and you have destroyed the last.

He could not take the chance. The promise might not keep.

Anyway, he felt a little guilty even thinking about it. Tony had been gone scarcely two winters now. Fifteen years Tony had shared his life, and the hurt was deep. Time only scabbed the surface; the wound was on his soul. Their line had reached its highest expression with Tony.

"That's your dog, Ben," Libby had said insightfully, from almost the moment he was whelped, "that's the one you've been looking for these forty years."

Tony had won seventeen times against the best in open and amateur cover dog trials, the greatest dog ever to carry the Willow Crest banner. The line had culminated with Tony. It had taken seven generations of meticulous breeding.

When Tony died, he had told himself that it was finished. The line had lapsed apurpose and he should leave it lay. There would be no other Tony, as there had been no other Bess, nor Cindy, nor Pat.

Yet each, in turn, had earned its place. Regardless of how impossible it may seem at times, you find there is more than one door to your heart.

Was that still true, even now? Was there enough of him left to give?

A hawk soared high above the meadow, screaming its supremacy to the breeze. In its cry was both defiance and loneliness. The shadow of its flight traversed the yard and evaporated among the trees. He retraced it in his mind, toying with the inference.

Libby hadn't left much room for another woman. But the nights were still long. And the first frost of autumn still turned his eyes toward the hills.

He could just give it up. Just quit. But his dogs never had . . . not once. Or he could just barter the time away arguing himself to his deathbed and choking on regret. Either way he wouldn't escape it.

Ben Willow hungered for one last dog.

There were things, Ben Willow supposed, that were more pressing. His eyes had found the east fence line and the rickety stand of posts that stretched away toward its corner. Half were rotted at the ground. Worse, the corner itself was spent. It was a chore past its due. The ramshackle brace he had slapped on to shore it up was an eyesore. Those same two brown-speckled heifers had busted out twice in three weeks, and the last time that confound Charolois bull got hed up and took out with them. It had taken a full day, half a night, and Walter Smothers's quarter horse to corral them again. Forkin' a horse these days was more production than he had props for. The fence needed a proper fixing. Even the neighbors were ragging him. It was time to be about it.

Clyde Wood was behind the counter at Southern States, humped over the computer and glaring at the monitor screen like it had spit on him. He cocked one eye over the rim of his glasses and registered recognition, then held up a finger to Ben. Tapping the keyboard a few more times like a lazy rain pecks at a puddle, he squinted hard, shrugged, and relinquished.

"What say, Ben," he piped.

"Ain't. Might come back at me."

"Uhh-hmn," the store manager acknowledged with a gratuitous chuckle.

"You got cause with that thing?" Ben asked, pointing at the monitor.

• "Hell, Ben, ain't no livin' with 'em. If you go to put sumpum in it, it tells you can't, and if you fine'ly get it to swallow it, it gets tangled up in its innards and you can't get it back! But there ain't no being without 'em either. Buckeye's agrowin', Ben."

"Yeah, I reckon. Where's Christine? She's the better part of this operation anyway."

"Sick!" Clyde vexed. "Oughta know better than to leave me here unarmed."

Pleasantries fashioned, the air clear for business, Wood peered over his glasses again. "Whatcha got," he asked.

"Twenty-six four-inch, eight-foot posts and five four-by-fours, treated . . . five pounds of staples . . . and five bags of Sakrete . . . and some bootlaces."

"Gonna fine'ly fix that east fence, huh?" Clyde punched the keypad and frowned at the screen again.

Ben looked at him hard. "Not you too."

"Oh, no, not me. Nettie. Ev'r time we're by there on the way to church Sundays, she locks an evil eye on me and says, 'When's Ben Willow gonna fix that fence?' Like I had sumpum to do with it."

Ben smiled. "You could if you'd come out 'bout six-thirty tomorrow mornin'."

"Busy, Ben, bizzeee."

Grinning, Ben started for the door. Clyde was a good friend. Milton Wood, his father, had been one of the first people Lindsey and Sarah Willow had met when years before they and their get had arrived in West Virginia, and easily the most colorful. When Clyde came along, he hadn't fallen far from the tree. Some years later Ben had needed a blade for a harrow. By then, Clyde Wood was already a fixture at the farm store, as much a part of the inventory as the washtubs, horse feed, chicken wire, and other paraphernalia stacked around its walls. Earthy as a mule in new ground, Clyde, from the beginning. The two had struck an easy acquaintance, despite the twenty years that separated them; in time it had minted into a deepening friendship.

Used to skip Sunday preaching regularly, an age ago, he and Clyde, when the hills were mint green with the first breath of spring and the trout needed tending.

"The Lord ain't there today, Ben," Clyde would say, as they slipped past the church on their way out of town. "I 'spect we'll find 'im up yonder in them hills, where any God-fearin' man oughta be."

Now they skipped whatever else was in the way, like farm stores and east fences. Clyde was no May banty anymore himself.

There was a thing else. You could go the river with Clyde Wood. He'd be there.

In the summer of '63, there had been an outbreak of scarlet fever on the Whitmeadow. Cameron Whitlaw, his wife, Jessie, the baby, and three of their five young ones were taken ill. Those were poor folk out there, with little more than a jar of beans and a pot to pee in. A man down meant a family out. Cam was on his back for five weeks.

Jessie's grandmother, Ila Johnson Bishop, had been a friend to Verdie Wood once, in an impromptu moment when badly she needed one. On a Whitmeadow back road at midnight, Verdie Wood had been alone with an ailing Model A and a three-month-old boy. There were three men. They were not there to help. Ila Bishop had arrived almost angelically out of nowhere, with the fires of Jehovah in her eyes, and stood them down. Sent them packing.

Clyde had never forgotten the story, nor the tremor in his mother's voice as she related it. Clyde Wood had shunned the quarantine and all concerns of personal welfare, and for two months in the small hours of every morning had carried get-by provisions to Jessie, Cam, and a lot of other folks down and out on the Ladder Run when nobody else would. They had never forgotten him for it. Neither had the town.

"Say, Ben," Wood called suddenly. "I almost forgot . . . did you know Pete Rush?"

"Uhnnt-uh, not that I'm aware."

"Was a grouse hunter, I hear. Thought you mighta run into 'im."

"Nope."

"Well, you grouse hunters tend to favor your own comp'ny," Clyde ventured. "He moved here from Taber City no more'n five years ago. Probably why. Has a sister out on the McAlister Road.

"Anyways, she was in here the other day an' told me he died 'bout two months ago. Aneurysm or somethin'. Said about five months before that he'd gotten another setter pup. The pup's still in a lot in her backyard and she don't know what they're goin' to do with it. None of her folks hunt and says she just ain't got time for a dog.

"She was askin' me if I knew a body that might be interested. Way she talked I think she would give the pup to the right fellow for the trouble. Thought I'd mention it. You're out of dogs, ain'tchee?"

"Yeah. Probably ought to stay that way," Ben replied. He could feel the slight stir of excitement in his chest. "She mention the breeding?"

"She didn't know. Thought she 'membered some registration papers."

"No matter," Ben said, pushing open the door. "Thanks, Clyde."

"Come see us, Ben," Wood offered.

"Same," Ben Willow returned vacantly, already lost in thought.

Reaching the truck, he climbed behind the wheel, stuck the key in the ignition, and settled against the seat.

He would never understand it, how things came to be. Your mind settles in on something supposed and suddenly, in a rush without a reason, life lays it square in your lap for real and dares you to wonder why. When you do, there's only one answer. And only a fool ignores it.

But here was the very situation he feared. Betrayed, bewildered, and alone in a strange and uncaring world was a gun dog robbed of its birthright. He didn't know anything about Pete Rush, but if he was a grouse hunter he certainly hadn't intended it that way. Intended or not, it had happened. Fate was saying he should take a hand. If he did, it could easily happen again. Pure chance was one thing. Defying it was something worse. A dog could not know the difference between intention and happenstance. All it could know was abandonment, and abandonment felt a lot like betrayal. A single betrayal by someone to whom you entrust your heart is enough to upend your world; a second is more than even canine faith can absorb. Was Somebody taking that into account?

Besides, if he was going to give in, he'd rather start with a sixth-week pup. Nothing was sweeter on God's earth than puppy breath, and no bond stronger than the one built from first love. No use being hampered by a kennel-shy foundling or someone else's ghost.

He fought it for a time, knowing all the while it would win. The limits of his concentration ran little more than the rope of his dilemma. Three weeks later and three fence posts in the ground, it was all that he had thought of night and day. He had wandered the hills restlessly with the sun, reviving favorite hunts with each of his setters, searching for the precise spot of a point, a flush, a fall, and a retrieve, trying to remember to the moment, to the feather, to an emotion, how it had felt, begging an answer. It had always been his idea of Heaven, going back and being able to relive one day of choice with each of his shooting dogs, the single most exquisite hunt of their days together. Someday he would do that, he hoped.

Several times he caught the booming rise of birds, and twice caught the shadowy wisp of their departure. He wondered if they were of the past or the present. He had sat with the moon through the small honest hours of false dawn, asked of it the essence of devotion and mortality, and where each must find its limit. And each night the answer was the same. The only end to love is death, and to forfeit love is less than living. He was a man without a matter. He was a clock short a mainspring.

You can deny your heart only so long. It was early on an October Saturday when Ben Willow sought out Susan Rush Devron. The tires hummed along the pavement of U.S. 219 as happily as the tune droned along in his throat. From a cloudless West Virginia sky a dazzling sun had climbed just above the Monongahela foothills, lighting the goldenrod and lady's thumb across half a mile of lush and billowing meadow, skipping along the meandering ribbon of the Greenbrier River on sparkling footsteps, and setting the vast headlands afire with vermilion, orange, and gold. He had finally come to terms with himself. It was eight-thirty in the morning and the eighty-third year of his life. It was a fine fall morning, and it would have been Libby's seventy-ninth birthday. Somewhere on the mountain a grouse was drumming from the sheer exhilaration of it all. And somewhere just a few miles ahead maybe there was still a foundling puppy that was willing to believe again. If the good Lord would permit, he wanted to live a while longer.

The Old McAlister Road left 219 at Spencer's Flat, snaked two miles down the grade of Little Mountain, funneled through the one-lane bridge at Rose Creek, and opened into the Tenyion Valley. Cattle dotted the roadside pastures, tranquilly grazing the floor of the valley and speckling the lower slopes. Beneath towering breastworks of fall color, scattered farmhouses nestled affably against the flanks of the shouldering hills, huddling a brood of barns and outbuildings at their skirts like hens mothering biddies. Here and there children played, housewives hung laundry, and tendrils of blue smoke climbed from smoldering leaf piles. Deeres and Fergusons wormed their way along the paths between the fencerows, drawing wagons laden with firewood or shuttling bales of rolled hay. Here and there a buzzard drifted lazily overhead. Another country Saturday.

Ben Willow was in no hurry. The closer he got, the quicker his heart pounded, the slower he drove. He glanced at the odometer; only three-tenths of a mile now. Why he should be nervous he was uncertain, but he was. It was that inane tingle you got when you were about to do something dubious, wondering all the while if you really should, knowing full well you were going to and excited to your toes at the prospects.

He was there before he was ready to be. On the left, an unmarked mailbox stood atop a leaning cedar post grown over with a morning glory vine. A few small flowers dallied, their dainty purple trumpets still fully opened and glistening with dew. To the right an open farm gate announced a dirt path that wandered away between a ragged lane of oaks to a white house on the hillside. At its entrance rested the old horse-drawn hay rake that was his landmark, crusted with a patina of age and rust, and bearing a small lettered sign: DEVRON, RT. 3. His heart thumped his throat at the sight of it. Braking and slowing, he started to turn, then let the truck roll by. A mile later, when he circled Ammon's Bros. store and started back, he was still chiding himself for being so absurdly timid. At eighty-three, what in the hell was left for a man to be scared of? He thought about that for a moment and quickly dropped it.

He forced himself onto the path this time, past the hay rake and the farm gate, and eased slowly up the hill to the house. Set amid a magnificent grove of white oaks, it was a large, two-story clapboard on frame over a native rock foundation, country plain and neat with a respectable coat of whitewash. He stopped at the front walk and studied it more closely. Scattered along the eaves of the porch that rambled around three sides were hanging baskets of ferns and strawflowers; to a corner trellis behind a last flush of bloodred blooms clung a summer rose. Beyond the porch rail, a pair of gingham-cushioned rockers and a deacon's bench invited a modest setting of company. A row of white beehives stood at the fringes of the side yard.

Apparently, someone was home. There was a red Nissan Pathfinder under the tractor shed.

Cutting the truck engine, he searched immediately and diligently about the surrounding outbuildings for a dog lot, but did not see one, nor did he hear a dog barking. He wondered if he was too late.

He had known Vance Devron only casually, from his association with the bank, but had never met his wife. Vance was a shade shy of haughty, tolerably decent, but always a little too sold on himself. If his widow was anything similar, this was going to be a bit stiff. Whatever, he would manage. Only the setter mattered.

Acorns popped underfoot as he picked his way to the front steps. The yard was littered with them, green yet. It would be a good year for mast, and squirrels, and deer. He gained the steps, mustered himself onto the porch, and took the final three steps to the threshold. Gathering himself, he opened the screen and tapped politely on the door. A moment later there was a rustle of motion inside, and then a faint creaking of floorboards beneath a cadence of muffled footsteps. The door jarred, caught for an instant, then swung partially open. A middle-aged woman stood there, inquisitively confident. On the borderline of pretty, she was tall and slender, in a flannel shirt and jeans, a scarf at her neck. Her features were soft, her eyes large, wet, and bright. She took him a little off guard, particularly in the flannel shirt. Libby had loved flannel shirts.

"Ms. Devron?" he inquired courteously.

"Yes." Her voice was light and pleasant.

"I'm Ben Willow, from over Travis Mountain way. Clyde Wood at Southern States said you were in there about a month ago and mentioned a setter pup. I'm wondering if you still have it?"

"Yes," she replied tentatively, "she was my brother's. He died three months ago."

"He was a grouse hunter, I understand."

"Oh, yes. He loved it. He was like the wind on the mountain fall and winter, blowing hither to yon through the woods. Him and his dogs. About the only time we saw him was Thanksgiving and Christmas. Do you grouse hunt?"

"Well, I've been known to," Ben said, smiling awkwardly, a little ill at ease. Susan Devron was more than he had expected. "I'm always careful who I mention it to. Some folks consider it an affliction," he followed.

Susan Devron chuckled cordially. She was working on her own assessment, beginning to warm to this man and his gentle manner. There was a genuineness about him. She pushed open the screen and stepped onto the porch. Ben politely retreated two steps.

"Pete, that was my brother's name, moved here from Vermont a few years back. He fell in love with the Alleghenies, and particularly the long bird season, but I don't think he ever got over being homesick," she explained.

"That's the way of it," Ben observed.

"Are you native West Virginian?" she asked.

"Might as well be . . . but no, Missouri originally," he answered. "That was long ago."

She had her brown hair, he noticed, pulled back into a ponytail. She looked younger than her years. There was life and living in her eyes.

The conversation stalled for a moment. They glanced away across the yard to the valley below. It was vibrantly green now, brightly lit with sunshine. A breeze stirred past, coaxing a fragile melody from the wind chimes. On the road, a truck pulled slowly by, trailed by a wispy spume of dust. Susan Devron threw up her hand and waved.

"The puppy . . . you have an interest, I take it?" she asked, turning to him.

"Yes, I think so," Ben offered, "dogs have meant much to me. Clyde said you might consider placing her with someone."

"And the nature of your interest," she inquired.

"The pleasure of her company, really," he said honestly, "if the feeling is mutual. A hunting companion, someone to share an occasional word."

"There have been others, Mr. Willow," she disclosed. "For one reason and another I have not been inclined to let her go."

He had guessed as much.

"I do need to find a home for her, but I want it to be the right one. I owe my brother that much. And to tell the truth, I've become a bit attached to her myself. But I don't hunt and I'm hard pressed to find the time she deserves."

"Yes, ma'am."

She smiled openly, at the "ma'am" it seemed. "My apologies, Mr. Willow, I didn't mean to lecture."

"You weren't," he assured, his admiration rising. Susan Devron was definitely more than he had expected. She was reminding him of how a man felt in the company of an engaging woman, and of how much he missed Libby.

"Do you have other dogs?" Susan Devron asked.

"No . . . no more," he replied. "I lost the last one two years ago."

She could read the trace of emotion that traveled his eyes, the significance in the word *last*. There was little need to ask more.

"She's out back," she said. "I'll show you."

He followed her off the porch and through the oaks to the barn. She walked upwind and once he caught the sweet smell of her, mingled with the fresh breath of morning. The memory was ageless. From the throat of the barn drifted the nurturing scent of the stables, the warm, musky spoor of horses, orchard grass, and hay. On the wind that blew from the mountains came the replenishing redolence of another autumn. Ben Willow was thankful to be alive.

A shed roof traversed the off side of the barn. It sheltered an old mule wagon, assorted farm implements, a winter's worth of alfalfa hay, and, at its southwest corner, four small dog runs. They were situated to gather the warmth and light of the afternoon sun, and were now forlornly in shadow. All were empty, save one. In it, he could see the diminutive white form of a solitary English setter, sitting quietly, facing them. Within his chest anxiety welled, the excitement of momentary reality, and close upon it a rush of empathy. The sadness of the scene was inescapable.

"Jenny . . . *Jenny.*" At Susan Devron's soft beckoning, the little setter made her way meekly to the gate, reared up on the wire, and thrust her muzzle into the woman's hand. Her tail beat gladly, but unenthusiastically. She was happy to see someone, he could tell, but it was happiness short of expectation, exuberance wrung dry of hope.

She was a slight little thing, scarcely more than thirty-five pounds, but deep of chest and clean and lithe of limb. Tricolor, she was modestly ticked and classically marked, with a full black mask washing into rich tan along her cheeks and muzzle and an oval patch loosely riding on one hip. She seemed to pay him little mind. He offered her the tips of his fingers. She sniffed them for a time, then licked them. He spoke to her and she looked into his face. Her eyes were soft, level, and engaging, pleasantly absent of timidity. He wondered if the fires still burned beneath them.

"She's about ten months now?" he asked.

"Yes, that's about right. She was an eight-week pup when Pete brought her home. That was in March."

"Do you know if he had her out any . . . to the woods, I mean?"

"Maybe a little before he died. I'm really not sure; I know he was looking forward to fall."

"Well, it wasn't likely," Ben said, "it was comin' summer and she was young."

The pup had backed away, watching them intently, listening to their voices.

"I brought her here the morning after Pete died," Susan Devron explained. "I'm afraid I've done little more than visit her once a day, to feed, water, and clean."

"I brought a check cord," Ben said, "do you mind if I get her out a minute?"

"No, please. She'll probably be ecstatic. I've been afraid to, for fear she might get loose and run off."

He eased open the gate and stepped into the run. The small setter retreated two steps, shrank slightly into herself, and studied him. "Jenny?" He spoke her name once, then again, asking acceptance. "It's all right, girl," he assured her softly, "nothin' bad from me."

There was a tentative acknowledgment at the extreme of her tail. He eased within arm's length and lowered himself to one knee. She stood without cowering, neither advancing nor retiring. Ben gently extended the back of his hand to her muzzle. She examined it by nose for a time, warily cutting her eyes the while, then accepted his hand behind an ear. He teased the silky hair there as a man toys with the soft curls at the nape of a woman's neck, traced the curve of her shoulders in soft, soothing strokes, and, scarcely touching the loft of her coat, caressed her back and flanks. He could see her eyes soften, feel her slender body submit. He spoke her name once more, in a whisper. Of sentiment and supplication, he had learned long before. A man asked the affection of a dog in the same tender manner he sought the love of a woman.

It did not escape Susan Devron, as it could not any woman.

He slipped the check cord from his jacket, lifted it to her nose, and snapped it to her collar. Struggling momentarily with his cramped old muscles, he urged himself to his feet beside her. Playing the rope out, he walked to the gate, pushed it open, and stepped aside.

"How 'bout it, girl?" he invited.

The puppy stood quizzically for a moment, registering the invitation, but uncertain of its sincerity. Ben returned to her, reassured her, and nudged her with the cord. She took three questioning steps toward the open gate and faltered, then gathered herself and bounded outside.

He was ready and still he was almost jerked from his feet as she hit the end of the cord. As suddenly, she was on her toes and her tail was dancing and her eyes were ablaze. She whirled and fought the rope, pleading against its restraint. He followed her in a series of stuttering sprints, as each time the rope slackened she jumped ahead, reached its limit, and stood trembling with excitement. A grasshopper took wing and then another, and she lunged hard after each in succession, testing his elbows. Then she was hunting them, flash pointing, rooting them out, dragging him along at each new flush. Flushed as well by the thrill of it, exuberant as the puppy he followed, Ben Willow was back in his element.

He stopped her, knelt again, and called her name. She turned reluctantly from the end of the rope, then ran to him. Placing her front paws on his leg, she thrust a wet, happy tongue in his face, while elation skipped through her eyes like sunlight on dancing water.

"Life ain't so terrible, huh," he said to her. She was only there for a moment, and then off again to rope's end. But in that moment the bond between them was spoken, and nothing short of mortal eternity would break it. Within that moment, he had felt her honesty running to the very soul of him, and the immense weight of his promise.

Ben Willow gathered in the frenzied pup and managed his way back to Susan Devron.

"I've just made a promise to this pup, Ms. Devron," he said, "that I'd like very much to keep. I'd like to take her with me. I'll try to do by her what your brother would have done."

Susan Devron fought the tears welling in her eyes, and lost the words, but she nodded. They looked at each other for a fleeting moment longer, Ben Willow and Susan Devron, for they would never meet again. Between them a zephyr of mutual admiration passed, and a trace of something more, then vanished again to another time, another place.

Fifteen minutes later, the truck hummed happily back along 219, and there was the same tune in Ben Willow's throat once more. Beside him was a small tricolored setter, pressed firmly into the hollow between the seat and his leg, uncertain still, but a little less lonely.

"One more time, Libby," he vowed, "just one more time."

He drove half a mile more, whimsical with afterthought.

"Knew all along, didn't you?

"Well, tell 'em to hold the angels for a while. I ain't quite ready."

Come Tuesday week, enroute from the mailbox, Ben Willow was arrested by the back porch rocker again. So it had been every day for the past nine. It was always friendly company, the old, weather-beaten rocker, compelling now that Jenny had come into his life. From it, he had an open view of the kennel, and an opportunity to adore her at length. It was right, after all, a dog about again, slowly opening another door to his heart, creeping past his defenses. Interred in his conscience, the ghost of apprehension still wandered. But less restlessly now. For once more he was taken with life and love and living. For the first time in six years, he could stanch the melancholy.

A cow bawled urgently, several times in succession. He gazed across the pasture and located her, a white-faced Hereford, satisfying himself that nothing beyond the ordinary was amiss. The rest of his little mixed herd was peacefully feeding. Presently, the Hereford quit her complaining and joined them. He considered her a few seconds longer. She seemed satisfied.

It troubled him when any one of his cows was in distress. He admired his cows. They were a barometer of well-being. When all was right with them, the world was generally tolerable. He liked to watch them, minutes on end, grazing in the green grass, flicking the flies aside with their tails, twisting their necks around and splaying their feet, and stretching with all their might to lick and rub an itch. Or just puddled in a bunch under a shade tree placidly chewing their cud. Most of all, he loved to watch the calves in spring, gamboling the hours away — running, kicking up their heels, bucking. He and Libby would sit for hours sometimes enjoying them.

While he was about the cows he'd as well go deliver the new mineral block to the pasture. The one on duty had been licked to a frazzle. He forced himself up, sidled to the shed, climbed in, and cranked up the old truck. He pulled to the pasture gate, got out and undid the rusty old latch chain from the nail, pushed the gate aside, and shooed aside the by-standers. Quickly he jumped back in the truck, eased into the pasture. One black steer refused to budge from the path. Ben Willow blew the horn and rooted him in the butt with the bumper, grinning when he bolted away jumping and kicking.

Driving to the small water hole under the willows, he disembarked, lowered the tailgate, and kicked away the spent salt block from the stob. It looked like a Fudgsicle somebody had worried to the last lick. Bracing and using the spring of his legs, he wrestled the new one off the bed of the truck and set it firmly in place. The cattle had gathered close around, cu-rious of the goings-on. Ben picked up a smathering of the old block and held it out in his palm to the nearest Angus cow. With a coarse purple tongue, she sponged off his palm, then continued up his forearm. It felt like wet sandpaper, raspy and tickling.

When he got back to the house, the rocker had waited. He sat down again, studying the little setter again with amusement. She had unearthed a centipede, grasping it in clenched teeth, shaking it earnestly, then gin-gerly depositing it back to ground. Again and again she repeated the in-quest, a puzzle on her face, until finally she put a shoulder to ground and wallowed on it.

Ben smiled. Puppydom's answer to crawling intrigue: "When in doubt, roll on it!"

From inside the house, the wall clock struck the faint half note past noon. He forced himself temporarily away to the kitchen. Rushing a turkey sandwich together, he left off the lettuce and tomato, and poured a stout cup of hardened cider from the icebox jug. Returning to the chair, he chewed a lopsided corner from the sandwich, settled back on the rockers, and relished the first, sharp bite of the cider in his throat. Momentarily satiated, he balanced the cup and the remainder of the sandwich on the porch railing, and reached for the long, blue legal envelope that rested there also.

His eyes danced across the return address: DEVRON, RT. 3, BOX 220. Fishing his knife from his pocket, he slipped the blade beneath the fold of the envelope, and opened it. Inside, atop a Field Dog Stud Book registration certificate and a certified pedigree, was a delicately penned note:

> Ben,
> *Thought you would want these. I forgot to give them to you when you were here. Best to you and the puppy.*
> Susan Devron

Ben considered the slip of paper in his hands for several moments, wondering at its magnetism.

Finally he set it aside and spread open the pedigree.

"Hey, Jenny," he exclaimed, "look at you!"

Pete Rush had known good dog flesh. The fourth and fifth generations rippled with Grouse Ridge greats — John, Will, Robert — and the newer blood was colored with equal celebrity: Tomoka scions through blue hen bitches, down to her sire, Grouse Ridge Storm, the recent Grand National Grouse Champion on the Gladwin grounds.

Glancing toward the kennel, he caught the gaze of the little setter, riveted back at him. She must have caught her name.

"Yeah, I'm talking about you," he called.

There was a tentative, acknowledging tail wag at his voice, a moment's lingering, and then a return to the centipedes.

Ben could feel the emotion welling. The rapport between them had rooted deeply in the last week. He brought her in each evening at suppertime. She sat by his side, naturally polite, never pushy, and accepted the fare he offered, her tail thumping in gratitude. In the small hours of the new morning, he would feel the comforting warmth of her, nestled against the fold of his legs. At breakfast she played with an empty Special K box, banging it gleefully against the walls, rooting it across the kitchen, shaking it mercilessly into shreds. Atop the dark and ancient toenail scars of her predecessors in the soft pine flooring, she left fresh white impressions of her own. Upon the long-suffering arms of the dilapidated La-Z-Boy in the living room were her newly deposited tooth prints.

All was right again and Ben Willow could feel it to the marrow.

A mere nine days they had been together, and already she was restoring to him the essential portion of his life he had banked for lost. It was time now. Tomorrow they would go. He and Jenny. To the mountain.

· 3 ·

Seven Step Mountain had been hallowed ground from the first moment Ben Willow laid eyes on it . . . from the first November morning some thirty years before when he, Cindy, and Trip made their way there. Arrested by the transcending beauty, they had halted on a neighboring hillside to watch the sun struggle over its shoulder and light a warm yellow shimmer in the chimneys of mist towering over the Bitternut Valley on its one side and the Whiterun on the other. The headland itself arose as one of the many vertebral spurs along the spine of the Alleghenies, but against the pale sunlight they could easily count the seven distinguishing benches that stepped to its peak. Thus came the mountain's name, from the roughshod men who logged the vast treasury of virgin timber from the hills amid the huff and clang of mighty Shay locomotives. Looming upgrade at the five-mile mark of the Bessie Morton switchback on the old Greenbrier, Cheat & Elk Railroad, the descent from its summit likewise signaled the tumble-run to mill and camp at the end of a torturous day.

The Step was one of the most treacherous stretches on the line, and men had died there, when chains popped as great logs shifted and even the best of honed wits could not escape their revenge. Or when the bitter blizzards descended mercilessly on the sawmill outposts for a fortnight, wringing life from the weak and sickened. There had been knifings and shootings there, too, when the timber was being brought down by lumberjacks frayed to the quick, and tempers ran hot. But there were stories, as well, of an incredulous trove of game about the wild and rugged expanse of the mountain: grand tales of partridge, deer, bear, turkey, and cougar. He had heard them time and again, from the grizzled and withered men who had outlasted the wrath of the mountain. Until at last he was moved to go there, to find and feel what was left.

Its peculiar attraction for grouse, he had been told, lay in the lush green "salad bowls" that flourished along the tiny streams of the many hollows that pocked its flanks, and those prospered uniquely, perhaps, from its relatively shallow limestone substrate. So, at least, Ben had presumed. Whatever the reason, he had recognized the inference almost immediately. Grouse were largely vegetarian, the young birds quickly developing a lifelong craving for greenery once they outgrew the juvenile necessity of six-legged protein. Particularly in winter, after the thorn apple orchards and grapevines were spent, the birds would seek the shelter and profuse vegetative larder of the hollows. And so it had proven.

They had moved thirty-six grouse on the Seven Step that first day. He could remember it vividly, not quite to the bird, but close enough. They had urged the truck up the old lumber paths to the three-quarter mark on the mountain. From there they had worked afoot the thorn apple orchards, the brushy draws, the multitude of wild vineyards, and the hidden hollows, climbing and climbing, traversing here and there pockets of immense spruce, hemlock, beech, and maple, awesome first-growth monoliths that had escaped the saw and seemed to touch the threshold of Heaven. A brace of setters can be one dog heavy on grouse, but Cindy and Trip had been as close to flawless as a wild bird hunt gets. Fourteen times they stood game, gracing the mountain, and nine times of fourteen they watched more than one bird away. Once four birds had taken flight almost as one, thundering up through the undergrowth, departing unscathed as he spent one barrel into an interloping spruce and was uselessly late with the second. He had laughed at himself then as he did now. As it was, two cocks had fallen to ground much sooner than he would have desired. The shooting had been both the best and the least of it, as it always was. Had Ben Willow wished, he could have taken other birds, but aside from legal legitimacy and opportunity, or the many occasions the birds might beat him, his lifelong ethic dictated no more than three birds to the hunt. And there were those days, when his mood was mellow and the mountains pleaded to him, when he chose not to shoot at all.

He had banked the possibility of a third and last bird until near sunset, though they had an arduous return and would not make the truck before dark. Such things troubled him less then. Then he was young and strong, indomitably confident and proud. Then he had been a mere fifty-three. And Libby waited at home in a warm yellow kitchen.

Stopping at the brink of a deep hollow, he had savored the medley of the bells, and contemplated the falling sun, and appraised the distant purple swells of the hills. Already there were dim pinpricks of light in the darkening valleys. He registered almost subconsciously the abrupt silencing of Trip's throaty cowbell, and, shortly behind, the absence of the tinkling brass Swiss. He had found Trip pointing into a huge blowdown under a tangle of grapevines at the edge of a rhododendron thicket, and, seconds later, within an intervening finger of laurel, the small, lofty stand of the little rump-patch bitch. They were locked as certainly into their promise as gun dogs could be, and there had been little doubt of the bird. It whispered away over the tip of the thicket in a terse, dusky blur and there was only time to rush the gun up and ahead and *pull*. The bird had faltered slightly, then winged on a long downhill glide into the shadowy void below.

He could hear the tinkle of the bitch's bell again, traveling over the brink and into the hollow, receding until it was lost. Evidently she had marked flight, and was rushing in its direction.

"Find 'im, girl," he called, "dead bird, dead!"

Gathering up the dog, who was happily immersed in the latent ground scent, he had hastened after her.

Descending the steep slope, he had stopped several times, straining for the sound of her bell. All was silent but the low moan of the wind on the ridge far above. He had kept going, down and down — sliding, palming saplings to slow the momentum, and walking the edges of his boots — until suddenly he found Trip out of hand also, and himself strangely alone. The stillness was like death, the light dim. Cocking an ear, screwing his face into a contortion, trying as he might, he could hear nothing. Nothing but the silence. On he had gone, deeper and deeper into the throat of the hollow, and there was nothing but the same endless, disconcerting hush.

"Trip! . . . *Cindy!*" He rarely spoke in the woods, but now he shouted. The two words momentarily shattered the quiet, then were as quickly swallowed by the dusky basin of the depression, and all was deathly still again. He had felt himself shrinking into the vastness of the mountain, growing ever more uneasy.

"Hyeayh, Trip! *Heayh*, boy!" He wanted to see his male dog then, needing the reassuring boldness of him. And the staunch, devoted presence of the bitch. He wanted to know they were okay.

At last he had broken onto the green floor of the hollow, beside the silvery trickle of a small stream fringed with scattered, feathery spruce. It was a beautiful place, destined to become the most cherished place of his hunter's heart, but he could not know it then. For once, of the few times in his life, Ben Willow was worried. Never before had two dogs become so abruptly and so utterly lost to him. Almost an hour had passed since he had left the ridge. He was wishing now that he had not shot at the bird. But it had scarcely been his election. It was a snap decision, governed more greatly by instinct than conscience.

"Cindy! . . . Hyeah *Cindy!*" he yelled, once, then again. The hills soaked up his voice as a sponge blots spilled water.

Minutes within the penetrating silence that followed, with his thoughts running close to despair, he had heard it. The deeply muffled bark of a dog, somewhere yet below. So indefinite was it that he was unsure at first, of the sound or its direction. But then it had arisen once more, and he was certain.

Running and stumbling toward its source, he was drawn deeper and deeper into the hollow. He could hear it more distinctly now, though still distant, the staccato chop of a dog at bay.

As he rushed toward it, the stream grew to a babble among the glistening gray rocks of its bed, and the steep, skirting hillsides fell to mere friendly shoulders. Within the trek of a hundred steps, the slope gentled and the dense screen of green and silver spruce thinned and abruptly opened.

At once, he had found himself at the head of a small green meadow, filled with the placid light of the setting sun. The modest glade had once been larger. The forest had used the passing years to advantage. New growth had pressed the clearing to its center and there, it seemed, an equilibrium had been established, so that while much of its perimeter was now overgrown with saplings, a goodly fraction of its core remained largely open and unsullied. It could not remain that way forever, of course. Gradually, the forest would win.

The meadow composed a humble portion of a sweeping hardwood bench, lightly stippled with rhododendron, and to either side, as far as he could see, the bench belted the waist of the mountain. The incandescent ribbon of the little stream wandered its center, catching the colors of the molten sky and pouring them over the brink of the mountain, and beyond, the headlands sprawled away in soft cobalt layers to the horizon.

Upon the meadow lay the remnants of someone's life. There was the stump of a chimney a peaceful walk from the gurgling water, and beneath it, partially overgrown with vine, the blackened bones of a house. About its modest courtyard, rusty shards of tin roofing were haphazardly strewn by the wind, and here and there lay the scant, decrepit remains of animal shelters and sheds. Like steadfast mourners, an ancient spatter of crooked and silvered apple trees stood by the corpse of the house, abiding in the intermittent comfort of a southern exposure. Two had succumbed also, resting now pitifully along the ground, the grotesque stubs of their naked roots clutching little more than mountain air. At the base of the largest, in a veritable frenzy, were his dogs.

Trip was digging and tearing at the base of the rootball with all his might, and Cindy, whom he had heard, thank God, had retreated in his wake to announce her unmitigated frustration in an endless pummel of barking. He had started quickly toward them, the muffled growling and whining of the incensed dog, who had now thrust himself far beneath the rootball, growing all the more frantic.

The bitch happily acknowledged his approach in wriggling tail and body language, but only momentarily, immediately renewing the din.

"Cindy . . . Cindy!" he admonished. "What in the world, girl?"

At his voice, Trip struggled wildly to extricate himself. He erupted for an instant, eyes blazing, tail whipping furiously, disheveled and covered with dirt, muzzle to ruff. Then he was ripping at the roots anew, worming his way underground again, snorting and whining with vengeance.

"All right, boy," he said, "hang on, cavalry's on the way."

It had to be, of course. The crippled bird had come to earth here, seeking refuge under the root hollow of the old tree, working its way beyond jaw range.

He had tried to roll the heavy trunk aside but could not, and resorted instead to a hasty search for a lever about the bygone homeplace. As he looked, he uncovered the legacy of a simple existence. The blue-white glint of a half-buried Mason jar, a rusted fragment of a spackled washbowl, a plain and paltry chip from a broken plate. The usual extent of human immortality.

Finally he found the better portion of a rafter, which might serve the purpose. Working the butt of it beneath the trunk of the fallen tree near the root base, he kicked a rock in place for a makeshift fulcrum and put his shoulder to the working end. The trunk budged meagerly and a root popped.

"Back, Trip!" he warned. The panting dog, already alerted by the slight shift of the roots, had withdrawn. Both he and the bitch were hard by and poised, engaging the ensuing strategy.

Another root popped, and the trunk gave noticeably this time. The dogs stabbed in, and back, circling and whining, as he had put his weight behind his wager, and there was yet another snap, and the tree rolled suddenly free. In a dusky flurry, the grouse had fluttered for the safety of the woods. Both dogs had overtaken it in a moment, and from the melee, Trip triumphantly emerged with the bird in mouth. Ben had accepted the wing-tipped hen softly, pained with the bewildered resignation in her glistening black eyes, and wishing that the kill could have been clean. It was never easy, this. He slipped an open palm around her breast, inserted fingers and thumb into the small depressions beneath her wings, and squeezed. The warm, perfectly russeted body in his hand shuddered and relaxed, there was a final momentary flutter of wing beats, and she gave her life up to him. He sat wondering for a time of his right to take it.

He had shared the bird with Cindy and Trip for a spell, then slipped it into his game bag with the others. The quest was complete.

He had looked about him then, intently, for the first time. It was beautifully serene, the bench and meadow, in the catch of twilight. A faint wash of light and color lingered in the southwestern sky where the sun had passed, the wind had fallen to a whisper, and it was very still again. The chill of evening was rising. The dogs had relinquished the hunt and had drawn close about him. Night was pulling a vast blanket of darkness over the hills.

He wondered of the people who had lived here, of the things that gave them reason to live, of how and when and why they had wandered onto this remote corner of the mountain and decided to call it home. He wondered, too, of the country as it must have been when they came, of the supreme wildness of it. Of the grouse and turkey that must have found their way to their humble Thanksgiving table. Life would have been forbidding here, at times, and the existence fragile, but it had been of their choosing. There was too much humanity invested there in the little meadow for it to have been otherwise. They had come in search of something, not in escape from something. He imagined they had been happy here.

Walking to the brink of the bench, gazing out across the swelling nightfall, he felt the first icy twinge of loneliness in the night. Immediately, he thought of home and Libby. They must be on their way. They had climbed high and hunted at will. They would be a while coming down.

"This could only be the seventh step of the mountain," he said to himself, letting the subtle revelation sink in for several moments.

He glanced above to the soaring ridge where an hour before he had wing-tipped the grouse. Higher yet stood the grand zenith of the mountain. There was a thing about being high and free, alone on a mountain with a dog and a gun. A thing that had come into his heart when he was a boy, and belonged as nothing else ever had. A thing that had never left him, and never could.

Turning, he retraced his steps, dogs at heel, to the hoary old orchard. Its surviving inhabitants loomed grotesquely. It was almost dark now. Time to leave, he reminded himself. But he could not force himself away. Something more had begged him to tarry. He ambled about the dilapidated homeplace, pulled along the edge of the murmuring stream to the point it left the mountain. Once more, he stood by the brink of the bench. Once more he told himself he must leave. It was then that he saw it. There was a small depression of earth there, thick with green moss and speckled with blue shale, and at the crown of its length and height was an aged and listing headstone.

Chalked and pitted by time and the elements, burdened with lichen, its face appeared anonymous at first notice. Captivated, he had pulled his flashlight from his pocket and knelt alongside it. There were words there. With his hand, he brushed and swept the knap of the stone until he could begin to make them out. The words stared back at him:

SAMUEL THOMAS

Brushing more vigorously, he had searched diligently for the numbers disclosing Samuel Thomas's time on earth. There were none, nor any other intimation of his existence. Only a crudely cut, terse, and piercing inscription under the feeble beam of the flashlight in the eerie cloak of dusk:

Live your own life, for you shall die your own death.

Ben Willow had felt a crushing tightness rush upon his chest. It had caught and squeezed his breath until it was ragged. Afterward, his stomach had run queasy, and the sweat had grown upon his brow.

It was minutes before he had recovered.

He looked about at length for other graves, but could find none.

There had not been a family here. Only a man, a solitary man. He would ask endlessly, in years to come, of this man, of how he came to rest there, and no one would know. Perhaps someone who became sickened with bringing death upon the great trees. Whatever, whoever, Samuel Thomas might have been, he had planned this, gathering his own headstone and cutting in the words and planting it here before his death. He could feel it.

Suddenly, he had wondered with a chilling shiver whether anyone was buried here at all. A man who died in this distant and desolate place certainly couldn't have buried himself. The work of a friend? Maybe. Maybe his bones simply lay moldering under the leaves on the side of the mountain, scattered about by the wild creatures that had been his neighbors. Maybe he had known it would come to that, which explained the headstone and the warning he left there in a few fearful words.

It was well past midnight when they had made home. From the last turn in the drive, he could see that the kitchen light was on. It triggered a stabbing pang of guilt for worrying Libby so, the one person who cared most about him in the world.

She met him at the back steps as the truck came to rest.

"I called Clyde about an hour ago," she had spurted, her brow gravely furrowed, "he's probably out looking by now.

"And Nate Mason," she had added.

"*The sheriff?*" he had returned incredulously.

She stared at him, eyes welling.

"I'm sorry, Libby," he said genuinely, "I never planned to be this late."

Ben doubted that Clyde was out looking for him. They knew each other too well. As for Nate, he wasn't likely to exert himself short of a murder.

"There're occasions when an apology just isn't good enough, Ben," Libby had countered. The words stung.

"Sometimes you show so little concern for my feelings," she had lamented, starting to cry. "You're never here when I need you. You're always off in the *damn* woods."

There was little he could say to that at the moment. He would try to make it up over the days and years, which counted most.

Libby had wept almost uncontrollably then.

She collapsed against him, sobbing. He wrapped his arms around her and held her tightly, his shotgun still in one hand behind her back.

"I'm sorry, Lib, really." He had kissed her and brushed back the loose wisps of hair at her forehead. "I've been late before, you know," he reminded her softly. "I don't think I've ever seen you so upset."

Libby had gathered herself then, and looked into his eyes.

"Your mother called two hours ago, Ben," she said gently. "Your father's dead."

The remainder of that night had been the hardest of his life. The surprise and shock of the loss staggering. He had kenneled the dogs and rushed immediately to his mother. The house at 357 Birch Street still smelled the same and looked the same as he had pushed open the front door and stepped into the front room, but already he could sense the emptiness, feel the distance. It could never ever be the same again, and he knew it.

There was a pale shaft of yellow crossing the hallway from the back bedroom. He made his way there. Libby had hesitated at the threshold as he entered. His mother was lying on the bed, seemingly comatose. She looked dreadfully frail in the half-light of the small, single lamp. It had been her, in fact, whom he had worried most about. She had been sickly most of her life. Cora Medlin . . . dear old Cora . . . who had seen him and every other member of the family through one crisis or another as long as he could remember, was by her bedside. She had a crumpled ball of Kleenex in one hand. She labored up from her chair when she saw him. They hugged and clung to each other for several moments.

"Yo' daddy's done made Heaven, Mr. Ben," she said, "th' Lord done called him."

Choking on the lump in his throat, he had broken then, moved by an immense swell of gratitude. He had sobbed uncontrollably on her shoulder, while she patted his back as she had so many times when he was hurt and only a boy. He held on to her, wanting to be the boy again, not wanting to let go, of home and childhood and the happy days when life still had all its pieces.

He could hear Libby behind him, crying also, and he had remembered his station as a man, and forced himself back.

As he quieted, Cora had pulled to arm's length.

"Dr. Allen's gave your po' mama something so's she could rest," she told him. "If you could've seen her after she foun' yo' daddy . . . she was pitiful, just pitiful."

"She . . . found him?" he had responded hesitantly.

"Yessir, 'tween heyh an' th' barn. He went down there to see 'bout that peaked filly an' never came back."

He winced inside, taken with the image.

He had knelt by his mother's side then and tried to talk to her, but discovered her numb and strangely imperceptive. She was pretty well under.

"Dr. Allen say she be 'round by mornin'," Cora assured him.

Dan Allen had tended the family miseries for about as many years as Cora had watched over its well-being. He knew well how Sarah Willow felt about intervention drugs. As Cora said, it must have been bad.

There was nothing more he could do there, until she was aware again.

He and Libby had returned home, to call his brother in Ohio, his sister in Omaha, and Andrea and Steve. And then he had collapsed into his grief.

He had been glad that the greatest welt of it came in the small hours, with Libby, before the day dawned and friends and neighbors arrived, meaning well, but hardly comprehending the part of him that hurt most and wished to remain undisturbed.

It was four in the morning and he was bone weary. It had been twenty-four hours since he had arisen the preceding morning to seek out the mountain. The hunt had been long and hard, its revelation penetrating, its aftermath devastating. He was going now on nerve alone. But he was far from sleep.

He had known that his father would not live forever, that the years were growing short, and that someday this hour would come. He wished he could have been there at the end, and worried that he had not. But he could have as easily been home in bed, and it would have happened no differently. That was the hardest part of it all. There had been no time for good-bye.

He had cared for his father, deeply, and sometimes envied his constancy, but had hardly known him outside the parameters of convention.

Forty-five years Lindsey Willow had worked in the coal mines, at someone else's anvil, scraping together day by day a hardscrabble sustenance for a wife and three kids, and not once in Ben's estimation had his father allowed himself to really live. Everything he did, everything he was, was for someone else. Folks get to Heaven that way, of course. He was respected in the community, devout on Sunday, responsible to a fault, but where was the passion that drove his soul? Where was the thing that made Lindsey Willow Lindsey Willow, that set him sufficiently apart when he was alone with himself, that filled the deepest void of his being? Every man must have that.

In all the years they had never talked as men, only as father and son. Now they never would. He wished he could have known his father also as a man.

Maybe the thing that had driven Lindsey Willow was little more than it appeared — simply the thing of being accountable. For some men, that seemed enough.

For years Ben had followed his father's footsteps, working for the mines. But it had never been enough. The only thing that had ever been enough for Ben Willow lay beyond people and most folk's idea of accountability . . . beyond towns and tolerance, beyond walls and welcomes, beyond striving and seeming, beyond once-a-week church pews, beyond conformity, contrivance, or convention. Even beyond Libby, it had seemed.

The only thing that had ever been enough for Ben Willow was freedom: freedom for the insatiable wildness at the marrow of his soul to wander woods and water and high places. Freedom to hear the wind whisper the conscience of the mountain, to catch the rhythm of hearts that beat from breasts wilder than his own, to meet the honesty at the edge of night, and grasp the clarity of sunrise at the rim of morning.

He had loved Libby completely. She replenished his life in the times between. When he was away he longed for her, in much the same way that he yearned for the wild places when he was too long at home. Yet once returned, soon he would leave her again. Within the course of a day or so, the magnetism would swelter until he could no longer be sane or happy, until it drew him from her. She loved and wished for him more than he deserved, but still he went, for going was life itself. And always she waited, too wise to force the choice.

Nevertheless, there came invariably the guilt of it when he lost someone close, as it had then with his father's passing. Libby, as always, was right. It had taken him time and again from her and others he loved, when tamer men stood hearthside and convenient. So many times, when by rights he should have been there for someone, he was not. Even as Andrea was born, he had been belatedly enroute from the Canaan, waylaid beyond intention by the strength of the woodcock flight, and more careless than he should have been of the moment. The September Clyde had been gravely ill with pneumonia, still he had departed for Montana and another bird hunt, his heart torn between allegiance to an old friend and the relentless beckoning of tameless places. Clyde could have died. And still he had gone. His old friend would have understood, he had told himself. But even to the degree that this was true, it was also presumptuous.

He could not always understand the whole of it himself. In truth Ben Willow was a deeply sensitive man, who knew how to love. Yet always he went, as always he would. He could not have stopped any more than the sand could desert the sea.

So he remained forever within the grasp of it, and those whose burden it was to love him bore the endless task of forgiveness.

"I love you, Lib," he had told her that morning, humbled with consciousness. "You complete my life," he had pleaded, "please never leave."

She had comforted him as only she could, and assured him that she would not.

Then, in a moment of deeper candor, she had recanted. "I hope I go first," she had said, "I could not bear living without you."

"You just promised you would never leave," he had argued.

"I won't," she had said, kissing him lightly, "until it's time."

"It will never be time," he had declared desperately, taking her hand.

They had talked until dawn about the age-old enigmas of life and dying, time and being, of first death and last wishes. Of where they would be buried. He had always assumed, as Libby wished, that they would be together. It was only right, it seemed, to spend eternity beside the woman you loved. Even in death, then, despite the vow, you could elude the parting.

As with the few times before, the questions became rapidly uncomfortable and fathomless, and they had abandoned the inquest before it was concluded. Particularly then, it was as well, for the night had changed him. He could sense the truth, if not the completeness, of it, and even as he had held her hand and poured his love earnestly into her eyes, there had crept into his mind a troubling modicum of doubt.

For, throughout, he had been unable to discard the weathered headstone on the bench of the mountain, nor its mesmerizing admonition:

LIVE YOUR OWN LIFE, FOR YOU SHALL DIE YOUR OWN DEATH.

He told her of it, of course.

"It was meant to happen, Libby," he had said. "I don't know why, but it was meant to be."

"It frightens me, Ben," Libby had said intuitively. "There's something very lonely about it."

They had discussed at length its mysteries. But neither he nor she could know then just how profoundly it had affected him.

Two days later, immediately following his father's funeral, Ben Willow kissed his wife deeply, told her once more that he loved her, and departed again for the Seven Step, with a dog and a gun. He was gone for four nights and three days.

He never went back to the Bluestone after that. He never sent notice, and no one came looking. As he thought, the mine could operate without him. He tended his beehives, minded his cattle, and carved his wooden bowls from the exquisitely figured wood that resided beneath the bark of the trees that fell upon the mountainsides. It was enough to piece together a comfortable life for himself and Libby, and, moreover, to pay the price of freedom, freedom and happiness as he had never known it before.

The words on the headstone became without compromise the creed and pattern of Ben Willow's life, and he wandered through the seasons as he wished, with a rod in spring and summer, a gun and a setter in fall and winter. And the words took him again and again to the mountain and Samuel Thomas's meadow. And always Libby was there, when he returned home, waiting for him.

But then there had come the day, six years before, when all too suddenly she could wait no longer, not in flesh, and would never again, and only then had he comprehended how life could barely be possible. And it was possible only because of Tony and the birds and the mountains.

Now Libby lay under a stone of her own, as did his mother and father, and Trip and Cindy, and Tony, and all the others. As, rightly, he would soon also.

A man could no longer flush thirty birds in a day on the Seven Step. But he might move a dozen or more, and there was the ceaseless magic of the place. It was still wild and remote, designated federal wilderness area, free of intrusion from motorized, four-wheeled vehicles. Short their raucous, gnawing ATVs, few had the grit or inclination to venture there. He hoped it remained that way forever.

He was too old, likely, to challenge the Step. Or so Andrea had been telling him for the last dozen years. On his seventy-fifth birthday, she had successfully applied to the DNR on his behalf for a senior citizen's access permit, which, along with the disability privilege, granted the only exceptions to the motorized vehicle prohibition. It was something he would not have done on his own, for had it been up to him the exception would not have existed at all. The spirit of the mountain was too precious to be gifted by conciliation, to him or any other man. But she had made him promise to use it, and finally he did. Admittedly, without it he might not have made Sam Thomas's meadow again. Even then, however, he conceded only to the extent of the fifth bench, leaving the truck by the prone black hulk of a fallen chestnut and climbing the rest of the way on foot when he dared the top. The climb to the little green meadow was the price of the pride that kept him going. When he was no longer able to make it, and that was gone, it would no longer matter anyhow.

Within those concessions, challenge it he did, and would, as long as there was steel left in his legs and breath in his chest.

Tomorrow he and Jenny would go there. Tomorrow, he would show Jenny the mountain.

4

A head, at the break of the ridge where the dense rhododendron breached, a grouse thundered away. Seconds later, a setter pup broke cover, springing wildly about the slope in hyperextended bounces, tail popping like an overwound metronome.

"Ehhyyeee, Jenny . . . a little point in there, huh?"

She threw a gotta-be-kidding glance his way that scarcely qualified as an acknowledgment, and whipped back into the thicket. Minutes later, he heard another bird go out, and then another.

Ben Willow laughed out loud, turned his face momentarily to the bright blue sky, and offered thanks with his eyes. His heart was light again and so were his feet, and they had started in on the third bench of the mountain shortly past eight o'clock, working the small draws to either side, and never letting up. It was ten-thirty now and they had moved birds all the way. Not in numbers like this, but steadily enough to prime a pup.

Now Jenny was completely out of hand, inebriated temple-over-toenail with bird scent and scouring hill and hollow as if someone had just disclosed the secret of her existence. A few outings more and it would come to her that Ben Willow was to blame, and he would grow in her heart and soon she would favor him with the considered presence of her company. One day after that she would encounter the hot fragrance of a bird, something would catch inside, and suddenly she would slam into artistry against a hillside. She would hear the rhythm of his steps on the leaves as he advanced to her side, the bluster of the bird from the cover, and the loud, stabbing noise again. The grouse would not fly away as always before. It would fall from a scatter of wispy feathers and she would dash to it, and for the first time know the sweet taste of it in her mouth. He would coax her to him and ask her to surrender it, and without seeming too easy she would comply. He would caress her silky head and tell her that the sun and the stars rose in her eyes. And she would become a gun dog in much the way a girl becomes a woman. To him and only him she would betroth herself, within the most genuine and loyal union on earth.

But for now, he was happy that she was passionately hunting and hunting naturally to the front, and learning how to stir the birds. A puppy was a promise, and sometimes a promise was almost as good as its delivery. His spirits soared with the innocent, unfettered exuberance of her.

"Yeeahupp, Jenny . . . *whewoo, whewoo, whewoo.*"

He heard the jingle of her bell — paws on leaves. Closer. Kneeling, he waited for her. Bounding from the thicket she started toward him, then veered as she sensed his purpose, slashing across the front and quartering into a draw ahead.

He wanted to get his hands on her. She had been down long enough first time out. "Never give a puppy enough," he was thinking, "always keep 'em hungry."

"Awright, Miss Jenny," he said to himself, "stay on till you decide better. Me, I'm havin' a sandwich. If you get here in time, might be a smidgen left."

Picking his way off the bench and easing down the slope, the old man made his way to a small mantel of rock that jutted from the side of the mountain. There he deposited himself, nestling into the hollow of the hillside. A November chill stiffened the air and there was a sharpness to the wind, but the morning sun was streaming in and the stone shelf beneath him was luxuriously warm. Letting himself go for a minute or so, he closed his eyes, allowing his muscles to go limp, and basking in the sunlight. He was a trifle tired, but too content to give it further notice. He dug the turkey sandwich from a vest pocket, peeled away the wrapping, and took a bite. It was so good his jaws ached.

In a boisterous rasp of toenails and flying bark, two gray squirrels ringed mad vertical spirals around a neighboring oak tree. Almost eye level, a large black buzzard was drawing idle circles in the air over the valley below.

"It's a good day to be alive," he was thinking, amending the notion in virtually the same instant. "Any day now's a good day to be alive," he reminded himself with a smile.

"Hey, Jenny," he called whimsically, "I'm down here when it matters."

"A puppy on a mountain," he mused, "a bird or two." Folks could have the rest.

"When I was eighty-three, it was a very good year . . . a very good year for blue-blooded pups with long silky ears . . . *that nosed up the grouse,*" he crooned, mimicking the Sinatra tune he had always admired, exaggerating the final syllable.

Nonsensically giddy, Ben Willow was. He couldn't help it. He was in love again.

There was a renewed patter of paws on the leaves above, a hesitation, another brief patter.

He let her worry a few seconds longer.

"Here, Jenny," he said softly.

The patter gave to a mad dash. In seconds she was in his face, eyes burning like bellowed ingots, licking him profusely. As quickly, she tried to lunge away. He caught her collar, hanging on as she bucked, snapping on the check cord.

"Whoa, girl," he chided, "birds need a break. Here . . . saved this for you."

Still full of hunt, Jenny refused the chunk of bread and meat. He laid it on the rock at her feet. Presently, she picked it up and swallowed it as a second thought, dancing the while on her toes, whining and alternately trying the cord.

Ben considered the morning and the tricolored puppy a while longer, then urged his complaining frame to its feet.

"You'll do, Jenny," he concluded, "you'll do."

Becky's Creek, Baker Sods, the Elklick, McGowan's Mountain, Hobson Run . . . they made them all, Ben and Jenny. Maybe a bit less spryly than before, in his case, but they made them. Calling on old friends, walking hills and hollows that harbored a few grouse and fifty years of memories. Some had changed, of course, land and people, and some were gone. A comfortless word . . . *gone.* Milt Nesselrod, Lindy Thompson, Bessie

Moser, Moor Coltrane — folk of his generation — names and visages that had been as much of the hunt then as the covert itself — all *gone*.

There were no Treadwells left on the Kettlehorn, none living anyhow; Cordiah and Nonnie had died within a few years of Libby and Cordiah's brother Samuel; Joshua, Jeff, and Nan had moved away over time, until the entire clan had departed. Hard to believe.

Cordiah Treadwell had been a fine old man, crusty and hard as flint, but steady as the seasons. Their first meeting would have made the books. Ben had pulled to the barn where the old man and the boys were putting up hay. The passenger-side window in the truck was partially lowered, and Hank and Molly were up and whining with their heads stuck out.

He had gotten down and sauntered to the wagon, waiting for a cordial break in the work rhythm. It never came. He had lingered there, discrepant and uneasy, as the boys stole cold glances and the man never wavered or even looked up.

"You'll not take a dog and a gun on my land," old Cord had muttered in a level tone, while he still stood there like a blemish on a bluebonnet — before Ben could utter a simple hello.

He wasn't even sure he had heard correctly. "Pardon?" he had inquired meekly.

"I said I'll not have your dog or gun on my property," the grizzled old man had reiterated, as remotely as before, never once acknowledging him openly or resting the pitchfork.

Ben had simply turned away then, walked back to the truck, and started back down the path to the road.

He was halted halfway by two Hereford steers, recently liberated by an obvious break in the pasture fence. They stood obstinately in the middle of the path, stared apathetically at the truck, and refused to be budged when he crowded them with the bumper. Half a dozen accomplices, cows and calves, were crowding the gap. A couple of hours and the entire herd would be adrift.

He had climbed out and shooed the problem back into the pasture, straightened the fencing, and propped the broken post with a pole against a rock. He did it as habitually as if it had been his own. Then got back in his truck.

As he turned on to the gravel road and accelerated, he had caught the faint blare of a horn. Braking, he searched for the source. It came from the hill above, and the barnyard. A small figure in overalls, dwarfed by the distance, was standing there beckoning with the terse curl of an arm.

He had backtracked to find Cord waiting for him. The old man's face was still as stoic as eternity, but he offered his eyes this time, and acquiescence.

"I think maybe I'll reconsider," Cordiah Treadwell had said. That was the extent of it; he had returned to his work then.

Ben had left two birds and his thanks by the house when he came off the Kettlehorn that night. Nonnie, a tiny woman as unstinting as she was slight, had accepted both and bid him welcome another time.

From there had grown a respectful alliance between Cordiah Treadwell and Ben Willow, and Ben was careful never to overstep it. In time it swelled to friendship, accumulated Nonnie and Libby, and flourished. Ben remembered fondly the many times in Nonnie's warm kitchen on frosty mornings before a hunt, sopping up sorghum molasses with a buttermilk biscuit, swapping farm doings with Cord.

So it had been in one manner or another with Milt, Bessie, Lindy, and Moor, and the others who had bestowed the privilege of their holdings. And now, though many of them were gone, there were kin who recalled a man, always with a dog, who came calling for the privilege of a partridge hunt, and came properly.

A man belongs to his land. The only thing of greater privilege you might ask was for his wife or his dog. Ben Willow had never allowed himself to forget that.

Without exception, Ben and Jenny found a welcome and a way. Even to the Kettlehorn, the whole of which was now in deed to Barstow Properties, Inc., a speculation company. He had left his old truck in front of the glass-fronted office in Elkins, rolled the window partway for Jenny, and shuffled in with little hope.

As he started up the walk, Jenny threw a fit, bouncing in and out of the window, pacing the seat, barking and straining to reach him.

"Jenny, Jenny! Hush that fuss," he admonished, walking back to her and mildly roughing her ears.

When he turned again, he could see a young woman watching from behind the glass. She had soft blue eyes and ash blond hair, he found, when he reached her desk. Immaculately clad in a charcoal business suit with a scarf of figured, burgundy silk, she wore her beauty elegantly, in a way that could pull a man breathless. With an air of confidence and authority, she smiled a greeting.

"What would be nice now," he thought privately, "would be a fifty-year refund."

He took her for the company secretary. The name on the shiny brass placard read DIANE S. CRANFORD.

"Miss Cranford," he offered, extending a hand, "I'm Ben Willow."

She took his hand, started to say something, then hesitated as if she decided it less than important. There was something absorbing about this old man with the most striking head of silver hair she had ever seen.

"I have a puppy who wants to be a grouse dog," he explained, "and I'm encouraging that. In times past I hunted the old Treadwell place . . . the Kettlehorn. Cord Treadwell was a friend. If we could go there again, to hunt I mean, I'd be obliged. I'm hoping I might gain permission."

"And your dog?" she asked, appreciating the play of words and reciprocating.

"Ma'am?" he begged.

"Your dog's name?" she repeated, a tease in those engrossing blue eyes.

Ben grinned. "Jenny," he said.

She hesitated another moment, a slight wash of wonder on her face, and looked out the window toward the setter. Smiling again, she took a thin slip of paper from her desk drawer. Writing a few words and her name, she handed it to him.

"Yes, Mr. Willow," she said brightly, "I believe you may have access to the Treadwell tract, and best wishes to you both."

He thanked her sincerely, was detained momentarily by her beauty again, and then pushed his way past the door.

As he left the building, another attractive young woman was entering. She carried a small cardboard box filled with drinks and sweet rolls. He nodded a hello and she acknowledged pleasantly.

"Okay, Miss Jenny," he said as he made the truck and climbed into the cab, "we're in business."

As a matter of course, he unfolded the slip of paper in his hand and glanced over the words:

Ben and Jenny Willow have exclusive hunting rights to Kettlehorn Mountain.

J. Allison Barstow, Pres.

Ben Willow mused a moment more, smiled to himself, and looked a last time toward the glass-fronted building. Five minutes later his old truck had escaped Elkins and regained the trail to Travis Mountain.

In the same few minutes, J. Allison Barstow had accepted a Pepsi and a danish, relinquished the reception desk to her secretary, and returned to her office. She was lounging against an executive chair, sipping the cola, and replaying the past quarter hour. Grinning, she reached for a reminder pad and jotted herself a note. She would have to tell the staff, especially the security people, that she had reconsidered her decision to restrict all extraneous ingress to Kettlehorn Mountain. They would be surprised, at first, since she had seemed so adamant.

Then the phone rang, calling her back to attendance, and immediately she was immersed in the less rewarding transactions of necessity. Twisting a finger around a wisp of hair at her forehead, she listened dispassionately to the solicitation at the other end, wrinkles growing in her brow as she detected its artifice.

She pivoted slowly in the chair as the conversation thickened, turning away from the desk to fashion a denial. As she did, her eyes hovered over a nineteenth-century mahogany credenza and held for a moment on a small, ornate frame of gold. Within it was an image from a moment less harrowing: a picture of a distinguished man with silver-gray hair, an English setter, and a little girl the family had called "Jenny."

5

Jenny Willow pointed her first grouse on the Kettlehorn the following Monday. Granted, it happened briefly, but it was headway. Ben watched her from the logging path below as she went birdy, worked the wind to the edge of a laurel thicket, and ran headlong into instinct. Slamming into point, she stood beautifully for about four heartbeats, then bunched and jumped. He popped a .32 blank as the bird blew out the other side, rolled back over the top of the thicket into a fast-crossing oblique in front of him, then pitched over the rim of the adjoining hollow.

"That one might have been in trouble with the shotgun ashoulder," he told her. "Stay about your good deeds and we'll fetch it along."

There were other points in the weeks to come, and each grew in dedication until soon he was able to approach her, and there came a day at the tag end of March, when the first blush of spring was on the trees, when she stood on the fourth bench of the Seven Step and allowed him to reach her side before taking the bird away.

"Progress, Miss Jenny," he observed, "progress."

It was time then. Ben Willow took her out of the woods and home.

That summer he instilled "whoa" as you would place a bookmark in a hymnal, certainly enough to establish the verse, gently enough to respect the religion. In return, the little setter's faith in him never wavered, only deepened, and she had simply to understand his bidding to accept his will. Soon she would stop at any beckon, standing happily and confidently, relishing the ensuing praise. Even in the off time, apart from their training sessions, when she rushed the guineas in a fit of mischief, a sharp "whoa!" would plant her midbounce. At least until the clattering cacophony gathered wings for the mulberry tree, and sometimes want overwhelmed warning. Then, with stoicism and a bit of indignance, she would await the inevitable consequence, being picked up and shaken briskly. Restored to the site of the transgression, she would pose in compliance, the tip of her tail ticking an exaggerated concession.

"Look at her, Libby," Ben would whiff satirically, "proper as Peggy on a payday."

A minute later and reemancipated, she was quickly prospecting again, devil-take-tomorrow.

Notwithstanding the vagrant heifers that still compromised the neglected pasture fence regularly and required intervening forays on Walter's quarter horse, the balance of her lessons had been accomplished as comfortably, and with the last of the tomatoes drooping forlornly from the spindly vines in their derelict garden, Miss Jenny was ready for finishing school.

In September, Ben Willow fashioned a small recall pen and enclosed it in two-by-four wire at the swell of the little meadow west of the house, at the stoop of the woods. Of a purpose, it had not seen the mower the summer long, and now stood beautifully in overgrown orchard grass, butterfly weed, and sedge. He was pleased to find Henry Armfield still in the quail-rearing business, and managed to procure a dozen eight-week-old birds for no more than the price of a poplar dough bowl for Maggie.

"Another pup, Ben?" Henry had inquired, drawn to the tricolor setter whining impatiently in the cab. The "pup" was showing undue interest in the transaction, and particularly in the curious sounds coming from the wooden crate that he had deposited behind the cab.

"Yeah, reckon she'll do?"

Henry Armfield knew setter dogs like he knew Morgan horses. He read the fire that danced in those hazel eyes, the way Jenny looked deeply and assuredly into his own, the clean, on-the-toes muscular carriage of her.

"She'll do," he declared.

"Course she thinks she's got flushin' rights now," Ben remarked. "You know the story."

"Oh yeah . . . Judd was three years comin' to an understanding. Wore me out. Ended up the best dog I ever had."

"I remember Judd," Ben said, "partic'ly that day on the Stonelick."

"He'd pointed that old cock bird five times before, Ben," Henry replied in a livened rush, "and ever' time it was the same. The ol' rascal would hang the edge of that laurel thicket in those grapevines, an' ever' time Judd established a claim, he'd flip home and Hiawatha into that thicket, hoof the length of it . . . musta been two hundred yards . . . and slip out the far end.

"I never knew for sure till that day. Never saw 'im. But I figured as much."

"Well, ol' Judd called his caper that day," Ben averred.

"When he broke off that way, I knew somethin' was 'bout to happen. 'Cause he had that bird nailed at the outset. He just never did that 'less he could better his possibilities.

"Prettiest sound I ever heard, that bell travelin' the back side of that thicket, 'specially when it stopped on the other end. Then yours a minute later. Which dog was that, Ben?"

"Cindy."

"Yeah, Cindy. They were shinin' like corn silk when we made the corner, in the mornin' sun, weren't they, Ben? Jacked hard into grouse. Some days I'd give the rest of my life to see that ag'in, Ben."

"Pretty decent shot you managed, too," Ben recalled. "Mighty good for an old man with a corn-shucker Ithaca."

"Hell, it was *your* shot," Henry returned crisply. "He flew right down your barrels."

"Yep, but it wasn't my bird," Ben said, smiling. "Good days, Henry, good days."

"I hated to kill him, Ben. He's not there anymore. Course, damn, he wouldn' be now anyhow; that was near twenty years ago. I'm not there anymore either's the hell of it. Gettin' tired and feeble, Ben.

"Good thing you needed these birds now. Prob'ly quit foolin' with 'em a'ter this fall. Too much trouble.

"Had a lot a gumption, that old bird. I've still got his fan in the den, on the mantel, over Judd's old collar."

The back screen slammed, and Maggie Armfield came bustling down the walk, carrying a paper plate covered with aluminum foil. She was a rotund little woman who still managed a bounce to every step. She wore a flowered gingham dress and her hair was pulled tightly into a bun, which made the smile on her red, round face all the broader.

"You're lookin' thin, Ben Willow," she appraised. Everyone was thin to Maggie.

She thrust the paper plate at him.

"Pineapple upside-down cake," she announced, eyes sparkling, "fresh yestiday. Take it along for supper."

"Thanks, Maggie, you know it's a favorite."

"I know Libby used to make at least one a week," Maggie remembered, "and who put her up to it."

Ben was pained by her words. Libby was on his mind a lot lately.

"Well, Jenny'll think I've taken root," he ventured, smiling, but rushing away from the moment. "Better be along."

"Make it a little more often, Ben," Maggie said, sensing his discomfort. Ben kissed her lightly on the crown of the cheek. Then she turned for the house, her copious hips swaying an unconscious rumba.

He smiled again. Maggie was a marvel.

Henry shuffled along with him to the truck and lingered by Jenny's window. He offered her a hand to consider, then caressed an ear as she consented. Her tail thumped the back of the seat with a tempered rhythm of caution and gratitude.

There was a wistfulness in the scene that Ben could hardly misinterpret.

"Grouse season's comin' in a few weeks, Henry," he said spontaneously. "Jenny here should know which side of the gun she's s'posed to be on by then. I'll swing by one day. We'll go to the Stonelick."

Henry continued to study Jenny for a while, almost as if he hadn't heard. Then he turned slowly. The eyes of the two old friends caught and held briefly, and the honesty was more than either could bear.

Henry returned again to Jenny for a time, then back, leaned heavily onto his cane, and extended a palsied hand. Ben reached to meet it. There was a fight for words, but they never came.

He would remember vividly in days to come the image of three clasped hands, gaunt, pale, and splotched, covered with blue veins that bulged and wandered like mole trails. He would remember the years that flowed between them, both backward and forward as they stood there . . . what had been and what could never be again.

He watched from the seat of the truck until Henry was halfway to the house, then turned the engine over and coaxed the old pickup slowly down the path. When it reached the mailbox, he turned left onto Mabry Road and accelerated. Gravel crunched under the tires, a slight breeze sprang through the window, and dust mounted. Only then did his attention reach the moment.

Jenny had left the passenger window and was taking stock of the paper plate, her nose testing the temptation.

"Hey Jenny, sumpum good," he teased.

She looked at him, wagged an inquisitive tail, then turned back to the plate. Venturing a paw, she scratched gingerly at its edges.

"*Jennny,*" Ben cautioned. Registering a brush of disappointment, the setter pranced to the passenger window and stuck her head back into the wind. The rush of air made a caricature of her ears.

A mile more and it was he who couldn't resist.

"Awright, Jenny, if you insist," he said. Jenny, innocent, still had her head out the window.

He peeled the foil back. The cake was golden and moist, almost gummy. He pinched up a fingerful and rushed it to his mouth. A portion of it landed in his lap.

With the wonderfully familiar flavor, the memories flooded back. Of Libby, aproned in a fragrant kitchen late into a Saturday night, feigning aggravation and shooing him away from the stove. Of family and friends clustered tightly around a Sunday table, of the blissful buzz of idle gossip, of Andrea with an Easter basket, of the grace spoken over a blessing of beautiful foods. Of Libby pulled close against him in a warm bed at the end of the evening, when everyone had left, and Andrea was in bed, and the house was still again. Of their soft, whispered words as they measured the day. Of their last kiss before sleep.

There was a wet, black nose in his face. Jenny was back.

Almost unconsciously, he removed the foil, spread it over the seat, and scraped a mound of cake onto it. Setting the plate on the dash behind the wheel, he watched absently as she gingerly sampled a chunk of pineapple, then a morsel of the cake itself.

He returned his eyes to the road.

"Libby, Libby," he exclaimed softly for what now must be the hundredth time, "where did it all go?"

There was another question, even more disturbing, that Ben Willow did not voice. It had festered for months, at the deepest corner of his soul. Amid Jenny and all the newfound happiness, it was, ever more, silently tearing him apart. The dilemma and the solution was his alone, the most agonizing choice of his lifetime. And he could talk to no one of it, not even to Andrea. He had struggled with it endlessly, yet he could not bring himself to finally grasp it, to bring it to resolution, though in his heart he knew what the answer must be. But there was no longer time for defer-ence. It was on his mind constantly now. It must be settled soon. It might come to bear tomorrow or ten years from tomorrow. But someone must know and he must find the way to put it to rest and go on living in the time remaining.

· 6 ·

W hoa, Jenny," he cautioned softly.
The little trisetter was transfixed before a gathering of orchard
grass and goldenrod, eyes smoldering with arrested desire,
nostrils pulsating rhythmically with the aroma of discovery. One foreleg
was cocked and a faint breeze teased the feathers in her twelve o'clock
plume. She had been standing for a time. Short tendrils of drool were
forming at the corners of her mouth, and she leaned heavily against the
wall of scent.

Ben moved to her side, then stepped in front. Her muscles bunched
and she rocked forward on her toes.

"Whoa!" he admonished sternly.

Heedfully, she went motionless again.

He took another step, let the air rush through his teeth in short bursts,
and kicked tentatively at the cover. Another bunching of muscles, then a
stagger-step. He returned to her. Picking her up, he shook her lightly, then
set her back in place.

"Whoa!" he warned once more.

She was locked tightly again. He rubbed her flanks and styled her pose to perfection.

Stepping in front anew, he reinstituted the flushing attempt.

Fired with anticipation, the setter swelled, about to blow.

He kicked the trigger then. With a thump, the trap tossed one of Henry Armfield's hen birds up and away in a flurry of wings and feathers. Behind it was a blur of tricolor setter and a rapidly lapsing check cord. Farther yet was an eighty-some-year-old man with two planted feet and a prayer.

Jenny hit the end of the tightened rope full on and flipped end-over-applecart onto the grass. Instantly, she was back on her feet, tail popping, whining, straining, and bouncing against the restraint.

Ben Willow, thrown off balance with the jolt, caught himself in a couple of wild rooster hops, then hung on mightily. His arms and shoulders had been wrenched, jerked so violently the sockets ached, and his head was spinning. But he still had his dog!

He walked himself up the cord to her side, hoisted and shook her briskly, then carried her back and dropped her where she had stood before.

"*Whoa! Jenny,*" he reiterated, stroking and styling her, then stepping away.

He let her stand and think about things for a while.

She wasn't exactly reformed; he was sure of that. She was boss-bull confident, her tail ticked jauntily, and when she cut those eyes, there was a blaze in them that said it was a long stint to staunch. Moreover, the way the muscles were knotted again, the "whoa" might come loose any second.

"Look, Jenny girl," he argued, "we got to come to an early understandin'. I ain't got the ballast I used to."

She rolled her eyes again. They were cocked like the hammer over a percussion cap.

"Oh, God," he thought.

Well, one more episode. That'd be about his limit this session.

He tapped her on the ear, led her what seemed a safe distance from the marked bird, let go his end of the rope, then hit the whistle.

Tearing across the meadow, the inebriated setter whipped merrily in and out of the breeze, tail clicking with every bounce. Grabbing the tree line, blistering the edge, she rebounded off a corner, and cut a happy circle.

"*Bird,* Jenny, *bird,*" he sang, whistling a staggered covey call to egg her on.

Pumped to a relentless frenzy, she scoured the field again, racing with abandon from one clump of promise to the next. Suddenly as a shot, she ran headlong into her nose. Her hindquarters gave way, skidded a full 180, and clawed for traction. Pushed upright, forward, and probing, she was slammed into point like a quickened bolt slaps home a rifle cartridge.

It pulled him momentarily breathless. Jacked nettle-prick high, she was swollen so intensely her eyes bulged.

"Whoa, Jenny," he cautioned.

He moved to her, caught up the end of the rope, and simply stood there, relishing the spell that had enveloped them both. He lived for this. For these fleeting few moments of completion when the rest of the world was suspended elsewhere. When expectancy trembled on nothing more than the invisible, vaporous link between a pointing dog and a few hidden ounces of feathers. When his heart was young again with its spontaneity, and aquiver with its apprehension.

Putting a hand behind her rump, he nudged her against the scent. Stiffening, she resisted.

"Good girl, Jenny," he praised. "Whoa, now."

Easing in front of her, Ben kicked at the weeds in measured motions, working toward the trap. Jenny gathered and rocked, but stayed.

A hot rush of anxiety filled his chest. His conscience was protesting vigorously. "Keep it up, you old fool," it argued, "get a broken leg to go with your broken head."

A deft toe flick and the bird was out.

Immediately, Jenny broke, dashing madly by him.

Mechanically, the old man yelled *"Whoa!"* gritting his teeth and bracing himself for the collision.

In the same instant, the outgoing cord snagged fast on a broken root. It was one of those rare quirks of providence that unravels at just the right instant and sends dog trainers to church on Sunday. It brought Jenny up short and hard and, most important, before she expected it. Jerked violently backward for the second time, she thumped the ground soundly. She was up at once, looking for the bird, but shaken a mite this time.

Ben went quickly to her, caressed away the embarrassment, restoring her dignity and poise.

"*Whoa*, Jenny, *whoa*," he repeated, grateful for the happenstance and using it to full advantage.

Soon her tail was registering gladness again. Maybe a shade less merrily. The fires in her eyes stilled burned, though they had fallen slightly.

This was the way of things, he reminded himself. To bring the desire down only enough to beg devotion to the gun. Still, it was a loss of innocence in a respect, and there was in it a thing that never failed to sadden him a little.

Rubbing her flanks a final time, he tapped her ear, and heeled her back to the kennel. Halfway there, he stopped, pulled her to him, and hugged her.

Progress grew rapidly from there. Soon she was reliably staunch, and he could walk in front of her with regularity, put the bird out, and fire the pistol. She would stand through it all, lofty and tight, and mark the flight. If there was a regression at all, it amounted to little more than a step or so, and each time it happened and she was set back in place, she became more certain of her station. She hit her birds hard and stood back off them, and soon it would be time to put her back in the woods again.

Ben Willow could scarcely wait.

On the last day of September, he celebrated his birthday. The celebration amounted to hardly more than an extra cup of coffee and a slab of buttered corn bread in the old rocker on the porch, a few lean words to the Almighty about the privilege of still being about, and an early-morning walk with Jenny down a lazy country path. The day was splendidly beautiful, and already there was a brush of color on the headlands. He could not have asked, or wanted, for more.

He wandered back through his life as they walked, dwelling here and there in the places that held special memories. And when he had gathered a number of them together, he realized again just how fully he had lived. And how very empty now his world would be, were it not for Jenny.

Alt Hoover jostled by with the mail around noon. He was running ten minutes to the good. So they had talked about the weather, buckeyes and rheumatism, and Glady Martin's egg custard pies until he was back on schedule. It lifted his spirits.

So did the three greeting cards Alt delivered, especially the one with the Dusseldorf postmark.

There was a pastel landscape on the frontispiece, of mountains, a blue sky, and a winding river. Inside was a bit of verse that did a reasonable job of expressing a suitable emotion for those who did not have time to compose their own. There was a short, handwritten message:

Miss you Daddy,
Wish we could be there today. Hope it's the best.
Happy Birthday!
   Love, Andrea & Steve

Well, they had their own life to tend. A world away. How he wished he could see her, though. She was the closest thing to Libby he had.

For a moment Ben Willow suffered himself to wonder on what might have been, had there been grandkids, had they settled a few miles down the road rather than on another continent.

The afternoon passed uneventfully. He split some kindling, checked his beehives. Soon evening drew near.

It was time to haul up another round bale for the cows. There was just enough time left in the day. He ambled to the back shed and climbed up onto the seat of the tractor. It was a Massey TO-35, one of the early take-off models from the '50s, into its third coat of paint. You'd not know it, for that one too had faded away to the color of a weathered brick, except that it was chipped in places to allow speckles of white to show through. It was old like the man who claimed it, and like him also, it managed. As with the Case and the Farmall before it, Ben Willow had rehabilitated it back to respectability, for a multitude of chores about the farm. It was fitted with a three-point hitch and now that the mowing was largely done for the year, the bush hog attachment had been replaced by the bale fork.

Ben pumped the clutch free, shifted both gear cases into neutral, and punched the starter button. The motor ground for a few seconds without catching. The old man yanked the throttle once, punched again. This time there was a promissory pop. One more dose of the clutch and it caught in a series of pops and sputters, until it warmed to a throaty hum. Ben gave it another minute, then shifted to low case and reverse and backed slowly out of the shed. He pointed the hood up the path through the side yard that led some four hundred yards through the woods to Billy Voncannon's hay field. Billy allowed him the few large bales he needed each year in turn for a bucket of honey.

He pulled into the field amid the cloud of grasshoppers that arose from the front tires, wheeled and braked the Fergy into position in front of the nearest bale, then backed up and speared it securely with the forks. The hay was still freshly sweet, had suffered little rain. The scent of it was another of the small things that graced a rural day. Satisfied the bale was in place, he ratcheted the lift lever to the top, frowning as the tractor labored to hoist the hay round clear of the ground. The hydraulic seal on the lift was leaking again. One day when the grouse left off he'd have to tear it down and fix it proper. Tenuously, at least, it was holding.

In first gear low Ben let the Massey crawl its way along to the pasture. The bale was bigger than the tractor. Together they resembled a tumblebug struggling with a ball of manure. The cows saw him coming; the lot of them had loped up and were waiting. As usual, he had to shoo them away from the gate, and then they were ornery about it. They crowded in behind him as he drove through, trotting along and trying one and another to steal a mouthful of the fresh hay. When he dropped the bale into place and pulled away, they closed about it in a rush.

With the departing sun arrived the loneliness. He walked to the kennel for Jenny. She erupted in an exuberant scoot, happy to be free, tucking her tail and running flybys around the yard. She bounced about him with play in her eyes, begging him to chase her. He clapped his hands at her and feigned a pounce. Flybys again, half a dozen in an unbroken string.

Ben dropped to a knee. She flew to him, sticking her nose in his face and baptizing his ear with a wet tongue.

"Thank God, Jenny," he said, "for little setter dogs."

From the porch, they watched as dusk thickened, twilight gathered, and the day closed. So ended the first day of the eighty-fourth year of his life, a melt of happiness and melancholy.

Supper was a tall buttermilk, corn bread, and sweet potatoes. Afterward, he set a bowl of Purina by the wood box for Jenny. She liked to eat some of it at bedtime and save the rest for breakfast.

An unseasonable chill had settled upon the house. He collected a lightern knot or two, found a match, checked the damper, and lit the first fire of the season in the woodstove. Opening the bedroom door so the heat could wander in, he returned to the kitchen table, picking up the latest issue of *American Field* from the huntboard. Jenny sprawled on the kitchen floor and worried the cardboard tube from an exhausted roll of paper towels. He watched her idly for a minute, listening to the muted crackle of the flames inside the firebox. Spreading open the *Field*, he scanned the recent trial reports. Dave Hughes prospered in the cover dog trials. He had met Dave once, on a Pennsylvania excursion, when he was still actively following the circuit. An enthusiastic young man then, with good dog instincts. His success had been no surprise.

He read until his eyes tired. The stove was humming now, its iron belly belching mumly as it digested its fill of oak and hickory. He could feel the soft caress of the radiating heat. Jenny was dozing, her flanks quivering periodically in gentle spasms. He sat with his chin in his palm, studying her appreciatively for several minutes. Then his mind subsided into a contemplative drift, as a librarian through a card catalog, and settled . . . as it always did with evening . . . on Libby.

If she were alive, they would retire to the side room now, and rock by the hearth until Seth Thomas struck nine and a half. While the flicker of the fire danced softly off the walls, and the night wind sighed around the eaves. Talking over intimate little corners of their existence. She'd have a lapful of knitting or a needlepoint project. He'd pull a pipe, carve on a bowl, loose shavings clinging to his socks.

It was eating at him again, the relentless dilemma his soul had forced upon his heart.

What would he tell her now, if he could, of what he was feeling? And what would she say? Most important, what would be the thought held and perhaps unspoken at the depths of her heart? She would sacrifice for him. She always had. That alone did not clear the way. It only made it the more difficult. Could she not expect the same from him? Particularly now. After all, the issue was eternity.

Does the covenant of a man to the woman who has loved him with the better part of her life truly end with death? In ceremony maybe; never as a matter of the heart. He was still drawn to her with every breath he took.

Was it even possible to reconcile what he contemplated sufficiently to complete his life in peace? It had the whisper of a betrayal, and that was next to unbearable. Yet it would be Libby herself who would be closest to understanding.

Was that a vindication or simply another supplication for sacrifice?

Of its own, his mind raced backward, searching for a counterpoint.

It found the headstone in Sam Thomas's meadow, as hauntingly as in the first moment he had discovered it.

LIVE YOUR OWN LIFE, FOR YOU SHALL DIE YOUR OWN DEATH.

The question was not living now; it was dying. But the message was the same, and as ever, he could not let it go. There was a thing about dying that was every bit as important as living.

He was groping helplessly with that certainty when the phone rang. It was on its fifth summons before it gained his attention and the seventh before he decided to lift the receiver. It was Andrea. The impact of her voice at that moment was almost overpowering, so delicately feminine. He closed his eyes tightly for a moment, while the emotion peaked, unable to speak.

"Hello, Daddy?" she asked for the second time.

"Hey, Andy," he answered earnestly.

"I was afraid I wasn't going to get you," she said with relief. "How are you? Happy birthday!"

"Celebrating again," he said, "now that you've called."

"Eighty-four!" she declared with mild amazement.

"Yep, it's found me again," he replied.

"I miss you so much, Daddy."

"You too, sweetheart."

"Are you okay?" she asked once more.

"Must be," he said lightly, "I'm still here to congratulate myself."

She laughed.

"How 'bout you and Steve?"

"We're good. We were in Paris again last week," she proclaimed buoyantly. "Stayed at the Relais Christine on the Left Bank. Rose petals and honor bars. Pretty tony for a country girl, huh?"

"I reckon. But I could've told 'em you were comin' when you were twelve years old."

"Were the stars in my eyes *that* obvious," she wondered.

"Only when you were awake," he said.

He could sense the smile.

"We're hoping to get there Christmas. It depends on Steve's portfolio clients; they can be pretty pushy. But he's trying to clear the calendar."

"That would be grand, sweetie," he remarked. "Jenny wants to meet you."

"How's she doin'?"

"Braggable. You need to come and see for yourself. We'll hunt the mountain."

"You're not still climbing the Seven Step," Andrea admonished.

"Just on weekdays," he said.

"Don't know what I'll do with you," she scolded.

"Not a lot from Germany," Ben Willow said to his daughter. "But come home and we'll see if you're still Andy. Course I'm a trickle slower than I used to be."

"I'll try to keep up," she promised with a chuckle. "I'd love to, Daddy, I really would."

"This must be costing you a fortune," he suggested.

"Not really," she said. "Anyhow, it doesn't matter. Guess I had better go soon, though. Got to get the day going here in a couple of hours. Just wanted to drop by with a birthday wish."

"It's meant a lot, Andy," Ben said. "And the card."

"Daddy, there's also something I've been meaning to ask you for a long time. I manage to forget it somehow every time we talk. But the other day I thought of it again, and jotted a reminder by the phone for the next time I spoke to you. I'm not sure how you'll feel about it, though."

"Nothin' chanced, nothin' gained, sweetie," he invited. "All I can't do is say no."

"Do you remember that knit shawl Mama used to wear all the time when I was a girl? It's in about every picture I have of her then. It was lavender, I believe, bordered with white lace."

"About the color of larkspur in June," he said. "The lace was hand knit."

"You remember it then," she said.

"Yes, I remember it."

"I think it must have been very special to her," Andrea said.

"Yes, Andy, it was very special."

"I'd love to have it, Daddy. It would mean a lot to me . . . You may not want to part with it?" she followed, after a hesitation.

"No . . . it belongs with you, Andy. I'll send it."

"Thanks," she said.

Andrea offered her good-byes then and a final birthday wish, and the phone clicked dead, and there was an empty dial tone where the soft, beautiful voice had been only moments before. He placed the receiver back on the hook as the loneliness rushed in again.

He sat for several minutes reflecting on their conversation, then urged himself up out of the chair. Making his way to the bedroom, he switched on the lamp. Jenny followed. She stood by his side, her tail swaying casually to and fro, as he opened the middle drawer of the butternut dresser. Inside, neatly folded, was the lavender shawl. He gathered it up gently, dropped himself into the neighboring rocking chair, and laid it over a knee. Jenny sniffed at it curiously, then circled three times and sprawled across the pine floor.

He drew the tips of his fingers across the softness of the yarn. He had given it to Libby the night he had asked her to marry him. A ring was beyond his means then. He had gotten it in exchange for a small, walnut keepsake box he had made for Mattie Caviness. She had knitted it for him and meticulously fashioned the lace on a hand loom. She was the best in the county and everyone knew that, including Libby.

"It's nothing fancy, Libby," he had said, "but it'll last the years. And so will I."

She had betrothed her life and love to him that night, as he had to her, and the shawl was the symbol of that pledge. She had worn it habitually during their early years together, and long after Andy was born. Later she had relegated it to significant occasions, and finally tucked it away to safeguard it from further wear or harm.

She would retrieve it sometimes late of an evening. He'd reach the bedroom, and she would be just sitting there with it around her shoulders, with tears in her eyes. And he would hold her, and it would be pressed tenderly between her bosom and his chest, and through it he could feel the soft beat of her heart as he had that first night.

Andy was right, of course. He did hate to part with it. But it needed to be cared for when he was gone, and he would send it to her — the sooner the better.

He did not know how long he had sat there. Somewhere during the course of his absorption he had dozed. Aroused from a light slumber, he blinked himself awake. The shawl had fallen loosely into his lap. Jenny was in a tight ball at his feet. He stirred slightly, rubbing a heavy hand over his face. The chair creaked and Jenny rose stiffly to her feet, hunching stiffly, then stretching, first one hind leg and then the other.

She stared at him blankly, then walked over and plopped with a thud onto the rug at the foot of the bed. He watched her, dryly amused, then returned soberly to the shawl, considering it anew. He rubbed his hand over his face again. It stopped on his chin, and he sat in an idle daze for several seconds. Finally, rubbing his cheek with four fingers and yawning, he lifted the garment carefully and draped it temporarily across one arm of the chair.

Tomorrow, or day after, he promised himself, he'd put it in a box and send it to Andy.

Rocking forward, he dumped his weight onto his palms and pushed himself up. Stepping to the dresser, he arranged the shawl neatly back into place and started to nudge the drawer closed. It was then, in the gleam of the lamp, that his eyes found the single strand of auburn hair. It was deeply meshed with the pelt of the yarn, and there was only the glint of the one small protruding loop that disclosed its presence. He caught it between his thumb and index finger and gently pulled it from the cloth. It was long and wispy, burnished the color of pine resin by the light.

He blinked against the burning in his eyes. How he had loved that fiery auburn hair — the play of firelight through it in a darkened room.

God in Heaven, if he could only collapse the years and put time and place together again. There was little telling how long the strand of hair had rested there; certainly before the snows had grown to snuff out the fire. Libby was yet a vibrant, young woman.

Almost incredulously he studied the wisp of hair.

He still could not find it possible, sometimes, to believe that she was gone. She must be upstairs in her sewing room, or busy in the kitchen, or out hanging the wash. She did that, he recalled whimsically, long after they had acquired a dryer. He had loved her quaint and quiet ways. The subtle little intimacies they shared. The way she pursed her lips when he touched her and she begged for him.

He had loved everything about her.

Laying the tiny strand back upon the shawl, he pushed the drawer shut. He sat again in the rocker for a time, then readied himself for bed.

Long after he had retired, the honesty of the darkness tortured him. His attempts at sleep were tormented by ceaseless fits of conscience. He slept only in stutters, awakening again and again with the burden of the dilemma. Twice he got up and tried to quell the anxiety with subterfuge. The first time he retreated to the porch and gazed for long minutes at the stars, separating the constellations and recalling their meaning. The air was cool and crisp, and should have cleared his head, but didn't. A meteor seared across the heavens, starkly brilliant upon the obsidian sky. Then it was as suddenly gone, only punctuating the solitude. Next, he had collapsed into the leather sofa by a soft lamp with a Buckingham book, and tried to escape for an hour in its pages. But escape had been impossible, and Jenny had come finally, to question his absence.

Now he was abed once more, trying yet to force his mind away. But he could not. He lay there dreadfully riddled with worry, tossing and turning. Twice the clock struck the hour, and it would not subside. The night was endless.

Stifled by the hopelessness, he could endure it no longer. Driven to compulsion, he shoved the clammy covers suddenly aside and sat up again. He was in a hot sweat. In the pressing blackness, he could feel the dank heat of the perspiration that beaded thickly upon his forehead. There was a slow, crawling trickle down the valley between his pectoral muscles.

He switched on the lamp, squinting at the abrupt harshness of the light. Lingering on the side of the bed, he mustered his wits, then stumbled to the bathroom and bathed his face, neck, and chest with a wet washcloth. The cold, frank caress of it was only a transient salvation. For a truthful minute, he stared at himself in the mirror, then acceded.

He would face it now, tonight.

It would wait no longer.

Blunted with fatigue, Ben Willow shuffled back to the bedroom, found his pants, and dropped heavily again on the side of the bed. Laboring one leg into place, then the other, he hoisted the cuffs indolently above his heels, worked the britches sluggishly up his thighs and over his scant buttocks, and hooked the waist button. Scratching a temple, his eyes searched the room for his shirt. It was on the cedar chest where he had left it. He pulled himself upright with the help of the footboard and steadied his way to it. Retrieving it, he buttoned it on and stuffed the tail under his belt. Stooping cautiously to pick up his boots, he started for the door.

Jenny was questioning him with sleepy eyes. Leaning, he fondled her ear with his spare hand.

"Strange doin's, huh girl?"

The inquiry was still written deeply into her gaze.

"What you get for livin' with a quare old man," he said.

She got up and followed him into the kitchen. He slid a chair from the table, invested himself in it, and laced on the boots. Nonchalantly, he noticed that his fly was still agape. He stood and tugged the zipper tight. Solemnly, he downed a glass of milk and a banana, handing Jenny a piece of cheese and half a biscuit. Then he made his way to the back threshold, pulled his jacket and hat from the peg, and opened the door.

Jenny bumped past his ankles, clamoring for the porch screen. Ben pushed it clear and stepped into the darkness. Ebullient, the little setter bolted for the pasture.

"Jenny!"

Recoiling abruptly, the fading, white blur forced itself to a halt and turned.

"Come! Heel!"

Dropping her tail, Jenny complied, perplexed with the reprimand.

"Sorry, girl," he apologized, "not just now."

She read perfectly the strain in his voice, and with canine grace, excused the moment before as if it had never happened. Hugging his side of the truck, she accepted the opened door, and climbed onto the passenger seat.

Bending left out of the driveway, he drove lethargically to the stop sign at Jacox Crossroads, swung the truck right off Traver's Creek onto the old Hillsboro Highway. The road was empty and lonely, his headlights small against the night. Against a sea of black, the truck seemed infinitesimally insignificant, eminently vulnerable. The feeble glow of the dashboard instruments cast a ghostly pall upon the cab. The softened hum of the tires and the drum of the engine barely disturbed the silence. Only the brief, mournful complaint of the brakes periodically pierced Ben Willow's abstraction. And each time, he lapsed as quickly back into his purpose. For he knew only what he was compelled to do, and little of how.

It was only a mile and a half more to Shandy Road. So deeply absorbed was he that the tiny roadside sign emerged into consciousness almost before his mind was prepared to acknowledge it. He braked abruptly, swung the wheel, then mechanically pressed the foot pedal again. A curve and a hilltop later, and in the right half of the windshield the indistinct, chalky perception of a small building seeped into the periphery of the headlamps. Slowing, he guided the truck into the narrow gravel drive that encircled it. As the sweep of the lights peaked, it grew into a modest clapboard chapel with a proud wooden steeple.

7

Shiloh Church was virtuously whitewashed, eminently Baptist, and 137 years devout. On Sunday mornings when the weather was faithful, it sheltered a fervent congregation of forty-three, counting children, visitors, and recent births. Built shortly before West Virginians were rallied to war, and left for another place of the same name from which many would never return, it was initially christened Belk's Chapel, for Benjamin Belk, the itinerant disciple who settled these hills and was most constructive in its origin. After the Virginia Campaign, it was rechristened, in honor of the bravely dead. It had served its wildwood community well. Withstanding the passing decades, it was a comforting and joyous retreat, and in its tiny sanctuary had been consummated the commerce of human spirits for six generations; through sin and consecration, union and re-union, birth, life, strife, and death it had stood as staunchly as the mountain folk who were its foundation.

And just beyond its back door, beyond the small picketed cemetery, the mountains soared in eternal stair steps to Heaven.

He had first met Libby there, when she was nothing more than a slip of a girl, and he was barely a hand-me-down into long pants. They had played there together as children, at family reunions and Sunday noonings, running and jumping at tag and go-seek, and turning rocks in the stream for salamanders and hellgrammites. She had fallen once, and gashed her knee on the edge of a jagged stone. It had bled frightfully, and she had cried, and he had picked her up — he but eleven and she just seven — and carried her the whole of the hundred yards back to the churchyard without ever putting her down. The grown folks and kids alike had clamored around them, and after that she was his Princess and he was her Galahad. It was there when they had lingered closely beneath a spreading beech, when first she had come to him as a woman, and first he had kissed her, lightly upon the lips. It was there they were joined under God two years afterward, and, incomprehensibly, there now that she was buried.

Behind the church, at the bend of the circle where a faint path embarked, Ben Willow stopped the truck and cut the engine. Jenny hurried over, standing with her paws in his lap. He put an arm around her and pulled her snugly into his armpit, then sat there for a time in dark and utter silence, searching himself one last time. But he was exhausted with thought, and his mind stalled, and he simply surrendered. Forcing himself to move, he pushed Jenny away and groped for the window handle. Finding it, he cranked the glass partway down, then pulled the door lever. Old and stubborn, it grabbed halfway. Bumping the door frame lightly with his shoulder, he tripped the latch.

Expectantly now, Jenny was crowding his shoulder, her excited breath beating against his cheek.

"No, girl," he reproved mildly, "you have to stay."

Gently admonishing her back, he slowly swung open the door and stepped down onto the gravel.

Despite the caution, Jenny was nudging the small of his back, poised on the edge of the seat to jump down.

"No, Jenny, get back!" he snapped, more brusquely than he meant.

He pushed the door into her face, forcing her to retreat. She looked at him through the window. Even in the darkness, he could see the disappointment swelling into her eyes, and it hurt.

He made his way around the hood, onto the buff ribbon of the path at the edge of the woods. He stopped there briefly, to look back. He could scarcely see the small white figure through the window, watching him away. But he could feel the tug of her. He hesitated a few seconds more, dropped his eyes to his feet, then turned and walked on.

Beyond the shallow copse of woods, at the hem of the mountain, lay a diminutive clearing of slightly less than an acre. Perception would have rendered it even smaller, pressed hard as it was by the forest on two sides, towered over by the single, great maple at its center, and contained in part by picket fencing. It loomed from the night in an aberration of netherlight and shadow, much as an illusion. But for the mere sliver of a moon, barely enough to scatter pale beams through the black lace of the treetops, it would have been formless. The meager gift of the moonlight, however, was sufficient to divulge the scattered gray headstones of a small country cemetery. They rose from the night like awakened sentinels, to stand solemnly over lives wagered and spent, dreams brought to earth. With each few steps he took, another rank would rise, and pass as eerily behind him.

They pressed closely around him as he stopped under the shadow of the draping red maple, to ask boldly of why he was there. And when he knelt by the small mound beneath the one that read ELIZABETH CHANDLER WILLOW on the one side and BENJAMIN FRANKLIN WILLOW on the other, he knew they understood, for they drew away to respect his reverie.

He sat there beside her for a quarter hour, among the leaves that sifted occasionally down with the night breeze, and could say nothing. The constriction in his throat was overpowering, and the welling in his eyes unrelenting. His sinuses clogged and his breath labored in heaves through his mouth, and he was so taken with emotion that his teeth chattered.

"*It was good, Libby,*" he managed finally in a tortured whimper.

The words would not come again for a while. Only the tears.

When they subsided, his eyes rested blearily for a time on the empty space on the stone under his name, faintly lit by moonglow, where someday, not distantly, the final date would be cut that would bracket the measure of his life. And then on the small rectangle of ground beneath.

"What do I say, Libby," he asked aloud, "how do I tell you?"

"Say it as you feel it, Ben Willow, nothing less, ever," she would have said, he thought. She had said it before.

He cradled his forehead heavily in his palm, then pulled his hand down his face until it covered his nose and mouth. He sighed deeply through his fingers, dwelling momentarily on the single whippoorwill whipsawing at the fringe of the mountain. The whippoorwill would be gone soon, he thought absently, he and his brethren, until spring.

"I wasn't always there, Libby," he said, "... but you were always with me."

It came out awkwardly. He was stumbling. It was even more difficult than he had imagined. They were destined to be together; they had believed it from the start.

"It will always be that way," he continued, "regardless of the distance between us."

Partly then, more than anything, he wanted simply to leave, to let things be as they had left them. Torn as he was, however, his heart would not concede. Not the part of it where the wildness burned.

"I was only good for a few days at a time, Libby, you always knew that.

"I had to go back. It was the only way I could go on.

"I have to go again, Libby . . . *please understand*." His voice broke and he sobbed as uncontrollably as a child, whimpering between the spasms.

He shook his head helplessly. He could go no further. The words would not come.

Ben Willow got up to leave, tears streaming down his face into the hollows above his jaws.

"I *loved* you, Libby," he said from the depths of his heart. "Thank you for loving me."

He turned then, and started away, between the somber sentinels again. He had taken only a few steps before he was compelled to stop. He looked back at the lonely gravestone and the blackened shadow of the three words on it, and the faint lump of earth beneath it.

Of all things tangible and intangible that life had delivered, he had cherished her most. All but one. And never before, not in flesh or blood, had it been a threat to her.

When he reached the truck, Jenny was beside herself, wriggling with joy and dancing on the seat. Tonguing his face thoroughly, she tailed an intoxicated tattoo against the backrest.

"Jenny, Jenny," he chided thankfully.

He twisted the ignition key and the engine caught after a few cranks. Completing the circle, he coaxed the pickup over the rise of the shoulder back onto Shandy Road. Tomorrow, he would see Clayton McAlister, and afterward, he would ask Clyde Wood for more than a friend had the right to.

A mile more and not yet home, the world caught up with Ben Willow, filled him with awe, and begged him to pause. Killing the motor, he allowed the truck to drift to the shoulder and coast to a stop. Exhausted, he sank against the seat, invited Jenny into his lap, and turned the window down. To the east, like a freshly lit candle in a cathedral, a faint, white light was rising. It grew above the rim of the highest ridge in the emptiness of the night, billowing cautiously higher and brighter. On a fragile breeze it traveled the clear, chill air, giving shape and form to the land, awakening the sleepy notes of the cardinals, stirring the crows to wing. Collecting the wispy clouds, it stained them gray, and pink, and purple, and blanched the skirts of Heaven pale blue. Behind the clouds rose an aurora of lemon, and between the mountains and the sky, a thread of molten gold.

Magnificently loomed the gleaming cap of the sun. Edging above the horizon, it spilled in soft rays across the countryside, through chimneys of mist from the valleys, onto the hillsides, over the meadows, painting the colors into a new day. On and on it spread, like an artist's brush upon an endless canvas, and every touch was vibrant with autumn.

At the center of the small cemetery behind Shiloh Church near Shandy Crossroads, it painted vermilion fires into the top of a maple tree, and through the tree blew a maiden rush of morning wind. Like scattered sparks, the red leaves swirled, then stalled. As one by one they trickled softly to earth, onto the single grave at the foot of the headstone marked Elizabeth and Benjamin Willow.

It was the first day of the tenth month. Across the whole of the Alleghenies, October had arrived.

8

"Pup ain't hard to look at," Clyde Wood observed laconically.

Jenny stood tiptoe tall and trembling, eyes riveted to the drift of feathers from the quail Ben Willow had just downed. Cocked for go, but faithfully steady, she awaited the tap on the ear that would release her boiling instincts.

"Packs your pipe, huh?" Ben Willow quipped as he moved to her.

"Uhhmn."

"Fetch," Ben ordered tautly, touching the galvanized setter lightly with four fingers.

Breaking explosively, Jenny raced to the fall, fussed with the mingled scent, then scooped the bird from the grass. Tail awag and prancing, she trotted the thirty yards back and delivered crisply to her mentor's hand.

"Awright, Jenny, *good girl*," he praised, rubbing and patting her flanks. Proud of herself, she shook vigorously from stem to stern, then wallowed happily at his feet. When she got up again he slipped on the leash. She danced, wanting to go again.

"Five days, Clyde. Come Monday," he pronounced.

"Oh, God," Clyde mocked gravely, "you haven't heard. Grouse season's off this year, Ben, canceled! Governor's wife's an unmitigated hunter hater. Got PETA in tight on the lobby list. Trendy these days, you know."

"Guess I can't be expectin' my name on the inaugural ball register, then," Ben placated.

"Course you know politicians, they're blamin' it on the fire hazard," Clyde explained. "Can't have a bunch of folks out wanderin' the woods kickin' up public fires.

"Hate it, Ben. Truly do."

"What about Laughton Hodges?" Ben queried whimsically. "Hell, he used to wear it out, grouse and 'cock."

"Reformed man, Ben. Seen the error of his ways. Still hunts 'doodle, I'm told, but not in the woods."

Ben grinned and shook his head. "Must not want to get reelected, then."

"Laughton ain't worried 'bout reelection, Ben. Not now. Just made the mansion; biggest margin in West Virginy history. He can promise and piddle for a while. That's what politicians do, you know, Ben . . . promise and piddle.

"Next year, now, you may get to go."

"Two, Clyde," Ben warned, holding up two fingers and chuckling, "two farts short of the outhouse."

"Gospel, Ben, gospel," the storekeeper said, framing his shoulders with his palms.

"Then we'll go to Pennsylvania," Ben vowed.

"Off there too, Ben. Went Democrat."

"Then Quebec," Ben whiffed.

The two old friends looked at each other for several seconds, mutual grins breaking into mild laughter.

"You know, good behavior might get you an invite," Ben cautioned. "When's the last time you went?"

"Last time you had a dog," Clyde admitted.

"If you're gonna let that little Superposed twenty-eight wither away, might as well give it to me," Ben kidded, "I can do it some good."

"Hell, Ben, you're too old to buy green bananas. Just be a waste. I've kinda taken a favorin' to Josh Chadfield, Ben, Therman's boy, prob'ly leave it to him."

"Josh's a good boy," Ben agreed. "He'll do right by it in a few years. Well, meanwhile, come and go ahuntin'."

He looked down at the little setter, digging another hole. "Jenny's ready, I think," he mused, "you'll like her."

"Already do," Clyde said. "And I just might do it. Right now, I've got to get along though, Ben, got a directors meeting at the store at seven."

"Hang on a minute," Ben instructed, starting for the house, unsnapping the check cord and calling Jenny to heel.

He was back shortly with a jar of fresh honey. "Put this with a biscuit," he offered.

"You're a credit to creation, Ben," Clyde allowed, "hope you're a year in Heaven 'fore the devil knows you're dead."

Ben shook his head, grinned.

They walked slowly to Clyde's truck, pausing at the driver's door.

Ben laid a gentle hand on his friend's shoulder.

"Thanks, Clyde," he said.

"You're sure about this," Clyde Wood asked for the last time, resting a reciprocal palm on Ben's extended arm.

"Yes."

He stepped back to clear the way as Clyde climbed into the cab, started the motor, and rolled slowly away.

"Regards to Nettie," he remembered. Clyde acknowledged with a terse wave, then faded away down the road.

A brief sinking feeling overtook Ben Willow as he stood there, watching Clyde away, washing over him like a wave and spending itself on the shore of his conscience. Partly relief, partly melancholy. It was done. Now, before he died, he was ready to live again.

There was some small concern that Clyde was pushing seventy, and might not live himself to fulfill their accord, but Clayton McAlister was a young man, and he had left further instruction should that eventuate. He hoped it would not. An important thing, a man's last wishes. Clyde would do it right.

He could put it to rest now.

Jenny was waiting for him at the screen door, wriggling with his return. Impatient with her confinement, she whined and pawed, begging out.

"Jenn-*eeee*," he scolded insincerely, cracking the door and letting her onto the porch.

She gamboled around him, toenails clicking on the boarding.

"Here," he urged, stooping. Both knees cracked. She squeezed herself between his legs, almost bowling him over with her exuberance. He caught himself with his off hand, pushed himself upright, then unbuckled the beeper collar and removed it from her neck. He had let her wear it on recent training sessions, so she could become accustomed to the noise. He much preferred the thrushlike melody of a small bell, but his ears were no longer up to that, and it would be important to get quickly to her when she pointed the first few times. She was dependably handling the backyard quail, but wild birds in the woods were another thing, and she was yet young and flighty. A canny old cock bird could swiftly undo a lot of training.

He hooked the beeper collar over the banister, walked to the rocker, and sat down. The lagging sun was saying vespers over McCathern's Knob, the sky above it fading slowly to indigo, the light draining out of the glowing hillsides.

He was bone tired. He could feel the strain of the past few weeks. But at long last, October was here again. He could feel that too, seeping into him. Gradually, it was strengthening both fiber and fortitude, and he was being reborn with the mood and march of it, with the bracing, bell-clear mornings when the sunlight was so pure and its energy so unimpeded that the tops of the trees were cut against the sky as vividly as his life was cut against time, and every day, and every hour, and every minute pleaded for the living. Reborn with the mellow height of each splendid day, when the vibrant colors literally melted off the hills into the face of the river and pooled in the hollow of the valleys, and the bees gathered in the goldenrod and hummed happily on the lazy, golden air. With the beckoning of the mountains, the prospect of grouse, the company of a dog and a gun, the promise of November.

Only a few more days and he would give himself to it, as totally as a man could become one with his nature; soon he would hold it, as closely as you can possibly hold the thing you live for and not despoil it by familiarity.

He could hear a flutter and cackle from the side yard. Jenny had put the guineas to roost. It had become a matter of daily mischief.

"Hey, Jenny," he called softly.

Seconds later, she took the steps in a bound, clattered across the porch, and plopped her front paws in his lap. She looked him fully in the eyes and strained to reach his chin with a wet, black nose.

"While you were about your rat killin'," he said to her, "I was onto important things, like where we're gonna go openin' day. Important thing, you know, where a man and his dog spend the first day."

She knew by his tone that he was teasing her. She backed partly off his lap, cocked her head slightly, and grinned, her eyes squinced shut and her lips pulled into an exaggerated arc above her teeth.

Ben loved a dog who grinned. Jenny was only the third of seventeen over the years who would truly do it. It was a beguiling thing, a special gift.

"Think that's gonna buy forgiveness, huh?"

She sat in front of him, riveted to his eyes again, tail gently sweeping the porch flooring.

Body and soul she adored this man, this man who had come to her as a stranger with the thoughtfulness of a friend, who had invited her to share his life and treated her with kindness and respect. This man who had allowed her freedom and being again, who placated her simple desire to stay by him both night and day, and who had awakened the blazing passion within her and given it liberty for expression. As unequivocally as the beat of her heart, she was entrusted to him, and as eternally as her life would allow, she would abide with him.

"What's your vote," he asked.

Jenny studied him with questioning eyes, her ears listing at his voice.

"We could try Becky's Creek. It'd be reasonable on a creaky old man and we moved a tidy sum of birds in there last winter. We could work off the creek as usual . . . hunt up the ridges and down the hollows."

The setter looked at him intently.

"Well, yeah, they'd be a lot of leaves on the trees. You're probably right, more of a November haunt. 'Bout Thanksgiving.

"McGowan's Mountain? Well, maybe. That's about as high and as pretty as it comes. Some of the leaves will have dropped. Nary as many birds. Wouldn't have anything to do with Chrissy Blankenship, would it? She gave you a molasses biscuit last time, as I recall. And an oatmeal cookie.

"I know. We'll drop in on that long ridge on the back side of the Baker Sods. There're grapevines galore up and down the flanks and several old homeplaces with apple trees. We could hunt it to the end and then drop off and backtrack the foot of the mountain along the edge of all those old woodsy meadows behind Jacob Franklin's cow pasture. A judicious puppy could gavel up a bunch o' birds along there.

"Course I'd have to find one first, that wanted to go," he said, smiling at her.

"Can't forget the Kettlehorn or the South Fork either. Always good, whichever. If we go to the fork, we can pack along a fly rod and stash it by the water and come noon, when we've made the round, we can tie on a hackle and trick a brown trout into supper.

"Tell you what: we'll hunt the Kettlehorn and invite Ms. J. Allison Barstow along. Wouldn't that be the cat's pajamas?"

He hoped facetiously for a reaction, but he had lost his audience. Jenny was halfway down the steps, off on another exploration.

All the conversation was idle nonsense, of course, as if there were actually some debate. Whimsical augury, to gild the occasion.

The joke was on Ben Willow anyway. The irony of the matter was, had he asked, Jenny Barstow would very likely have come along, thank you, and two Jennys and the distraction of all that lovely blond hair would have played heavenly havoc with a grouse shoot.

9

Monday, come opening day of Ben Willow's sixty-ninth grouse season, was as glorious an early-autumn day as God could create. They were happy as wasps on watermelon, Ben and Jenny Willow, wallowing up the fifth grade of the Seven Step in the International on what was left of the timbering paths. As he had known they would.

Seven-thirty into the new day, the old truck grumbled along in four-low as the slope steepened, whining in and out of its gearbox as it alternately found and lost footing among the rocks and washes. Higher and higher it labored, until finally the gradient yielded and they were welcomed onto the long, gentle bench. Beside the massive corpse of the friendly chestnut, Ben applied the brakes, and it eased to a stop.

They tumbled out of the cab into the stiff, cold air, their breath condensing into clouds as around them the world fell away. In the blue haze beyond the mountain, ridge rolled into ridge, billowing to the distant horizon like wind-churned waves on a vast inland sea. From scattered valleys plumes of mist were rising, steeping slowly up through the pale yellow shafts of the waking sun. Across the sprawling miles, feeble splotches of sunlight were beginning to grow upon the shadowy landscape, kindling a sleepy glow in the mottled tapestries of hardwoods and evergreens. And upon it all was a reverent hush, much as the silence devoted to a morning prayer.

Over the fold of the Cheat, far away, came and passed a tiny, momentary glint of reflected sunlight. And behind it, another. Scarcely visible, a pair of hawks were hunting a careless breakfast, drifting in and out of the shadows. High and free.

In a jubilant rush, Ben Willow's spirit clamored to freedom again as well, released by the wonder and immensity of it, the wild, tameless, uncompromising defiance of it. Eleven months each year he languished, hoping that he might once more come to this moment.

Somewhere below, a million people were stepping into another day, jostling for a moment's liberation from a world contrived of boundaries. Here, there were no boundaries, only destinations. Destinations of the mind and the heart. Destinations governed only by determination and self-reliance and desire.

Turning to the truck, he reached for his old Parker, cradled in the gun rest behind the seat. It came to him with a belonging. He lay it gently on the hood and reached for the tattered old canvas vest behind the seat. He pulled it on, hesitating partway, gratified by the soft rattle of the shells inside, then snugged it in place around his collar.

Jenny, meanwhile, was still racing around in fits of exhilaration. He could hear her in the underbrush, making a short circle in the hollow below.

"Jenny!"

He heard her trickle to a stop.

"Jenny, here," he repeated softly.

An intermittent patter of feet, and a slight hassle of breath, and she topped the crest of the path in return. Running almost to him, she wheeled and impatiently started off again.

"Hey! Close, Jenny!" he cautioned.

Backtracking reluctantly, she came to him this time.

"I know. I know," he acknowledged, grabbing her collar, "but give an old man a chance and he'll tag along."

She pivoted, twisting his fingers in the collar.

"Ouch! Dammit, Jenny!"

Hanging on, he pulled the check cord from his vest with his other hand, snapped it on, and tied it to the bumper. He shook his numb fingers. She lunged against it repeatedly, whining.

"Could be you'll need me, you know," he reminded her. "Who's gonna shoot all those grouse you're gonna point?" He rolled his eyes heavenward.

She had calmed slightly at his voice, leaning against the taut cord, tail wagging furiously.

Ben rummaged behind the seat again for a moment and extricated the two brown paper bags that had been covered by the vest. He stuck one, then the other in the game pocket behind his back, slapped on his old Filson hat, and slammed the door.

"Okay, Jenny, just one more thing," he said, working the beeper collar out of his pocket and fastening it around her neck. He fumbled with the switch before he felt it trip, and held her for a minute to see that it was working. The signal was programmed for point only. It was less obtrusive that way, and also less annoying.

"I wish this were a bell, Jenny, but these old ears just won't allow it . . . so bear with me now and hang on when you stand a bird and it goes off, 'cause I'm comin'. It just takes a spell."

Jenny looked at him as he talked, still whining restlessly in her throat. He popped the snap, freeing her again. She bolted away down the path for a distance, then halted and checked for him.

The old man was behind her, his gun on his shoulder and a gleam in his eye, and somehow she sensed the difference this time. He fingered the whistle on the end of the dilapidated old leather lanyard around his neck and blew two sharp blasts.

"Bird, Jenny, bird!"

And Jenny Willow shot off the side of the path into the hollow that led to the streambed below, on the first cast of the first morning of her first grouse season.

It was indescribable really, the feeling inside, from following a dog again on a mountain path, from the pinch of pinfeathers he found in a vest pocket as he walked along, from the set of the gun on his shoulder. The morning sun was streaming boldly in now across the path ahead, the warm drafts rising. The trees on the hillside were shot through with orange and red and yellow, and the ground below as well, where the leaves had fallen. Somewhere up ahead a grouse was astir, and a puppy was afoot to find it.

It was humbling. Overwhelming.

You could relate bits and parts of it to other men who understood, who had been here, and even then there was a part of it that was so elusively tied up in spirit that it was indefinable.

He saw his dog climb out of the hollow and quarter across the path onto the forward hillside, which would open soon into an old overgrown clearing, where once a house and barn had stood. A few rotting timbers from the old barn still rested there. At woods' edge, the opening had encouraged a scattering of wild grapes, which occasionally pulled the birds from the forest and the patchwork of rhododendron above. Jenny, he was pleased to see, obviously remembered it. Good dogs always did. She was hunting beautifully. Her desire burned like a torch.

"Good girl, Jenny," he praised silently.

He could feel the pull of the grade in his hamstrings. His lungs were beginning to pump. It was a grand sensation. But he was slow, so much slower than once he had been, and he had to pick his footing carefully, for his step was not nearly so certain. Progress was a series of compromises with the terrain. He had learned to accommodate it, but he would never come to accept it.

Several minutes and three hundred feet farther, where the path intersected the lower side of the little clearing, he suddenly caught the piercing summons of the beeper collar. He turned his head right and left for a fix on the sound. It emanated from the hillside above and slightly ahead. He hurried as best he could toward it, excitement flooding his chest and pushing into his throat. He had gone only twenty yards or so when it stopped. He halted and listened, but could hear nothing. He eased on up the slope until he neared the edge of the timber. The little setter was whipping back and forth between field and the woods, temporarily incensed with ground scent. He had not seen it, but he knew what had happened.

When he neared her, he hollered "whoa!" at an accommodating moment. She pulled to a stop, then surged ahead.

"Whoa!" he yelled again. This time she stayed.

He leaned his gun against a tree, picked her up and set her back down a few feet to the rear, then went through a flushing ruse in front of her. The bird was gone, of course, but he wanted simply to remind her, calm her a bit, and regather the hunt.

"Got a little too close, huh," he observed. A faintly sheepish tail beat was his answer.

"You got to remember now, you're not huntin' those pussyfootin' pen-pampered quail. Proddin' tail feathers in this neighborhood's gonna keep you in trouble."

More wagging.

He tapped her on the ear. She stabbed forward, frittered with the ground leavings a few seconds longer, then bore away to resume the hunt, tail popping.

On they climbed. Thirty minutes later he caught the russet flight of a bird gliding low and away across the end of a thorn apple orchard. Jenny wasn't in sight, but he had heard her a minute before in the vicinity. He imagined there had been another wreck. She appeared, wild-eyed and overwrought, about the time he reached the area where the bird had passed.

"Hey!" he yelled. "Settle *downnn!*"

He could tell by her demeanor she was guilty, but to what degree he was uncertain. Like the old field trial adage: "You can't judge what you don't see." He always gave the dog the benefit of the doubt in such instances. If you started jerking a dog around every time a bird flew, you'd soon have an overcautious neurotic full of false points.

An hour later they were still climbing. Ben pulled up for a blow. His calves were cramping, his heart was thumping against his ribs, and beneath the light jacket his shirt was clammy. But they were above the seventh bench now. The bigger part of the journey was done. When he had first found the little meadow, he had assumed the bench fully girdled the mountain. Later he found that it dwindled at little more than the halfway point on each side. It had dawned on him then that he had not crossed it going up, and that of course was the explanation.

He stood watching Jenny work in and out of a small draw clustered with laurel. She went birdy and stopped twice, pointing for an instant each time, then moving on. On each occasion, his hopes rose and sank.

They needed a bird. A bird that would lay to her point and that would flush within reason, that he might bring to earth so that she could see the whole thing transpire as it was meant to be. He hated to beseech the Lord for such a favor when another creature's life was in the balance, but he did as sometimes he had before, silently praying that it would happen.

Jenny left the draw and hunted on, slicing the grain of the slope. He trudged after her, angling gradually uphill toward the crest of the mountain, toward the narrow spine of the ridge that rimmed the vast black hollow. The hollow that tumbled to the meadow, that had swallowed Trip and Cindy so mystically that evening thirty-one years before. His legs were pithy now, aching and quivering with the exertion, his breathing labored and wheezy. He would have to hold up at the ridge and rest awhile before he could attempt the descent to the meadow. Thankfully, it was only a short pull farther.

He had mustered the wherewithal for the next few yards and taken the lead step when he heard the shrill blast of the beeper collar. It was not far ahead, maybe even on the ridge itself. He felt the rush of adrenaline, found the footing beneath his boots, and urged himself up. Hastening his way with his free hand, pulling himself tree to tree, circumventing great, jagged upheavals of rock, he struggled to reach his dog as quickly as he could, hoping the bird would lay. With each passing second that he fought to get there, he was beset with the fear that the steady pulse of the beep would suddenly go quiet, that he would fail her or that she would break or that the bird would grow nervous and leave her.

At last the slope yielded and he topped the ridge. The beep was piercing now, only forty or fifty yards beyond. He gathered his strength and pushed on, shaky and stumbling, straining for the first glimpse of her. But it was thick with rhododendron, broken only in patches, and he could not see her. Finally, when it seemed from the din of the beep that he would stumble over her, the cover opened into a modest pocket at the fringe of the hollow. Jenny was standing thirty feet shy of a tangle of vines and broken limbs, starkly white under a splash of sunlight against the blur of the depression. The wind was in her face and she rested proudly against the scent, so certain he was sure.

"Whoa, Jenny," he said quietly as his breath staggered. "I've . . . got you."

The little tricolor setter stood rigid, true to her training, eyes glistening behind her full black mask.

This was the moment he had waited for. He had come to it hundreds of times before and the next was as fresh as the first, and each was as unique as the dog who struck it, and the scene that framed it. Nothing of God's creation had ever thrilled him more deeply, nor completely.

His heart was beating unmercifully as he fingered shells into the gun and advanced. His chest was taut with anxiety, his forehead sweaty with anticipation. The pressure now was his. Jenny had done her part. The rest was his.

Jenny moved slightly, drawing up a trailing hind foot and bringing it to rest beside the other, squaring herself.

"Whoa, girl," he whispered.

As he moved, he was reading the lay of the find. The bird would likely slip out low and drop off into the hollow. He paused and backtracked a couple of steps, circling behind the pointing setter until he could redirect his approach to advantage, hugging the break of the ridge. With luck, he would catch the departing bird just as it left the cover and skylined itself against the head of the hollow. The double gun waited at a practiced angle across his chest, resting lightly in his hands, the thumb of his right hand on the safety. He picked his way, steadily but carefully, riveted to the cover ahead.

"Please, God," he warned himself.

He had taken but two steps beyond Jenny's shoulder when the knot of vines ahead clattered with a buffet of tangled wings. Reflexively, he pivoted as the gun came to ready and he fought to distinguish the form and motion of the rising bird. For a procession of harrowing moments the grouse beat frantically to free itself of the cover. The delay broke his rhythm, undid his timing. Suddenly the struggling bird exploded, banking and whirling back over them and speeding away into the hollow. The shot from his right barrel splattered high. He saw the shot cut the leaves, though he had tried mightily to pull the muzzle under the dropping bird. He never had a chance to trigger the left. As he twisted to hasten the follow-through, the loose stone under his left heel rolled and Ben Willow crashed to the ground.

Jenny had stood until then. The improvident and headlong commotion was more than she could stand.

Ben Willow had lost his wind. The force of the fall was, for a time, incapacitating. He felt the sinking feeling in his stomach as Jenny shot by, but could muster not a word, which might have been futile anyhow. His first thought was not for himself but simply that the moment was spent, the opportunity lost.

He lay there for several seconds, gasping for breath, putting himself together. Gradually he pushed his upper body aright. He was badly shaken. His left shoulder blade was numb from the blow of the landing, and there was a dull, growing ache in his left arm below the elbow. He peeled his clothing back and examined the arm. It was abraded and so painful that he feared it was broken, but decided finally that it was not. When his breathing leveled, he reached for the Parker and pulled it into his lap. He knew that it had hit hard, indeed absorbed much of the fall. Fortunately, perhaps, but he grimaced as he appraised the damage. There were fresh white gouges in the dark, burnished walnut of the buttstock, and a slight chip splintered off the forearm. He inspected the barrels for dents. They seemed unharmed.

He laid it on the ground again and picked himself up. His legs seemed okay. The fingers on his right hand were stiff where they had been banged against the pistol grip. All in all, however, it could have been much worse. At least he was still mobile. They wouldn't have to send a helicopter.

In a week or two, he would mend physically. The sickness in his stomach would take far longer. Jenny had pointed and held her first grouse and he had failed her. He had not expected the riotous flush. But he was accustomed to the unexpected in grouse shooting. He had taken many birds far more difficultly presented than this one. It troubled him deeply. That he was no longer as adept, of course, was long since less than a revelation, but when he failed at something when before he would have never, and particularly when he blundered at the thing in which he had most greatly excelled, it was devastating. Ben Willow was uncompromising, most of all with himself. It would gnaw at him, demoralize him, until and if he could exact some semblance of salvation.

Moreover, this was a setback. He had worked hard to steady Jenny without diminishing the fire. The next time she pointed, it would be harder for her to stand flush and shot, and require more pressure to assure it. It was just one more rather-not-happen that would work to undermine the regimen of steadiness he had instilled. He worried too much about such things maybe, of a moment anyhow. He had been training dogs long enough to know that if you keep tapping at it, it was a lot like raising kids. Mostly, though it sometimes gets sidetracked, they want to please you. Show them the right and steady of a thing, and they'll come back to it.

He listened for her below, but heard nothing. Several minutes had elapsed since he had fallen.

"Jenny!" he called. "*Jenn-eee!*"

He could hear her coming presently, below the break of the hill.

She trotted in happily. Ben tousled her ears and patted her flanks.

"I'm sorry, girl," he said. "I'd offer an excuse if I had one."

She looked him in the eyes as she was prone to do. He tried to read the message there. Nothing about apology that he could tell. Just "let's do it."

Well, he didn't deserve one anyhow.

"Awright," he agreed, climbing to his feet, "your lead . . . long as it's downhill."

Still shaken and unstable, Ben admonished himself down the slope, catching a sapling now and then to slow his descent. Jenny was crisscrossing the front again with the regularity of a pendulum, showing occasionally in the cleft of the hollow as she inquired of one side, then the other. He reached the floor of the grade and the small basin clustered with ferns, where the wispy green spruce clustered and the little stream was born. It shimmered along ahead in a reflective trickle, gathering the colors of the leaves. Again he was taken with the utter stillness of the place, so profound that it was disquieting. He could feel the sense of privilege swelling inside once more.

He continued to descend with more enjoyment now as the slope receded, trekking the gentle fall of the stream as it acquired small, sparkling rivulets from creases in the adjoining hillsides. Once he heard a bird go out. A minute later Jenny exited the vicinity, suspiciously happy, then saw him and whipped back into a hunting ruse. He studied her closely. Not enough to warrant an arrest . . . but sufficient to prompt the injunction.

"Look *out*, Jenny!" he rumbled. "I need redemption, not retribution."

She halted for a moment, looked at him, then bounded back into cover.

Ben Willow smiled, more amused than disconcerted. She was learning how to sweep the dirt under the rug, the little gyp, though she was as yet comically inept.

Three hundred yards later he almost stumbled over another bird. With no help from Jenny this time, it sprang aloft in a thunderous blur of feathers almost beneath his feet, blowing by his head so closely he could see the startled black bead of its eye, and quartering swiftly away up the hillside. The Parker came up, around, and settled, held for a moment, then wavered. It was tempting, but defeating. He had neither need nor desire to drop an aimless bird. He'd wait for a point. Jenny must learn they were a team.

"Whup, Jenny!" he cautioned, asking her to close, for she was becoming a bit ambitious as the hillsides receded. "One day you're gonna learn why I'm back here," he said to himself.

He chirped three times on the whistle.

Jenny checked in and out, working comfortably afront once more.

Ahead the spruce was beginning to thicken, the billowing green limbs shingling into a shadowy curtain. Shimmers of sunlight gilded random feathery branches with gold. The stream had found its voice, tumbling along now in a gabble. He could feel his pulse quickening with anticipation. Of the myriad places he had wandered in his sporting life, none had ever affected him so completely as this.

A flight of deer scattered before him, sketches of tawny hide and bristling white flags. He stopped to listen. In old days he could have caught the rattle of hooves on stone as they scrambled wildly up the hillside, and then the abrupt hush as they paused above to listen. Now he could hear nothing but the water and a timid wind.

On he rushed, as old men rush, with his heart dangerously ahead of his feet. It was not far now. Already, Jenny was there.

It happened almost before he knew it. With the same thrilling suddenness the veil of spruce drew away, perception overtook reality, and he was standing again at the crest of Samuel Thomas's meadow.

Below, Jenny was holding inquest at the ancient orchard, by the darkened mound of the old homeplace, threading figure-S's between the bent gray trees. Probably a bird there recently. Beyond her, the last bench of the Seven Step poured itself over the side of the mountain, and the layered ridges grew away to the horizon, hovering under a blanket of blue haze. The meadow was still lushly green and cast upon it were scattered splashes of red and orange and gold, where the leaves had ridden to rest on the October wind. Among them the sparkling stream meandered.

Neglecting his watch, Ben Willow glanced at the sun overhead. It hung twelve-thirty high in a faultless blue sky, the air laundered so purely by the building pressure that it shook the senses. On lightened steps, he ambled his way to the small stone bench by the stream that Sam Thomas had built from three slabs of granite. It glistened with flakes of mica in the bright sunlight, while beside it the water sang happily by.

Ben laid his gun to one side in the thick green grass, pulling off his old hat and dropping it alongside. He stretched mightily, with his face thrown to the sun, closing his eyes and drinking in its warmth and the caress of the breeze. Relaxing again, he let his eyes ramble the semicircle of his surroundings, lost in its serenity.

Jenny was unaccounted for now. He called her. She had decided to check on him for she came almost immediately, rushing in from behind the decaying rubble of the house, welcoming his touch. He slipped three fingers under her collar and punched the beeper off.

"What say, girl, no grouses about?" he asked, tousling her ears. She wriggled and tugged against his restraint, asking to be off again.

"Nope . . . nope. Dinnertime. Let's bank the hunt and drift a while."

He pulled a worn latigo leash from his vest, black and slick with age and use, and lashed with scratches. Snapping it to the ring on Jenny's collar, he tethered her to a nearby maple sprout. It was handier than he wished. He looked around him, disconcerted by the number of others that had sprung up in the last five years. One day soon, despite Sam Thomas, the little meadow would give itself back to the forest. Sobered, he dwelled on the thought for a moment, then swept it aside.

By then it wouldn't matter, he guessed.

Jenny was favoring a paw. She was down on her forelegs, attacking it with her teeth.

"Here, girl, let's see."

Ben caught the paw between his fingers, carefully parting the pads while the setter licked his fingers.

"Uh-huh." A brier had worked its way deep between her toes, embedding itself into tender skin. He grasped it between two fingers, eased it out, and held it up for her to inspect. She snuffled it with her nose, to see what part of her came with it.

"Nothin' you need to keep," he assured her, pitching it aside and stepping away to the edge of the gurgling stream.

Intrigued, tail lolling, she watched as he laid the back of his shriveled old hand gently against the water. The current rushed around it, clean and cold. Satisfied, he removed one of the paper sacks from his game pocket, taking from it a small corked bottle. The liquid inside caught the sun, glinting purple. He immersed the bottle, resting it among the rocks, pleased at the eddy of water that encircled it. From another pocket he took a folding tin cup, pulled it open, and lowered it to the water, letting it slowly fill. Raising it to his lips, he drank, shutting his eyes to relish the bracing ecstasy of it.

Replenishing the cup, he balanced it on the stone slab and seated himself alongside it. For long minutes he sat there, staring idly across the distance, considering the unencumbered gift of the mountain and the meadow, the sun, the wind, and the sky. The setter and the shotgun. The set of the old Filson hat, the woods-worried leather of his boots, the years of tooth marks on the mouthpiece of the old Bakelite whistle. The wisps of feather he found hiding in the crevices of his shooting vest.

There could never be enough of it. Were he to live another hundred years, there would never be enough.

He wondered sometimes, in this day and age, how he came to be this way. Deep inside somewhere . . . someway . . . thank God, a primordial gene had spiked. He cherished the times it separated him from the world.

He would never understand the realm below. How some men could forsake something so utterly consummating and genuine as this and return to life in a world crowded with pretense and manipulated animosity.

The planet was full of such men, of course, and women, and always would be. People who so enjoyed the charade and the chalice that they had carried themselves hopelessly distant from their origin. It was why there were great cities, towers of commerce and bastions of industry, trendy eateries, and millions of town houses and condos all in a row.

But they borrowed from the earth things they could not possibly return. The debt had mounted so geometrically that even the manipulators had found it necessary to accede a natural dependency, making one-handed politics of it. While the other gorged on in exploitive gulps, with wanton gluttony.

One day, perhaps even in the next hundred years, it would be gone. One day they would miss it. The peace that once lay somewhere in the woods just beyond the back door. When it had shrunk to little more than a pittance of public parks. The sanction of a few million acres would prove insufficient to satiate the homecoming of a trillion people.

He looked to Jenny, enjoying the quizzical expressions of her eyes as she watched a leaf twirling on a twig. Jenny worried little of such things, he thought.

Useless anyhow.

He shook the afterthoughts from his head, freeing his mind to travel at will once more. It brought him back to ground, as always, not far from Libby.

Pulling a small, folded square of checkered linen from his pocket, he let it linger in his hand a moment, then shook it loose and allowed it to settle casually over the stone table. It fell, bright blue and white, over the gray granite and onto the green grass. Pleased with the impression, he dug his sandwich from behind his back, peeled open the Saran Wrap, and laid it on the cloth. He failed at his first attempt to rise, settling back helplessly onto the stone. His legs had stiffened. The morning had been taxing. He tried again, nudging himself aloft with the strength of his arms. Steadying himself, he shuffled to the stream. Stooping, he retrieved the little bottle, now beaded and deliciously chilled. Making his way back to his seat, he recovered a small shot glass from a final upstairs pocket of the canvas vest. He pulled the cork and tipped the bottle. The blackberry wine inside poured a rich reddish purple.

He placed the shot glass beside the sandwich and appraised the result. Then frowned. The tin cup was out of place. He discarded its contents, pushed it closed, and returned it to a shirt pocket.

Now.

"Whatcha think?" he asked of Jenny, riveted to his every move. She wagged her tail and wiggled and danced on her front paws against the leash.

He reached for the sandwich. Met midway by a reproving notion, he hesitated. Urging himself up again, he crossed the stream and collected a handful of red and yellow leaves from the meadow. Returning to the make-shift table, he moved the sandwich and wine to one side and let the impromptu bouquet spill loosely onto its center.

That was for Libby. It had been Libby's idea . . . the tablecloth and the wine at each opening-day nooning, in those wonderful years before An-drea was born and life thickened, when Libby was young and carefree and had hunted with him. When they could hardly endure a parting. When they had laughed so easily under the sky and toasted the sun in some small, hidden clearing high above the patchwork of farmland below, with Thorn and Thistle sprawled at their feet . . . and drank to the birds and the day.

"Special things deserve special favors," she said, never satisfied until a delicate wildflower or a sprinkle of autumn leaves graced the occasion.

It was the soft, ethereal touch of a woman, and he had savored the rit-ual from its beginnings, continuing it faithfully through the years. It was as crucial as the hunt itself.

He raised the glass to the sun, turning it, inciting sparkling splinters of light through the translucent red-purple of the wine.

"Honest men and bonnie lasses, Libby," he proposed . . . "setter feath-ers and grouse on mountains."

He sipped the wine, sharing the sandwich between times with Jenny, and just drifting, like the leaves that sifted by on the wind. There was no place to hurry, no thing to attend. Only life itself, which had grown far more dear.

He finished with a Winesap apple, folded shut the pocketknife he had used to slice it to quarters, and got up to find a soft place in the grass of the meadow near Jenny. He lay on his back, palms clasped under his head, indulging the ebb of fatigue from his muscles and the dampening of his breathing. Shortly Jenny conceded, turning three times before she col-lapsed into a ball. Sometime between contemplating the infinite depth of the crystal blue sky and supposing the fate of the afternoon hunt, Ben Wil-low faded from consciousness into sleep.

He awoke with a start. Jenny was on her toes, barking furiously, strain-ing in staccato stabs against the end of the leash. He strained for the source of the commotion, but his eyes were bleary and he had to massage them with his fingers before he could see clearly. A skunk had left the sanctuary of the old homeplace rubble and sauntered streamside for a drink. He watched, amused, as it stole cautious laps between furtive glances at Jenny. Finishing, it scratched an ear, then whirled and hightailed it on nimble toes for its den.

"That's all we need, Jenny, a row with a polecat. You'd like that sumpum awful, wou'dn' you?"

He looked for the sun and found it lower than he liked. His watch heightened his displeasure. It was approaching three o'clock. They'd never make the truck before dark.

"Damn," he thought.

There were days when it wouldn't have mattered in the least, but they were gone. He hadn't anticipated a flashlight and an old man had no business stumbling around on a mountain in the dark. He was angry with himself. He had meant only to drowse; he had been more weary than he realized.

Quickly, he gathered the lunch leavings, folding the checkered cloth and replacing it to his pocket. Snapping Jenny free, he prodded the leash into his game pocket with one hand while he picked up first his hat and then his gun with the other.

Jenny made a dash for the skunk haven, but he managed to warn her off.

"Bird, Jenny, bird . . . bird in here!" he called, directing her to the west end of the meadow, toward the truck. They would take the bench to its completion, then travel the ridges, avoiding as much as possible the in-and-out climbs of the deep winding draws. It was the shortest way back, and mostly downhill.

Intoxicated with freedom, the setter fled the meadow swiftly, boring ahead into the woods.

For a brief minute Ben stood by the spot of earth covering Sam Thomas, feeling it run through him again. The headstone listed ever more precariously, so chalked and encrusted with lichen that the spellbinding words of its inscription were almost illegible. Next time, he told himself, he must straighten the stone and brush it clean.

He forced himself away, after Jenny. He paused again at the tree line and looked back over the little meadow and the shadowed corner of the grave site. He sighed, hoping there would be a next time, and turned and walked away.

He caught the white blur of the setter, fading to the front some seventy yards out. She was flying and reaching.

"Hey, Jenny, remember I'm back here," he yelled, fearful that she would outrun his hearing and point out of kin.

It struck him then, like a loose board and his heart jumped into an anxious knot at the cleft of his throat.

He had forgotten to turn the damn beeper collar back on. Jenny was running silently. As much ground as she was covering and as slow as he was, barring a miracle, he'd never find her if she pointed . . . not in time.

Dammit to hell! All the hours trying to get a dog on track, and then you yourself throw the switch on the spur line.

She closed twice in the next thirty minutes, and each time he tried without avail to call her in. She was yet young and strong with hunt, defiant, not out of disrespect but desire. He had encouraged that, not the defiance but the desire, worked mightily to leave the fire burning. He'd not start hacking her now. Without desire, you had nothing. Dampen it and it was like removing the patina from a hundred-year-old piece of heart pine furniture; you could never quite regain the original luster. He'd wait on her. If the chance came on its own, all and well.

Besides, shooting birds had long ago become the least of it. It was thrilling, watching her burn the front. At intervals, she'd show, a flash of white with a merry flagstaff, always well forward. Jenny hung the ten-to-two front as well as any dog he'd ever had, even Tony. A cover dog did not by necessity have to hug your feet. Its job was to find birds you would not on your own, and to please you in the doing. It was a thing to be highly valued, not easily attained — the stretching-forward casts, each building on the other. The trait was virtually innate. You could teach a dog to quarter, and you could encourage it to be front-running, but you could not infuse the natural, sixth-sense ability of always knowing where you were and forever turning to the front, no matter the range. A dog ranging ambitiously forward was hunting for the gun as surely as a dog underfoot; it was not obligatory that they do it within the distance of a shotgun charge. Not a pointing dog. Not Ben Willow's dog.

If a front-running dog went missing, at least you knew where to look.

Still and yet, there was always the chance of walking by a standing dog unseen, or a limb find on a puzzling tangent.

He worried mightily of losing Jenny on point. Losing a dog on point was the most abominable travesty in Ben Willow's constitution. Particularly a young dog. It was nothing less than a betrayal. You trained a dog to hold, to wait unerringly for you. It was a trust bond, the promise you made from the first day you asked a dog to abandon its instincts. When a dog pointed, it was your obligation to get there in a reasonable span of time. If you did not, you could hardly blame the dog for ultimately reverting to its nature. Then it was six steps backward for the three you had managed forward.

Reaching the end of one ridge, he negotiated the small rocky saddle to the next, pulling up to listen for the travel of his dog. She was showing regularly, but it was imperative to stay as closely in touch as possible. Almost on cue, she emerged from a laurel thicket, crossed the ridgeback below, and rolled out through open hardwoods to the first of several thorn apple orchards ahead.

"Nice, Jenny," he thought.

There was almost always a bird here. He hoped so now. Jenny had been humping it for an hour without a contact.

The afternoon had softened. The sun was growing weary; an hour and it would tag the horizon. Its warm mellow light was gentling in on the northwest slopes, where the thorn apples grew, while simultaneously the lusty breath of evening was beginning to steep from the forest floor. The blue haze over the far headlands was washing to violet where the shadows deepened between the cusps of the hills.

He dropped slightly downslope to the first of the hawthorn thickets. For the first time, Jenny closed and checked by to locate him.

"Back from Newark, huh? How's the weather?"

She acknowledged momentarily with body language, then bounced on.

"Find 'im, Jenny . . . *burrrd.*"

It failed to register that he had missed the opportunity to trip the beeper collar. The cover ahead had grown birdy and his blood was up.

So, still, was Jenny's. She was stitching briskly in and out of the cover, ambitiously sewing one cast onto another. He wove his way along the high edge of the thorn apple thicket as rapidly as his tiring legs would carry him, trying to stay in contact with her. His feet were heavy and his hamstrings ached as if they'd been beaten. Had it been his — he mused — this notion that an octogenarian could philander with a puppy?

He laughed, teasing himself with the answer.

It had been five minutes now since he had seen her. He prodded on, intently searching the cover, reaching a slight swale. It furrowed its way downhill for some two hundred yards, widening and deepening as it went, bellying at its completion to a small green basin of maybe an acre or more.

Outcroppings of rock dotted its length, along with scattered splotches of brier and saplings, but otherwise it was relatively open, wedging the thicket aside right and left. At the center of the small basin the earth was richly blackened with moisture where water collected. It was an alluring little intercession, secretive in the falling light, and whispering with promise.

He still had not seen Jenny and was growing anxious. He had that swelling feeling that she was pointed. Pausing, he pursed his lips, whistling softly. Once more.

Nothing.

He remembered the beeper again then, and cursed himself for the second time.

She might yet be ahead, but his instincts were drawn below. He surveyed the prospects. He'd have never thought twice of it fifteen years ago, simply sidling down, checking out the possibilities, and then cutting the slope back to the top. At seventy he was still hunting the Shickshinny on the day shift and two-stepping Libby breathless come moonshine. But that was then and this was now. Now he had to rest twice before he walked to the mailbox.

He'd do what he had to, but damn a gimpy-assed old fool that forgot to turn a beeper collar on.

He hastened down the grade, working through and around the occasional patches of brush and brier, combing every pocket for Jenny. With every passing second he grew more apprehensive, certain now that she was standing somewhere on a bird, and fearful that he would not find her in time. The little draw was thicker with cover than it had seemed from the top, and on either side the thicket was dense. His eyes strained for a patch of white or the glow of her blaze orange collar as he pushed nervously on. The dropping sun had been swallowed by a billowing lavender cloud bank that blanketed the distant ridges; the light was failing. Dusk would be premature.

He rushed to and fro, crisscrossing the depression, searching and searching until his eyes burned and saw nothing but brush and shadow. At one point a sparsely grown pocket jutted like a pointed finger deeply into the thorn apple thicket. He sidetracked, hurrying around it with growing despair, tripping once and almost falling. Regaining his balance, he stopped, his heart pounding. He didn't need another fall! Pushing on again, he completed the loop to the swale, dropping toward the clearing at its belly.

It had been almost twenty minutes since last he had seen Jenny. She was a young dog. He couldn't expect but so much. A wash of frustration rushed over him, bringing him to the edge of tears.

The sweat had grown on his forehead and he could feel its sticky dampness in his undershirt, layered hot against his skin. It fanned his discomfort, abetting the anxiety. And still dusk hastened, beginning to mute the landscape.

He reached the little meadow, larger than it had appeared, checkered with weeds and brier. He looked frantically for Jenny. Nothing.

He halted at its center, at wit's end, combing his senses for a proper bearing and coming up dry. How had he missed her? In one of a hundred places, of course, depending on how boldly she had taken the thicket. Once here, he had been certain that he would find her. She would have hunted it and he would have found her on an edge. It was beautifully birdy.

He could backtrack up the hill. Worming through hawthorn thickets this late would be futile, even dangerous. You couldn't see. He'd have to stumble over her. If she was still standing, which he doubted. Actually, he was expecting her to come in at any moment, *looking for him.*

His heart was sinking. This was not how the day was to go. Not opening day. Not any day.

He had come to the point of desperation. If Jenny hadn't pointed and simply stretched out of kin, or if she had pointed and broken off, she would be anxiously looking for him now. She was anything but an outlaw, bold but always with regard for his whereabouts.

Glumly, he gave up. Ben Willow was not a man accustomed to voice in the woods. But he was unstrung, maybe more distraught than once he would had been. A dog amiss was forever troubling, but Jenny's absence for any time was almost unbearable. Digging his whistle from beneath his vest, he blew three long blasts, waited a few seconds, then called.

"Jenny . . . Jenn-y . . . *Hey, Jenn-ee!*"

Turning 180, he hollered again.

"*Jenn-eee!*"

The loudness of his voice shattered the stillness of the mountain, rolling into the draw below and echoing from the offside slope.

A minute grew, then two. Ben cupped an ear, listening for the rustle of feet, the hassle of her breathing. All was quiet.

He started to call again and stopped midnotion, deterred by the stillness, so foreboding that it defied disturbance.

If she was near, she had heard him. If not, she was running lost and he must find her or move and allow himself to be found.

Disheartened and drained, he slowly began the uphill climb back to the ridge.

All the work. All the building. All the coming to a fitting moment. And this. Twice he had failed her, in a day. Maybe . . .

No. He wouldn't, couldn't, allow himself to think that way. There had been troubling days when he was younger, too.

He was past worrying about a misspent point. All he wanted now was to see her again, to know she was okay. To lay behind the failing, gather their resources for another day, another hunt, when hopefully fortune would run kind again.

Somewhere in the vast, shadowy hollow below, he heard a big owl whoop. In the distance, another murmured a reply. It found the boy in him and an uneasy shiver traveled his spine. It would be dark soon, and this was wild, lonely country.

He spurred himself upward, veering to dodge a copse of brier and stubble, drawing to the murky edge of the thorn apple orchard. He ached with fatigue, to his bones, and his legs were spongy. He made the sidelong pocket where the jutting finger pointed deep into the thicket and faltered, pulling up to rest.

For a minute or more he listened. The woods were deathly quiet. Queasy with anxiety, he shook away the reticence. He must call again. His fingers found the lanyard and then the whistle. Slightly off balance, spraddled awkwardly over a tumble of rock, he shifted uphill. Raising the whistle to his lips, he gathered his breath to blow.

In the same instant he started to exhale he saw it, through a tiny, open window in the limbs, a diminutive, ashen blur in the murky corridor between the briery perimeter of the pocket and the inner thicket. So shadow choked were the entangled branches of the hawthorns that he looked away, and then back, before he was sure. His heart jumped! He forgot fatigue, forgot the mountain, forgot the world. Stooping and worming his way under the outlying confusion of branches, forcing aside the snarl of thorny limbs, he fought his way closer. In a flood of relief, he was overwhelmed. It was Jenny!

She stood faithfully, pointed just inside the heavy clabber of briers. Her tail had wilted to nine-thirty, and she was trembling and swaying on her feet, but she was still intensely tacked to body scent. How long she had been there he could only guess, but it had been a while. Likely she was there when he made his way through the first time. How he had missed her was puzzling, but it would not have been difficult in the muddled cover.

"Oh, God." He shut his eyes to the welling emotion and exhaled.

"Got you, Jenny," he called softly, reassuring her. She flagged lightly, acknowledging.

Sixty years of grousing read the lay of the find, steered his determination, crafted his strategy. From the certainty of Jenny's stance and the security of the cover, he was sure the bird was there. But he was in an abominable position. He couldn't even get the gun up. He had to back away and work around to the outside of the thicket into the pocket itself. Then he would have a chance. It had to be fast; dusk was thickening now.

He turned and moved as quickly and unobtrusively as possible to escape the thicket, fearful with every step that he would hear the thunder of the departing bird. At last, with relief, he broke into the open pocket.

The Parker abreast, he neared the point of Jenny's stand. "It must go right this time," he told himself. The briers were dense. There was no hope of wading through them.

"Whoa, Jenny," he cautioned.

He kicked at their edge, tensing with the rattle, anticipating the bluster of the bird.

It did not come.

He kicked again, vigorously sideswiping the matted stalks. Nothing. Save the cutting tension of the suspense.

He checked for Jenny. She had not moved. His mind raced, gnawing at the dilemma. Two ways he had trained Jenny to break off and relocate: a tap on the ear or one short, shrill note of the whistle. He fingered the whistle, bringing it to mouth. There would be some confusion if she were hard against the bird, but she had been standing nose to feathers a long time. He was betting she would go. If she was canny enough to make a grouse dog, she'd understand. Instantly, he hit the whistle.

The briers rattled and jumped as Jenny stabbed forward, then clapped with a cacophony of stifled wing beats as the startled grouse thundered up and through a tangled bower. The bird shot skyward, flinched, twisted and rolled hard right, then pasted itself flat against the dusky ceiling of the thorn apple thicket and streaked diagonally away for the ridge. Ben Willow's old gun had jumped to shoulder at the first clatter of feathers, pulled up through the rising silhouette, bucked fruitlessly, then corrected crisply right as the bird rolled and peeled. Sweeping after the fleeting shadow, it swung through and past, and jumped again. There was a flash of fire from the muzzle and the crash of the shot thudded into the hillside. In virtually the same instant the blur of the grouse blew limp and ragged against the air and tumbled on its forward momentum into the thicket.

It had happened so quickly that reality had yet to overtake impression. He stood, still with the gun to shoulder, waiting for it to catch up. With it came a tide of gratification.

Jenny had burst into the open pocket with the first shot, bouncing and whirling, wildly searching for the bird. She never saw it, for it was well away, but she caught the swing and direction of the gun, and the bark of its second charge. Immediately she had slammed headlong through the briers again back into the thicket, hunting recklessly for the fall.

He could hear her, stuttering through the undergrowth, scrambling figure-eights.

"He's there, Jenny. Dead . . . dead bird, dead!"

He could hear the furor of her search intensify, bore more deeply into the thicket.

"Find 'im, Jenny. Find 'im," he urged, strident with excitement.

Suddenly, she stopped. There was a rustle, a stabbing clamor of motion, a moment of silence.

Then the staccato patter of paws, happy paws. Jenny Willow emerged triumphantly into the heavy dusk, a wing and a head on one side of her jaws, a foot and fan on the other. She minced about him in a circle, tail aloft.

"Uh-huh. Goes better with the gun around, hey?"

She laid her ears back and paraded all the happier, wagging her tail.

He knelt, cradling his gun with a knee and elbow and extending a hand. "Come, Jenny . . . fetch!"

Unhesitating, she came to him. He caught a wing with his fingertips and begged the question. "Give!"

Resisting for a moment, she looked at him with the reluctant eyes of a child, then let the bird drop loosely into his grasp. It was a grand old cock bird, perfect of condition and full of feather. He shifted it to his off hand, pulling Jenny close into his side.

"Good girl, Jenny, *good girl*," he assured her, stroking her ears and neck.

It was one of the most perfect moments of his life, as every other of its kind had been. Of them all, however, perhaps this was the most poignant, because he could easily have deprived himself of it. Have died never knowing it again. Have unknowingly forsaken Jenny.

He studied her eyes . . . the beautiful hazel wonder of them, the peerless gift of them, as she worshiped first the bird and then him . . . saying a prayer that no one could hear.

If that was maudlin, he thought, to hell with the shallow son-of-a-bitch who never knew a dog well enough to know otherwise.

Burning for the bird, she was crowding now, trying to get her mouth on it again, nearly toppling him.

"No, Jenny," he reprimanded quietly, holding the bird aloft.

The fires had been ignited and they would never be extinguished, not while she breathed.

He collected himself and stood, shifting the Parker to the crook of an elbow, and the partridge to his other hand. He was taken with the beauty of each bird, though in essence all were alike. The rich, dark plumage of its epaulets, the black bands of its fan. Jenny was politely removed, still alert for an opportunity.

He looked around him, taking stock of the diminishing light. The depression below was barely visible now. It would soon be dark. The moon was up, but on its back in a feeble crescent. They were a long way from the truck. It would be a tough go.

Somehow, that didn't matter as much as it did, Ben Willow thought, as he glanced again at the grouse and then at his dog, and slipped the bird into his game pocket.

Spending himself sparingly, he made to regain the ridge. From there he could see the distant lights of the farmhouses below, and fix his bearings. Jenny fell to heel of her own, drawing close beside him. Around them, the night wind whispered strangely through the trees. A red fox yipped a hunting song. Overhead, the stars pulsed in an obsidian sky. They trod alone in a netherworld of black, mildly melancholy, faintly afraid. Gone the day. Homeward the hunters.

It was well past ten when they finally reached the truck. It loomed from the darkness, first as a foreboding hulk and then as a well-sought friend. Finding the slot, Ben undid the lock and swung wide the door. The cab was dark as the night, the interior light long since defunct. Jenny clamored up onto the seat. Doffing his vest and swinging it in behind the seat, he followed. Fumbling for the ignition switch, he nudged the key home, and tripped the switch. The engine turned, sputtered, then died.

He pumped the accelerator and tried again. Grabbing, it rumbled to life. He pulled the light switch. Outside, the headlights drove aside the darkness and within the dash lights awoke with a friendly glimmer.

He urged the gearshift into reverse, feathering the clutch. When the hood pointed south, he shoved the knob into first and, braking with the engine, crept slowly down the path for home.

A few yards on, he flipped the heat switch. The night had grown brisk.

· 10 ·

An hour before on the same evening, Clyde Wood had started home from another directors meeting at the store. He hated the damn things. They never amounted to more than a fractured evening and a cold supper. If they'd leave him the hell alone, he could keep the spokes in the wheel.

He swung the LeSabre onto 58 and pushed the speedometer back to forty-five. For Clyde Wood, the dial might as well have ended there. For years, he had found the world drifted by quite efficiently at that pace. Who in hell was ever going 120 any damn how? The speed limit wasn't but fifty-five!

He was in an irascible mood and knew it. Lester Wiggins had floated his usual Founder's Day motion, and they had whipped a whole hour agitating over how to pry Calvin Hoover loose from his stubborn insistence that there "warn't gonna be no goldamn concrete statuary in his heifer run." It happened that Calvin, like it or not, owned the birth site of Ogden Nance Patterson, rumored to be precisely dead center of Calvin's quarter-million-dollar breeding pen. Patterson, it was further purported, for those who pretended to care about such things, was Buckeye's town father. For years now, Lester, to whom the members had entrusted the gavel, and who was coincidentally the incumbent mayor, had brandished it over their brows in favor of a fitting memorial. Neglecting to accede, as Calvin cogently asserted, that "there was awready a statuary of Chief Clawin' Bear on the courthouse lawn, and he was stompin' these parts two hunerd years 'fore Patterson found his mama's tit."

Truth be known, the aforementioned statuary was at best a replica of the elite Tuscarora warrior, in fact a wooden, storefront Indian that the town council had rescued from a fire sale in Stonewall and had bronzed. Granted — though Lester, to the disdain of the town leaders, often used this disclosure to discredit status quo — that held little sway with Calvin.

How the business quorum of Southern States got mixed up in all this to begin with was simply a vagary of small-town politics and a few whereases.

Point was, every time the damn thing came to the floor Clyde was designated to carry the declaration of the board to Calvin. Now he had it to do again. He'd as soon slap a bull in the ass.

On the good side of the ledger, Therman Chadfield had dropped by the store during the day to pick up some crankcase oil, three sacks of sweet feed, and a link pin. Young Josh was along, he had found, as he had accompanied Therman back out to the loading dock. Josh would be about ten now. The boy was wondering over the selection of steel traps — coil springs, long springs, and Conibears — hanging in a bunch on the wall nearest the door. He and Therman had stopped there for a moment.

"Boy thinkin' about goin' into the fur bus'ness, is he, Therman?" Clyde joked. Josh grinned self-consciously.

"Been a varmint through the henhouse lately," Therman explained, "killed three of our best layin' hens. Told Josh here if he'd catch 'im, there'd be a dollar in it for him. Toward that rifle he wants. He's sat up for 'im a night or two with my old shotgun."

"'At so," Clyde said.

"Yep. No luck though."

"Killed three of your hens, huh?" Clyde repeated.

"Ate a little o' one," the boy volunteered hesitantly, "just left the others lay, bloody and all."

"Weasel, likely," Clyde said after an instant of thought.

"Prob'ly," Therman agreed. "Maybe a 'cat."

"Don't think 'cat," Clyde had said.

Clyde had walked to the boy's side, fingered through the chains and jaws, and picked out a couple of #0 Victor jump traps. Handed them to Josh.

"These'll be about right," he declared. "Boy on an expedition's got to have the right possibles. Set 'em light."

Josh looked at his dad, not sure what to say. Clyde read his mind.

"Reckon we can just put 'em on yer daddy's bill," Clyde promised.

Josh looked at his dad again for an okay. "Thank you," he said to the storekeeper. Clyde nodded.

He had watched the boy struggle to load one of the heavy sacks of feed into the truck. Stubbornly, Josh had managed. Good boy, Josh.

Come to think of it, the day had gotten by and he never had tallied the steel traps. He doubted he would.

Almost missing his turn, Clyde hit the brake and cut the wheel hard, swinging onto Traver's Creek Road. When he reached forty-five again, he could faintly discern the murky promontory of McCathern's Knob ahead on the right. He slowed again and looked left, off the stretch of shoulder where Ben Willow lived. The dim bulk of the house and barn pulled by. The house was completely dark. From the bare illumination of the single security light, he strained for the shed and the glint of Ben's old International. The truck was missing, or appeared to be.

Strange. Not the absence of a house light, for the chickens had to brush Ben off the limb to go to roost. But the truck. Ben was never far from his old truck.

Mildly concerned, Clyde Wood pulled into a farm path and went back to check. He switched on the courtesy lamp and glanced at his watch. Nine-twenty. His brow furrowed.

He pulled into Ben's drive, wallowed the ruts up to the shed. It was indeed empty. Leaving the motor running and the lights on, he climbed out and walked to the house. The sounds of his steps on the porch boards were annoyingly loud in the darkness. He rapped on the door.

"Hey, Ben!"

He waited for a minute, listening for sounds from inside. It was uncomfortably quiet.

"Hey, Ben. Ben Willow!"

No response. He walked back to the car, looked around one last time, and lowered himself in. Turning around, he drove slowly out to the highway, contemplated the situation a moment longer, and turned apprehensively for home.

Nettie was waiting, supper warm in the oven. He pecked her on the cheek, hello.

"Lester Wiggins again?"

"Umm-hn."

She busied herself with the table and his meal.

She could tell, after fifty years, that her husband was troubled beyond Lester Wiggins.

"Something else?" she asked quietly.

"I came by Ben's. His old truck wasn't there."

"Odd," she agreed. "Maybe Peck Watson's working on it."

"Ben wasn't there either."

Nettie Wood thought for a moment, but said nothing further.

After supper he read at length, a Louis L'Amour western, finally tiring and leaving Kilkenny on the verge of a showdown with the Poke Dunning bunch.

He tripped the lever and sat upright in the recliner, slowly stroking the declivity between his lower lip and chin with two fingers. He was still troubled with Ben. He sat a minute longer and reached again for his glasses, and the telephone.

Seth Thomas was striking half past midnight when Ben Willow stabled the old truck in the shed, dragged himself from the cab, and plodded the remaining twenty steps to home. Propping the screen aside with one foot, he let Jenny past and squinted at the key ring in his hand. After a moment he found the thin, worn old house key, then the back door lock. He pushed the key home and twisted. The door gave. He nudged it open. It was delightfully warm and familiar inside. His fingers patted a clumsy circle about the wall, and found the light switch before he meant for them to, inundating the kitchen with a blinding burst of light.

He closed his eyes for a moment, then blinked away the burning. His vision was still bleary and clouded with fatigue.

Jenny was standing beside him, begging with her brown eyes. Even they were tired. He walked to the refrigerator, slid open a tray, and procured a piece of cheese. She accepted it gingerly and made for the hallway, no doubt as to destination. A moment later he heard her jump onto the sitting room couch. The leather creaked as she arranged her bed, then quieted.

He laid the shotgun on the table, slipped off his coat and hunting vest, and hung them on their pegs. Holding the tail of the vest with one hand, he ran the other into the game pocket for the grouse. Carrying it to the sink, he pulled his knife from his pocket and drew it, leaving the entrails where they fell. He gave briefly to the fatigue, resting for a minute against the counter, then shuffled a weary path back to the door. Stepping back out into the chill air of the porch, he reached for his bird strap and hung the feathered carcass from the clothesline. He'd finish in the morning.

Coaxing himself to the bedroom, he sprang the light switch there, then turned for a last look about the kitchen before flipping the switch behind him. Jenny heard him and followed, jumping onto the bed and plopping heavily onto the covers.

"Long pull, huh, girl."

Head on a paw, she hardly acknowledged. It was time for bed.

Asleep on his feet, he tottered to the end table, unbuttoning his shirt, pulling it open as he went. Collapsing on the side of the bed, he bent to work on his bootlaces. Then remembered the Parker. He closed his eyes and sighed.

In a hazy stupor, he somehow found the wherewithal to stand again, find his way back to the kitchen, and run a quick oily rag over the gun. He would not remember that he had done so come morning, wandering in and out of the doubt like a vessel reckoning in a drifting fog. Wondering and wiping it again. But he had . . . the boy who was Lindsey Willow's son, who perchance harbored more of his father than he knew.

He had groped his way back bedside even more mysteriously, was kicking off his trousers when the phone rang.

Dazed, he was long seconds registering its flutter. Glancing at the clock, he grew mildly alarmed. He picked up the receiver and answered weakly.

The voice on the other end was hesitant.

"Ben?"

The inflection was strange. Then familiar.

"Clyde? Something wrong," Ben asked.

"You taken up 'possum huntin'?"

"What?"

"'Possum huntin'?"

"You called at one in the mornin' to ask me about 'possums?"

"Pretty slick animals . . . 'possums, Ben. Diversity's in nowadays," Clyde said matter-of-factly.

"Oh, God," Ben muttered, wiping a heavy hand over his face.

"Well, what were you doin' out in the dark?" Clyde demanded.

"Grouse huntin'! Open'n' day. I told you three weeks ago."

"In the dark?"

"Oh, hell." Ben sighed. "We were late off the mountain. Jenny pointed right at dark and I was a while findin' her."

"That so."

"What's your sudden interest, you old fart. You wouldn't come with me."

"Hell, I wanted to, Ben. Busy. Bizzeee."

"You're gonna 'bizzeee' your gimlet ass right into a grave," Ben declared.

"Where'd you go?" Clyde demanded again.

"Seven Step."

"Andrea's gonna shellac your behind over that," Clyde observed with a cackle.

"She doesn't have to know," Ben warned.

"Aw, Benn . . . you know I won't say anythin' apurpose. Course now, if she's to ast I'd be in a pickle, knowin' now like I do. Maybe it'd be better you hadn't volunteered it."

Ben realized he had taken the bait again for the thousandth time.

"I'm too tired for this. You got any other reason for callin' other than 'possums?"

"No. No. I just happened to drop by your place two hours after the hens went to bed and you weren't with 'em. I's just curious. Me and the rooster."

Worn as he was, Ben couldn't smother a grin.

Beneath the usual nonsense, he could tell that Clyde had been genuinely concerned.

"Tell me 'bout Jenny."

"Nice, Clyde. Really nice. She had that bird for a long time. First one she's really held for keeps. I walked past her twice, I think, lookin'. Finally gave up right at dark . . . just got lucky. Backtracked right into her. Got the bird too!"

"Flew into a tree, did it? They forget where to look sometimes."

Ben refused to reply.

"She brought it to me . . . gorgeous old cock bird," he said instead.

"I'd have loved to have been there, Ben, really would," Clyde replied. "I'm goin' one day soon."

"Anytime, Clyde. You can ride in the dog box."

"You sound whipped, Ben. Get some sleep."

The phone clicked dead.

He kicked his remaining leg out of his trousers, sat inert for a moment, then toppled back onto the bed. Mustering his last will, he crawled under the covers.

Sometime during what was left of the night, he awoke long enough to turn off the light.

Ben Willow was three days recovering from the Seven Step. It was grand, and a morsel of life he would not have missed, but it had wrung him out terribly. Much more than he had anticipated, and the inference was demoralizing.

He had hoped for one last go at the Shickshinny, to walk it with Jenny and prove to himself that he still could. He knew now that he would never make that hunt again. It was beyond him and he knew it, and that was the most insidious reality of all, for few things of his choosing had ever been beyond Ben Willow. He knew now, also, how arduous even a return to the seventh bench of the Step would be. He had done it and he could do it again. But within the thought there was a strange element of incertitude. Even a premonition. Would he never again see the little meadow or its tumbling stream?

For more than a week he found himself in a bout of depression, listless of life. He shrank within the circle of the house and barn, and did not hunt, nor for a time do any of the things that were typical of Ben Willow. He was a facsimile.

He would walk from the house to the barn to check the cows and Jenny would dash for the pickup, jump onto the tailgate, and dance with clicking toenails in hopes of a hunt, and he would simply speak to her and walk on. He would haul up the round bales, prop up the pasture fence, split the kindling, and go the store for milk and vitals, the things he had to do. But it was not life, it was existence.

And three times he made the trip from Traver's Creek Road to Shiloh Church, to the grave site under the maple tree.

He finally rescued himself on the night of the tenth day. Morosely, he packed off to bed and Jenny was lying there in her usual place amid the covers, and the fire was no longer in her eyes. It had diminished, and in its place was some of the same sadness he had seen there when first they had met. It sliced him to the soul.

He cradled his head in his hand and contemplated the state of his being for long minutes that passed into an hour. From the introspective came three words.

"I'm sorry, Jenny."

He looked at her for understanding, tried to read it in her eyes or in her demeanor, and was pressed to find it. On the morrow she would know. He would shake himself out of this misery and they would go back to the woods. He'd bury the pity, the regrets, anything else that got in the way of living. Never again would he allow himself to abandon her or himself for any reason. For, in essence, that was what he had done . . . drawn away from her and from himself. He'd fight the limitations, and never quit fighting them, until he could fight no more.

It was hard to say after that night who became the greater legend . . . Jenny Willow or the old man who followed her.

She would rival the greatest grouse dogs Ben Willow had known in a lifetime of grouse dogs, even, when he could admit it, Tony. There might have been a few who could shade her on birds, but then they had more opportunity in their day. None could have shadowed her on the ground. He found again that he could not resist the magnetism of the cover dog trials, for Jenny was worthy of the chance. He could not know the joy of handling her himself, and that hurt, but Brian Castion did. Castion was one of the foremost pros in the Northeast. Ben Willow had befriended him back when he was first breaking into trials and the young man had never forgotten it.

He was there two days after Ben Willow had called, and considered it a privilege. He left with even greater respect for both the old man and his dog.

There would be those who would never understand it, Clyde even, for it meant parting and deprivation, any moment of which was a precious sacrifice for an old man. One day, alone, at the height of autumn, was priceless.

"Hell, Ben, field trials're nothin' but vainglory," Clyde vented. "Pride over pragmatism. You oughta know that now better than anybody. Just enjoy her, Ben. It ain't like it's forever, you know."

Hell, he knew. All too well. But Clyde didn't understand, had never been there, had never known the incomparable flight of spirit that rides the brilliance of a gifted, far-flung cast, the supernatural courage of mere sinew over impossible adversity, the hot, permeating thrill and magnificence of a quivering, elegant find. Only one dog in a hundred could give you that.

No denying it. It was fabricated vainglory. For many. Yes, he would admit it. He enjoyed the competition. If that was a weakness, it wasn't his only one. But truly, at its stem, it had always been about the dogs.

With one so gifted as Jenny, it was simply not within him to stuff the light under a basket. In her every triumph was his own. He knew how good she was.

What was greatness without its opportunity?

"For a while, Brian," he told the young man, "for a while."

Brian made the circuit with Jenny, and Ben Willow suffered the dreadful, empty nights without her so that she could have the chance.

From the first time Brian Castion put the little trisetter down, he could never get enough of her, and neither could the judges. When she pointed she was one spark short of a fire, and encouraged to sprint, she flew, electrifying galleries with cast after scintillating cast that lay forward with relentless purpose. Always hunting. Always finding.

Ben Willow had laid the groundwork well. In their first trial season, Brian Castion and Willow Crest Jenny became an undeniable force of reckoning.

She won at Venago, Dubois, Gladwin, and Marienville, Kilkenny, and Woodstock. And early in her second season, the fourth year of her life, Jenny Willow wore a title, and then a second, and only two months later, in spring, a third. The honors flowed, Top Dog awards, Cover Dog of the Year. She was nothing short of phenomenal.

Between, she hunted for the gun, for the old man she loved almost as dearly as the birds and the going. With BenGay, aspirin, and the plain hell-to-care country fortitude of a stubborn old Missouri–West Virginian, they made the rounds again . . . Becky's Creek, Baker Sods, the Elklick, McGowan's Mountain, Hobson Run, the Kettlehorn.

"Once more," he told her, "if never again."

She learned to pamper him, to dampen the ground fires that had vanquished a hundred hardened field trial challengers. Adjusting to little more than flushing dog proportions, checking often that he was there, waiting as patiently as necessary for his arrival. The grail of her life was to please him.

By her fifth year Jenny Willow was renowned. Benjamin Willow was receiving absurdly extravagant offers from breeders a continent away . . . and flatly refusing each and every one. His heart was not for sale.

He himself was not unacclaimed.

Letters and cards sifted in from well-wishers throughout the Northeast and Midwest, field trial luminaries and just plain dog people, who somewhere along the way had crossed paths in a trial or bought a puppy or still read the *Field* and kindly remembered Ben Willow and Willow Crest Kennels from the old days.

And in the quaint corner of West Virginia he had adopted seventy-nine years before, which now had a regional university and an Appalachia Cultural Center, he had become a hometown celebrity. Without a semblance of politicking, he had more name recognition than the mayor.

Buckeye, as Clyde Wood had said, was growing.

"Big enough to draw Yankees, 'n' small enough to ast the man 'cross the holler 'bout the wife and young'ins," as Clyde put it.

Big enough that eccentricity was charming. Word grew, and to newcomers and old blood alike, Ben Willow was the most intriguing anomaly Buckeye could muster. This old man who forever drove a bird dog around on the front seat of a battered old 'National Harvester. This old man who still gamboled over the Seven Step with a setter who was some kind of a field trial champion. This old man who could still sit a cutting horse and round up stray steers. This stubbornly independent, white-thatched old essence-of-West-Virginia octogenarian who, it was said, spread a tablecloth on the mountain and said alms to birds and autumn leaves.

Buckeye was proud of Ben Willow, in a way that a town is proud of its roots. Boastful of its beginnings.

Suddenly, strangers were lifting a hand for no apparent reason, and everywhere he went he found a friend.

Somewhere in that woodpile, he suspected that Clyde himself was hiding, yet there was an undeniable flattery about it. A pleasant, home-spun belonging, kind of like Chief Clawing Bear on the courthouse lawn.

Mostly, it was amusing.

"Who'da thought, Jenny," he observed, "I've outlived 'quare' and made respectable."

Time turned on for Ben and Jenny Willow, and turned well.

There was a wispy stretch of nine days when Andy was in again, and this time they hunted for seven of them. Jenny had sensed from their first meeting that Andy was someone special, and the sincerity of her voice and caress won the setter's confidence. Jenny allowed the banked fires to flame those few days, and the brilliance flared.

"She's breathtaking, Daddy," Andrea had exclaimed, following the lick of her going with awe, "breathtaking."

"She's been the light of my life, Andy," he said, "for almost four years now."

"She was fortunate you found her like you did . . . gave her the chance."

"I think, really, Andy, she found me somehow. And gave *me* the chance again."

"Whichever," Andy said earnestly, turning to him. "I'm so very glad."

She had closed to him then, in a hardwood highland of Becky's Creek, and he had held her in his arms, and he could feel her gun clasped against the small of his back as she must feel his, and there was a symbolism in it that cut him to the quick. An honesty. Because it was the closest they would ever come again to where they started. On a mountain, in a woods, in the quiet. For a fleeting moment she was his little girl again, and Libby was alongside, there once more.

He fought back the tears so that she would not see.

Parting to arms' clasp, she looked at him slyly.

"Clyde tells me you've been up the Seven Step again," she said, grinning.

"Damn old Judas goat! Said he wouldn't tell."

"Well, I did have to wheedle it out of him," Andy admitted.

"Uh-huh, I'll bet . . ."

"Do you really think you should, Daddy?" Andy asked.

"Live your own life, Andy," he had told her gently, "and grant me mine. There have been, and will be, things you will not always under-stand, as it is and will be for those who care for you."

She searched his face a moment longer, then conceded with a tight smile.

They had left it there.

Jenny had come in to see who or what was holding up the hunt.

Then Andy had left, to go so very far away again, and although every fiber of him wanted to hold her there and never allow the parting, he could not. For always, for each of us, life must fall to the words on the stone in the meadow of the Seven Step.

So he watched her go, leaving unspoken the words that would have hurtfully contrived to keep her, though there was a disturbing finality about her leaving.

He pined for a day, then collared the Judas goat and dragged him to the woods, he and Jenny, ignoring the protests. Clyde remembered he liked it, and then they had to put up with him regularly. Until his arthritis worsened and quashed it all.

So passed the eighty-seventh and eighty-eighth years of an old man's days, and Ben Willow was painfully happy, so consummately fulfilled that it scared him. It was the Indian summer of his life.

· 12 ·

The following year, with September and a new trialing season at hand, Brian Castion retired Jenny Willow. He had worked her through August and found that his heart was no longer in it. The decision was in no way acquiescent. She was still a major power, veritably at the top of her game. But she had gone the distance. There were no peaks left to climb. Only one. And that was at home. Ben Willow was failing.

He was persevering valiantly, but he was slipping and Jenny needed to be there for him.

"She's done it all, Ben," he told the old man, "take her home, just enjoy her. You've both earned that."

And with great reluctance, Brian Castion walked away, biting his lip until the blood ran.

The old man had sat for a time, relishing the reunion, but slightly melancholy, also, at the passing of another era. There had been many.

"We've come a ways, Jenny," he told the setter beside him, catching a silky ear with two wishful fingers. "God willing, we'll go a ways more."

That night Jenny slept on the bed again and the next morning she neatly undid another Special K box, and after that she put another generation of guineas into the mulberry tree.

"Letting your hair down, huh," Ben Willow called from the porch.

She broke off and pattered up to his chair, tongue askew.

He rubbed her head.

"Whatcha think all those judges you golly-gagged would think about it?"

She turned away, ignoring him, sight pointing a goldfinch on a thistle stalk.

He studied her whimsically. Grand, the thought that she was home for good.

"October's hard by, you know," he reminded her. "Good things happen in October . . . like red leaves and grouse apples."

He watched her sink a little as she watched the goldfinch away.

"Don't know 'bout goldfinches," he teased. "Be hard to hit . . . all that flittin'. Know anybody 'at wants to go, grousing I mean?"

Jenny looked at him and wagged the tip of her tail.

"I could use a partner . . . My nose's been off a spell."

He reached for the cup on the banister and sipped a swallow of hot coffee, steadying the trembling cup with a second hand. For a moment his eyes caught and held the age splotches. They must make the most of this season, he thought, he and Jenny.

He watched her circle and lie down at his feet, remaining alert for something awing.

It was not beyond Ben Willow that time was closing the window. It had never been. But he had not forsaken his vow after that day on the Seven Step, not once. He'd never bowed to pity again. And he wouldn't.

They had not been back to the seventh bench since that day. They'd hunted the lower reaches of the mountain below the old chestnut blowdown where they always parked the old truck, but he had not attempted the uphill haul to the top. Maybe, in truth, he was a little afraid. Of what, he wasn't even sure. Wearing himself out?

Hell, he'd done that all his life. The only difference now was, it took less to do it. And longer getting back.

It was pulling at him. Hard. Both the place and the dare. He wanted to see the little meadow again, the dimpled stream, commune with Sam Thomas one more time. Know what it felt like to be really high again, to consort with the clouds.

"It's to do, Jenny," he promised himself.

When the calendar said it was legal, they hunted another autumn away. Sometimes under the mists of the mornings, sometimes in the long shadows of the afternoons. Ben Willow was digging up memories. The Fiddleback, Spencer's Knob, all the secret, hallowed haunts, even a two-day pilgrimage to the Canaan for woodcock.

Thrice, when they were in the vicinity, they stopped by Shiloh Church. Jenny would watch from the truck window. The old man would stand quietly by the gravestone under the maple tree for a time, with the leaves sifting down.

October washed past, golden and giddy, November and Thanksgiving, ruddy and mellow, bringing December, moody and gray.

Shortly past first light on a Tuesday two weeks before Christmas, Ben Willow pushed open the screen and stepped onto the front porch, sidling to its northwest corner, where for fifty-seven years he had weighed the promise of each new morning. For most of those years he had been accompanied in that task by an English setter. This morning was no different.

A hint of sunrise lay pale and cold behind a thin quilt of clouds in a pewter sky. On the air traveled a peculiar, dampened chill.

"There's a front comin', Jenny. Tomorrow, or day after. Birds'll move."

He could hear the slight, rhythmic thump of her tail against the wall.

There was a longing in the morning, a wistfulness. He had known it before, but never so intensely. It called to him. He strained for its message and it advanced and receded vaguely in and out of consciousness, never quite reaching his grasp. Until finally he understood, and it was as though it were saying,

"It's time, Ben Willow."

He wondered for several moments, his mouth slightly open, his tongue working the underside of his lip.

And then he knew.

He turned abruptly and strode for the door, Jenny bumping his heels.

"Shake your britches, girl, we're going up the Step."

Hastening to the kitchen, he threw together a turkey sandwich, grabbed a Winesap, crammed them in a Ace Hardware bag. He stuffed the bag into the old vest, pulled it off the peg, slung it over an arm, and dampened the stove down. Grabbing his coat off a chair, he draped it atop the vest and, like an overloaded maître d', sidestepped to the corner for the Parker. Crab-walking across the kitchen, he managed the knob with a thumb and two fingers, and pulled open the back door. He slapped on his hat and punched the screen aside with the gun barrel. Jenny shot through.

Gaining the porch, he held the screen at bay with his back and the buttstock, pulled the door to, and turned the key. Only then did he stop to pull on his vest and coat, taking a long breath and exhaling, watching his breath fog the air. From regalia to ready, the whole affair had taken less than five minutes. Ben Willow was a man on a mission.

The National's wipers swiped madly as it bounced up the path to the road, kicking up gravel. Its engine roared and the pedal hit the metal. By the time it passed Carter Jenkins's hog house the speedometer needle was dancing the dial like a puppet on a paddle. Behind the wheel an eighty-nine-year-old man was grinning as mischievously as a teenager, and a seven-year-old puppy was drawing abstract noseprints on a still-foggy windshield.

Around them the world was still yawning. It was always inspiring, watching it awaken. When all was anticipation and the dreams of the day had yet to unfold.

The morning lay thick and cold upon the countryside. Fingers of smoke ventured slowly skyward from huddled farmhouses. Frost crusted the meadows. Here and there, small bundled figures were making their way through prebreakfast chores. Trickles of hungry livestock loped from pasture to barn to meet them.

Inside the cab of the truck, the tired old heater roared mightily, barely intimidating the chill. Ben Willow worked his fingers; they were numb and clumsy on the wheel. He exchanged hands, thrusting the exposed one into his pocket to thaw. Finally, he dug out his shooting gloves, jerked the right one on between steering maneuvers, then snugged the left with his teeth.

On they sped, the tires singing happily as the miles peeled by. In tune with his heart.

He felt good this morning. Richly alive. Relishing the reunion ahead.

Jenny was still puppy-poised, rocking in and off balance with all four feet on the edge of the seat. He smiled.

"I'm a pretty smug old dog myself, Libby," he exclaimed silently. "Off ahuntin' again . . ."

He peeled off 38, onto the gravel of 2410, then onto the forest service access road leading to the fourth step of the mountain. Embarking there, the truck clawed its way up the old timbering paths a level higher, pulling to rest beside its friend the chestnut log. Ben bumped open the door with his shoulder and Jenny clamored by, across his lap.

"Hey now!" he warned, too late.

She raced away.

"*Hey!*" he hollered.

She braked hard and returned halfway, prancing, whining for release. "You're just all out of hand, this mornin', hey. Heel, Jenny!"

Reluctantly, she came in, moaning, hurrying him with anxious glances, dashing out and back.

God, he loved that kind of passion. If you could just find it in people.

He pulled the Parker from behind the seat, then the sandwich bag, depositing the one to his shoulder and the other to his vest. Excitement swelling, he snugged his hat down, pushed the door to, and turned for the day.

He ambled a short way along the path, mellow with the morning, just embracing the mountain. Jenny chafing at heel.

It was grand . . . being here. Being back. Being alive.

Far below, over the winding river of the valley, a skein of geese pulled through the sky, *kee-onking* glad tidings to the new morning. He could see their extended wedge against the darker valley floor, stretching and closing, drifting alternately in and out of the mist through filtered sunlight.

He could feel his spirit peaking, soaring with release. He was as wild as any one of them. High and free again. He looked at the prancing setter beside him, wired with exhilaration.

"Awright, Jenny girl, unkiver us a grouse."

He hit the whistle lightly, thrilling as she tore away. Powering to the front, she laid forward out of sight, then flashed white against the distant laurel for a second as she whipped right up the hillside.

He followed slowly, conserving himself, estimating his strength against the day ahead.

Five minutes later, she remembered who she was hunting for and closed to Ben Willow range, falling into pattern. Quartering comfortably, opening biddably when the opportunity arose, she made for the old homeplace clearing at the height of the slope. Where she had pointed and bumped in her maiden season, when first he had carried the gun.

"Find 'im, Jenny," he called, blowing a rollout whir on the whistle. He caught himself. The last thing an old man needed to do with a dog of Jenny's ambition was to hit a whistle. It was habit, ingrained for fifty years. The setter accepted it with a caveat.

Ten minutes afterward, Jenny was pointed. He heard the beeper trip. He was a while getting there. She was standing almost where she had that first day, pledged decisively just inside the woods line. Two birds went out before he was set, slightly apart, right and left. Jenny watched them up, swelling onto her toes. He lost the first as it leveled low among the trees, then caught the second off his left shoulder as it topped its upward spiral and banked for the clearing. It fell cleanly to his single shot. He could hear its death flutter as he released the setter for the retrieve.

Delivering to hand a prim little hen, Jenny accepted thanks, shook herself, and rolled in the leaves.

Sent on, incensed with desire, she clicked ahead.

Birds were astir. Less than an hour into the hunt, she had her second find. He watched as she went birdy on the hillside above, the quickening pulse of her tail, the tautness of her quest. Boldly cautious, she hastened forward, unraveling the warm, lingering spoor. Baffled momentarily, she corrected, stitching back and forth, working the breeze for a cue. It reached her nose, snapping her sideways. Throwing her head high, weaving her way into the scent, she feathered steadily through broken fingers of laurel. Twice she stiffened, then roaded ahead. The bird was running.

Ben was moving now, hurrying ahead, trying as he would have in old days to circle wide, get in front of the bird, place himself for the shot. He was ill equipped to do it now, but he was trying, stumbling as he picked his way and tried to keep an eye on his dog at the same time.

She had stopped again, lofty and riveted. He adjusted, cutting in slightly. Now, once more, she was moving, mincing forward on cat paws. He had closed the distance. He was almost abreast of her, though forty yards below. She halted again, solidly midstep, a forepaw afraid to gamble the ground. She was twelve o'clock high, blazing with intensity.

"Awright, Jenny," he acknowledged softly, "I'm up."

Up, but laboring for breath and less than easy on his feet. Ben Willow was off step and astraddle a small log when the laurel thundered thirty yards ahead and the shadow of the grouse exploded through a confusion of bottle green leaves, caught a pocket of light, and burned russet and gold for a split instant. Purely of reflex he whirled, twisting from the hip. His arms swept upward from his chest and the Parker leaped to shoulder in the same moment that his cheek found the stock. It settled for less than a second before pulling him off balance, at the very limit of his lateral axis. In that instant the muzzles gained the silhouette of the speeding bird, and he pulled.

The shot thudded against his shoulder and the hillside, reverberated into the hollow. As a single pellet from the chilled load of Federal $7\frac{1}{2}$s found its mark. Faltering, disoriented, the bird pulled vertically skyward, higher and higher. It battled gravity for a suspended moment — wings beating furiously — then toppled.

He watched, touched by remorse, as the grouse fought to survive and lost. It was an awesome thing, a head-shot bird.

He clucked to Jenny. She had marked the flight and was on the bird in an instant, returning full of prance.

"Show-off," he said as he took her offering, a large cock. The perfect compliment to a fine, mixed brace.

The little setter shook vigorously.

"Jenn-y, good girl!," he praised, pulling her against his leg and patting her side soundly.

He glanced upward. "Hey. Whatcha think o' that, Tony? Nice piece of grouse doin's."

Wasn't bad himself. "Pretty tight, old man," he sang out loud.

He chided himself for being boastful, but even a spurred rooster found the gall to crow. When the younger cocks of the walk wore him glum, and suddenly he cornered a loose hen.

He turned the bird to its back in his hand and smoothed the breast feathers, then nudged it into his vest. How many grouse had he stuffed into that old vest? He wished he could go back and count, day by day, dog by dog.

It was eventuating into a sterling morning. Young still, with birds at the cleft of his back, two already, probably the third if his shooting held. An hour or so more and they could laze in the meadow, chew a sandwich, and watch the clouds by. Relive each flush and feather.

Jenny was already ahead, quartering the draw. He pushed on.

Not thirty minutes later she was pointed again in a small damp hollow. A woodcock tittered away. Ben leaned into the rise and then dropped the gun slowly back to port, his face lightening.

"Another time," he vouched. Today, it was grouse.

Onward and upward.

Two hundred yards on, another grouse went out. Blowing from the hollow below and crossing the next ridge. Jenny was no-fault on the opposite slope. He watched it away.

Detouring around a dense wall of rhododendron, he climbed on. Slightly perturbed.

His strength was waning and it annoyed him.

He had crosscut the grade with every opportunity, but still his spindly old legs were beginning to ache with the ascent. His lungs were pumping, harder it seemed than they should, and his heart was thumping. Resigned, he pulled up to rest, parking on a stump. He sat the butt of his gun on a knee, cradling the barrels in the crook of his arm, while he caught his breath and patiently picked loose the wrapper from a piece of hard candy. Cherry. The flavor burst sweet against his tongue.

Overhead, a militia of crows were giving a big redtail how-for. From a secret hollow, a woodhen joined the din, drubbing a crescendo on a hollow trunk, then shrieking devilishly at the deed.

Jenny clipped back to check on him. Her eyes warmed as she neared. Rushing up, she laid her ears back and pushed her head between his knees.

"What say, Jenny girl. No grouses locally? Betcha a scrambled egg in the mornin' they'll be one on the ridge."

The hardest climb of the journey lay just ahead, up the steep rocky slope and the sliding shale to the cap of the mountain and the winding spine of the ridge, which he would ever mark by that first climactic day with Trip and Cindy. The ridge that guarded the hollow, where the tiny stream that watered Sam Thomas's meadow grew from the rocks and first whispered the lesson of the stone.

Jenny studied him briefly, looking earnestly into his eyes.

Only a dog, he thought.

He tousled an ear. What a godsend she had been.

He pulled out a couple of the Kraft Singles he'd brought for her, tearing off slices and doling them one by one to stretch it out. She was silly over Kraft cheese. And spaghetti.

Cheese downed, she dropped and wallowed, running her muzzle under the leaves and snorting. Then she lay flat on her side, cutting her eyes up at him, beating the ground with her tail.

"Flirt."

She wagged the harder.

Up suddenly, she shook nose to tail-tip, ready to go again.

"Awright, you're the leader. Just remember the old jaywhacker who's doin' the followin'."

Jenny bounded away, upward, the muscles knotting as her hindquarters bunched and pumped against the incline.

He extended both legs and flexed, stretching the muscles until they burned mildly, then dropped them and pumped each once in turn. Standing, he located the Pepsi among the grouse in his game bag, uncapped it, and downed a brief swallow.

He could see the broad, mottled face of the slope looking down on him through the notch of the saddle above, massive and imposing, its great hulk dwarfing the lesser hill between. Black-green veins of rhododendron wandered its wrinkles like a congress of gypsy tribes, trailing around and between the staggered gray monoliths of rock. Vaguely, under the timbered skyline along its summit, he could discern the long backbone of the ridge. He wished he were there.

He wiped his mustache casually with his sleeve.

He could bear due east, skirt the mountain, and catch the bench. Come into the meadow from below. It would avoid the arduous grind to the ridge. But Jenny was already enroute there, and there lay the pinnacle of the challenge . . . and the birds . . . for they loved the head of the hollow and the warm sun and green thickets and blowdowns of the ridge. He had never taken the easy way to any destination. It was not Ben Willow.

He wanted to come to the stream and the meadow as he had that first day, and each time since; to have it unfold before him as he remembered it. To feel again at least a semblance of discovery. To earn the privilege of it, by conviction, not compromise.

He gathered his resolve and started after his dog.

Negotiating his way up the remainder of the hillside to the saddle, he reached the monumental old-growth spruce that paralleled the seventh bench. He paused for only a moment, laying his hand reverently upon it and craning upward to its staggering zenith, then dropped into the narrow draw beyond. Jenny showed several times, sweeping nine-to-three, going birdy once in the salad greens that floored the draw but making nothing of it and hunting on. He rested shortly, watching her away once more, enjoying the grace of her going and obliging momentarily the spell of indigestion at the pit of his chest.

"Bird in here, Jenny . . . watch *clo-s-s*." The encouragement came almost involuntarily.

Conserving himself as he pushed along, he accommodated the small headland that stepped to the great slope. It towered ahead now, like a biblical Goliath.

He had lost Jenny temporarily, but now he had her again, already well above him on the soaring hillside, cutting the grain, questioning the clot of grapevines bordering an expanse of laurel.

Steeling himself, he started upward, step over step, thigh over thigh. He jacked himself up the merciless incline until his withered legs burned and his calves threatened to cramp. Up and up, until his breath grew congested and ragged. Reaching the quarter mark, he sidetracked thirty feet to reapportion his ascent past a large jut of rock. He paused to breathe and glanced upward again, throwing himself momentarily off balance, falling back a step or so to gravity. He leaned with the grade, planted a hand on a knee. For a minute he hung there, gathering his strength, soliciting his will. With a push and an oath, he drove himself on. A tumble of shale blocked his path. One up, two back, he fought the rotten footing in slipping, stumbling, energy-sapping steps, crabbing to its perimeter, shifting the Parker to his left hand, using his right to pull himself ahead by anything he could grab.

His mouth was cotton dry. The burn in his legs had worsened to a searing ache. Breathing laboriously through his mouth, he hesitated, looking above. Almost halfway yet. He found another piece of candy and stuffed it past his lips, rolling and sucking it to stimulate saliva.

Ben Willow was into himself now, dredging the deepest reserves of his spirit, where the heart and courage of his dogs lay.

He would make it by God! . . . he would make it.

Rolling his shoulders, he stretched his torso. There was a nagging tightness in his chest. Through a corner of his mind, a thought of Libby effervesced. He caught sight of Jenny again, high ahead, nearing the top. Felt his resolve bunch. His legs stiffened under him, and pumped on. A torturous forty yards, then twenty more. Climbing, faltering, then climbing again. Gradually he was winning. He could sense the massive bulk of the mountain below him now, the crown of the ridge close above. The triumph rising.

He dug on, sweating profusely, determined beyond consciousness. With every pull, he gasped in coarse raspy breaths for air. But the air wasn't coming fast enough. His heart was pounding, and the exertion was squeezing his chest painfully, relentlessly.

He had to stop. Had to rest. Pulling his hat off, he stood straddle-legged on the slope, blowing. Sweating. The pain in his chest was intense. His whole upper body hurt, it seemed. Even his neck and jaw ached. Feeling for the Pepsi, he took a long pull, and another, and put it away.

Fretting, he wanted to push on, to regain contact with Jenny. But he felt suddenly weak, with a touch of nausea at his stomach, a little light-headed. He would rest a bit longer. He took four or five quaky steps to a slab of rock, lowered himself with a hand. He felt queerly. Vulnerable. Something sinister was suggesting that he would not make the ridge this day, nor any other day ever again. That he would not walk Sam Thomas's meadow, nor hear the happy gabble of the stream, nor the sweetness of Andrea's voice, nor see another sunrise of another morning.

He fought it away with the strength of his confidence. He had pushed too hard, yes. Gotten carried away. But he'd sit a minute, let his old body catch up, then go on. Jenny would be back to check on him shortly. He'd call her in and they'd sit a spell and then make the top. He'd done it before. He'd do it again. He rested the gun in his lap, took his hat off again and laid it atop a knee, pulled his bandanna out and mopped his forehead.

He was stuffing the bandanna back into a pocket when he halted abruptly, stiffening. His face tilted slightly upward and his eyes rolled inquisitively right and stalled. Riveted, he listened with all his might.

"Point!"

He could hear the urgent pulse of the beeper from the ridge. Jenny!

Sixty-four years of conditioning backed the mandate. A collage of a thousand beautiful images, floating across the seasons, spurred the response.

Ben Willow slapped his hat on his head, gathered his gun, and struggled off the rock. Somehow, he would get there. Somehow, he was going to make it. Jenny was honest. Jenny would wait for him.

He reached into himself and grabbed the hill. He fought it with the last reserve of strength his stubborn, hard-crusted old will could muster.

But time had run the river. He had taken little more than a dozen dogged steps when suddenly he could go no farther. His heart was pounding its way through his ribs, and there was a crushing, crippling pain at his chest. His breath caught violently; nausea writhed in the pit of his stomach. The whole of his body ran fever-hot, engulfed in a smothering, consuming rush. He felt himself go weightless, felt himself falling.

Desperately, he caught the trunk of a small maple, clinging, the Parker dropping from his fingertips and clattering sickeningly among the rocks. The limbs of the trees spun above him in the growing dusk.

And in his last few moments of rationality, all the fears of an old man's years came crashing down around him, the one above all others.

"No! . . . No! . . . Jenny . . . *Jenn-eeee*," he pleaded feebly, futilely, while the strength ebbed from his fingers and he lost his grasp on the bark of the tree, and consciousness, and slumped, limp, to the ground.

Long strands of white hair spilled loosely against the leaves as his old canvas hat rolled away. He lay upon his back, one leg drawing slowly under the other as his body stiffened, relaxed, and quieted. Briefly his eyelids fluttered and a last inaudible word escaped his lips. Three times more his chest rose and fell, then stilled forever.

In the eighty-ninth year of his being, Ben Willow had died where most completely he had lived, upon the hills of home, with a dog and a gun. Though the time was not of his choosing, no man could ask for more. He had lived his own life and died his own death.

Fifteen feet away, the old Parker had come to rest also, barrel angled upright against a small face of rock, almost as if someone had set it there.

· 13 ·

The little setter bitch stood high on the ridge that capped the Seven Step, grouse in her nose, waiting patiently for the old man to come up. Waiting to hear the broken patter of his footsteps on the leaves. To feel his approach and have him step alongside, and hear him speak softly to her. To feel her body tense as he moved ahead to put the bird up, to savor the blaze of desire at the report of his gun. Waiting for the dash to the fallen bird.

Waiting, and waiting. As the minutes passed slowly by, ten, then fifteen, and the beeper blared, and the ache in her torsioned limbs grew.

She waited and listened, but oddly, could hear nothing of him.

Twenty-five minutes now. The body scent of the grouse was still strong. Ensconced deeply within the clutter of vines that littered a ragged blow-down, it was held by the invisible thread of jeopardy between fright and flight. But the setter had lost much of her initial character. Her tail drooped nine-thirty and her body had been drained of the immediate electricity of the find. The muscles in her hams quivered involuntarily with fatigue. She shifted to redistribute the strain, bringing a hindquarter and forepaw gingerly forward. She rocked on her feet for a second as she settled.

He should be here by now. Always, he had come.

But still she could not hear the familiar cadence of his approach, nor catch the smell of him on the breeze as sometimes she did. She was nearing exhaustion. Torn with plight. Boxed into a confounding predicament of discipline, instinct, and depletion. One last time, she questioned her senses for him, vainly.

Submitting, she gave to instinct. Taking three stutter-steps forward, she reestablished. The scent had grown.

Three minutes more she stood there, drinking in the spoor, listening.

Mesmerized now by the immediacy of the bird, she ventured one step more, and another, crouching with stealth, until the hot stream of scent assailed her instincts so totally and abruptly that she was stove instantly motionless. In the same moment, peril prevailed and the grouse thundered from suspension, lofting itself free of the tangled cover and striving on whirring wings for survival.

Jenny swelled, eyes blazing, marking the flight as training regained a hold. She watched as the bird leveled — habitually anticipating the shot — following its flight as it glided the crest of the ridge and lowered itself deep into the great hollow below.

She stood for a full minute before she realized the absence of the old man again. Then hesitantly broke and fussed for a minute or so over the steaming ground scent. She hunted the area for a short time more, less than seriously, until the pull of his absence grew into a summons.

Backtracking, she followed the eave of the ridge, stopping periodically and listening. She could hear nothing but the sigh of the wind and the screams of the agitated jay birds in the trees overhead. Moving on, she trotted along the ridge, restlessly now, back to the point of her climb from its plummeting back-side slope. She stood at its rim, looking and listening below. Not a sound of him.

She started down, the hunt forgotten now, wanting only to find him. Worried, she zigzagged the hillside, searching futilely for his track, working her way gradually back in the direction where last she had seen him. Always before there was the sound or sight of him, for he moved at leisure, and it was little trouble for her to find him quickly and easily.

She stopped again, at length, tail half-mast. Listening, whirling, and listening anew. Anxiously now, she swung laterally left and down, querying the slight crosswind that meandered the slope. It was in that manner that she found him. The faint, familiar musk of him.

Pivoting into the wind, she quickened her pace, hurrying at the speed of her nose. It carried her quickly to him. Bounding happily in, she sought the sight of him, the familiar welcome of his stance, the ubiquitous word of greeting. The wonderful, completing company of him. And then her world collapsed. For there was more than the smell of Ben Willow — there was the squalor of death. It stiffened the hackles at her back and brought her up steps short. A growl of apprehension rumbled deeply in her throat. In the leaves a few feet ahead, the old man lay faithlessly, lifelessly inert.

Bracing against her haunches, she ventured a cautious step toward him, and another, her nostrils pulsing, trying to unravel the strangeness of him. She sniffed him closely toe to head, wavering at the edge of retreat, finally backing away.

She knew death, had encountered it untowardly before. Always, it was disturbing. Disarming.

Perplexed, she stood at bay, yearning to go to him, unnerved by the utter absence of response. Inclination clashed with instinct. Perceptibly, devotion overran dilemma.

Returning to his side, she sniffed at him again. His body was barely warm. Scratching at his chest — once, then again, she urged him to move, but he would not.

Confused and frightened, she retreated again, circling and sniffing evasively of his hat and gun.

For a time she remained close, expectant that somehow he would rouse. But the familiar voice and gentle hands of the man she loved and trusted more than any other in the world lay strangely upon the ground and refused to respond.

Presently, she drifted a short distance away, receding into instinct again. She wandered within the radius of a few hundred yards during the remainder of the day, hunting absently, addled by his absence. There were flitting lapses when she expected him to appear, and yet he did not.

She returned to him three times in the course of the afternoon, but each juncture it was the same. She could not find the old man she had known and adored. Only the vacant senselessness and the sinister stench of death. Just a cold mound of flesh lying in the leaves, that somehow looked and smelled like Ben Willow, but somehow wasn't.

Abandoned now in forty square miles of wilderness, she was once again alone. The old man who would have moved Heaven and earth to have it otherwise was now a part of neither.

In good part, he had been permitted the last wish of his life. In another, he had only lived his worst fear. Who could say why?

Only time and the mountain.

In the final minutes of the December day, the sun suddenly brushed aside the veil of clouds it had worn since its rising, flooding the southwestern slope of the Seven Step with warmth and light. It fell upon the small green meadow and for a short time lit the crystal highlights of the tumbling little stream, disclosing the last, crumbling protrusion of broadaxed logs where once Samuel Thomas had lived. Then the clouds billowed once more and slowly the yellow fingers of the sun were withdrawn. For a fleeting moment, they touched softly upon the brink of the seventh bench and the small table of earth that rested there. And the stone. It lay on its face in the green moss, its back crusted and gray, its words returned to earth. It was not long fallen. The upheaval of dirt at its base was yet soft and loose.

14

In the growing dusk, Jenny returned despondently from the ridge back to the place the old man lay. He had been the heart of her life and it still wanted to beat there. The chill of night was swelling. The mountain was growing vast and lonely. The wind moaned through the trees.

She scratched out a depression in the leaves by his hat, circled twice, and curled herself into it. An icy breeze rippled the guard hairs of her coat. Hours later she shivered herself to sleep.

Deep in the starless night, the wind grew, tossing the tops of the trees overhead like switchcane, strutting the ridge in a great, bullying bluster. Intermittently, limbs cracked like rifle shots and whumphed discordantly to earth. Leaves whirled like snow in a crystal shake-toy, flying before rip-winds that chased across the slope.

Jenny tucked more snugly into her tail and trembled against its anger, until it unsettled her so that she rose as a matter of course and moved timidly to his side. She hesitated over him for a moment, then lay down again, balling herself snugly into the cleft between his arm and chest. There was no warmth there and little solace. It was simply all of him that was left.

The wind howled the night away, until its breath was spent in the final hour before dawn, dying to a whisper it trailed off into damp, flickering breezes. The woods quieted. The chilled air drew thick and close.

First light found its way onto the horizon, seeped across the hollows and into the limbs of the trees overhead, gray and feeble against a somber sky. It suspended itself between the night and the day for a time, neither gaining nor losing it seemed, merely waiting. Until there came a first, soft tic upon the leaves, and another, and another, until their sum was a gentle patter, as the rain came.

It fell in wet, careless drops upon the sightless eyes and the unfeeling face of Ben Willow, onto the tattered old canvas vest at his chest, the old double gun standing forlornly amid the rocks. Onto the setter, lying there among them. She raised her head, blinking against the spatter, then tucked deeply again, pushing herself hard against his body and into the loose folds of his jacket.

She persevered there for most of the day, soaked and shivering, with her coat plastered to her skin, and the water on the slope swelling endlessly into runoff, twisting itself downhill and under her bed in cold, wet rivulets. Pooling there until at last it was too comfortless for even devotion to endure.

Distraught, Jenny pushed herself up with stiff hindquarters and stretched. Shaking violently, she unburdened her sodden coat, the water flying in sheets from the rolling skin of her back. The rain fell mercilessly on. She shook again, to the tip of her tail, so hard that she staggered, whipping the circulation to life. Sniffling of him once more, she found little that was familiar. The beating rain had washed most of the scent away.

Restrained by loyalty, stymied by confusion, she lingered a few seconds longer, then wandered slowly away down the hill.

He had been the one constant in an inconstant world. She had loved and trusted him implicitly. But he was no longer here. She must search for him elsewhere.

Throughout the remnants of the day the rain persisted. Mist thickened in the hollows, climbed the flanks of the headlands, shrouded the shadowy treescape. Dusk came before its time, and in its unearthly half-light, the Seven Step brooded its way into a macabre night.

15

Ed Brickett wallowed pillar-to-post on the seat of the jouncing forest service Blazer, cursing the ailing defroster and fighting desperately with one hand to wipe the fog from the inside of the windshield with a balled-up jersey. His other was clamped to the steering wheel, wrenching the tires out of the holes. A boulder loomed suddenly ahead. He stabbed the brake, barely dodging it. The Blazer fishtailed precariously and jolted in and out of a rut. For a wild moment the headlights stared off into the oblivion of the thousand-foot drop below, then lurched back onto the road. Spinning the wheel, he stalled the slide.

"Dammit to hell," he shouted, cursing himself now for staying as long as he had. He knew better.

The logging path from the top of the Step was slick and treacherous, rotten with mud and loosened rock. He had pushed the truck to the seventh bench shortly before day to cruise a section of hardwood on the DNR's small-game management schedule, then ignored the rain and decided while he was there to reconnoiter a stand of second-growth spruce. He had ended up spending the day, glad for a respite from office minutiae, and fascinated, once again, with the mountain. It had been a long time. He knew the road down would be mean, but then he was a man used to mean, particularly when it came to rough weather.

"Fool—you're a damn fool, Brickett!" he vowed, laughing, whipping the wheel to avoid another cavernous wash.

Mountain born and bred, he'd been raised on the Shickshinny. Townfolk had called Daniel and Sallie Brickett lunatics for living on the 'Shinny, but lived they had, with seven kids—he among them—a few pigs, and three used-up lumber mules, with ice and snow as neighbors for five months of the year. A little rain wasn't so bothersome.

Contrarily, the rain battered the windshield until there was little left to see. The wipers flapped vainly. He braked, waiting a minute until it dropped off again. Then wallowed on. The truck bucked in and out of a deep hole, throwing him almost to the roof.

"Lord and Lizzie," he vented.

Two hundred yards later, he came to the fork. He swung left. He was below the sixth bench, past the worst of it now. A piece farther and the road got better. Beyond the fifth step, it even got a lick and a promise from the road crew.

Slipping and sliding, he maneuvered his way through the hairpin at Skillet Rock. Dimly ahead, the path fell away from the headlights, leveling. He was on the fifth bench. Into a short stretch of flatwoods.

Vaguely he caught the slight glint of the headlamps against wet metal, then lost it as the road swung away. When the lights settled back, he could see that it was a truck, just off the path . . . dark blue or black, for he could just distinguish it from the night and the pouring rain. He slowed and pulled alongside. It was an old blue, navy-refugee International, and he recognized it at once.

He rolled the window down, searching the gloom for signs of a presence, then cranked it quickly up again. It was dark as pitch, pouring bucketsful, beating in a roar on the cab and spattering in a drenching onslaught through the open window into his lap.

"Old man's pushing the pedal tonight," he mused.

He sat a minute longer, listening to the low hum of the radio and the slap of the wipers, debating. He should wait a few minutes more, see that the old man made it in all right. But he was woefully behind himself. Debbie would be putting supper together about now, watching for the lights of the truck in the drive, wondering why he was late. Worrying. He didn't want to be any later than he was already going to be.

Besides, he had had her in the back of his mind all afternoon. One of those days. He wanted to hold her, feel her. It was a school night; the kids would be to bed early.

Ed Brickett rolled down the window again, stuck his head out in the rain and whooped a mountain hello.

"*Whhhaaaee!*"

He listened. Nothing but the incessant din of the rain.

It was still early, really, just after dark. The old man might have holed up under a rock shelf to wait out the downpour. If anybody knew the Step, it was Ben Willow.

He hesitated a moment longer, thinking of Debbie again, contemplating the rain and the dark, and eased away.

For a fleeting moment he entertained a nebulous wisp of motion just inside the woods, and even thought he heard a curious noise. He crept to a stop, peering ineffectively into the night as the fog and rain blotted the headlights, decided he was mistaken, and drove on.

The beeper collar tripped to silence as Jenny stepped cautiously from the woods and onto the path. The shrill pulse of the collar had been an endless annoyance, but now, at last, it was dying. She shrank against the cold, driving rain, watching as the truck receded. She had reached the old International just before dusk, but did not find the old man there as she had hoped. Disconsolate again, she had crawled under the chassis to escape the rain and wait. Sooner or later he would come.

It was there that she had first heard the growl and whine of the truck engine and watched the frenetic approach of the headlights through the deluge, until she had grown fearful and slunk away into the woods like a landfill mongrel, hiding until it left. It was behavior totally out of character, for when she had been with the old man she had welcomed the advances of humankind, even strangers with a caring hand. But he was no longer there and little of her world was the same.

Throughout the weeping night, she remained under the old truck, tucked and forlorn, while the rain beat a mindless tattoo on the metal bed above. Day dawned wet and cold as well. A massive low-pressure front had stalled over much of the Northeast, Kentucky to Delaware, inundating Appalachia with near-record rainfall. Reinforced as it fell by a plunging surge of Arctic air, there was promise of worse.

The morning progressed blustery and gray. The thermometer fell and noon brought the pinging spatter of sleet. Under the truck, the little trisetter huddled still, hungry now, and much alone. By midafternoon a dry snow was falling, in fine, dense flakes that pledged to linger. It whispered down, gathered into blurred, gyrating swirls by instantaneous gusts, painting the path into a pale suggestion and the woods patchy white. It grew upon hill and hollow, rift and rill, and on it rushed to the ground. By dusk it had prevailed, muting the face of the mountain, catching the ghostly glimmer under a clabbered sky and reflecting it back coldly blue-white. Dreary was the land and vast its emptiness, as night descended, and on the snow fell.

Throughout another long and shivering night, Jenny lay unhappily under the old truck, bunched against the inner rim of a wheel in the lee of the searching snow. Numb with cold, hurting with hunger, she could not understand her plight — how suddenly the world had caved around her — only suffer it. Endure it. Hope and dependency were giving way. Reverting to an instinct older than man, deeper than domestication — the will to survive. At her canine core, a wildness stirred.

Dawn broke wickedly. Windswept, icy, and bitter. Stiffened by cold, stifled by overcast, it crept in as if the day dreaded to follow. It found only a slight, round depression under the bed of the old International, already indistinct under the blowing snow. The setter was no longer there.

Half a mile below, wet and shivering, Jenny paused on the rim of a frozen ridge. Kneeling on a foreleg, she chewed anxiously at the ice ball in her pad. Standing, she blinked, wincing against the merciless, stinging onslaught of sleet and snow. It hissed about her evilly on the still, frigid air. Behind lay an aimless set of tracks, ahead the swirling, milky loneliness of another hollow. Aside from the incessant frenzy of the elements, the landscape was lifeless.

Desperately hungry, dispirited by hopelessness, she had surrendered her vigil at the first allusion of light. She wandered now, restless, instinct against fate.

All day she searched for something to soothe the gnawing burn at her gut, with no more fortune than the partially eaten carcass of a yellowhammer, deposed from the talons of a red-tailed hawk. It was pitifully little. She could feel herself weakening. The snow was crusted, yet too frequently she floundered brisket deep, and the effort necessary to free herself sucked at her dwindling energy reserves. As did the constant, stabbing cold, increasing the burden for body heat.

She had been in peak condition, muscle and sinew, with a minimum of fat. Pared perfectly for intense bouts of strength and endurance within the period of a few hunting hours, but ill prepared for the unexpected ordeal of deprivation, depletion, and survival that had been forced upon her, and had continued now into days.

Dusk found her three more miles from the world she had known. From all that was kind, all that was warm, all that was of comfort. Now she clung to its last fragile remnant: life itself. Adrift in a void of white, she wandered on instinct. Traveling eastward and downslope, toward the farmplace and fields they had hunted on the second bench, searching for something familiar, and as she knew she must, something human.

She had managed to find water under the spews of ice in a rushing stream, but had found nothing further to eat. The ravenous burn in her stomach had given way to a hollow, throbbing insistence, dire and uncompromising. Weakening, dangerously chilled, and sensing the onset of starvation, she grew frantic. Soon, if not already, her meager store of subcutaneous fat would be exhausted, and her tortured body would begin the deprecating process of consuming itself. And still the blizzard howled around her, and still the snow fell, as once again darkness grew.

The night that followed was cruel. The temperature plummeted until the glacial air squeezed the snow into a fine, biting sleet. It sizzled against the icy crust of the earth, almost as if it were born of fire rather than ice. Roaring like a raging giant across the frozen, desolate slopes, the wind wrung the trees until they moaned, allying with the brittle cold until again and again great limbs splintered overhead. Nothing walked and nothing flew, and all of life shrank, shivered, and waited somewhere beneath the wrathful blanket of the storm.

In a small cavity beneath a dense gathering of rock, Jenny endured the long, excruciating hours preceding morning. Desperate for shelter with the falling light, she had been fortunate. Squeezing herself past a hairline fissure, she had discovered the tiny sanctuary, free of snow and compact enough to conserve a modicum of body heat. It offered scant comfort. Inside, the piercing cold remained brutal, and time and again the icy breath of the wind huffed its way between the cracks and swirled in numbing drafts over her body. Drawn and stiff, the little setter shivered uncontrollably, so violently upon occasion that her teeth chattered. She was alive, and that was a fair bit to ask on such a wilderness evening.

But where was the warmth of home, and all that she had known, and most of all, the kind and gentle old man she cherished beyond life itself? She did not contemplate these things. She only knew the pain of their absence.

A wave of queasiness pulsed through her vitals. Behind it was another. They recurred frequently now. Her weakening body was feeding upon itself, metabolizing the energy for basal existence . . . for breathing, for caloric heat, for heartbeat. Again, with morning, there would be the demands of necessity, in addition. Moving, hunting, searching. She thrust her muzzle more deeply into the tuck of her tail. With morning, she must find food.

At last the faint light of day grew slowly upon the mountain. A dull gray glow formed in the cracks between the rocks, barely beginning to illuminate the interior of the little cavern. Jenny was aware, of course, but what semblance of comfort she knew was in her tuck and she was reluctant to break it. She could no longer hear the howl of the wind, nor the serpentine hiss of the sleet — just a very faint rustle on the quiet air. She lay for another hour, constricted with cold, clinging to the bit of heat trapped at her belly. Until finally she acceded to her body's bidding. She must move if she was to live.

She uncurled reluctantly, and stood. Stretching fore and aft, she fully extended and tensed one hindquarter, then the other. The activity brought another bout of queasiness, and a gnawing spasm of hunger.

Wriggling through the narrow cleft in the rocks, she left the haven of the tiny cave and stepped into the morning. The whole of the earth was white. The sky was still low, somber, and overcast. Tight layers of ashen clouds were stacked like twisted bedsheets along the horizon. A whisper of sleet lingered, but no longer with malice, and while it was yet bitter cold, the wind had waned, leaving the chill less forbidding. During the long and heartless night the fury of the storm had diminished, and now there was evidence of life. Above the tops of the trees over a distant ridge, a travel of crows lifted and dipped its way along, gabbling to its scouts of its progress.

Jenny scanned the expanse of the surrounding landscape, testing the freshened air with her nose. There was nothing of sight or scent that was familiar. Her wits had not failed her. Hardly four hundred yards below, overburdened with snow and ice, lay the remains of an ancient rock wall and near it the rotting slivers of chestnut timber that once had been a home. Where once, when life was intact, she had pointed a pair of grouse before the old man's gun, and he had managed the both of them. She had brought him one and then the other, and he had thanked her, and the circle of her existence was both closed and begun anew.

Minutes later, hollow with hunger, she would pass within a few feet of the very spot. But he would not be there, as he had not been elsewhere. All that she had known of him had vanished.

Travel was easier this morning. The crust of the fallen ice was frozen hard — though that was of dubious advantage, for it also imprisoned and obliterated the grass and brush that might have harbored a meal, however meager.

Reaching a thorn apple thicket, the little setter lingered for an hour, hunting desperately under the bare and bony trees. Several times, beside protruding clumps of grass, she detected the faint scent of a mouse beneath the ice. Scratching wildly, she tried again and again to dig through, until there were bright flecks of blood on the snow from her bleeding paws. But there was little use.

With midmorning Jenny found the pale, narrow ribbon of the access road that traveled the third step of the mountain. The air temperature had moderated slightly. It was snowing again, thick and white. Sparrows were moving. They flitted nervously along the shoulder of the road ahead of her, searching also. Following for a distance, she stalked them, slavering, trying vainly to get close enough to catch one, leaping high into the air and snapping so hard at a straggler that her teeth clicked. But they were too fleet, and finally she gave up, sensing the need to conserve herself.

Leaving the road, she wandered the woods again.

Shortly after noon, along a laurel thicket in the valley of a hollow, she came suddenly upon a grouse. She whirled and pointed. The bird was close, the air heavy with body scent. For a time she remained as frozen as the world around her, suspended within the clash of instinct and habit. But quickly she remembered. She was hunting for herself now, and gravely. Gauging the distance to the bird, she measured the chances of catching it. Her hindquarters bunched, her body rocking for balance. Now! Exploding — muscles bunching, body stretching and arching — she heaved herself at the hot center of the scent stream. Landing upon the startled bird, she snapped wildly as it sprang up past her muzzle, wings buffeting the tangled laurel in a disordered attempt at flight.

By a fraction of an inch, she missed, the terrified grouse flapping all the harder to escape, rattling against the frozen leaves, loosening a shower of snow. Jumping, flailing with both paws, Jenny managed to slap it down. Instantly, she was upon it, seizing it in her jaws and clamping. For a moment it seemed that she would be successful; she felt the flesh give under her teeth. Then the feathers tore loose and the bird somehow wallowed free, fighting again in ramping wing beats to depart the ground. Avoiding this time the prison of laurel, it thrust itself ponderously upward into the open fringe of the hollow.

Recovering, Jenny fought recklessly to stop it. Twisting and heaving, she strained to hurl her muzzle into the fleeing bird. So narrow was the decree of chance that her jaws brushed tail feathers. Nothing more, as gravity claimed the battle. She landed awkwardly, thudding upon a fore-leg, her muzzle grating harshly into the ice.

Her sides heaved with the exertion as she watched the befuddled grouse beat laboriously away into the hollow. After a moment, Jenny shook herself.

Withering, she turned and walked away, then broke into a worried trot.

Ever, her hunger grew.

Throughout the afternoon, ridge and hollow, she hunted desperately, turning up little. With the approach of evening, she crossed the track of turkey and trailed it for a way, but the spoor evaporated at the roost. Dark-ness came, forcing her once more to shelter. She squeezed past the mat-ted arms of a drooping spruce, and balled herself into a knot at the base of its trunk. All night the snow sifted down. She could hear the rustle of it in the dark. She slept fitfully, the demon at her gut pulsing away, feeding at the weakness of her body. Already she was growing gaunt, the skin of her flanks hollowing between her ribs. Steadily, inexorably, her plight was worsening.

Jenny stirred with daybreak. She left the relative comfort of her bed under the spruce, pattering in anxious, aimless loops, frantically searching again for something . . . anything . . . to eat. Two hours along and more than a mile removed, she had found nothing more than the trace of a squirrel, which had ventured beyond the cozy den of a tree hollow only long enough to excavate a stored nut.

Pressing on, she roamed the saddle of a neighboring ridge, then cross-cut its slope deep into the adjacent hollow. Coursing the frozen streambed at its belly, she paused to drink from the gurgling water that tumbled through a small, open pocket in the ice. It was colder here. Less inviting to prey. She climbed to the top of the shouldering ridge.

Half an hour on she came to a small clear-cut, perhaps two years into succession, fringed by another perhaps twice that age. It was alive with small birds, juncos and sparrows, and the latent spoor of rodents. Nosing about, she zigzagged her way from one snowy clump of grass to the next, senses whetted. She was not the only hunter afoot there. A young gray fox stepped into a crisscrossing deer trail, halting as it saw her. For a few seconds each surveyed the other, until the smaller canine grew nervous and padded quickly away.

Jenny picked her way on, pawing and snuffling, tail flicking with anticipation. Struck by the hot scent of a mouse, she froze, listening intently, then pounced, driving her muzzle deep into a snow mound. She missed, raised her head, cocking an ear, then plunged her nose back into the snow, rooting and snorting. She tore at the grass, snow and debris flying behind her. Unearthed, the startled mouse squeaked and jumped, fleeing for its life, appearing upon the snow and scampering furiously for the next hole. In a bound, Jenny was upon it, snatching it up and crunching.

There was a small squeal of distress as she felt the tiny body pulp under her teeth, and then the faint, salty sensation of its blood was upon her tongue. She swallowed it in a gulp, slavering profusely at the first warm morsel of food — scant as it was — that had reached her shrunken stomach in almost a week. She returned instantly to the task of another.

Fifteen minutes and two misses later, she managed a second. Prospecting for the third, she edged closer and closer to a small hump of white secreted perfectly beneath the grass at the trunk of a cedar tree. Its ears were plastered along its back and aside from the almost imperceptible rhythm of its breathing, its only motion was the telling pulse of a flurrying heartbeat against the paper-thin skin of its chest. Closer the setter, closer and closer.

Then came the rush of fate that brought equally mercy and hell.

Surrendering to fright, the hare exploded from its bed, bursting past the setter's nose and digging for safety. Astonished, Jenny bolted after it with all her might. Yipping, closing the distance, she strained for the last few feet that separated them. In the same instant, they reached the thicketed fringe of the older cut-over. The setter lunged and snapped. Sideslipping and leaping, the hare dodged by a snippet the clicking jaws.

It should have been decided. Hostage to her momentum, Jenny crashed against the dense undergrowth under an avalanche of snow. But in the frenzy of its final leap, the hare had entangled itself within a plait of grapevine. For the space of seconds it floundered, but fatally. Just as it bounded free, Jenny was upon it.

Shrieking dreadfully again and again, pummeling the setter's face with blows from its powerful hind legs, the terrified hare squirmed to free itself. Jenny ended it as the bones broke under her jaws; the body pumped a few times more and went limp. The tantalizing taste of flesh and blood again.

The struggle between the two creatures had been mortal, but spiteless. It was simply that the one must die that the other might live.

Satisfied that the hare was finished, Jenny deposited it to the ground. Placing one paw on its shoulder, she tore it open ravenously, and began to feed. As suddenly, she stopped, as the hair over the length of her spine climbed into stiff, gray hackles.

· 16 ·

Not fifteen feet removed was a huge, brindle mongrel. Shabby and coarse, its back was bowed and roached, its lips wrinkled into a snarl over bared white teeth. From deep in its throat rose an ominous, guttural growl, and its tongue worked nervously back and forth between stiletto canines. It was as wild and rough as the mountain, and there was little doubt of its intent. Within moments, seven of its followers had slunk from the underbrush behind it. As lean, rangy, and rapacious as the alpha male, summoned as their leader by the agonized shrieks of the dying hare, they bunched with gnarled, menacing threats.

Growling fiercely in return, bushing into as formidable a display as she could manage, Jenny held her ground. There was hell's chance that the bluff would work, and no possible way she could stand against the pack. But she was starving, and she would not simply relinquish her first substantial meal. The brindle male began to advance, step over step, popping his teeth. Close behind drew the pack. Jenny grabbed up the rabbit in her mouth and crouched, continuing her warning from deep in her chest. With an infuriated, curdling snarl, the mongrel lunged.

Jenny spun and whipped sideways, eluding his chopping jaws and racing away through the thicket. Incensed, the pack sprang behind her. For the length of the cut-over, she held her own. With every jump she could hear the clamor of their pursuit, but her diminutive size allowed her to nimbly navigate the dense cover, even with the burden of the hare. Reaching the open woods, she tried to turn and dash back into the thicket, but the pack had split and blocked her path.

Over open ground, it was hopeless. Quickly they overtook her, and would be upon her in a matter of yards. She dropped the hare and raced on.

She trotted to a halt at a safe distance, turned and looked back. The hulking male was hunched over the rabbit, tearing at it. Huddled about him were the rest, waiting for the chance to arbitrate the remains.

Forlornly, she trotted on.

She had traveled less than a quarter mile, and had barely begun to hunt again when she heard the frenzied, intermittent yip of the pack. She watched as it topped the ridge that she had crossed but a few minutes before, and trickled down its slope on her trail, a broken, black ribbon flowing against the snow. Closing behind her.

The pack was desperate, as desperate and hungry as she, composed of castaways and outlaws, and gathered for survival. They would kill her if they could, and tear at her flesh as they had the hare's.

Jenny ran — down the precipitous, off side of the hill, deep into the shadowy gorge below — careening through snarled knots of rhododendron, clawing and sliding her way across the icy tumble of rocks at its floor. Cutting the grade of the far slope for a distance, she turned, grabbing the steep incline, scratching and pulling her way vertically to the fringe of an immense thicket of laurel. Only then did she pause to listen.

For moments, there was nothing. Then a piercing yip, and another. Closer now than before. The pack would not be shaken. Tempered by famine, rib-sprung and hardened by grinding marathons of endurance that had worried deer to ground, the conquest of a kennel-pampered setter, even at peak condition, was hardly more than a sprint.

Jenny pushed her weary muscles into flight, threading herself into the confusion of the thicket, weaving through its gnarled, darkened midst in a frantic ploy to escape. She could hear the muffled hassling of the leaders now as they reached the laurel, the throaty, yippy whine of their excitement. They could gauge her proximity, sense the encounter.

Clambering through the scrambled limbs, the little setter clung to the delusion of the thicket, trying desperately to lose herself in the gloam and tangle. And with every motion the scent-laden air, laced with heat and fear, remained behind to betray her, as invisibly as it had betrayed grouse to her point. Dangerously close now, she could hear the rush of the dogs behind her, the rattle of the ice-stiffened leaves as the stems were knocked aside. She hurled herself on, careless of the buffeting brush, fighting for a margin of safety. And when it seemed she might manage it, the thicket suddenly shattered into the stark, threatening brightness of the full snowscape.

She wanted to double back, to reach again the fragile security of the laurel. But in the heavy going of the thicket, the pack had dispersed, fanning on either side of the leaders into an impossible gauntlet.

Into the open woods she fled, willing burning, listless muscles into a last, desperate sprint. Hard after her closed the pack.

A hundred yards — two. She could go little farther. Her body was spent. Faltering now, she struggled to hold the pace, barely able to summon the substance of another stride. The pack was gaining. The measure of her life had drawn to scantly more than a few feet. She could hear the swell of them now, fast behind her . . . the stiff huff of their breath, the thud of their paws on the hard, crusted snow, the whimpering frenzy of their bloodlust.

There was nowhere left to turn.

Abruptly, Jenny whirled and bared her teeth and faced the onslaught of the mongrel pack.

In a maddened din, led by the brindle cur, they slashed hellishly into her. So enraged that the snarls jammed and gurgled in her throat, Jenny flung herself recklessly against the forward three. With a wicked thump, their bodies knotted in midair. Slashing, tearing, clashing with fury. It lasted little more than the second of the collision. Knocked sprawling by the bulk of the cur, the setter rolled and tumbled, her feet flailing wildly for footing.

They fell upon her, trying to seize and overpower her. Scrambling to her feet under them, Jenny spun, slashing, cutting, emitting a fiendish shriek. Before the explosion of her wrath, they fell back, circling, first one and then another dashing in and tearing. Pursuing the advantage, trying to incapacitate her, seeking a deathhold. From Jenny's ear, split from curl to tip, a gash at her shoulder, a sliced foreleg — from the punctured faces and torn necks of the mongrels, and from a long ugly slit in the flank of the cur — thick red drops of blood spilled into ragged circles on the snow. Jenny whirled, first this way and that, spoiling their purpose, growling furiously. Around them, the balance of the pack yipped a frenzy, pacing and circling, urging the kill.

Hastily, the big cur dashed in, feigning an attack. Jenny met him head-on in a crescendo of slicing canine teeth. Sidestepping and dancing, he avoided her. But in the same moment, the shepherd and the hound slashed at her hindquarters, ripping a three-inch gash deep into the muscle of her thigh. Whirling again, crying with a mix of pain and rage, she rushed both attackers, scattering first one and then the other. Sensing her confusion, an outrider dashed in, then another, snapping and retreating. Jenny whipped back and forth, countering ineffectively, her bewilderment growing with the confusion of the assault. The brindle cur was at her again, tearing in and away. Then the shepherd, then the hound. Bitterly, with unleashed fury, Jenny spun and fought. Parry and thrust, pack and prey, and upon the trodden snow the red stain grew.

Torn and bleeding, Jenny battled desperately. It was simply a matter of moments now before their numbers prevailed, before they would over-whelm her. But it would not be easy for them. Some would pay. She would defy them until they ripped and choked the life from her.

From the rear, the shepherd was upon her. Spinning, she snarled and sliced, throwing him off. In the same calculated moment the brindle cur slammed into her shoulder, knocking her to the snow. Instantly the three were upon her. Beneath their wicked teeth, sensing the end, Jenny fought with all the might she could muster. Tearing at their forelegs, clawing at their bellies with furious hind legs, slicing and cutting at any piece of them that moved.

The little setter fought with the last measure of an indomitable heart. But she was smothered under them, unable to gather her feet, while they tore at her. She could feel the last vestige of her strength being shaken from her body, feel herself falling limp, as the deadly, slavering jaws of the cur reached her throat.

The next instant was split like a tree under a lightning bolt — in a thud-ding, thunderous roar — and the chest-hide of the cur blew open into a ragged, gushing hole, spewing a swatch of blood and gore upon the snow. And behind the one roar, virtually crashing into its reverberation, came another. And another. The hound was shrieking pitifully, dragging its hind-quarters in circles, the macerated stub of its backbone and the silvery thread of its spine pulped and gaping at its hip. Even as it cried, the re-mainder of the pack scattered in a panic, racing for cover while another of them thudded lifeless onto the snow, its vitals jellied from brisket to rec-tum. Another crashing roar and the hound slumped to its forequarters, its neck sliding uselessly to rest upon the snow, while behind it lay the gruesome red trail of its final, agonized moments. One terrible last time clapped the thunder, and with it a mournful and piercing succession of yelps, fading as the refraction of the thunder itself through the hollows. And when the last echo had fallen away, there came a stillness upon the mountain, not unlike a moment of mourning.

17

L itton Thorne lifted his elbows from his knees and leaned comfortably back against the trunk of the great white oak, shifting the Brown-
ing BAR rifle to his lap, staring at the inert forms of the dogs on the
snow below and assessing the quality of his shooting. He blinked owlishly,
his eyes bleary and bloodshot with hangover, the stubble on his jowls scrag-
gly as scattered metal filings.

Midmorning had brought the first signs that the storm was breaking.
The air was less keen. Grudgingly, the temperature had ascended; a fresh
west wind hinted that it might edge the thirties by afternoon. The day had
brightened, sweeping away some of the gloom. There was still snowfall,
but it had trickled to straggling flakes, and periodically there rose a faint
halo behind the glazed clouds where the sun would be.

Thorne was a coarse, hatchet-blade-thin, hawk-nosed man who lived
by the signs. He had left his shabby tarpaper cabin near Tin Creek as the
sky lightened, driving to the foot of the Step, strapping on snowshoes, and
trudging up the mountain to this spot on the second bench where deer
were known to cross. He sat the saddle of a high ridge, where he had been
for the last two hours, hoping for some fresh meat for the larder.

He raised the rifle again, bringing the scope once more to his eye. The setter was still prostrate, alive maybe. He thought he could see the shallow rise and fall of her sides, but he couldn't be sure. Even if she was, she might be beyond help.

While he had the rifle up he glanced over the carnage, bringing the glass to rest on the big cur. He could see the thick splatter of blood behind it.

A grin broke across his mouth. "Drunk or nay, Litton, you shore-hell shot the lights outa that one," he told himself proudly.

He had seen it all unfold. The chase. The stand of the setter as it was brought to bay. The fight. He had watched with mere amusement, curious of the outcome. Only in the last decisive seconds had he seen fit to intervene. His motive was hardly noble, and in no way an act of mercy for the setter. And he might have waited too long at that.

It was just that setters loose on mountains were most often grouse dogs, and a man could turn a grouse dog into folding money.

Thorne popped the spent magazine from his rifle, pulled a box of .300 Winchester Mags from his coat pocket, and shook it open on a thigh. Pulling the long brass cases from the box, one by one, he reloaded, thumbing each into place so that it would feed properly into the action. He inspected the result with a mechanical eye, turning it side to side. Satisfied, he returned it to reserve in the chest pocket of his coat. The primary clip he retrieved from his lap, where it had been hastily deposited during the heat of fire. This he likewise fingered and replenished, replacing it to the fold of his pants. A last cartridge he pushed into the chamber, clicking the bolt shut, and flicking the safety. He stuffed the cartridge box back into his pocket. Looking idly about, he gathered up and aligned the magazine to the loading port, palmed it to a stop, then cuffed it home with the heel of his hand.

Planting the butt of the rifle firmly in the snow, he braced against it and pulled himself erect. When he had stretched the kinks from his legs and back, he retrieved and refitted his snowshoes. Remembering the spent brass, he set his rifle against the tree and went about collecting it. There was no hurry. If the setter was still worth the trouble, fine, if not he'd simply find a stick, knock it in the head, watch it kick, and keep on prospecting. Although he had relished the shooting, he'd spent enough deer rounds; they cost too damn much to be wasting on dogs.

He glanced around one last time. Satisfied that he had found it all, he pocketed the brass, then picked his way down the hill toward the dogs strewn around in the snow.

Below, Jenny lay dazed and listless, yet adrift in the impassive vacuity between life and death. Her eyelids blinked apathetically. Her sides lifted and fell in a feeble rhythm with her lungs. Her once silky coat was torn and bloody, her tricolor muzzle cut and punctured to the bone, matted with blood and saliva. Both ears were split and still bleeding profusely. The large muscle of her thigh, ripped by the teeth of the hound, was slit from belly to tendon, and a wicked gash at the base of her tail had torn the hide aside to expose the blue-white cartilage of her hip. Numb with pain and shock, she had neither the senses nor will to rise.

She was only barely aware of the steady crunch of the man's steps as he neared and the careless edge of his voice as he spoke.

"Huhgh." Litton Thorne huffed the summary of his appraisal. "Shoulda shot sooner," he told himself.

He nudged the setter with the wooden bow of his snowshoe. There was little response. He nudged again, more forcibly. Jenny stirred, attempting to rise, then sinking back to the snow.

Thorne grunted again. "You're prob'ly short the worry," he grumbled aloud.

He looked around for a stick, seeing nothing suitable for a club, dumbly realizing that there was two feet of snow on the ground.

"The butt of the rifle would do as well," he admitted, pardoning himself.

He raised the rifle, muzzle first, tensing, ready to deliver the blow. It was then that his slow brain was reminded of the collar.

He hesitated, then lowered the rifle and squatted on his haunches, cradling the firearm across his hips. With cracked and callused fingers he opened the buckle and slid the orange collar from the setter's neck. Holding it to the light, he squinted at the brass nameplate.

Thorne recognized the name immediately.

"Umgh," he grunted again. He looked again to be sure. "Hafta be careful with this one," he warned himself.

Reaching again, he unfastened the beeper collar as well. It wore no nameplate and was no longer working, but it might with a fresh battery, and the worth of it would fetch a fifth of whiskey or a carton of chewing tobacco.

Standing, he stuffed both collars into his pocket, fishing in the same motion for a fifteen-foot length of camo cord.

Jenny was beginning to regain her senses, trying to find her feet.

"You may be worth messin' with after all," Thorne observed. He had a buddy two counties removed. That'd probably be far enough. "Hell, if nuthin' else, the old man'd drop a pretty penny justa git you back."

He pushed her down with a knee, deftly flipped a slip knot into the cord, and made a loop. He slid it over the setter's head, snugged it to her neck, then urged her up.

She stood uncertainly, staggering. Thorne jerked the cord tight around her neck, holding her upright. Tentatively, she gained her balance. Thick red blood still dripped from the sodden tuft of hair at the tip of one ear. Her body tottered, emotionless and unresponsive.

He let her stand for a minute or so as he took stock of the other dogs. He studied over the bulk of the brindle cur. On impulse, he set the rifle aside and removed the heavy, serrated survival knife from the sheath at his belt. A few deft whacks and he had severed its brittle backbone at the hips. Slipping the straps of the canvas knapsack from his shoulders, he spread open the sack on the snow and stuffed the bloody hams inside.

Unless he got lucky on his way back, there'd be no deer today. He needed something for supper. Dog was not a thing unknown to Litton Thorne's table.

Ponderously, he lifted and shifted the bulging knapsack back into place, a fresh bloodstain seeping through the canvas. Retrieving his rifle, he slung it over a shoulder. He glanced around briefly, then stepped to the setter and grabbed up the cord.

"C'mon dog, time to travel."

Jenny stood unresponsive as he started away. Reaching the end of the makeshift leash, Thorne halted, jerking on it. Jenny complied, her spirit as limp as the tail behind her. Following for several yards, she floundered, lagging to keep her balance. Thorne jerked more angrily on the cord, dragging her behind him until she failed and was pulled headlong into the snow. He jerked again, attempting to pull her to her feet, but slid her instead across the ice.

Jenny lay upon the snow, no longer caring. For a moment, Thorne debated again the worth of her life. Then, cursing vehemently, he stooped, gathered two legs in each hand, and swung her roughly over his neck and onto his shoulders.

Litton Thorne hesitated only once between there and his truck. Beside a dense and deep copse of rhododendron, he paused to pull Ben Willow's collar from his pocket and fling it as far into the black thicket as he could.

18

Susan Devron hummed along with Andy Williams on the radio, her attention glued to the road, her hands grasping the wheel. She drove modestly, though she was anxious to get home, glad for the All-Terrain Goodyears Kevin Howard had mounted on the Pathfinder for her only a month before. The roads were treacherous with snow and ice, and would be for several days. She had driven the snow before, of course. If you lived in West Virginia, you drove in snow or you didn't go. And folks had to go. Still, it always made her nervous.

At least, this storm was breaking. The snow had dwindled to a few lingering flakes now. It was supposed to clear overnight. Morning promised blue sky and a pink sunrise.

Thank God. She was glad to be alone and about with herself again. She dearly loved her sister, but an icebound week with Martha and Oprah Winfrey was five days past the limits of her patience. What was the old saying? — "One day fresh, three days stale."

Martha would have been better put with some kids, she thought. But then, who was she to go on about kids?

Three days was all she had planned when she had driven the three hours to Clarksburg the Monday before. A short visit to deliver gifts and wish her holiday cheer. Now it had been eight days since she had seen Route 3, McAlister Road, and her Christmas tree and savored the songs of the season without interruption. Christmas was a family time, but other than Martha she had little of that left, and she had learned to relish the season by herself. Although it was sometimes lonely on Christmas Eve. But not for family.

Then the storm had blown in and stalled into blizzard proportions, and there she was: stove up for five more days with Martha and the TV set.

"Ummmh, Nat Cole," she announced to herself.

"Chestnuts roastin' on an open fire, Jack Frost nippin' . . . ," she crooned along.

She had left earlier that morning, with the first hint that the weather was improving. Martha had a fit, certain that she would slide off the side of the mountain and kill herself, and funerals were awfully depressing at Christmas. But then, that was Martha; Martha would drown in an April shower.

"Yuletide hymns being sung by a *choir*, and folks dressed up . . ."

Little more than an hour now. She glanced again at the fuel gauge and frowned. She'd have to stop for gas soon. She was angry at herself for not taking the time when she first left Clarksburg, but she was in a hurry to be off, and actually had more than enough to get home anyhow. But two hours of unanticipated, creep-and-stop delay behind a jackknifed semi on 79 had left things on the iffy side of maybe.

She was still unhappy with herself. There were some things a woman just didn't leave to chance. Now she was in a pickle.

She thought of the possibilities. There were really only two, Grady Skeen's Vesco station just beyond the Craigsville crossing and Ray Thompson's BP a mile short of Ansted. The BP was by far the more desirable, but she was worried about making it, and being stranded roadside in ice in the middle of nowhere was hardly an agreeable thought. She didn't particularly cater to the Vesco notion either. It was a filthy little place, an independent operation of nothing more than two pumps and a stick-built four-by, always with a few cobbish men hanging around. She'd stopped there with Vance a time or two, once even daring its squalid bathroom, a pleasure she'd never afford herself again. Skeen himself, though obscenely obese and dirty, had acted a rather decent sort. *Act* was probably the word. Rumor was he was the slickest fence in Randolph County.

Well, she'd left herself little choice. She'd stop and get done with it and get out. Besides, she wasn't traveling alone. Lady Smith was in her handbag.

It wasn't that much farther. To the southwest, though still distant and vague, she could distinguish the Seven Step, its pinnacle cloaked in steel gray fragments of the storm. Craigsville was slightly northeast of it. No more than fifteen minutes.

Ten miles along, the sky was darkening again, the white face of the landscape sobering to stony gray. She glanced at her watch. Two forty-five. She'd still make home before dark, though dusk would come early without the sun.

The tires hummed steadily on the ice. The chill had grown. She levered up the heat a bit. Casually, she studied the rear mirrors. Only the one other traveler in sight, for the last twenty miles, a red Jeep Cherokee. Irregularly there was someone headed north. She leaned forward, turned up the radio, and retrieved the thermos of hot chocolate on the seat in the return motion. Pinning it between her thighs, she loosened the lid and raised it to her lips, taking a lengthy sip. The thick, rich chocolate was warm and soothing upon her tongue and throat. She took another sip, glad that Martha had insisted.

Susan Devron smiled. A woman could manage, she mused, with a little chocolate.

Ahead, at the bottom of the grade, where the narrowing ribbon of the road lapsed to a thread, she could see the Craigsville caution light blinking. Slowing, she screwed the lid back on the thermos and returned it to the seat. A minute later she passed the crossroads, concentrating on the right shoulder for the gas station.

There it was, a dingy, bantam clapboard with two windows, duller now than the white of its surroundings and no bigger than an adequate smokehouse. Under the sparse wing of its porch were two antiquated gas pumps with one-way access, and on the fascia board above was a blue VESCO sign with a matching horizontal stripe for respectability. The snow was only partially cleared from the pumps, and around the space of its tiny pull-off, three trucks were parked. She noticed a small knot of men gathered by the tailgate of the one nearest the door.

Susan Devron braked, then as quickly lifted her foot from the pedal. She glanced again at the gas gauge, not wanting to accept it. Desiring simply to drive on and take the risk. But the needle had collapsed into the red, hovering against EMPTY.

Almost past the turn, she pumped the brakes again, fishtailing. Leaving the road, she pulled into the pumps. The three men at the pickup turned to appraise her a moment longer than necessary, then turned away again to their conversation. Seconds later, they exploded into a muffled outburst of laughter. The inside of the station was faintly lit. She sat inside the Pathfinder, waiting, until it was obvious that no one was coming out. Once more, she thought of leaving. But it was to do.

She gathered up her handbag, buttoned the flannel shirt at her neck, then popped the door latch. Stepping out, she slung her handbag over an arm, snugging it close to her body. Once again, the three men were looking. Angrily, she could feel the hair crawl along the back of her neck. Pulling aside the body flap, she opened the gas cap, reaching for the nozzle of the pump marked PLUS. She fumbled it, then tripped the dispense lever, and pushed the nozzle into the tank. The pump vibrated to life, laboring noisily as she squeezed the handle control. It was old, feeble, and painfully slow. It worked in spurts, the black hose bulging and bucking with each pulse as if the fuel were being gulped by the tank rather than pushed by the pump. The eyes of the charge dial blinked as the black numbers clicked excruciatingly by. And for Susan Devron, each long moment dripped with self-consciousness.

She pumped only the several gallons needed for home, replaced the pump nozzle, and capped the tank. Locking the doors of the Pathfinder, she crossed the pump island and walked briskly past the impolite stares of the men to the threshold of the station.

She opened the wooden door and stepped inside. The air was hot and close, thick with tobacco smoke. Three other men sat opposite sides of a wooden desk in the right half of the small, single room. Each held an unfinished hand of cards. Between them were disheveled stacks of papers, yellowed invoices skewered on a note pin, an old mechanical calculator, a spare piston, a couple of empty soft drink bottles. Behind them, she could hear the muffled thump of the fire burning in a big iron stove.

Skeen occupied the business side of the desk, his back to the fire, dwarfing a diminutive cane-bottom chair like an elephant on a thimble. His piglike eyes were expressionless, pocketed over hambone jowls and glued to his playing hand. Beneath his soiled T-shirt and suspenders, his monumental belly rose and fell, lapping more crudely over the waistband of his pants each time he exhaled. Clenched between his teeth was the blackened stub of a cigar. For moments he said nothing.

Ill of ease, Susan Devron glanced furtively about the room. In the far corner between several old tires was an ancient Coke machine, atop it a soft drink bottle inverted into a small glass of water to fashion a makeshift barometer. Alongside was a wire rack filled with assorted cakes and oatmeal cookies, widemouthed jars stuffed with nabs.

Grady Skeen suddenly slapped two cards to the table. Startled, she jumped.

"Two," he demanded of the man nearest the deck. "Yes, ma'am," he offered loudly, his swinish eyes swinging, working uncomfortably the length of her before they rested on her face. "What can I do for you?"

"Eighty-forty in gas," she said, extending the bills and correct change in silver.

Skeen made no move to rise, flopping a heavy arm across the desktop, the ponderous flab under his tricep rolling and quivering like Jell-O. He opened a hammy palm. His companions offered no accommodation. Still studying their cards, they sat dumbly with their backs to her. She leaned between their shoulders, dumping the money into the fat man's hand.

"And what else can we do for you?" Skeen invited.

His tone was edged with insult. She wanted only to leave.

"Nothing, I'm sure," she said. Turning, she walked to the door, opened it, stepped outside and pulled it fast behind her. She could feel her heart thumping and the heat of her anger rising.

The walk back to the Nissan took her closely by the men at the pickup. In the periphery of her vision, she could sense their simpering stares. Like an ingot bellowed in a forge, her ire flared. Impulsively, she turned and glared back at them, watching with satisfaction their gaze wilt and fall away.

All but that of the churlish, cadaverous man with the cold eyes. The cold eyes held her captive, like a snake holds a bird, until she felt herself shiver and pull away. But the retreating sweep of her eyes caught upon a small gray form at the cab end of the open truck bed, and she was compelled to look back. The three men had separated slightly and she could see between them now. It was a small dog, by all appearances a setter, pitifully spare and bedraggled. It was huddled apathetically upon the bare metal floor, in the black grime between a dishevel of petroleum cans, a clutter of filthy sacks, and a chain saw, and about its mien was the heartrending gloom of utter hopelessness. She saw the poor creature only for the space of an instant, and her impression was that of another shamefully abused animal, but there was something more, something irrepressibly familiar.

Reaching the Pathfinder, Susan Devron slid quickly behind the wheel, slammed the door, and tripped the auto-lock switch. The solid thud of the bolts was reassuring. Starting the engine, she pulled immediately away onto the highway. Thankfully, she could see the dingy image of the station fading away in the side-view mirror. It had been much the ordeal she had imagined, and she was glad to be rid of it.

Gradually, she was conscious of the radio again. Bing Crosby was crooning "White Christmas." She teased a strand of hair, beginning to relax. Putting her mind to ease. Except for the haunting visage of a small dog huddled on the cold, filthy, metal floor of a pickup, with hope of nothing better.

She could not escape it for hours after she reached home, nor in the night that followed, nor for the preponderance of the ensuing day. It was more than the simple burden of sympathy; there was wrapped within it a supplication. Vainly, she struggled to understand it.

And finally it came, in a breath-wrenching strangle of horror.

"Jenny!"

· 19 ·

For the third time of the afternoon, Clyde Wood pulled off his glasses, dropping them on his desk atop the General Accounts ledger, and falling back into his chair in a wheezy belly laugh. He had barely recovered when again his eyes strayed uncontrollably to the folded newspaper on the credenza, sending him snorting into another convulsive fit, laughing and trying to smother it until he was literally gasping for breath. He was over the edge, crazy as a coot in cranberries.

Christine Roberson, at the service counter just outside his office, passed an apologetic grin to Cliff Boyette, who had momentarily forgotten his transaction for a spool of barbed wire and was snickering infectiously himself.

"Keep it up and I'm calling Poponaoplis at Mental Health," she called.

"Ummmhh," Clyde moaned, managing to stagger to the door. One look at Cliff and he had to retreat again, bursting out again.

Christine sadly shook her head.

"Private, or can anybody have a chug?" Cliff inquired.

Christine smiled and rolled her eyes teasingly. "Say Cliff, how's Ginny?" she returned with exaggerated inflection. Cliff grinned.

Ms. Roberson knew full well the pander in the pansies that had driven Clyde delirious. She and only she. Secretly, she was four feet and eleven inches immersed, right up to her cherubic little neck. But the incriminating crux of it may as well have been locked in Fort Knox. Twenty-eight years she and Clyde had counted chickens at the FCX and her loyalty was beyond reproach.

She received the invoice from the printer, tore off the store copy, and handed Cliff the customer duplicate. He headed for the door. Christine dropped the store carbon into the in box on the way to Clyde's door, stuck her head in his office, and cocked an eyebrow. Behind the hand that cradled his chin, he chortled anew through his nose. Turning, she pulled the door closed and demurely greeted the next customer.

Clyde flipped another page of the ledger, reached for an exaggerated bass, and busted loose singing. "Fly in the buttermilk, shoo fly shoo, fly in the buttermilk, shoo fly shoo . . . Skip to m' Lou, m' *dar-lin'*." He couldn't help himself. The mayor's fuzzy bag was between the bricks and he was shamelessly demented with the image of it.

For twenty years, Lester Wiggins had garnished his Christmas Eve deification with Bushmill's Irish Whiskey. It would have been twenty-one had not Darth Tysinger of the *Pocohontas Inquirer & Chronicle* gotten involved. But then, that was the whisker in the whiffle.

"Chicken in the bread pan peckin' up dough . . . chicken in the bread pan peckin' up dough . . . skip to m' Lou m' dar-lin'." Clyde was humming in and out of his gloating like a chigger under a camisole.

Christine yelled through the door from the customer counter: "Clyde — what's the price on four-five-eight-seven Wolverine work boots?"

"Eighty-seven fifty," he called back. He could hear the low buzz of her gossip with a customer. God bless small-town expediency, he thought.

The needle that had knotted the knitting was $28,643.49 worth of horse liniment.

It came to journalistic attention the day Darth came interviewing. Just exactly how, since it was password protected, no one could say. But a holiday order for a hundred bottles of Absorbine for a man who didn't even own a horse — waiting to be filed under the pseudonym "Periwinkle" — had an odor no hungry reporter could sniff and ignore.

Darth, of course, had no idea at the time that he would stumble into the local equivalent of a Pulitzer Prize. The mercantile trade since Thanksgiving had been the most lucrative in Buckeye's history and Lester simply saw an opportunity to boost the municipal image. All Darth knew was that

Lester had somehow convinced the editor that toy joy in Buckeye was newsworthy.

From the beginning, he had considered the assignment plebeian, dry as a Sunday-morning wine bottle. Moreover, it had little chance of impressing Chet Phelps, who held the strings on the feature desk across the valley at the *Charlottesville Times & Record*. He was looking for an excuse to desert, when in a remarkably intuitive whiz he hatched the notion that a little philandering among December sales invoices could resurrect the destiny of a desperate man. Citing a bunch of ledger numbers for gross revenues was about as personable as Scrooge before the Ghost, but 200 Christmas trees, 127 boxes of stick candy, 11 toy John Deeres, . . . now there was something somebody could make Christmas of.

Poor Christine could have been no less appalled had he laid a hand on her thigh and asked the number of steps up her bedroom trellis. For two decades, the only thing more sacred than the company records had been her retirement account. Flustered, she fled for higher authority.

Rushing into Clyde's office, aghast, she had whispered breathlessly, *"He wants to see the sales invoices!"*

Considering her proclamation gravely, Clyde had finished tapping the dottle out of his pipe.

"Do say?" he had grinned.

"Yes! What do I do?"

"Well, I say we give 'em to 'im."

"What?"

"Well, Lester said to give 'im anything he wanted," he had responded. He could still hear the pompous old son-of-a-bitch: *"Chronicle's* comin' over this afternoon, Wood . . . this needs to go well [as if it wouldn't] . . . help 'em any way you can."

"But it's still in there," she had cautioned, whispering again.

"What's still in there," he had asked unnecessarily.

"You know what . . . I haven't had a chance to password it yet, much less purge it to your desk file," Christine had confided desperately.

Clyde had smiled.

"He'll find it," she had warned.

Clyde Wood had looked at her without a word, just a supposing twinkle in his eye.

Gradually her face had lightened and a smothered laugh gushed past her lips.

"God," she had exclaimed, rolling it out through her teeth.

Clyde chuckled. He stifled it, only to have it burst loose again. And again. Before he knew it his body was convulsing, falling back into the chair once more, his head back and guffawing. Collapsing forward to his desk, he pinched the bridge of his nose between his fingers and shook his head.

Rich! Rich!

From the beginning, twenty years before, when he had finagled his late daddy's chair on the company board of directors, Lester Wiggins was a shiny little two-bit piece who thought he was a dollar. Burdened with making up the difference, he was as plastic as the bumper on a Subaru. As good as he was, however, he sometimes found it difficult to juggle roles and keep the play on the stage.

No less than a month after he had assumed residence in the boardroom of Southern States, he was a politician in a pickle. Hard into the horserace for a seat on the town council, he wanted something awful to throw a party. The camber to the council chamber was Samuel Bolivar Sullivan. "Bol" Sullivan, resident city father, was a crusty old Irishman who'd grubbed out a small fortune in mining dollars on his own and married more. Moreover, as legend had it, his great-grandfather held the stake that Ogden Patterson smacked into the ground to lay the town corner.

Other than Blanch Parrish when his wife, Constance, wasn't looking, Bol was known to fancy foxhounds, fund-raisers, and fine Irish whiskey. Information that had not been wasted on Lester Wiggins.

The garnish in the gambit was Bushmill's 1608, which to Bolivar Sullivan's satisfaction was the finest barley whiskey this side of The Water. Once Bol was captive, Lester would unstopper the Bushmill's, see that he got the first shot, and propose the most rousing toast to prosperity since King Richard at the Round Table.

Blanch had consented to sing the siren song and the stamps were being licked when the preacher called and of a sudden Lester found himself a Sunday benediction away from the deacon's pew at the New Light Baptist Church. First he had smiled smugly at the details of his anointing ceremony and the next minute he was mortified. Ten minutes before the phone had rung, he had called in an order for enough hooch to float Calvary. One whiff of that by the scripture-thumpers and he could kiss Heaven good-bye. Immediately he had called and revoked the order; five minutes afterward his heart quit pounding.

"You kinda see where I am here, don't you, Wood?" Lester had asked pitifully.

"Shipwrecked two snorts short o' salvation, 'pears to me," Clyde had observed neatly, a grin lurking behind his lips.

Lester had shot him a hard look, shifting nervously in his chair. "Well, that's one way of putting it."

"What's another way o' puttin' it?" Clyde had prodded.

"Well, a man needin' a hoist past a hard place. I thought," Lester had said slowly, his inflection lilting, "if maybe we just ordered it through the store and got Clarence to run it out to Clegg's on the delivery truck like anything else, it'd kinda get me off the cross and back in the congregation so to speak.

"Remove any chance of embarrassment to the Reverend Pugh and the good folks o' the church, you know.

" 'It' meaning the hooch, of course," Clyde had clarified.

"We'd just order it, like store inventory," Lester had explained frugally.

"And just how much wobble water you figure it's gonna require to wash you into city hall?" Clyde had asked.

"No more than fifty bottles," Lester had responded meekly.

"Fifty bottles!" Wood had howled. "And just how do you propose I sail that past the auditors?"

"Well, I thought we'd just mark it horse liniment," Lester had remarked.

Clyde Wood had fallen back into his chair dumbfounded. "Horse liniment! Well, why 'n hell didn't Clegg Redding just order it himself? Ain't nobody considerin' him for deacon, I'll guarantee."

Lester had hemmed and hawed. "Well, you know . . . Sally's big into the Women's Exchange, and if word got around, it wouldn't look just right."

"Look," Wiggins had added impatiently, getting up and crossing to the door, "you figure out how to get the beans in the basket. I'll see it weighs a bushel."

Clyde Wood had never forgotten his parting comment.

"Your sister Thelma's youngest boy, Thad. Christine tells me he's applied as an associate at Cranford, Hicks & Gladding. Jett Cranford and I were dorm mates at UNC. He'll probably call."

He should have gone directly to the board then. But he'd as well have dug a six-foot hole and put himself in it. Craven Wiggins, dead as he was, could still have called a lot of notes.

He grinned again. But that was rust on the running board now.

It had taken twenty-one years to soap the slate, but given a leg up,

Darth Tysinger had done it in little more than twenty minutes. Five minutes to trip over an outstanding purchase order for one hundred bottles (need had doubled the number of bottles over two decades) of Absorbine @ $2,755.73. Ten minutes beyond that to enter the password *periwinkle* into the PC and locate seven more like it. Only five after that to crawfish into W.D.L. and back out one Lester Dalbert Wiggins. Granted, it had taken two days yet before Darth finally trailed to tree the proposition that Carlson, Carlysle & Morton, Esqs., brokered a different kind of horse liniment, and almost a week before he had E. Stancil Bennington of Thomas, Bennington & Pfeifer, CPAs, by the short hairs. But once he had figured out that Stancil had done the numbers for old Craven Wiggins, too, the frog was in the frying pan.

By then he had called his editor with a headline and scotched front-page space for the hottest scandal to hit the *Chronicle* since Blanch had flown a pair of crotchless step-ins on the mirror of the governor's limousine.

The story had hit the Regional Affairs edition that very afternoon, and an hour later Lester Wiggins couldn't buy a cup of coffee from a dispensing machine. Margie had gone into hiding, Peyton, Wiggins & Lautimer had the phone off the hook, and the city council was in emergency session debating impeachment. Every news reporter from here to Richmond was scrambling with the supposition that the shoo-in for the Fourteenth District had just sabotaged agriculture, and rumor had it Calvin Hoover would declare for mayor by the middle of the week.

Yes sir, Lester was a fox in a fix!

Clyde cackled again. It was more than he could stand.

"*Whooo-ee!*" he vented, forgetting himself, slapping the top of the desk so hard with the flat of his hand that he knocked the paper clip bin to the floor.

He was on his hands and knees rounding up paper clips when the phone rang again. "Damn," he thought — it was worse than a colicky baby. Ignoring it, he continued his search. Christine could screen it at the service desk. He was thinking of leaving early anyhow. It had been a rare day. He'd go home, share it with Nettie, and tip a shot of horse liniment.

Christine Roberson pulled her eyes away from the computer monitor, dropped her pencil to the pad, and reached for the phone for the umpteenth time. That's all she'd done, it seemed, since noon. Talk to pushy people who had to speak to Clyde.

Frazzled, she mustered the mettle for the stock salutation — "Merry Christmas, Southern States" — and braced for the worst.

It was not what she had expected. The voice on the other end was polite and genuine. Shaken and grave. Her eyes narrowed and her mouth pursed as she listened.

"One minute, please," she replied, punching the phone on hold and rushing immediately to Clyde's office.

She found the portly little store manager still all fours on the floor, rump hoisted as indelicately as a winking mare, puffing and peeping under his desk like he'd lost the key to Christianity. Any other time, the impulse would have been irresistible.

Wood rolled only his head, looking up at her from where he was with a catty-cornered grin. He was still mucked in mirth, silly as kitten scamper. Suddenly, even the prim Ms. Roberson was ludicrous. From this angle, she looked like an inverted clothespin.

He was ready to burst loose again when his eyes fixed on her face. Twenty-eight years of reading Christine's moods arrested his conscience like a latent referendum.

He pushed himself awkwardly to his feet, using the desk corner as a crutch. He looked at her again.

"What?" he asked.

"Susan Devron on two. You need to talk to her," Christine Roberson said.

Their eyes held briefly as he moved around the desk to his chair. He sat down and pulled himself to the phone, then punched line two and cautiously picked up the receiver.

"Ms. Devron? Clyde Wood here. What can I do for you?"

"Mr. Wood, I'm calling you because I know you to be a good friend of Ben Willow's."

Wood paused a moment. The woman's voice was quivering.

"Yes. Ben and I go back a ways," he replied tentatively. Curiosity pricked, he waited for her to continue.

"Does Mr. Willow still have the setter. I mean, is she with him now?"

It was an even more curious question, Clyde thought, after all this time.

"Jenny? God, yes," he answered.

"Right now?" she came back immediately.

Taken with her terse reply, he reconsidered for a moment.

Truth be known, he couldn't say for sure. He'd been so occupied with Darth Tysinger, Lester Wiggins, and the holiday rush, he hadn't even talked to Ben. He'd been meaning to get by with a box of horehound and a decanter of Daniel's, and invite him over to supper Christmas Eve. But he hadn't gotten it done. He felt suddenly guilty. Nettie had reminded him twice.

"It'd be a safe assumption," he assured her. "Ben'd as soon be without his next breath as without Jenny."

Wood sensed the hesitation on the other end.

"What is it, Ms. Devron?" he asked.

"I know this is going to sound strange, Mr. Wood," Susan Devron said, "but yesterday afternoon about three o'clock, I'm virtually certain I saw Jenny at Grady Skeen's Vesco station out on Route Sixteen near Craigsville. She was tied in the back of a pickup truck with three men around it. One of them was the most hideous person I've ever encountered."

Clyde Wood could feel his breath catch, his flesh crawl, sense the sudden vise grip on his stomach.

The woman had paused, waiting for his response. It did not readily come. She proceeded to explain.

"I was on my way back from Clarksburg. I was forced to stop there for gas. I only saw her for a moment. I was alone and afraid to stay there any longer."

Wood knew Skeen's place well, of course, not from association, but by reputation. A filthy little place full of filthy people, wolfers, drug heads, and thieves, attracting the absolute worst humankind could muster.

"I haven't seen her since she was scarcely more than a pup," Susan Devron continued. "I was all night and most of today before I was sure. But it was her. I *know* it was her."

Clyde let the words sink in, then asked the woman to describe the men and the truck as best she could. The truck she could remember vaguely, an older pickup with dark blue paint, and even less of two of the men. But the third Susan Devron recalled vividly. The third she could never forget.

It was Wood's voice that shook now. "Thank you sincerely, Ms. Devron. I've got to go," he said gravely.

"Clyde . . . ," she urged as he started to hang up. He paused.

"Clyde . . . she was pitifully thin and bedraggled. I think there was blood on her coat."

He paused a moment longer, with the receiver suspended above the phone, then dropped it loosely from his hand to the cradle.

Clyde Wood was hot, nauseated. He held his hands out, palms down, in front of him. They trembled uncontrollably. His heart was thumping against the wall of his chest, and his breathing was shallow.

There would be no more humor in this day, nor for many to follow.

Something was dreadfully wrong. He fought for control, his mind racing at the possibilities. Susan Devron could be mistaken, but even as he gathered up the phone again, at the marrow of him he knew that she was not.

The line had rung fifteen times when he hung up. Ben could be about the place, chopping wood, feeding chickens. But his heart would not believe that.

He got up from the chair, grabbed his hat and coat from the rack.

Christine Roberson glanced up from the counter. Wood's face was tight and bloodless. There was commitment in his step.

"I'm leavin'," he announced, without stopping.

"What is it, Clyde?" she called.

"Ben Willow," he answered without further explanation, and walked out the door.

Clifton Thrip was perusing the ax handles in the bin by the office door. Clifton could talk the ears off a deaf mule, but not today. Almost rudely, Wood brushed past the overtures and extricated himself. He'd make amends later.

Avoiding further detainment, he followed the dimly lit hallway to the rear of the store and found the rim of light around the back entrance. He opened the door and stepped into the day and the cold, blinking as he paused to fish a pair of jersey gloves out of a pocket and pull them on.

The bulk of the storm had passed the evening before, but the morning sun had not lasted. The sky had clabbered over again with the tailing low, and, once more, snow flurried intermittently. It was showering now as he walked to the Bronco. Caught and tossed by a brisk west wind, the confusion of white flakes swirled about him like wheat chaff blown from a combine.

He pulled the driver-side door ajar, climbed into the Bronco, started the engine. It roared briefly, then sputtered and died. Wood cursed. It was a good old truck, but it had always been cold as a whore on credit. He pumped the accelerator, spun the key again. Once again, the motor roared. He feathered the pedal, nursing the faltering engine to health. Impatient at the delay, he let it warm past the choking point.

He was worried. Gravely worried. There was no way in Satan's hell Ben would let Jenny out of sight if he could help it. And nothing short of calamity could force the setter from Ben.

Leaving town, he crossed the Wolf Creek Bridge and swung south onto the Clarington Highway. He pushed the Bronco up to a normal forty-five. The oversized wheels hummed. He was driving faster than he should. The main roads were stiff with ice and snow, and would be for several days. There was only so much the equipment crews could do with two feet of frozen crust. The back roads would be weeks clearing, barring a warm-up.

He passed a piddling pickup and a laggard pulpwood truck, hurrying the seven miles by to Traver's Creek Road. It was not yet three-thirty, but already the light was low, the landscape dusky. McCathern's Knob was hidden somewhere in the sagging cloud cover. Distracted, he failed to slow in time for the curve ahead. The Bronco lost its footing and skidded crazily. Backing off the accelerator, he steered hard into the slide, bound for the ditch. At the last moment, the big wheels grabbed and pulled true. Clyde breathed a sigh of relief. Out of the curve, he nudged it back to forty-five. Only a mile more.

The modest clapboard house and weathered barn loomed on the left. The house was shadowy. Except for a few chickens and the small huddle of cows in the side pasture, the yard looked forlorn. His eyes quickly jumped to the stall where the old International stabled. It was gone. Apprehension circled his stomach and hurdled into his chest. Queasy with anxiety, he swung off the road onto the path to the house, straining for a glimpse of life. Hoping against hope that he would see Ben round the corner, bucket in hand, under the crinkled old Filson hat.

He pulled to the shed, stopped, and got out, giving heavily to the pain in his left knee. He grimaced and steadied himself, allowing his legs to recover momentarily while he took stock of the grounds.

The air was still and quiet. The chickens were beginning to fly to roost. Bunched and waiting, the cows stared toward the house with hunger in their eyes. The round bale in the barnyard was exhausted. Vacant and morose, the mood of it. Wrong.

Wood hobbled around to the back porch, his leg catching with each step. It did that now, more and more.

He crabbed his way up the steps, noticing the empty rocking chair. Crossing to the door, he pulled aside the screen, rapped loudly on the door three times, and called stridently. "Ben? . . . 'ey *Ben?*"

He strained for the familiar creak of the floorboards, the rustling of the old man making his way to the door. There was nothing. Nothing but the pallid stillness.

Stretching to lay a hand atop the doorsill, his fingers groped for a moment, then closed on the key. He fumbled it in his hand, straightened it, then pushed it into the lock. He turned the key and fought the door for a moment. Giving finally, it opened into a dark kitchen. He found and flipped the light switch.

A small tribe of roaches hastily vacated the opened loaf of light bread on the kitchen table. There was a partially expended jar of Miracle Whip that should have been replaced to the refrigerator. Atop the lid was a dirty knife. The stem slice of a tomato lay pink and shriveling upon a stained paper towel.

"Ben," he called again, expecting no answer.

He made his way slowly toward the bedroom, afraid of what he might find. He found only the unmade bed, the covers thrown back. He canvassed each room, returning presently to the kitchen.

Something was dreadfully wrong. More swiftly now he was being pushed to accept it.

So painfully quiet, the house. He had been here many times, in this very room, sitting at this very table, sipping coffee or something stronger — come whim or need — and passing the day with his old friend. Something familiar was missing. Something beyond Ben. Evident by its absence. Roaming the room, he struggled to place it. Suddenly, the second time around, he knew. The utter silence. His eyes jumped to the old wall clock. The pendulum hung lifelessly below the supper mark and the weights rested on the bottom of the cabinet. It was dead.

Certainty clutched his throat. Time had stopped in Ben Willow's kitchen. In the order of life and living on a country farm, only one thing on God's green earth would suffer that to happen.

Clyde stepped to the sitting room, turned on the overhead light, and lowered himself to the edge of the chair. He could feel the pulse thumping in his neck, above the foreboding, prickling apprehension. Picking up the phone, he tapped out seven numbers.

He waited through the rings, the queasiness in his gut, until the connection was made.

"Sheriff's office, dispatcher. How can we help you?" a familiar voice declared.

"Mazie, this is Clyde Wood. Is Semp there?"

"Yeah, but he's wrapped up with some people from the SBI," the dispatcher replied frankly.

"Would you bother him? I need a favor and it won't wait."

There was a slight hesitation, then an accord.

"Sure. But you'll owe me breakfast," she vowed. "Hang on."

The phone went dormant for a time and a dozen suppositions flooded his mind. None good. More than forty years Ben had been a friend. His best, when others had wavered. Not so much that he was always around. He wasn't. Old Ben was a will-of-the-wisp. He knew his own mind and went his own way, and he never bothered anybody with the fixings.

A lot of folks didn't understand him. But then Ben didn't give a hoot in a haymow about what other folks understood.

What he'd always liked about Ben Willow was that a little of him rubbed off on you when you were with him. Ben had a rare way of looking at things. And he always left you the better for it. When civility lodged in his craw like dry potatoes and he needed to feel like a man again, he went to the mountains with Ben Willow.

No stick in the mud either, Ben. Always fun.

It was a hard thought, that something might bring all that to an end. And yet they were both old men. Old men who had lived past their expectations maybe.

But not beyond their hopes, he thought, as the phone sprang to life again with the burly voice of the sheriff.

"Clyde . . . Semp. What's turnin'?"

"I got a call a while ago, Semp, from Susan Devron out on McAlister Road. Her voice was tremblin' like a leaf."

He related the substance of their conversation to the sheriff, and the nature of the connection.

"I'm out at Ben's place now. Somethin's bad wrong here, Semp. I don't think anybody's been here for several days." Quickly, he related the reasons.

"You put it all together and it comes up sour. Somethin's happened with Ben, Semp. I don't know what, but somethin's happened."

"I wouldn' be too quick on that, Clyde. He's prob'ly just off huntin'."

"I got no doubt he's off huntin', or was, but not *this long* . . . "

"Hell, Clyde, you know old Ben. He's as flighty as a mayfly hatch. Likely he sprouted a wild hair and decided to hole up with somebody."

"Yeah, I *do* know 'im, Sheriff, and I'm tellin' you somethin's bad wrong!

"Oh, there was a time . . . you're rememberin' 'im from the old days. Hell, he's eighty-nine years old now, Semp. No, whatever way you scatter the shit here, somethin' stinks. No matter what else, he'd never let that dog out of kin."

"So what do you want me to do, Clyde? I got to get back to these people here."

"Start lookin' for 'im! That's what I want you to do."

"Wouldn't be the first time the sheriff's office's been ast to look for Ben Willow, you know," Semp vented. "Most times he ended up findin' us."

"Goddammit, Semp, I ought not to have to be convincin' you here. You owe Ben Willow as much as I do! If it was one o' those high-falutin' deep pockets out on Beech Ridge that stuck your reelection poster up in his front yard, you wouldn't be doin' all this garblin'.'"

"All right, Clyde, all right. Got any idea where we might start lookin'?"

Wood thought a moment and didn't like his conclusion. "The Step," he answered.

"The Seven Step?"

"Yeah."

"That's rough country, Clyde, and a lot of it."

"I know it. But that's where I think he is."

"What was he drivin'?"

"Dammit, Semp, you know what he was drivin'. He ain't got but one truck — that old blue International."

"All right, Clyde, damn! We'll get on it, okay."

"Now?"

"Now."

Clyde dropped the receiver back in place, waited a moment, then picked it up again. When he was sure he had the dial tone, he punched in another set of numbers.

"Nettie . . . me. Listen, I'm at Ben's. There's somethin' haywire here and I'm worried about Ben."

"What is it?" Nettie interrupted.

"I don't know," he replied shortly. "Ben's not here, and hasn't been for a while. There's bread loose on the table and soured milk in the refriger-ator. I've called Semp Mason, and he's promised to start lookin'. Mean-time, I'm gonna check a few places on my own."

"Clyde, you got no business out on a night like tonight," his wife pleaded. "Come on home and let the sheriff's office handle it."

"I can't," he told her adamantly. "Who would you have called if it was me?" he argued.

His wife lapsed silent.

"Don't worry," he admonished, "and don't hold supper, and don't wait up. I don't know when I'll be."

He knew she would do all three.

"Just look for me when you see me."

There was a slight pause. "All right," the soft voice conceded.

Now he felt guilty.

"I love you, 'Ettie," he finished, and hung up.

He had pressed Semp Mason. It was a favor he had waited to collect for some time. He had no doubt Semp would follow through, and expediently. Which was good, because he had every intention of letting the sheriff's office search for Ben. There was a thing inside that told him Ben Willow was beyond his help. But there was another matter that was not. At least he hoped not. Already it might be too late.

He had given his word to Ben. Ben had not lightly asked, and he had not lightly agreed. And he had not anticipated that it would come down to this. But he would never go back on his word.

If the time came, he had pledged, he would watch over and keep Ben's final wishes. Likely, that time had come. And of the several things he had promised, there was the one that Ben had bound him to above all others — they had clasped hands on it — to watch over Jenny.

20

Clyde Wood knew the piece of trash that Susan Devron had described: Litton Thorne. He was a bad one. If he was in any way involved, no good could come of it. He had been in and out of the state penitentiary since he was eighteen, for everything from grand theft to manslaughter. Five years before, he had been technically acquitted, though nobody understood how, in the rape and second-degree murder of an itinerant Mexican girl, and had been implicated more recently in half a dozen hate crimes against blacks and Hispanics. His daddy had been no better. He had killed his wife in a drunken rage when the boy was seven. He had never made it to the West Virginia gas chamber. These were backwoods folk and her people peeled him royally and stretched what was left from a locust tree before the authorities got wind of it.

The boy had been passed to a ne'er-do-well uncle, and brought up mean and hard. Until one day, when he was fourteen, he had bashed the farmer aside the head with a hickory ax haft and run off. The old man recovered and after a while they had just quit looking for the boy, because nobody really cared. So he made out on his own, hook-and-crook, working for the sawmills, and trapping and trading and hunting in the hills, and running with the wrong people. He'd been in and out of trouble ever since.

He'd been in the store a few times. Wood knew his sallow face and his cold eyes and that he lived in the woods somewhere off Route 38 at the foot of the Step. It all tied together.

Clyde Wood was not a brave man. He was but a simple storekeeper, old and round and bald, with modest hopes of peace and pension in the next year or two. He'd been in only one real altercation in his life, and that was in the seventh grade when he and Benny Thornburg traded fists over possession of a Barlow pocketknife his daddy had entrusted to him. It amounted to no more than token blows before the teacher had intervened. He had been scared to death then. The thought of a confrontation with a man like Thorne, especially now, was unraveling.

Clyde Wood was not a brave man, but he was an honorable one. In the worst of times, honorable men find courage. There was an anger growing in Clyde Wood that bled through the fear. An anger rankled with the premise that some molly-pandering maggot like Litton Thorne could put in jeopardy the most valued thing in Ben Willow's life. A living thing, moreover, that he had given his solemn word to guard and protect.

He could, of course, call Semp back and request the assistance of a deputy. But then he could have done that before. No. If the law was involved, then there would be the encumbrance of due process. Questions of search, possession, and seizure. The entanglement of "civil" rights. Thorne, he was sure, knew all the tricks. It could only amount to molly-coddling and delay, and two hours after they left the little setter would be somewhere in a shallow hole on the side of the mountain with her head caved in.

No. This was his to do. Alone. It was the only way. He had to deal with Thorne on his own terms and he had to do it immediately. It was Jenny's only chance.

He pushed his way up out of the chair and walked back down the hall to the kitchen. Despite the limp, there was determination in his step. He crossed the kitchen and stopped briefly at the door, intensely conscious, at once, of where he was. The house was still rich with the smell of the old man who built life and home here, who had loved a wife and raised up a daughter, and who in the winter of his years had asked for little else than a setter dog and another day on a mountain. The old man who had befriended him as none other ever had.

Then his jaw hardened and his eye twitched. Snapping off the light, he let himself out, and pulled the door tight behind him.

A reasonable man was being pushed beyond reason.

Thirty-five, forty, forty-five, *fifty* . . . the needle climbed the speedometer dial. Spumes of ice and snow flew rooftop high as the big wheels of the Bronco chewed the roadway and furiously spat away the remains. He left Traver's Creek, hit 219, was soon on 38. Dusk was mounting rapidly, the sky eroding to cobalt. Here and there in the escalating gloom of the countryside, scattered farm windows blinked pinpricks of yellow between the trees. There was warmth and shelter behind them. A warm supper. A chair by the fire. Kindness and laughing voices. No threat greater than the morrow. At home, Nettie was waiting, worrying. He wished he were there, with the softness of her presence and nothing more to fret over than the comfort of the evening.

Off his right shoulder now rose the great hulk of the Step, mute and menacing in the fastening darkness. Slavishly, the road bent to the will of the mountain, winding submissively about its feet. Rarely now, the yellow lights of a farmhouse. He passed one cluster then watched, interminably it seemed, for the next. He almost passed it — one brief twinkle in an ocean of darkness. Slowing, he ascertained his bearings, then veered off the road onto the farm path and downshifted against the drag of the snow. Two hundred yards later the narrow white corridor opened to a barnyard and the shadowy silhouette of a double-chimneyed two-story. He climbed cautiously out, hallooed the house, hobbling toward the door when he was known.

It took five minutes to get past the pleasantries with Clara, and several more to maneuver Brantley off to a corner and explain judiciously what brought him there. But in less than fifteen minutes, he was out the door and the Bronco was clawing its way back to the road.

Brantley had listened dubiously and warned him away from it, but Clyde knew now where to find Litton Thorne.

Three miles more and Clyde Wood passed the faint trace of the forest service trail that twisted right to Chandler's Knob, two miles later the steep, grinding curve that whipped itself like a roller-coaster rail into Ginseng Gorge. There were no yellow lights now. Only the vast, clutching darkness.

Look for a small, unmarked mailbox, Brantley said, and nothing more than a narrow hog path.

He passed it the first time. The mailbox perched obscurely atop a slender metal post, draped over with snow-laden branches. He never saw the path. After a few minutes, he knew he must have gone too far. Even with the luster of the snow, the inky darkness blotted the headlamps until it seemed they were scarcely more than a five-cell with weakened batteries. He got the Bronco hung up trying to turn around. He slammed it into four-wheel low and gunned the motor. Snow flew and debris rattled against the fenders, but the tires merely slid and spun. He could think of nothing worse at the moment than being stranded out here and alone. As long as he was mobile, he was in control.

Desperately, he shifted between low and reverse, popping the clutch, rocking and grinding. The engine roared and the chassis bucked and wallowed. Dirt and snow spattered the windshield. At last the big wheels grabbed, held tentatively, then caught. With a wrench, the truck lurched up out of the ditch, righted itself, and spun its way back onto the hard road.

He could feel his heart fluttering, feel the surge of relief as the Bronco answered his will again. He stopped momentarily, righting his resolve.

A few minutes afterward, Clyde found the mailbox and the slender path that led off opposite it into the woods. He backed up, then swung the headlights onto the path. Only a few feet of it was visible in the lights before it narrowed to nothing and was obliterated by the darkness, but there were fresh ruts cut in the snow. There was a fresh wash of heat over his body, a rising prickle of anxiety. There would be no turning around once he started. Steeling himself, he pulled the gearbox back into four-low again, nudged the accelerator, and eased the Bronco off the road onto the path.

Thirty yards later the deep, black woods had closed around him. The snow-splattered trunks of the trees arose one after another in the lights, ghostly and gray, creeping slowly by as if they were measuring him, then melted again into the darkness. The dash lights glowed eerily in the cab. The engine moaned in and out of the drivetrain. Saplings bent and twisted by the ice and cold brooded in claustrophobic gauntlets over the diminutive ribbon of the path, clawing like stiffened fingernails against the sheet metal of the cab as they were shoved away.

On and on wound the pittance of a trail, through rut and wash, until he began to wonder if he could be mistaken. On led the tracks before him, telling him that he was not. There was a plunging hollow ahead. Gripping the wheel, he guided the truck into a controlled slide down the pitted bank. The lights buried themselves momentarily into the snow ahead. He caught the glint of water. Bracing, he hit the accelerator and the Bronco wallowed its way through the small stream, bottomed on a protruding rock with a sickening thud, throwing him hard against the door, then gnawed up the knobby hill on the other side. He slowed to a crawl on the crest of the rise, collecting himself. There was a flat ahead, it appeared, on the toe of a lower ridge. Above, he could sense the foreboding presence of the great mountain.

Deeper and deeper he bored into the shapeless, black cauldron of the forest. He'd gone a mile, he thought, maybe more. It seemed forever in the dark. Then, coming out of a dip and topping a saddle, the terrain gentled into a flat, on the toe of the low ridge. And for the briefest moment he thought he caught the glimmer of a light ahead. When next it should have reappeared, it was gone.

He thought he heard the barking of a dog. He lowered the window. Definitely a dog. From the sounds of it, a big one, a Dobe or a rott. Heavy, guttural volleys of woofing, one after another.

He took a deep breath, let the Bronco growl along in low, leaned over and felt for an object wrapped in an oily rag on the floorboard. He laid it on the passenger seat beside him.

Ahead, it seemed, the woods gave way a small clearing. He couldn't be sure. Everything was shrouded in obscurity. There were no stars, no moon, just the half-light of the snow. He let the Bronco creep on. Now he was certain. He could distinguish the approaching break in the trees, perceive the small patch of open sky emerging overhead.

As he drew closer, the hoary frame of a ramshackle shanty crept slowly from the trees, caught dimly in the sweep and aberration of the headlights. It had neither windows nor porch. There was but the vacant cavity of a sunken door frame at its center. There was something else, something peculiar and unsettling. His eyes strained to differentiate it, not willing to believe the image his mind was devising. A dead-man's brace jutted from one wall. From it something was hanging by a shank of rope, something round and swollen, about the size of a man's head. Below it was a macabre shadow not unlike the torso of a limp and lifeless human body. He could feel his pulse beat again, the hair at the base of his neck hackle.

The truck pulled closer. For a few moments, the lights played more fully upon the scene. From the swirling melt of light and shadow, reality separated itself abruptly from deception. The piteous torso dropped away, nothing more than the trunk of a posterior tree distorted in the refraction of light. However, the dead-man's brace remained. From it was stretched a length of rope, and knotted into the end of the rope was a swollen canvas knapsack stained heavily with blood. It had dripped for a time; flesh-colored icicles had coagulated at the bottom of the sack.

It was no more than a cache of food, surely, that Thorne had hung high enough to foil the night creatures, but it was no easy image.

The headlights swung past it into the clearing. At first Wood saw nothing. Then, almost imperceptibly, the low-slung shape of a small cabin grew like an emulsion from the darkness. At its periphery, a chained dog was whirling and snarling in a demented frenzy. It looked like a pit, huge, low slung, and blocky.

He eased to a stop a short distance away from the cabin. Porchless, it was more a shack than a cabin, with walls crudely laminated with tarpaper, totally black, absorbing the lights like a blotter drinks ink. It was as dark inside as it was out. Two small windows and a door allowed ready surveillance of the path and yard. He studied the door. The shadow at the frame seemed a shade wider than it should have been. He was almost certain someone was standing in the darkness behind it, watching and waiting. A stovepipe rose above the eave, but it was too dark to determine the presence of smoke. The yard was cluttered with junk and trash. There was another small shed, a smokehouse maybe, off the corner opposite the dog. A woodpile. Something else there that looked like a large, wire animal cage.

He dreaded the encounter ahead. For a moment he had an overwhelming urge to leave. Just turn around and drive quickly off the way he came. But he would not allow it. He knew better. If he buried his resolve and convictions here and now, and allowed himself to drive away, he might as well bury the rest of himself along with it. Because he could never live with what was left.

Clyde Wood cut the headlights and switched off the engine. The night went dark as a cave.

The din of the bull terrier was deafening on the hushed air.

Undoing the rag from the .357 on the passenger seat, he opened his coat and slid the heavy Colt Python behind his waistband. One button he refastened over it.

Taking a deep breath, he levered the door latch, freezing for a second with the sharp clap of the freeing lock. He eased open the door of the truck, braced against the armrest and the dash, and lowered himself cautiously to the snow. The damn knee pinched again, buckling painfully. Damn the getting old! Straightening, he stood in the silence for several seconds, his elevated breathing condensing on the frigid air.

He strained to listen for some closer sound other than the enraged dog. He could distinguish nothing. His damn ears were no good anymore.

The cabin sat stone cold and silent.

Finally his vision began to recover, pulling to recognition the vague shapes and forms backlit by the pale gleam of the snow. As it did, his eyes swept the yard. They found the obscure silhouette of the truck this time. It sat on the off side of the shed, blending almost perfectly with the night. He could tell little about it, other than it was an older pickup with dark paint.

The word stalled for several seconds on his tongue before he forced it out.

"Thorne?" Unanswered, it lingered on the silence. Then the pit went crazy again at the sound of his voice.

"Litton Thorne?" he called again when the barking subsided, louder this time.

The suspense was like a knife point. So intense that his ears rang with the rush of his blood. He knew someone was there; he could sense it. His skin twitched when at last he heard the thick, gravelly voice.

"Who's askin'?"

"Clyde Wood."

There was another lengthy period of silence, then the coarse, curt reply.

"Whad'a you want, Wood?"

"There's a thing, Thorne. We need to talk."

"So, talk."

Clyde's mind raced. Ever since he had left the store, he had been wondering what he would do when the time came. What he would do after he found Thorne and demanded that he give up Jenny. What if he refused — which was likely — what would he do then? He was no closer to the answer now than he was two hours ago.

One thing was certain. Nothing could be accomplished at arm's length. He had to get face-to-face with this man. Look into his eyes. Keep his wits and stay ahead of him. This was no Tuesday-evening board argument with Owen Roberts over how much alfalfa hay to inventory. It would be dangerous. But he had known that before he came. And now here it was.

He seized the moment.

Stepping away from the truck, he advanced slowly toward the dark rectangle of the cabin door, limping slightly with each step. He had never known a moment like this. The queasiness in his stomach pulsed like a hammered thumb, the heat of it clutching his body, the giddiness of it whirling in his head. His skin tingled with apprehension; taut with adrenaline, his muscles gathered at the brink of reflex.

He wondered what a bullet would feel like at the instant it ripped your guts apart and blew them out your backbone onto the ground. When you heard the blast of the gun, it would be done.

The bulldog was lurching and banging, throwing the entire weight of its body against the chain.

Step by anxious step, he shuffled closer to the door. He could make out the pale glow of Thorne's face now in the crack of the door, the intimation of his lanky body.

Clyde stopped a few feet from the man. "You al'ays talk from behin' the door?" he asked.

Disdainfully, Thorne widened the crack in the door and stepped through, tall and tight. His coarse, thin face was screwed into something between a smirk and a scowl.

The pit was incensed.

"*Shad up, dog!*" the scowling face hollered. The bulldog subsided to a few dribbling protest barks, then fell to a throaty rumble and retreated.

"Say it an' get out," Thorne muttered. "I ain't used to bein' bothered."

Clyde could feel his anger surging again, shoving aside the fear. He would not waste time with this man. It would do no good.

"Where's the dog, Thorne," he demanded.

He could not see clearly the cold, hard eyes set in their hollow sockets, but he doubted there was a quiver.

"What dog?"

"The one you had in the back of your truck yesterday afternoon at Skeen's place."

"I wadn' at Skeen's yesterday and I don' know what dog you're talkin' about."

"You're a liar, Thorne," Wood declared.

Thorne knotted like he had been slapped, then took a single step forward. "Look 'ere you old tin-pipe son-of-a-bitch, you're fixin' to coon a log you ain't got the ass to cross. Who in 'ell you think you are anyhow? Comin' in here like Christ A'mighty . . ."

The bulldog was growling again.

"I've 'ad 'bout all your shit I'll hear. Get your pearly ass on outa here!"

"You were there, Thorne, and you had a setter dog in the back of that truck out there. Ben Willow's dog."

"An' I'm tellin' you for the last time, Wood, I ain't seen no dog," Thorne swore. "Now git the hell off my property."

Litton Thorne had been accosted many times before about somebody's one thing or the other by a lot stiffer men than this shriveled-nutted old storekeeper. Many times before. It amounted to nothing more than piss on pulpwood.

He could play the game as long as he had to. They could blow smoke up his ass till it trailed out his ears; short the hard evidence, it was nothing but a bunch of pithless palaver. Thing was — he was trying to figure out how to hell the old man could have known. A witness could be a problem sometimes.

Clyde could sense the advantage. " 'Fore I leave, then, you'll not mind me lookin' around a bit," he said.

"Be goddamned if you'll look around," Thorne vowed. "What you'll do is take your muly-fuckin' ass down the road and not come back."

Thorne reached across his body, jerking free with his right hand the hatchet from the chopping block beside the door. He'd had enough of this. He'd put hard men on the ground before for less, hurt them, seen them crawl. Enjoyed it. And here was this one . . . some lard-assed, pansy-dicking town-titty marching in here and demanding what-for. He'd leave. He'd leave now. Or wish by God he had.

Cocking the razor-edged hatchet by his waist as he turned, Litton Thorne whirled to punish Wood, his eyes blazing with rage and cruelty. And froze, rocking on his toes to arrest his momentum.

Before him was a rigid, lard-assed old town-titty with a very big gun. He could see the faint glint of the snow reflected off its stainless-steel barrel, and it was pointed dead center of his gut.

Clyde Wood knew little of what was happening to him. He was past moral consciousness. Storekeeping and civility. Leaning on his good knee, he had the big Colt leveled at the thickest portion of Thorne, finger against the trigger, and it wasn't trembling. Suddenly, *vehemently*, he hated this man and all his kind. It was a seething hate that had lain banked and smoldering for fifty years. Kindled by playground bullies, fanned by the conscienceless disrespect of petty thieves and the obscenities of Saturday-night drunks, and fueled endlessly by the atrocities of molesters, murderers, and madmen on plain and decent people who went day by day bothering no one, attempting good and charity in the world. It flamed now, white-hot, and Clyde Wood scarcely realized it, but he was no longer afraid.

"You get one chance, Thorne," he warned, "you drop it, and drop it now, or so help me God, I'll blow your sorry guts through the cabin wall."

Litton Thorne was furious, but no longer certain of himself. Sorely, he wanted to try this old man. But the cactus prickle of anxiety was rising in his own throat now, and he hesitated, tottering on the cusp of indecision. Until his inimitable arrogance could stand it no longer.

"You ain't got the balls, storekeeper," he muttered, advancing a step.

He halted short of another. On the cold, brittle, breathless air, Litton Thorne caught the chilling, subtle click of a locking trigger sear. An instant short of death, he reappraised his predicament.

Clyde Wood's hand wavered, but negligently. The hammer of the Python was raised like the head of a viper over a 158-grain hollow-point cartridge, and his finger was half a second shy of killing a man. He might do it yet.

"I ain't askin' again, Thorne," he announced.

Behind the mask of darkness, at the recesses of the sunken sockets, hatred burned in the cold, cruel eyes of the thin man's face, but the arrogance had vanished. Always on the coward's end of true courage, Litton Thorne had never known raw fear before. The gut-wrenching, spit-thickening thought of violent death within the next moment, the agony that could precede it if it came more slowly. But he did now. And apprehension sang through his veins like the voltage in high-tension wires.

The hatchet slipped from his hand, falling with a soft thud to the snow.

"You can't do this, Wood, come in here and shove a gun in a man's face . . ." he gusted. "I'll have the law on you for this."

"I'm doin' it," Clyde declared, "and you can have whoever in hell you want to on me, 'cause it ain't figurin' to do a shit's wortha good. You're nothin' but a pus maggot, Thorne, and you been one so long, there ain't nobody around that don't know it. So you just do whatev'r in nay-bob you goddamn well got a mind to, and let's see how much cott'n it chops."

Clyde Wood was hot, almost irrational. "Get away from that door. Get out in the yard," he ordered.

The pistol had not wavered.

Thorne sidestepped into the yard, his long arms hanging loosely from his shoulders.

Clyde had little thought of what to do next. He needed a way to temporarily dispose of Thorne so that he could look for Jenny. He limped between the man and the cabin, keeping the gun at ready, easing his way to the corner and the woodpile. Scanning the yard as he went, he looked for a way. His eyes found the wire cage.

Thorne stood watching him, hatred surging, scheming again.

Watching him closely, Clyde crossed the few steps to the cage until he could distinguish it more clearly. It was heavy-gauge steel. It appeared to be empty, though not long ago something had been captive there. Even in the cold air, the stench was hideous. Rancid fat and dung. A bear maybe. Some people kept them along, to fatten and eat, or sell for the tourist trade. Thorne was the type.

The door of the enclosure was agape. There was an open padlock hanging on a hasp.

"Get in," Wood said.

"The hell I will," Thorne protested.

"The hell you won't," Clyde said, shuffling back over to the cabin door. Without relaxing his vigil, the old man stooped with effort and picked up the hatchet in his left hand. Struggling to win the advantage of his good knee, he righted himself. Returning, he tossed the hatchet on the snow near Thorne's feet.

The hammer of the Python was still cocked. He faced Thorne, steadying the big handgun with two hands and pointing it directly at the man's chest.

Litton Thorne looked at him incredulously.

"Self-defense, I figure it, Thorne. I came out here to ask you if you'd seen Ben Willow's dog and you went haywire and came after me with a hatchet. Ain't nobody out here but us, Thorne. Now you got till five to git in that damn cage, or I'm gonna put a bullet a cock's inch high o' your sack and blow your stuff clear t' Buckeye."

"You're fuckin' crazy, you old son-of-a-bitch," Thorne protested. It was cold, but the sweat was growing under his collar.

"Your gamble," Wood cautioned.

"One . . . ," the old man counted, lowering the weapon in his hands and steadying his aim to the man's crotch.

"Two . . ."

"All right," Thorne conceded, moving reluctantly toward the cage. Wood backed away, the pistol still trained on its target.

Thorne hesitated at the door of the cage, glaring at him. "Goddamn you, Wood, goddamn you to hell . . . you'll pay for this," he said, lowering himself through the opening. He crawled to the center of the cage on all fours through the layered, snow-crusted pork fat and dung, then crouched on his haunches.

Clyde pushed the door to, swung the latch over the hasp, replaced and snapped closed the padlock.

Thorne glowered at him. "You'll pay for this," he repeated, "you'll pay big-time."

Clyde ignored him. He could look for Jenny now. He let the hammer down on the Python and pushed the heavy pistol back under his waistband.

Turning, he limped toward the cabin, ignoring the bulldog, too. He'd look there first.

He had just reached the door when his body ran hot, and his stomach retched with the first wave of nausea. He was so abruptly weak he could hardly stand, and his muscles failed and his legs sagged, and a wave of heat rushed from his toes to his head. He reeled, stumbled across the threshold, grabbing at a chair. He was shaking so frightfully it buckled, crashing to the floor. Lurching sideways, he thudded hard against the wall. He turned and braced his back against the logs. And then the retching, rolling sea of heat washed through his insides again and he bent to the waist and vomited on Litton Thorne's floor. Again and again. Retching until he could no longer stand and sinking helplessly to the floor.

Too weak to rise, he lay there for what seemed minutes, managing finally to struggle back into a sitting position against the wall. He sat there exhausted, five minutes . . . ten, his heart slapping wildly against the wall of his chest. Clyde Wood was coming off his anger, and the reality of the preceding quarter hour was crashing down around him like shattered glass. Now he was alternately hot and cold, trembling more violently as the fear grew. He had been mad, blind mad. For the first time in his life, he had come within a firehouse instant of killing a man. Of blowing his insides to jelly, and reducing him to a pile of gore and cold meat on the ground. He, a balding, gone-to-seed old storekeeper who went out of his way to pull stray kittens out of the road. And the most terrifying thought of all was that he knew he would have done it.

He sat for another few minutes, gathering himself, sweeping up his courage from the floor and puttying it back together.

Outside, he could hear Thorne periodically ranting and cussing. He was glad the ratchet-faced bastard hadn't been able to see the truth of him the last several minutes.

Gradually, his strength returned. He pushed himself slowly up off the floor and, using the wall, pulled himself upright. Cramped and aching, his knees complained with his weight. He limped to the door, fumbled around the door frame in the darkened cabin, and found a light switch. Snapping it on and off, nothing happened. He hobbled outside, looked for the generator. It was close by the wall. He almost tripped over it in the dark. It was still warm. He jerked the cord, and it started immediately. Stepping back, he tried the switch again. This time, the shack was dimly illuminated by a single, overhanging sixty-watt bulb.

The cabin was scarcely more than a rectangle, crude and squat, with a shed-roof extension tacked onto the back wall. Basic mountain living, still, with a gallon of springwater in a spackled blue bucket on a makeshift sink, and a two-quart coffeepot steaming on the stove. But it was filthy, sullied with scattered trash and piles of clutter.

He moved slowly about the room.

He had been lucky. There was a gun in every corner, a BAR on the wall on a crude deer-antler rack. Why Thorne had emerged without one of them, he couldn't say. The man could not have known his reason for coming, and would have taken him lightly anyhow.

Whatever, he could see that Jenny was nowhere within the main room. He crossed to the door of the back room. Thorne had been in the midst of supper. There was a plate of stringy-looking meat on the table, side-dressed with a sweet potato, a can of beer beside it. He stepped into the offset. It was cool, almost chilly. He felt again for a light switch. When he found it, another single bulb glowed from a porcelain ceiling socket. There was a bed, a nightstand, a TV and VCR against the wall. Clothes thrown around. No sign of the setter.

He stooped awkwardly to the floor, grunting, letting himself down on all fours and checking under the bed to be sure.

"Jenny?" He called her name as a last assurance.

He walked back through the main room to the open door. He stepped outside again and punched off the thrumming generator.

Thorne was livid, raving. Clyde disregarded him as before, shuffling to the Bronco for a flashlight.

He looked around again for the next most likely place. Switching on the light, he crunched through the crusted snow to the small, dark shed. It was still flurrying, the fine, dry flakes sifting through the beam of the flashlight. There was a single, wooden button latch securing the entrance to the shed. He turned it aside and pulled at the door handle. The plank door was stuck at the bottom. Clyde stuck the flashlight in a pocket, braced his foot against the frame, and jerked harder. The door gave a little, a little more, grating and bucking against the sill, then surrendered. The shed was inky black inside. Clyde wrestled the flashlight from his pocket and threw the beam inside. It was void of life. Just a pile of rubble on the floor, a pair of hip boots, and a few old steel traps on the wall. A lard bucket or two.

He shouldered the door back in place, then wondered why he had bothered.

The pit bull was still going crazy—barking and lunging, rattling the heavy chain about its moorings—so infuriated that it was gurgling in its chest with rage.

"I told you there wadn' no goddamn dog here," Thorne shouted, " 'cept the one you keep worryin' over. Maybe he'll git loose in a minute, Wood, and chew your goddamned throat out!"

Clyde shuffled to the back of the cabin, searching here and there with the flashlight. There were some weathered wooden crates piled around, a few split to kindling, all empty. Some old tire rims and a few loose tools. A rusty, fire-blackened barrel full of garbage.

He flashed the beam around for a time. He was running out of places to look.

He thought then of the shed coming in, where the knapsack hung. He'd check that next.

A shiver of doubt skipped through his mind. What if Ms. Devron had, in fact, been wrong?

The shed at the opening to the clearing proved as devoid as the other, harboring no indication of a dog.

Clyde was concerned now. If Jenny was here, he should have found her immediately. Thorne would not have been expecting anyone. There was no reason for him to go to great trouble in hiding her. She had to be close by.

Unless, of course, she was no longer alive and the sorry son-of-a-bitch had simply thrown her in a ditch somewhere along the road. Susan Devron had said that she looked bedraggled and worn. Or the asshole might have already fenced her to a buddy a hundred miles away. However he had managed to get his grimy fingers on her, she was likely wearing a collar. Everybody knew Ben Willow. Even Thorne would have realized a bit of a predicament.

Wood was worried, but he was not ready to give up.

Shuffling through the snow back to the cabin, he sorted through the probabilities. It was cold. He was shivering. His pant legs were wet and his feet were freezing. He had nothing on but a pair of everyday work shoes. That was stupid.

He glanced toward the wire cage. Strangely silent, Thorne hunkered in the same spot near its center, emotionless.

The old man began circling the cabin again, his eyes to the snow, searching diligently with the flashlight. The pit bull was agitated again; he could hear it barking furiously behind him.

Litton Thorne had waited until the instant the old man rounded the corner, then dropped to his back in bear shit and renewed his efforts at escape. Every chance he got he had been kicking with all his might at the welded wire door of the cage, using the barking of the bulldog as a cover. He kicked again now, as hard as he could with both feet, until his teeth shook, and each time he did the steel latch slapped violently against its hinge and was snapped back by the padlock. It was holding, but it was old and rusted. And very, very gradually, within the tortured metal, a hairline rupture was building.

Clyde Wood minced along the perimeter of the clearing behind the cabin, foot by foot, reading the surface of the snow by the ray of the flashlight. There had to be a place, probably several, a distance from the house, that Thorne used to hide hot merchandise. For a man of his profession, they were essential. It would be virtually impossible to find them at night, or even in the daytime, on open ground, but with the snow there was a chance. About the only one left. The fat was in the fire. If Jenny was here, he had to find her now.

He reached the opposite corner of the cabin, where the pit was tethered, uncovering nothing. There was no sign or trace of travel. The surface of the snow was unblemished. Sensing his proximity once more, the bulldog strained against the chain, snarling. Clyde eyed the animal uneasily, only a few yards away. He was worried now more than ever, after all the banging, that the chain might give and he would have the irate brute to contend with.

As it was, he'd have to go back around the house to regain the front yard. He couldn't get safely by. The woods and the cabin crowded closely at that point, and within the throw of its chain the pit bull could reach either.

He reversed and started to retreat, then stopped, intrigued by a stray thought. Maybe that was intentional. Granted the light was feeble, but when first he had seen the bulldog, it had appeared to occupy a small alcove between the tarpaper cabin and the woods. Now, behind the shack, he had found a similar situation. Maybe the pit itself was a "front." A rather imposing one unless someone had a really stubborn interest.

Turning, the storekeeper skirted the menacing dog until he reached the edge of the woods. Or what seemed the woods. The understory was thick and foreboding, black dark and matted with ice-stiffened rhododendron. The beam of the flashlight survived only a few feet before the darkness swallowed it up. Under casual circumstances, he would never have attempted it. His toes were utterly numb now. He wondered how long he had to go till frostbite. He was an old man. It would be easy to back out and leave, say he'd done his best.

But he hadn't, not yet. He knew it and Ben Willow knew it.

Struggling into the thicket, he fought and crawled his way through the laurel, until his breath was ragged and his chest hurt. Until the sweat beaded on his brow and the whole of his body ached. He had gone only a few yards, but it seemed far more. Another bolt of pain shot through his leg. He paused, cursing anew, blowing. At least he could feel his damn toes again. On he squirmed, growing increasingly discouraged. The thicket seemed endless. A fool idea, this was.

Dropping the flashlight half a dozen times, he battled on, grunting and huffing his way in a rough semicircle behind the sounds of the frenzied pit. Again and again, he could hear the unnerving clap of the chain on wood as the dog lunged and was jerked short. Pushing on, he prayed it held. So absorbed was he with the task of the next foot, and so profoundly dark was the immensity of the world beyond the puny halo of the flashlight, that he almost crawled through the narrow opening that defined the path without noticing. But in his struggles, the shaft of the flashlight stabbed into the depths of it and abruptly he knew he'd found what he'd been hoping for.

And when he had clambered to his knees and examined the snow ahead of him, the old man's heart skipped into his throat. Imprinted into the white crust of the snow were the half-covered tracks of a booted man and a setter-sized dog!

Clyde Wood pulled himself to his feet and followed. The tracks led from the cabin, winding away through the thicket. For a moment they were confusing, and then he could see that they were overlaid at intervals by a second set, where only the man had returned. He could feel the mounting promise of his efforts. For another twenty yards, the path twisted itself amid the clutching darkness of the thicket and the footprints followed, and then terminated before another small shed squeezed into a diminutive opening hacked into the laurel.

The door to the shed was shut, secured by latch and padlock, but the throat of the lock hung open. Clyde stopped before it, his heart pounding with apprehension.

"Jenny?" he whispered. He could hear nothing inside.

He lifted the lock from the hasp and swung aside the latch. His breath caught as his hand grasped the door handle. Afraid to press the moment, he hesitated, then slowly pulled open the door.

The little setter blinked against the harsh brightness of the flashlight. It was her only response. She was unable and unwilling to do more. Torn from everything that resembled kindness, she lay apathetically, head on a paw — pitifully thin and unkempt in the middle of the junk-cluttered floor, shivering with shock and cold — affronted by a spent and greasy hock bone and a scattering of moldy bread scraps. Gaping red gashes lay raw and oozing on her hip, foreleg, and muzzle, and her coat was bedraggled and heavily matted with blood. Burning with fever and racked with pain, she was drawn deeply into her misery. Clyde Wood looked into her eyes and could find nothing more than despair.

The old man swallowed hard, felt the tears well into his eyes. Beneath the softer emotions, his anger surged. Goddamn the whory piece of trash that did this.

He could only guess at how she had come to be in such a desperate condition, or how it was that a pile of shit like Thorne got his hands on her. He could never know the full story, but he knew enough. Thorne had brought her here and Thorne had left her here, hurting and bleeding and untended, careless of whether she lived or died save the few dollars he could turn if she survived.

If Ben Willow were here, Litton Thorne would never see the light of another day.

"Jenny." He knelt and extended the back side of his fingers to her nose, speaking her name as gently as a prayer. She raised her head slightly, sniffing impassively and withdrawing, registering no sign of recognition.

Where on God's earth was Ben, and how . . . *how* . . . could this have happened?

He had glanced away with the thought, but his hand still rested limply on the floor by the setter's muzzle. He was conscious, suddenly, of the faint touch of her nose again. And when his eyes returned to her, the feeblest thump of her tail.

His eyes welled again. He smoothed the tuft of hair at her forehead gently, brushed back the matted ruff over her shoulders. It was still beautiful, the rich tan at her cheeks, the black mask.

"It's me, Jenny . . . old Clyde."

She was frightfully wasted. He could feel the bony protuberance of the occipital bone at the stoop of her skull, the sharp edges of her shoulder blades.

He lifted her muzzle with his hand, looked into her eyes, and begged her trust.

"I don't know how we'll do this, Jenny," he said, "but we're goin' home."

The length of camo cord still dangled from her neck.

"I don't think these old legs are up to carrying you, girl; you got to help on your own," he encouraged, laying the flashlight on the floor and urging her up with two hands.

Jenny struggled to her feet, tail tucked, hunched and listless. Clyde climbed back onto his feet. Coaxing her gently with the cord, he pushed open the door of the shed.

She resisted, not wanting to move, then took a tentative step or two.

"Good girl, Jenny," Clyde said, "stay with me. It's gonna get better from here. I promise."

She took another measured step, and another, pausing at the door, looking into the barrenness of the night. She was insentient from shock and pain.

Clyde stepped outside, keeping the flashlight ahead and out of her eyes.

"C'mon girl, you can do it."

The pit bull could see spasmodic flashes of the light, hear Clyde's voice. It was raging against the chain again.

"C'mon, Jenny."

Wobbly with pain, but wanting now to follow, Jenny was beginning to find her feet. She stepped out of the shed onto the snow.

At the same moment, he heard the resounding whack of the bulldog's chain against the crate, a sickening pop, and the horrifying crack and whimper of splintering wood. He knew in the instant what had happened. He could hear the closing rush of the infuriated dog through the thicket, the ascending, gurgling snarl of its rage, the violent whip of the chain against the brush behind it.

For the balance of his days, Clyde Wood would never know how he managed in those next few seconds. Somehow he grabbed up Jenny, catapulted her back into the shed, and boiled in behind her. Like a locomotive, the turbulent huff of the onrushing dog closed through the darkness upon them. The old man grabbed for the open door, fumbled the handle for crucial seconds, then swung it shut with all his might. Against the force of his leverage, the wooden door spun recklessly on its hinges for the frame. And wedged nine inches short as time ran cold, and the broad, demonic head and neck of the pit bull slammed through the closing crack by the brute force of its momentum. Knocked from his hand, the flashlight spun like a top on the floor of the shed, its beam whirling inside the tiny enclosure in a muddle of light and shadow.

Frantically, Wood braced his foot against the wall, pulling with all his strength, fighting to hold his meager advantage against the crazed fury of the pit. He could feel the powerful, tearing thrust of short muscular legs against the floor and the snow as the beast strained for him, trying to drive its thick black chest through the cracked door. Inches from his body, in the luminal netherworld of the flashlight, its curling lips and snapping stiletto teeth were unearthly.

It was hopeless. He was straining against the lunging dog with every ounce of resistance he could muster, and with every thrust of its powerful hind legs and shove of its stout forequarters it was gaining, worming its way into the shed. Clyde's strength was failing. Another few seconds and it would be academic. In the closeness of the small building, he would have little chance against the vicious beast. He glanced furtively for Jenny. She had withdrawn to a corner, her head turned to the wall.

Clyde Wood did the only thing left. Struggling to hold the door with one hand, he freed the other and worked the heavy Colt pistol from his belt. Shoving the muzzle of the gun flat against the brutish head as the dog forced its way through, he jerked the trigger.

The blast of the .357 was deafening within the tiny shed. The silence following it deathly. Clyde Wood had been thrown by the rebound of his effort against the back wall of the shed, momentarily insensate but for the ringing in his ears. In the ellipse of the flashlight, the head and chest of the pit were sprawled upon the blood-spattered floor of the shed, its hindquarters balanced over the sill onto the snow, its tongue slowly working within its still-bared teeth. Its forelegs twitched convulsively and just outside the door, its hind paws dug shallow, diminishing circles in the snow. There was a small, black hole in the side of its head. Beneath the uglier one under its jaw a dark red pool was growing.

The old man stared at the dog for a time, collecting himself. Then, as if remembering where he was, he struggled to his feet again and approached Jenny.

She had tucked herself into the corner and buried her head. She would not rise, and after several minutes of coaxing there was nothing left to do but lift her past the dead animal and put her down in the snow outside the shed again. He accomplished it, but now the pain grabbed his left leg with every motion. He gimped along the dark, winding path, persuading Jenny gently with the cord, waiting for her when she faltered, reaching the wooden crate at the side of the cabin where the bull dog had been chained.

He paused there, weighing the distance to the truck.

"You have to do it, Jenny," he told her. "I'm too old and wasted to carry you."

Stiff and hurting, she shuffled behind him, stopping every few steps, resuming with reluctance. Finally she would go no farther, and dropped to the snow.

For yet another time in an incredible night, Clyde Wood somehow reached inside himself and came up with the wherewithal for what had seemed impossible. He bent and stooped and struggled, managed to gather Jenny into his arms, and staggered back to his feet. He limped past the cabin, through the shadowy clutter of the yard, toward the Bronco. He tripped over the protruding edge of a washtub buried in the snow, almost falling. It was pitch dark, even with the contrast of the snow. He had stuck the flashlight in his pocket. He fished it out again with a fumbling hand, pushing it on, turning clumsily side to side to direct the beam. He tottered toward the dim silhouette of the truck, the setter, even in her depleted condition, growing ever more burdensome.

"Hang on, Jenny," he told himself, "we'll do this."

On he stuttered, sweating beneath his coat from the exertion.

"Almost there, girl," he vowed, "we're past the worst of it."

At last he made the passenger door of the truck. He paused, shifting the setter's weight one last time, gathering his balance. The faint beam of the flashlight swept erratically across the yard as he contorted, past the cabin, the woodpile, onto the wire cage where Thorne was huddled. Semiconsciously, his eyes followed it. And slammed to a halt. Like a photograph rising from an emulsion, the obscure impression grew on Clyde Wood's mind, emerging to reality, bursting into a icy facsimile of horror. Steadying Jenny in his arms, he twisted desperately, struggling to fix the light again on the cage. It swept awkwardly past and back, then settled. His certainty was so staggering he felt his blood run cold. There was an empty black hole where the door should be.

Litton Thorne loomed out of the night like a satanic phantasm. His bony face was gnarled with madness, and from his throat rose a shriek. Death walked his eyes, and with all his might he sidearmed the hatchet at the old man's skull.

Frozen with shock, Clyde Wood could never have reacted quickly enough on his own. Jenny, weakened as she was, had sensed the lurking man seconds before he had sprung. As he rushed in, she bolted with abrupt terror from the old man's arms. The thrust of her hindquarters against his chest drove him stiffly backward and Wood's feet shot out from under him as he crashed hard against the door of the Bronco and then to the ground. It was the only thing that saved him. The razor-keen blade of the whizzing hatchet hissed by his head, missing by a death-row prayer. The passenger window disintegrated in a tumultuous splatter of glass, and Litton Thorne ranted like a madman.

In a fresh moment of terror, the old man found himself flat on his back between the enraged man's legs. He was disoriented, his glasses askew atop the bridge of his nose. There was no time to think, only seconds to react. Desperately he grabbed for the Colt. Towering above him, Thorne recoiled instantly, jerking the hatchet back through the shattered window and cocking it above his head. He meant to bury the ax to the gory haft in Wood's brain and he meant to do it now. Clyde's groping fingers found the checkered grip of the pistol just as the hatchet reached the extremity of its travel above Thorne's head. For a second, the hatchet hung there on the hinge of doom. Then Thorne screamed another obscenity, dropped earthward on folding knees, and sent it hurling toward Clyde Wood's skull. In the same instant, Clyde Wood freed the big handgun from his waistband and shoved it skyward.

For the brief space of a millisecond, a ragged finger of fire belched into the night. The concussion of the muzzle blast thudded against the ground like the clap of thunder. The .357 hollow-point bullet tore through Litton Thorne, macerating his genitals, mushrooming into his bowels, devastating lungs and liver, and exiting in a jagged, lemon-sized hole where his spine had been. The man jerked as if he had met the end of a hangman's rope, lurched forward, collapsed, and rolled off Clyde Wood's chest onto the snow. He would never move again.

The old man lay stunned, on his back in the snow, his face warm and wet with spattered blood, not finding the will to move. So impossible were the last few moments that only slowly was reality dawning. He blinked, staring at the head of the hatchet. It was buried in the door of the Bronco at the bottom of a four-inch gash. An inch this way and Nettie Wood would have been a widow. He tried to absorb that.

He pushed himself to a sitting position against the rocker panel of the truck, his breath coming in gasps, the pistol in hand across his lap. Gradually, his senses were beginning to perceive the magnitude of what had happened. He looked at the dead man lying motionless and bloody less than two feet away. It was surreal, especially in the dark. This must be a dream that would soon climax, and evaporate in a shower of relief. It must be, but it wasn't.

He had come so close before and managed to avoid it, and after all that, somehow still it had happened. In less time than it takes to draw a breath, he had killed a man. He had known that his coming would be dangerous. But what was danger? Somehow, before, it had always lapsed short of death. He was a man unfamiliar with violence, and how naive he had been, with a man like Thorne. Now the unthinkable had happened. And, most strangely, now that it had, he felt little emotion, either way.

The man had tried to kill him.

He struggled to his feet, nudged the Colt back under his belt, bent and picked up the still-burning flashlight from the snow. He turned the beam on Thorne for a moment, studying the man blankly, then away, swinging it about the yard. He must find Jenny again now.

"Jenny?" He called her name, hoping that she had not gone far. "God, don't let me lose her now, after all this," he thought.

He found her after no more than a minute or two. She had stopped between the Bronco and the cabin and lain down again. The pain in his leg was agonizing. He limped toward her. She stood as he neared, disoriented and apathetic.

Bending down, he rubbed her flank, his fingers riding the washboard of her protruding rib cage.

"Once more, Jenny," he said, "trust me once more."

Slipping his arms gently under her, he lifted her. He took a deep breath, mustering his strength. With a wobble and a grunt, he regained his feet.

Without pausing, he reached the driver-side door of the truck. He lugged it open, held it aside with an elbow. Awkwardly, he leaned across and lowered Jenny onto the passenger seat.

He stood up, straightening his back, then climbed in after her. Switching off the flashlight, he poked it back into the console. With a turn of the ignition key, the engine spun to life. Punching up the heat, he flipped the fan on high and turned on the courtesy lights.

After a minute or two, he could feel the warm, welcome rush of the heat, countering the cold air that rushed through the missing window.

He sat a minute longer, looking at the setter curled on the seat, then picked up the bag phone. Stabbing in seven numbers with his index finger, he double-checked himself mentally, then tapped SEND with his thumb.

The phone buzzed four times, then connected with a voice.

"Mazie? Clyde Wood again. Is Semp still around?"

"No. He got rid o' the SBI and left not long after you called."

"I've got to talk to 'im. Can you git 'im on the radio?"

"I'll see," the dispatcher promised. "What's your number there — I'll have him call you."

Clyde fed her the number.

"Mazie?"

"Yeah."

"As soon as possible."

"Okay, sweetie, hold the pipe . . ."

He held the phone to the light again, squinted his eyes for END, and punched it back to standby.

Five long minutes later it rang shrilly. He fumbled it to his ear.

"Clyde . . . Semp. Mazie said you hollered. Hey, thought I'd let you know. We got a line on Ben. That is . . . we know where to start. You were right about the Step. A part-timer with the forest service, name o' Brickett, picked up our lookout on the scanner. Says he was up there just after the storm came in and saw Ben's old truck parked somewhere near the fifth bench. I'm roundin' up some people and we're gonna fall in on it first thing in the mornin'. Matter o' fact, I'm not far from the Step now. Had a paper to serve in Stidwell."

"Can you make a detour," Clyde asked, his voice quaking.

"I guess. Whatcha need?"

"I just killed a man."

There was a moment of dead silence.

"You just —"

"I just killed a man," Clyde Wood repeated, "Litton Thorne . . . I just shot Litton Thorne."

Another interval of silence.

Semp Mason's voice returned, stern and husky. "You there now?" he asked.

"Yeah."

"Anybody else?"

"No."

"I'm on the way. Wait for me. You told anybody about this?"

"No, just you."

"Well, don't. Don't call anybody an' don't talk to nobody. Not Nettie, not nobody. I'll be there as quick as I can."

The phone clicked dead. He hit the power button and dropped it back in the bag.

Clyde Wood leaned back against the seat, absorbing the silence.

He looked over at Jenny again, lying despondent on the seat. He was worried. She was terribly wasted, weak, and torn. But she was out of Thorne's hands, and she wasn't shivering as much anymore. Just as soon as he got though with Semp Mason and this nightmare, if they didn't throw him in jail, he'd call Dan Hudson, no matter the hour. Get him to meet him at the clinic. If anyone could see her through, it would be Dan Hudson.

Reaching over his shoulder, he lifted his boots off the backseat and sat them on the console, dropping the spare socks in them onto his lap. He squirmed around the steering wheel, untied his soaked work shoes, and peeled the wet socks off his lily white feet. He studied his pale feet. They were blue and shriveled.

He paused again.

Gathering up his right boot for no reason, he turned it in his hands for a moment and set it back, thinking grimly of the man lying just outside, cold and dead in the snow.

And of the day that Ben Willow had chosen to ask of him those things a man must finally trust to another, and of them all, the last.

"There may come a time," Ben had said. "*Whatever else,*" he had pleaded, "*see to Jenny.*"

He dropped his chin to his chest, took a deep breath, and cradled his head in his hand for a time.

Then he collected the heavy wool socks from his lap, leaning over and pulling on first one and then the other.

They were warm and dry.

21

They were three weeks getting Ben Willow off the mountain.

Just as it had seemed the weather was leavening, another onslaught of Arctic air blustered in from the north. By night, great oaks cracked like cannon shots, splintered limb to trunk by the relentless wedge of the cold, and by day skeins of ice grew on flowing water. Old folks, huddled to hearth, would pronounce it the bitterest in memory.

In its numbing grip, a team of local deputies and wildlife officers searched futilely for six days, using the old International truck as a benchmark. Floundering atop the deep and crusted snow, they turned not a trace. The storm had obliterated all before it, far below the softer surface left by the trailing flurries, beneath the stiff and successive layers of ice deposited by sleet and bitter cold. The sun shone weakly but could do little to warm the brittle air, and the wind blew merciless and lonely about the rugged slopes.

On the seventh day they submitted and went home. It was Christmas Eve.

By the day after Christmas, Semp had mustered reserves from the adjoining three counties and the West Virginia State Patrol, and counting civilian volunteers, the search party had swollen to well over a hundred. Divided into four equal ranks and utilizing GPS grids, it proceeded laboriously and relentlessly across the precarious, upper face of the Step, each man armed with a prod pole, a folding shovel, and a small pack of provisions. Until by the thirteenth day of the search, even the toughest of them was haggard, spent, and stubbled, and together they were still no closer to finding the old man than when they started. The mountain was an implacable, mind-numbing enormity of white, stiff and emotionless as stone. And despite all desire to the contrary, they were forced by greater logic to suspend their efforts until the stinging air mellowed.

It was only with the new year, in the first few minutes after midnight, that the probing vanguard of the southeast wind finally stole past the outposts of winter, pressing in gentle zephyrs across the Shenandoah, climbing above and beyond the bleak and frozen headlands of the Blue Ridge, claiming each succeeding hill and hollow. Close behind massed the great push of an immense Atlantic front.

An hour into another January, Semp Mason had walked reflectively past the back door, through his back pasture, past the knotted, black shadows of the cattle, to the swell of a small rise. He loved this place. Loved to stand as now and study the valley below: cold and blue in winter, fresh and earthy in spring . . . languid and green with summer . . . mellow and chill in the fall. Particularly he liked the frankness of winter. Across the disclosure of the barren landscape, as far as the eye could carry, he could see the glow of the burgeoning little towns, *his* towns, and in the dark expanses between them the scattered pinpricks of farmhouse lights, where folks, *his* folks, went about the chore of daily living.

Tonight there were more farm lights than usual, folks still sitting up taking stock of the old year, hedging their troubles and mulling their blessings, praying faith over hope that the one coming would bring better.

It was up to them, of course, and in the test some would prosper and some would fail. The rest would fall to fate.

There were times, Mason thought, when he wanted to be anything other than a law officer, when people did as they would, despite decency and the Good Book. And then there was most of the time, with the majority who were just the good, plain folks he'd been raised up with, who wished for peace and harmony and had entrusted a major part of that to him, when he wanted to be nothing else.

As his daddy before him, he liked the thought and order of that. When there was order. Now there was a thing undone. Ben Willow was troubling him, and he could not let it go.

Ben was one of *his* people. Despite the homogeneous facade of official-dom he was forced to don in the course of duty, he had been partial to old Ben himself. He was sure, now, that the old man lay somewhere under the ice on that cold and lonely mountain. It was gnawing at him, the disorder of it, the indecency of it. Over and over in his mind, he had pitted himself against the tremendous perplexity of the wild and rugged country, annoyed at how easy it would be to walk within a few feet of the body and never know it was there. Likely they had. Free of the deep and frozen snow cover, the search would still have been formidable. With it, their task had been nigh impossible. Even then, he had not wanted to quit.

But now he could feel the tease of the first temperate breezes against his face, and overhead the clouds were beginning to shift, exposing broken pockets of stars. Morning would bring the sun. If the weather seers were right, warm air would build in for the next five days, ushering tempera-tures well above freezing. With it would come the melt and, by everything within his means, the whereabouts of Ben Willow. He simply wouldn't quit until it was so.

He took a last, long look at the valley, storing it to memory. Distantly, vaguely, he could place the part of it where Ben and Libby had lived, see in his mind the quaint little farm on Traver's Creek Road, the old man and the dog in the yard. Andrea was there now, waiting for word. It must be very painful for her, the days wearing on. Setting his jaw, he started down from the rise, back to the house.

First thing tomorrow he would alert the search teams, the several agencies, arrange for the equipment and support, set the logistics in place. Day after, they would climb that damn mountain again — reexecute the entire hunt for Ben Willow from zero — and they would not come down without him.

By the eighteenth day, it had become one of the most intensive and punishing search and recovery missions in West Virginia history. More than 125 officers and volunteers representing a dozen state and local agen-cies were engaged, including volunteer firefighters from four counties, emergency management crews, aerial recon elements of the Civil Air Pa-trol, and two units of the local Guard. That was in the search alone. Scores of others were immersed in the considerable task of equipment, food, fuel, and supply, with three EMS units on the scene, and a Medevac team at the CAM Center in Charleston ready to put a chopper enroute at first summons. Altogether, counting Mazie Bullard and the fellow members of the Buckeye Ladies Auxiliary, who were putting together sandwiches in the kitchen of Hopewell Baptist Church, more than three hundred men and women were absorbed into the chore of finding Ben Willow.

Ben Willow, himself, would have considered that an extravagant bother, and abhorred the intrusion upon the mountain.

As predicted, a period of mild weather had prevailed for the five days since the search had resumed, the open sun plummeting from the clear blue sky, softening and diminishing the thick rime of ice and snow that blanketed the merciless terrain. But the melt was excruciatingly slow. In some places, on the shadowy northern slopes, the nearly four feet of ice covering the ground remained stiff and unyielding, thawing only enough to slicken the surface, making the footing perilous. At the expense of one broken leg, several twisted ankles, and sheer exhaustion, however, the quest had gone as planned. But unsuccessfully.

Mason was haggard, perplexed, and desperate. The warm air couldn't hold much longer. Already the return to winter was on the short-range maps, another assault of roaring winds and single-digit temperatures. The weather people could promise him two more days — at best — before the arrival of the front. He had talked to Clyde Wood again the night before, grasping for some better idea of the way Ben would have gone. And, now, once again, he had redirected the effort, returning to the brutal area as-cending the summit beyond the seventh bench, which lay above and west of where the old man's truck had been found.

It was midafternoon of the twenty-first day when happenstance had finally unearthed the instrument of disclosure. Throughout the previous evening the northwest wind had stiffened with the approaching front, its edge sharpened by the building cold. Dawn had broken under an ashen sky, and throughout the morning the clouds had layered and thickened. By noon the first shards of new snow were on the air. Relentlessly the gusts had continued to rage in great blasts across the slopes of the mountain, bending and torturing the trees, leaving them moaning and creaking above the heads of the shivering men who shrunk more deeply into their cloth-ing, held their long, ragged line, and persevered their way up the steep, rocky wall of the Seven Step.

On the slick and treacherous incline, one of them, a young man under the gray mantle of a patrol officer, had tripped over what he thought was a stob, pitching headlong into the ice. Angrily, he had picked himself up, glaring back at the offending object and cursing it as if it were aware. Like mist before a dry wind, his ire vanished and his heart jumped. The force of his boot had kicked away the disguising rind of ice, and he could see it perfectly now. It was the first two inches of a shotgun barrel.

Semp Mason had been two hundred yards removed on the adjacent slope. Within five minutes of the radio call, he was on the spot. Twenty minutes later, he was looking into the frozen blue eyes of Ben Willow. Immediately he patched through to Clyde, Andrea, and Steve.

Carefully, the body of the old man was extricated and carried by stretcher to the crest of the slope, then directed by aerial reconnaissance through a deep hollow to a small open meadow. In the blue haze of the rising evening, it was lifted off the mountain by helicopter and removed to the county medical examiner's office.

It would have been all and the same to Ben Willow had they left him there, where they found him, but there were certain things the Great Order demanded before a man could hope for peace. Things important to humankind, and wholly inconsequential to eternity. It must be determined that, yes, in fact, he was dead, and how that came to be, and there were reports to be completed and filed so the numbers could roll over by a digit on the vital records scrolls, the Social Security Administration would terminate the benefit payment, the state could go to the trouble of collecting whatever share of the estate it deserved, and the IRS could follow closely the distribution of assets. Not to mention the clerk of court, fiduciary institutions, creditors, and vendors to be duly notified, so that the debits and credits of a man's life might be neatly adjusted to the sum of zero.

In due time society was served, the body was released to the family, and Andrea arranged through Tom Pugh what was intended to be a small memorial service at Shiloh Baptist Church. Short of the Second Coming, the Reverend Randy Parrish and the resident deaconry could hardly have been prepared for the deluge of last respects. A day raw, wet, and blustery did little to dampen the resolve of the many who came. An hour before the service the first of them began trickling solemnly into the back rows, silent and pensive. Twenty minutes later the pews were filled to capacity, and those left standing began to line the walls. Side by side . . . mine workers and farmers and hill people and townsfolk, folks in tattered coatsleeves and fine silk ties, family friends, lifelong acquaintances and come-lately strangers . . . those genuinely grieving, and those slightly more than curious, admirers of the old man's folklore and eccentricity. All waiting to be led through the Valley of the Shadow, to leave there a thoughtful word for the deceased, and to be returned to the other side. There were others, not present, who had simply read the obituary over a cup of morning coffee at Sarah Gentry's café counter and registered to their mind a kind thought, mourning the passing of another bucolic bit of old West Virginia.

The preacher delivered a short and apt eulogy, consecrated and delivered a lost soul to the Lord, and voiced for the gathering a prayer of faith and salvation. A cappella, Irene Presnell offered a sensitive rendering of the old wildwood hymn, "Will There Be Any Stars in My Crown," soaring with the final chorus. In the piercing stillness that followed Andrea read softly the familiar verse from Frost: ". . . before a deep woods, two roads diverged, and I took the one less traveled."

Clyde Wood, Henry Armfield, and Joshua Treadwell were honorary pallbearers.

Afterward, Andrea and Steve returned to Germany, and, individually, succeeding the momentary reflection that one day it would be their own crossing, the rest of the congregation settled back into the balance of their lives.

A few weeks later Thelma Haskins, chief librarian for the Randolph County School System, would be surprised and mildly intrigued by the generous memorial gift from Susan Rush Devron. Twenty-five classic volumes of sporting literature, among them Buckingham, Babcock, Sheldon, Ruark, and Ford.

In the days and months that followed, the course of affairs grew routine again at the Randolph County sheriff's office. Walter Criswell, tax supervisor at the Buckeye Municipal Building, granting himself the honor as he had for seventeen years, hoisted the flag anew each morning. Folks who sinned on Wednesday went to preaching on Sunday. The *Courier Tribune* marched religiously to press every Thursday evening at seven o'clock. As to the life and times of one old man, it would have been surmised that the world was in closure.

But in Shiloh Cemetery, under the shadow of the solitary maple tree, its limbs bare and bony against a sodden sky, the small plot of earth beside Elizabeth Chandler Willow lay undisturbed. And in a security vault, on a shelf, in an interior vestibule of Pugh Funeral Home, rested a small walnut box. Inside waited six and a half ounces of fine, gray ash.

Clyde Wood had placed the phone back to the hook the afternoon Semp had called from the mountain, turning slowly to Nettie, staring as if she wasn't there.

"It's time for a crepe hanging," he had said, his face ghostly pale.

She had looked at him, at first with fright, then with a wash of understanding.

"Ben Willow's dead," he had finished, saying the words for both of them. Sinking heavily into his chair, he had not spoken again.

She had laid a gentle hand on his shoulder some time later, and left him be.

"I'm sorry, Clyde," she had offered. "Ben was a good man."

He had not come to bed that evening. Through the night, she had slept alone, one of the few times in their lengthy union. She had found him the next morning, still sitting in his chair, appearing not to have moved. For an hour she had gone about breakfast, put in a load of wash, mended a shirt, without so much as a word from him. She had gone to the garden, come back and sat at the kitchen table, snapping beans. Remembering the bedclothes needed a change, she had put the bowl down, wiped her hands on her apron, walked past him on her way back to the bedroom closet.

"Ben Willow was an old man," he had said suddenly. "*I'm* an old man."

The resignation had been complete, and it had stopped her midstep. At the moment she was of a loss what to say. She had stood there a few seconds, then walked on. There were words, of course, but none of genuine comfort. Not then.

Every day since, she had been trying to help him past it all, and he was beginning to come out of it, but it would take more time.

Nettie Wood watched her husband now over the magazine in her hands, as he carelessly knocked the dead ash from his pipe, digging the tobacco pouch from his pocket, and retamping the bowl . . . igniting a kitchen match with his thumbnail, his round cheeks hollowing and filling as he drew the flame into the bowl.

Three months had passed since that dread afternoon, and still he had not shaken it from his mind. He had recovered to an extent, but was yet grumpy and morose, far from his jovial self. Before, they would talk, in the evenings after the day was done, of this and that. Laugh and tease. But he said little now, and answered in single syllables. The terrible night with Litton Thorne probably had more play, too, than he was willing to admit. He had said little of it. She did not yet, never would, know the details. Knowing him as long and completely as she had, she still found it hard to believe that, with a man so docile and unsupposing as the one she had married, it had happened. But it had, and they had to live with that.

Abruptly, she was flooded by a wave of empathy, moved to offer something more, a helping thought . . . something.

"I heard a whippoorwill tonight," she ventured, "first of the year."

They had always looked forward to the return of the whippoorwills in spring. Starting in early April, they would steal a moment between evening chores and the house, stopping together on the back steps to listen. The first one was always the harbinger of harmony, its wistful, three-noted whip-sawing in the twilight of a tender spring evening a reassurance that the world was yet in order.

"In the wood ashes at the edge of the pasture. Early this year."

"Mmhhh," he acknowledged through an exhalation of pipe smoke.

She could see that he was off somewhere again, that he would not accept her enticement for conversation. She tried to ignore the rejection and absorb herself back into the magazine.

The house was quiet, the silence dragging monotonously toward bed-time. Accepting the company of the clock, she languished for a time between the words on the page and the rhythm and stroke of the pendulum.

"Do you think you could manage here by yourself for a time," he said, turning to her.

Startled by the question, her heart fluttered and she was a moment replying.

"I suppose . . . ?"

"I believe I'll move in to Ben's for a few days, 'Ettie," he finished, his voice earnest and begging. "It'll be easier with the cows, and there's the estate to do."

It was the "'Ettie" that caused her to question no further, to simply lay her palm on his wrinkled hand and capture his eyes with a tender gaze.

"Do as you need to, Clyde. I've abided here forty-six years. Thick and thin. I don't guess another few days will change that, either way," she assured him, smiling.

The thank-you was in his eyes. He brushed her cheek gently with the back of three fingers and withdrew, settling back into his chair.

Nettie did not look forward to his absence, for even a day. Or even an hour, it seemed, when you got right down to it, although the reality of that was absurd. She no longer liked him leaving for work every morning, or going to board meetings on monthly evenings. Now that they were older, and every day was a bit less certain than the last.

But for the first time, Clyde was moving past himself, accepting an initiative. For whatever reasons, it was a small step forward.

Clyde Wood was a troubled man. He sat in his old leather chair, reflecting upon what he had just said to Nettie about moving to Ben's and thinking just how he was going about it. It had been at him again, for the last two days. Ben's death. He could still hear Semp's voice, from the mountain that dark Thursday afternoon. Picture in his mind the scene the sheriff had described.

He had known from the moment Susan Devron had called about Jenny that Ben had come to ill miss, yet the confirmation of it had stunned him more than he had imagined. The finality of it. He knew there was no place on earth, given the end, that Ben would rather have been, but he missed his old friend. Ben had been the one bit of certainty in an uncertain world. Ben was Ben. No more, no less.

Ben had seemed as certain as Chandler's Knob, and it didn't seem any more right that he was gone than it was right that the mountain was still there.

They didn't see each other every day, every week, even every month. Not like when they were younger. They didn't walk the mountains like they once had, or worry the brookies as regularly, or chase bluetick coonhounds in the hours past midnight. Hadn't for a good while. But they *had*, for a lot of years, and *that* was what was important. That, and the certainty that Ben was there and that when he saw or needed him again, he would be exactly as the last time. That there was no need for explanations of absence, nor limp and belittling apologies — only the happiness of greeting him once again and basking in his company — a feeling akin to embracing once more the freshness that followed a summer storm or the first chill day of fall.

Within a mutual hatred of pretense, there had never been the slightest bit between them.

Ben had always been his hero, long before Ben had pulled Trafford Johnson off him in the dirt street behind the Merrymore Hotel one night and beat the living snot out of the big red-assed bastard. He had admired Ben's stubborn independence, his fearless grit and grind. He had always wished he could be more like him. But his cloth was of a different cut, and every time he had ever tried to be unduly serious about something he had always ended up laughing. He liked the humor in living. It lightened the day, and he went out of his way to find it.

He had loved to tease old Ben. Ben was always so serious.

Now all he had of Ben was Jenny. And that was a great deal.

He glanced at the setter, curled on the rug by his feet, fretted at an irregularity in her breathing, relaxed as it smoothed.

It had been close.

It was two-thirty in the morning when he had been released by the law

the night of Litton Thorne, and only then because of Semp, who had as-
sessed the scene and vouched for his story. He had rushed home to reas-
sure Nettie, then immediately called Dr. Hudson. Thirty minutes later the
white-bearded, bleary-eyed old vet had met him at the door of the clinic,
looking a bit like Santa Claus the morning after, a cup of coffee in his
hand, and an offer for a second for Clyde, which died with the first glance
at Jenny.

He had taken her from Wood's arms, carried her past the examining
rooms to the surgical station in the back. He had shaken his head, grunted
as he spread open her eyelids, stared into her eyes, turned her lip. Her
gums were bloodlessly pale.

For the better part of the next two hours, Dan Hudson had worked
constantly over the little setter, attaching her to IVs of glucose and whole
blood, cleansing and stitching the wicked cuts. Probing, feeling, and listening intently to the thump and squish of the organs through the stetho-
scope, posing sparse questions to himself, and pumping in the first round
of antibiotics and steroids. Throughout, Jenny lay on the stainless-steel
table with cataleptic detachment, her ribs etched deeply with each breath
against the pinched skin of her sides, her eyes frantic and fixed. Though
she was only mildly sedated.

"She still has signs of shock," Hudson had explained, reading the
question in Wood's eyes.

Clyde had remained by the table the entire time, numb and dazed himself, so aching with exhaustion and emotion he could hardly keep his feet.

"What the hell happened?" the vet had asked finally.

He had felt the heat of Hudson's ire, and had shrank before it. Surely,
the man didn't think he had anything to do with it.

He had related what he knew, realizing how little it was, what Susan
Devron had described, her condition when he had found her in the shed
at Thorne's. Ben's absence. Beyond that, he had declared, he was at a loss.

Impassively, Dr. Hudson had turned away to the sink, washing and
shaking dry his hands, finishing with a paper towel as he returned to the
table.

"Well, there's no mistakin' one thing," he observed, studying his pa-
tient, "she was in one hell of a dog fight. From the looks of those cuts,
more than one dog. It wasn't a roadside disagreement. They were tryin' to
kill her."

"Damn nearly did," Hudson concluded, balling the used towel up in
his hands and tossing it toward the waste can.

"Will she get through this?" he had asked, afraid of the answer.

"I don't know, Clyde," Dan Hudson had said, leveling his gaze. "She's in a bad way. By the looks of her, she's run the brunt of this storm. God knows what else. She's obviously anemic . . . probably advanced. I'll run the blood work shortly, and we'll see what else we've got. It won't be good," he had said, pausing. "Her heart's fairly steady, but it's weak. The shock alone may kill her, even yet."

Clyde had said nothing in reply, couldn't. After all that had happened in the course of the last twelve hours, he could not lose her now.

"What worries me most," Hudson was continuing, "is what may be going on inside. She's bruised internally — brutally — and likely as not there's some hemorrhaging."

Wood had stared at Hudson, and his eyes must have said as much as his words, because concern had registered on the veterinarian's face even before he had spoken. And he knew he was asking more than he had the right to.

"What was between Ben and Jenny . . . ," he had said to Dan Hudson, "it was like that between me and Ben. I killed a man tonight getting her here, 'cause Ben couldn't."

He could see the shock ripple Hudson's face, the droop of his chin. He had stopped then, lowering his head, eyes welling.

When he had looked up again, it had been in desperation.

"I promised Ben — about Jenny," he had said. "You're the last hope of keepin' it."

He had turned and walked out the door then, with the weight of the world on his shoulders, feeling as if the very breath had been sucked from him, and driven home in the faint gray light of dawn.

Jenny had tottered on the hinge of death for the next seven days. Even the dangerous doses of antibiotics and prophylactics Hudson dared could barely stem the toxins that swelled and swarmed through her ravaged system, and amid the havoc of infection, chances of her survival withered rapidly. But somehow, by tubes and needles, the wisdom of a traveled old vet — and something greater — she clung to life. As morning after morning, hope beaded and vanished like dew before a harsh morning sun.

Finally the grip of the fever had been broken, and a will grew again in her eyes, and slowly she had begun the fight back. Later, he had learned that Dan Hudson had slept the first six nights at the clinic, checking on her almost hourly. He would never forget that.

But just when it seemed the tide had turned, the reprieve toppled into relapse, and suddenly Jenny's lungs filled perilously with pneumonia. Once more she was drawn to the brink of a grave, and once more — night through day — Hudson struggled against impossible odds, and brought her through.

Gradually, she battled back. With another week, and solid food again, her strength rebounded. On the eighteenth day of her recovery, Wood had taken her home.

He had Dan Hudson to thank for that, and a lot more.

A month later he remembered he hadn't received the bill, so he had stopped by the clinic. Tillie Whittaker's daughter, Emmy, was at the reception counter, flustered when she found the billing record incomplete in Jenny's file. She had excused herself to look for Hudson. The elfin old vet had returned with her, glasses on his nose, a clipboard in hand and a pencil over his ear, humming as he let himself past the counter into the reception lobby.

"So, how's Jenny Willow?" he chirped, extending a hand.

"Not kickin' up a lot o' dust yet," he had reported, "but still in the race. Nettie's scramblin' a layin' o' eggs for her twice a day, and she ate half my bread puddin' last evenin', so there's hope."

"Good, good!" Hudson agreed. "You look a sight better'n last time yourself," the good doctor added with a chuckle.

"Ain't but so much you can expect," Wood had countered, grinning back. He *was* some better, with Jenny on the mend and since it appeared now he had been exonerated of any prosecutable wrongdoing in the death of Litton Thorne. There was still to be a formal inquiry, but no charges were being filed, the books likely to be closed on self-defense. At least he wasn't going to waste the short end of his life in the state penitentiary.

There was a brief lull in their conversation, so he broke to the chase.

"Thought I'd come by and settle up," he proposed, reaching for his checkbook.

Hudson hadn't replied for a moment. He had raised the clipboard and opened the file in an absentminded way, then closed it and extended a hand again.

Clyde had reached for it.

"You and Nettie come to dinner one Sunday," Hudson said. His gesture was obvious.

He still had the vet's hand. "I *already* owe you a lot more than money, Dan," he said.

"I know 'bout Ben Willow and his dogs," the old vet had exclaimed, fixing the storekeeper with his gaze, "and I've heard a bit also about his friend Clyde Wood."

Clyde had started to protest again, past the lump in his throat, then firmly shook the hand in his clasp, letting it rest. It was too generous a gesture, after all, that Hudson had made . . . and one no gentleman would refuse.

Jenny was well out of the woods now physically. Nettie had pampered her, like the child they never had. She was in good flesh again, her coat silky and supple, though the underlying muscles, always knotted before, and rippling, had atrophied with trauma and inactivity to spare and stringy. That would take care of itself, once she was about again. She had been almost a year old when she came to Ben, so she would be about seven now. On the far crest of the hill, but yet in her prime. What worried him most was her indifference. She had regained little of the white-hot zest for life, the indomitable will that had been her trademark. She would wag her tail obligingly, acknowledge the appreciation of their attention. Once she had barked halfheartedly from the porch at a neighborhood hound. But altogether she was far too complacent, as if her spirit were imprisoned.

Clyde was uncertain how much of that had to do with the ordeal she had been through, and how much of it had to do with Ben's being gone. Dogs grieve. He knew that. She had to feel the loss; they had been inseparable, heart and soul, for six years. If nothing else, she was confused and distraught by the absence of all she had known.

It was different with a gun dog, Ben had always said. A thing, of the bond between a hunter and a hunting dog, that carried beyond the heart. Beyond companionship, to life itself. The condition that each could live . . . *really live* . . . only through the other.

He realized that much of Jenny's malaise was made of his own. He himself had not gotten past Ben. Aside from the store, all he had done was sit, mope, and piddle.

He looked at the little setter again.

"Ben ain't comin' back," he said to her, "and he wouldn't take kindly to us sittin' around an' doin' nothin' about it."

The morning after they found old Ben, Clayton McAlister had been by to tell him something he already knew, that Ben had named him executor of his will. He needed, now, to be about the estate.

"You know Ben has a rather peculiar request in here, don't you?" Clayton had asked, handing him the envelope containing the will.

"I know," Clyde had said. "Don't know that it's peculiar."

"Well, I mean, it's *different*," McAlister observed.

"Ben Willow was different," Clyde declared.

Clayton had waited there a minute, mildly chastised.

"How'll you do it," he asked awkwardly.

"Jus' like he asked."

After McAlister had left, he had thought about how he would do it. What Ben had asked of him as they sat on the porch that day, before they had worked Jenny, still a puppy, on quail. It *was* different. *Perfectly* different. Though the request had taken even him by surprise. Libby. He'd always assumed . . .

So had Andrea. She had not taken it easily.

But he remembered the look in Ben's eyes.

He was less certain than he pretended about how he would do it. Now that it was actually come to pass. Mechanically, it was simple enough, maybe, perhaps the way Ben had suggested. They had laughed together over it, and then the laughter had died, and he had seen the pain in Ben's eyes, and he had known that it had not been an easy decision, but he had seen equally the resolve, how important it would be, in the end. It was left to him now, the final wishes of a man with an uncommon passion for life, and a singular notion of eternity. A man who had been, for forty-odd years, his staunchest friend. Hard as it had been, he'd kept his promise for Jenny. Now there was the one thing more. Jenny would be a part of it.

It would take some thought, and some time. And it would be done, the way Ben Willow wanted it done.

The behest was simple enough otherwise. Everything went to Andrea. He'd run the usual ad in the *Tribune* notifying creditors. Worthless waste of time and five dollars. Hell, Ben Willow hadn't owed a red cent in thirty years.

Now he needed to be about the rest of it. Luella McDowell had called from the clerk of court Monday reminding him he was due for the initial inventory.

He'd been feeding Ben's cows regularly, each night on his way home from the store. He ought to see about selling them, and some of the other things, and getting the money to Andrea. But he hated to. Ben had loved his cows almost as much as his dogs. Never could take 'em off, when the time came for putting some beef in the freezer. Always had Timothy Campbell come pick them up while he was off hunting. Then he'd pine for a month over the recently departed.

Clyde laughed despite himself, recalling the time Campbell picked up the wrong cow, Libby's Swiss brown heifer, and when Ben got home and found out, he'd taken out to the abattoir. The master cylinder on his old truck had been leaking for a while, and Ben came flying into the parking lot sliding sideways, hit the brake, and nothing happened. Suffering hardly a dent, the 'National took out the front office and the corner of the ladies' john. Nobody got hurt, but Sallie Stayman was sitting on the pot with her step-ins around her ankles. Jumped up terrified, tried to run — got tripped up in the hullabaloo and fell facefirst on the floor — dress over her head and that beautiful, bare ass shining like two sacks of flour hugging the crack of Heaven. It was the first thing Ben saw once the truck got stopped.

"Thought I'd reached the Promised Land," Ben told him afterward.

It had cost him a pile to fix the building and even more to repair Sallie's pride, but he rescued the brown heifer.

Anyhow, he'd been thinking about it for a couple of weeks — moving in at Ben's — maybe it would help, with Jenny. Tomorrow, he'd quit thinking about it and do it.

22

Clyde threw up a quick hand, uttered a terse malediction, and eased the Buick into a tight semicircle around Peavey Abbot's green Ford pickup, the nose of which was poked halfway into the intersection of U.S. 58 and Traver's Creek Road. When he had recovered the right-hand lane of Traver's Creek Road, he glanced at the side mirror. All he could see was an immense pair of hog balls on the ass end of a Duroc, through the slats of the wooden siding framing the bed of Abbot's truck. He couldn't remember a time he'd seen Peavey in twenty years that he wasn't hauling a boar hog. That's how he associated the man . . . hog balls.

It was a charming spring morning, fresh with an early-morning chill and the mint green blush of the hillsides. It had showered during the night, and now the first rays of the rising sun caught the sprigs of mist climbing lazily from the still-wet pavement, lighting miniature rainbows across the way ahead. Clyde Wood was feeling something that resembled anticipation, and it had been a while. He had loaded Jenny, his toothbrush, a sack of groceries, and a few clothes shortly after eight, kissed Nettie good-bye, and set out for Ben's. Jenny was on the front seat beside him, taking notice, too.

Besides the trips to and from the vet, it was the first time the little set-ter had ridden in a vehicle in many weeks. Perhaps it was kindling a mem-ory. Though still with reservation, she was enjoying it.

He could easily place his own enthusiasm. It was nothing more than he was going to Ben's, never mind his old friend wasn't there; he had been. Parts of him still were, everywhere.

Slowing at the rising visage of the little white house opposite Mc-Cathern's Knob, he turned beside the mailbox faintly marked WILLOW onto the path that led to the door. Daffodils were blooming gaily at the foot of the post, along the drive, here and there in the yard. Libby's touch; she'd always loved buttercups, as the old folks called them generically.

"Homey," she said fondly of them, "abidin'."

You could go all through the mountains now, find pieces of home-places two centuries to dust, nothing left but the stub of an old rock chim-ney, a few walking stones, maybe a mound of earth or two. But there'd be buttercups, descendants of descendants of descendants, thrusting their pretty yellow faces past the grass to the sun. Alive, living on, carrying on for the people who settled, raised up youngins, and died there.

The old International was sitting under the shed. You could almost ex-pect that Ben would come around the side of the house any moment, a bucket in hand, a setter by his side. But the setter was with him. He opened the door, grabbed his cane, and trickled out. Waited for Jenny to follow, then let the door swing to on its own.

He settled heavily onto his cane, took a long look around. The cows were loping up from the side pasture. The grass was coming in, but they recognized the old Buick from its mercy missions of the winter, and were still eager for a handout. He'd throw them a square bale or two once he got settled.

Ben's little patch of onions and fescue needed mowing. Jenny was ex-ploring it tentatively. He wasn't up to that old push mower of Ben's, but he'd call Joe Darden's boy, Wes, and get him over to do it. Wes was be-ginning to notice the skirts. He could find an easy way to spend the ten dollars.

Jenny walked to the old truck, put one foot on the running board, sniffed the door, then dropped away. Circling, she continued to investi-gate — the shed, the woodpile, a pile of feed sacks — but there was little spring in her step and her tail was lackadaisical.

"Jenny." He called her to him, and began stuttering along to the front steps.

His cane grabbed in a crack of the rock walk and wrenched him sideways, and the sudden force shot like a searing flame through his bum leg, threatening to topple him. He jerked the cane free and stabbed it hard ahead, arresting the fall. He exhaled with relief, cursing age and affliction.

Reaching the front door he thrust aside the screen, fumbling through his coat pockets until he found the worn, old brass key Ben had slipped onto a length of pigging string. It slid into the lock easily, and with an unfettered turn the door tripped ajar. He opened it and stepped into the sitting room.

Immediately, he was assailed with a foreboding emptiness. The house was quiet as the breath of death, and he felt like an intruder. A stranger who begged a welcome. He wondered if this was really such a good idea, coming to stay for a time. But this was about Jenny, and he hoped that here she would find herself again.

Standing aside, he let her pass. She nosed here and there, showing scant recognition and little emotion.

The sun was finding its way through the front blinds, casting faint pale shafts of lemon light into the room, but the house was yet dank and cold. Wood shivered inadvertently and made his way through the hall to the thermostat, rotating the dial gently with three fingers until the oil furnace kicked in with a thud and a hum. Ben had conceded to the furnace finally, at Libby's behest. Their mainstay had always been the old woodstove in the den, but Libby's thermostat had changed as well in the latter years, and she would sometimes complain of the kitchen chill. Ben would have walked the world backward for Libby.

Continuing to the back of the house, he glanced briefly into the den. It was as should be, except dim and largely empty. At the threshold to the kitchen, he flipped on the overhead light, pausing to let his eyes adjust and consider the surroundings. Jenny nudged the back of his leg. He let her pass once more. The little setter sustained her aimless inspection, sniffing here and there with seeming indifference, wandering into the dark portal of the bedroom. Intermittently, he could hear a bump and a snuffle.

He looked about the small kitchen for several moments, and then came the flood of reflections. So utterly bleak and bare, this room that always had beckoned so richly with anticipation and country munificence — that was once so alive with the spit and sizzle of link sausage and sunny-side eggs, the fortifying fragrance of steeping coffee, the smiles and chatter of breakfast prattle while first light grew slowly outside into the promise of a grand November day. So devoid of Libby's cheery "hello" as she hustled him in, invited him to a table crowded with steaming cups, biscuits and jellies, butter, molasses and grits, and bustled to and fro putting together sandwiches and an apple for the old man's coat. With frost silvering the windowpanes, the Parker waiting by the back door, and Ben rambling through his pockets, counting out blue Peter's shells, woods leavings and all, onto the checkered oilcloth. While the barks and whines of hopeful gun dogs from backyard kennel runs argued the urgency of departure, and prompted furtive glances at the old wall clock.

His eyes found it now, the old clock, and he realized that it was as life-less as it had been the afternoon Susan Devron had called, and he had rushed here looking about for Ben. With the consciousness came the same sinking, pithless feeling.

He moved instantly to it, opened the cabinet, and felt for the key. Winding mainspring and chimes, he started the pendulum with an easy finger. It caught and ratcheted into a uninterrupted rhythm, the familiar, gratifying double note of the regulating spur on the timing gear magnified by the stillness.

Clyde Wood listened for several moments, satisfied. The house had a heartbeat again.

Jenny had returned from the bedroom, attracted to the residual smells of the pantry. Wood left her to her business, tripping back to the car for the bags of groceries. He filled the coffeepot, loaded the percolating bin with Maxwell House, and set it on a warm burner. Digging out staple goods, he stocked the refrigerator. Pausing, he listened, then resumed, assuring him-self once more that the clock was still astir. Opening a bag of peanuts, he cracked a couple, downed them loosely. Jenny registered interest, and he handed her a single kernel. She took it gingerly, depositing it carefully on the floor. Studying it and him in turn, she pawed at it.

"Shouldn't run off," he chided, "but be ready."

Finally she ate it, then begged for another. He finger-fed her several more.

The bubbling perk and aroma of the brewing coffee began to capture the room. Warmth was rising from the work of the furnace. The house was becoming livable again.

Clyde made another dawdling trip to the car and fetched his notes and clipboard, leaving Jenny waiting at the front screen. Returning to the kitchen, he found a mug in the cupboard over the sink, checked the prog-ress of the brew, and, finding it finished, poured a brimming mug of coffee. He sat it on the table, and settled himself alongside, watching the rise and curl of the steam above the cup, and set himself to thinking about the tasks ahead.

The household inventory would be short and simple — a good place to start. Andrea and Steve had shipped back several items of furniture already, including Ben's old Shaker rocker, the pine huntboard that had stood in the corner where he now sat, and the lovely, hand-carved headboard and matching cherry wardrobe Ben had built for Libby on their twenty-fifth anniversary. Sundry bits and trinkets from every room that were of sentimental value, some of the china, most of Ben's wooden bowls. Just the bigger pieces were left, the house itself, the appliances, sofa and chairs, and the plethora of minutiae imperative to the pledge between a man and a woman across the years, and to mountain living — pocketknives and clothespins, shaving mugs and baking tins, shotgun shells and flour bins — make and matter that had somehow outlasted the sum of two lifetimes.

He busied himself most of the day wandering room to room, tallying this and that, opening drawers and delving into personal belongings that heretofore had been just that, jotting to paper the cold specifics of the account. The job was more formidable than he had estimated, enlarged by the ample moments he spent in rumination at one small thing over another, and by late afternoon — after an admittedly liberal lunch breather around the premises with Jenny — not only was the task less than half concluded, it was evident also that he had forgotten the multifarious contents of the attic. Weary and bleary-eyed, he limped back to the kitchen, sidestepping Jenny on the way, surrendering the day and tossing the pen and clipboard to the counter.

He glanced through the side window for the sun and, after a few steps left, found it. Flickering through the newly sprung leaves of a mulberry tree, less than an hour from its end, having traveled since morning almost the entire westerly crescent of the house.

Already the long blue ridges were grabbing at the swelling purple hemline of the sky, reaching to claim it. Dusk came quickly in the hills.

Urgently, he decided, he needed some air, a respite from four walls.

"Hey Jenny," he called to the setter deposited full sprawl on the hall carpet, "up and about it. We're chasing daylight."

She raised only her head, rolled her eyes, and looked at him over her shoulder. It would take more than his word.

Clyde bustled around the room as briskly as infirmity would allow, making a to-do of scratching up his hat, coat, and cane. But it was only when he cracked the back door that she took him seriously, elevating her-self to four legs. She stretched at length, before trotting through the open door, halting of necessity at the porch screen, her nose poised at the crack between the door and frame. Wood pushed the door aside and let her down the steps. Her egress was unenthusiastic. Rather than dashing away as the old Jenny, she trickled out and began a measured reconnaissance of the immediate backyard. She seemed uncertain, still, of her settings.

Clyde watched her regretfully, hoping for more.

At the far corner of the yard, a guinea also took notice, craning his neck and hautily shrugging his wings, fluffing his domino-like plumage and instigating a riotous cackle among his six cronies. Their ruckus cap-tured Jenny's awareness, and she studied them, making no attempt at pur-suit. Emboldened at a measured distance, they sauntered insolently along the perimeter of the wood shop before executing a dawdling retreat.

Clyde made his way to the pasture fence to meet the cows gathering there. Their clustering and lowing reminded him that he had not delivered the hay bales as promised. He hobbled to the hay shed, surveyed the stack, rolled an inferior square aside, and reached for the next. Then halted, with four fingers of one hand hooked under the baling twine, staring at a dim pile of something in the opposite corner of the building. Then real-ization set in and he grinned. No one forty years at the mercantile desk of a village farm store could mistake his own product. It was a sizable pile of Southern States' fence posts.

"Hummph," he spurted, relaxing his grip and letting the bale fall back in place, the grin growing into a smile.

He shuffled over for a closer look, stood with his hands clasped atop his cane, studying first the pile and then the dim eastern fringe of the pasture. Here and there he could distinguish the black stutter of decrepit posts, snaggletoothed in the fence line, splayed precariously short of collapse. Others had been crudely knee-braced to avoid an impending topple. He was reminded that he had made a casual note of the dilapidated condition of the fence two weeks before, worried that the cows would break out and of just how the hell he would round them up if it happened. He had won-dered then what the blazes happened to the new posts Ben had bought that day at the store six years before.

"Hummph!" he snorted again, breaking into a chuckle. He had won-dered. Now, here it was.

"Jenny, you know anything 'bout this," he asked of the setter snuffling an enticing crevice in the haystack. She extracted her muzzle, looking up at him and wagging her tail indefinitely, knowing only that he had spoken her name, having no cognizance of the reality that she, in fact, lay at the seat of the mystery.

He counted the individual posts in the pile. He couldn't help himself. He'd warehoused miscellany for so long it was first nature to compare a finger tally of a commodity on the ground with the other he retained in the pachyderm memory under the crown of his old bald head.

"Uh-huh," he muttered in an inference of guilt. Twenty-three posts. And what? Twenty-six that old Ben had gone home with that day. The arithmetic was plain enough and he smiled again. Three posts in six years . . . old Ben had replaced a grand total of three posts in *six* years. And just how old was Jenny now? Sneakin' up on eight. He glanced at the crumbling fence line again, threw back his head, and guffawed out loud.

It was something he, himself, would never have tolerated. But then there was Ben Willow, whose priorities followed his heart rather than his head.

Retracing his steps to the haystack, he gathered up and labored first one bale, then another, back to the edge of the pasture, clipping the bindings with his old Boker blade and tossing the loose fodder over the fence to the hungry cattle. Jenny remained close to hand, initiating only diminutive, lateral forays with short and indifferent missions.

Wood doted for several minutes on the feeding animals, thinking of whom he would call to negotiate their sale. Sheely Brubaker the most likely. He'd know who was buying. He'd call him first thing in the morning.

Just ahead of the setting sun, they skirted the house, meandering the yard until somewhere at the verge of the woods a whippoorwill opened a spirited, seesaw soliloquy. The old man's heart lifted.

"Nettie was right, Jenny," he said aloud to the setter, "they're back."

He listened with the same fascination he had when he was a boy. It was his grandmother who had told him, as she threw out the wood ashes by the edge of the garden, that the ol' wills would come there to wallow and sing. She was inviting them, of course, because they were an omen of good bidding . . . home folk, like bobwhites and thrushes and house wrens.

"They'll come," she had told him, "if you ask."

He still wasn't certain of that, but always since he had faithfully delivered the ashes to the fringe of the woods, seeking their twilight assurance.

"Listen, Jenny," he entreated, mimicking the singsong chant of the bird, *"all-is well, all-is well, all-is well."*

Jenny cocked her head at his lilted voice, acknowledging her name and the softness of his tone. There was something soothing about the words and the company of this old man who spoke them. Shallowly, it was stirring the recollection of another before him.

Buttermilk biscuits, damson preserves, two sweet potatoes, a glass of milk, and a can of chicken-noodle soup was the better part of supper, with a slice of egg custard to remember it by. Wood sat at length over the custard, dividing it meticulously into small bites and savoring each one, listening to the steady ticking of the clock and the equally mesmerizing munch of the setter over her dry food. It was akin to the sound of field horses over their grain bins at the end of a long and strenuous day of clearing new ground or snaking out the huge old chestnut logs that lay on the mountain. Coming up, his daddy always sent him to barn and care for the horses at twilight, with the toil of the day at an end, and he had loved to sit there, bone tired, and listen to them munch their oats and hay. Through the open crack between the great plank doors of the barn, he could see the soft yellow light of his mother's kitchen and sometimes her shadow as she readied supper, and he would tarry there in the cold with his breath on the air, relishing the comforting crunch of the grain under the heavy molars of the horses, ravenous himself, stalling and anticipating how right and wonderful it would smell and feel when he opened the back door and first stepped into the kitchen.

It had never felt quite that way since.

Finally he got up, cleared the table lazily, and trooped to the den. After a loose minute more he sat down in Ben's old easy chair, felt odd doing so, and was soon on his feet again moving about the room. With night came the loneliness . . . and the fear, and there was no escaping it.

There was still kindling and firewood in the wood box. He felt the need for a fire. Opening the door of the blackened old stove, he stared into the dark cavern inside, stirring the ashes with the poker to prepare a small bed. Upon this depression, on a twist of newspaper from the kitchen, he laid a few sticks of fat pine. Swiping a match across the iron rim of the firebox, he touched the little flame to the paper, watching appreciatively as a tiny plume of smoke lifted and then the fire erupted and grew, licking the kindling into a modest blaze. When his little fire was hardy, he laid in a small bolt of green hickory and then a chunk or two of oak. Closing the door, he adjusted the damper so the stove could freely breathe, and listened with satisfaction as the flutter inside its belly slowly bellowed, then roused to a muffled roar.

He resumed an aimless tour of the room. Shortly afterward, his ears caught the click of toenails on the bare hall floor, and presently Jenny wandered in. Clyde was pleased that she had followed. She circled the room vaguely also, and for a time the two of them made a restless pair. Until he recognized a familiar volume on the bookshelf, a Christmas gift, in fact from him and Nettie to Ben several years before. A copy of George Bird Evans's cottage masterpiece, *The Upland Shooting Life*. They had even gone to the trouble of gaining Evans's signature for the frontispiece, and Evans himself, fully familiar with Ben Willow, had contributed an eloquent and inspiring inscription in addition.

He pulled the book from the shelf and found Ben's chair again, and this time he allowed himself to relax. The rumination of the stove had grown to a steady, blissful hum, and he could feel the ascending warmth gathering the room. He watched as Jenny, too, turned and turned in ever-tightening circles over a braided throw rug, then collapsed in a heap, sighing deeply and tucking her nose inside the cozy nook between foreleg and hindquarter. He wondered of all the nights she had done the same with Ben. Not a lot of progress with her so far, not as much as he had hoped, but this was only the first day and maybe he was expecting too much. She had been through a harrowing trial. Perhaps the wounds left inside would *never* heal. But he had to believe otherwise.

Pulling his glasses from his vest pocket, he slid them on, then opened the book to the chapter titled "Men Who Shoot." It was largely about old-timers like himself, and Ben — bird hunters — a bit more refined admittedly, what with neckties and shooting jackets similar to those he wore to church on Sundays. The closest he had ever come to refinement was a tin Filson vest, and he had gotten that because he admired Ben's. But the sentiment of dogs and guns and birds was universal, and he enjoyed the salutary prose.

He read himself sleepy, thought about the tasks of tomorrow, and when he next awoke it was well past eleven and he had forgotten to call Nettie. It was too late now. He'd call in the morning.

Pulling himself up stiffly, he arose from the chair. Jenny stirred with the rustle of his movement, raised her head, and looked at him past droopy eyelids.

"Want to take a turn around the yard, girl?" he invited.

Seemed she did. Rising, she stretched mightily, fore to rear, finishing by fully extending and constricting methodically one hind leg and then the other. That accomplished, she followed him into the kitchen, waiting with beseeching eyes while he donned his coat and hat, and mumbled around until he had remembered where he had placed the cane.

Clyde exited the back door, grabbing up a flashlight as he went, then swung open the porch screen. Jenny rushed past and bounced into the yard, ran a few feet, then reversed and disappeared into the night. He stopped on the steps, cracking a stray peanut he discovered in his pocket, and noting with gratification the display of enthusiasm, however ordinary. She was glad to be out and so was he. It was a beautiful evening. The heavens were clear and bright with constellations, and all about the spring peepers were happily celebrating the birth of spring. Pitch dark, it was. There was a sliver of moon resting on its back, barely enough to throw shadows, but just sufficient to lend a spooky mystery to the rustle and movement of the cattle scarcely distinguishable in the pasture. Particularly the Angus, which were black as Satan anyhow.

He rummaged in his pocket for another peanut, eventually finding a fragment of one in the lining of his coat that had escaped the small hole in the toe of his pocket. He broke out the single nut and popped it in his mouth. A screech owl joined the chorus of frogs, its eerie, fluttering call rising on the air like a shiver up your backbone. From somewhere in the mulberry tree, a game rooster crowed a false dawn.

"Jenny," he called briskly. He had no thought she would run off, but it was time to inquire. In a moment she checked by him, then trotted on into obscurity again.

He stepped off the porch, working his way along to the small-equipment shed and the International. He opened the door. It smelled musty inside, like old man and cankered burlap. He wondered if it would start; the battery was probably dead. Another item on the list. The key was hanging on a nail by the kitchen cabinet. He'd try it in the morning. Ben had loved the old truck. Wouldn't hear of anything else. Switching on the flashlight, he examined the odometer: 287,346 miles. That was before they had ripped the speedometer cable loose nine years before on a hump of rock hiding in an ice storm. He was after Ben to fix it but he never did. Troy Miller at the crossroads kept slipping it past the inspection law every December.

"Don't need to know how fast I'm goin'," old Ben snorted, "just that I'm gettin' there."

"Argyin' with you's like stickin' a milk bucket under a bull," Clyde had harumphed at the old man. "One o' these days Semp Mason's gonna catch your Missouri carcass."

"If he does," the old man declared, "it'll have to be on the way back. Ain't got no time agoin'."

Stubborn old mule's ass, he thought. Wonderful, stubborn old mule's ass.

But that was as far as he got because suddenly the soft spring evening exploded with a thud and a horrendous crash, a stammer of furious growls, and then the slam, bang, clang, and clatter of metal on metal.

"Be damned," Wood muttered emphatically, jerking alert. The same instant brought another heavy crash and an explosive shatter of glass, and the hair bristled along the back of his neck.

"Great God A'Mighty!" he shouted out loud, clicking on the light and shuffling as fast as he could in the direction of the commotion.

There was yet another crash and a renewed series of frenzied growls, and then a stint of ungodly whining.

"God in Heaven!" Clyde exclaimed incredulously as he hurried along, sparing the cane and gimping in awkward, loping strides toward the source of the tumult. His heart was thumping like a drum. It had to be Jenny. What in Satan's blazes?

He could hear her distinctly now, alternately whining and growling, a curious mix of anguish and fury, closer still, and then the insufficient beam of the flashlight began to pick up vague bits of the disaster from the darkness: garbage cans asunder, a box of glass gallon jugs toppled and shattered, garbage and litter strewn here to there. At the periphery of the tragedy, writhing and wallowing along the ground in hysterical circles, was Jenny, whining and snorting with some peculiar affliction. And then it assailed him — in an overwhelming, inundating wave — the drenching, permeating stench of polecat. Wincing and stumbling, he beat an inample retreat, swinging the light in an awkward, sweeping arc. At the midst of the mayhem, it skipped past, reversed, and found the little varmint, scarcely twenty feet to starboard, hautily fortified against a nail keg. Cocked and poised for the next volley, it had its sights on the setter, and at the exact root of its bushy white tail the wrinkled pink ellipse of its defenses winked an unambiguous warning.

Wood coughed, almost gagged. He was already too late. Now Jenny was rallying, rushing to renew the attack.

"No, Jenny!" he yelled at the top of his breath, grimacing and shaking his head, trailing into a tortured grunt as another revolting wave stifled his breathing.

Desperately, the old man made a swipe at the setter's collar. Unfortunately, he caught it. At the precise moment the adjudicated skunk delivered the second judgment, Clyde Wood was jerked forward off his feet into the vanguard of the assault. His last and fleeting impression, within the misty halo of the flashlight, was the contracting pink muzzle of the enemy's ramparts and a viscous shaft of golden mucus, no less worse than imagined, speeding accurately and at considerable velocity toward the bridge of his nose. In the following instant, he dropped the flashlight and cane, overpowered by a fetid yellow fog.

Like incubated osmosis, the vile, vaporous excrement penetrated and deposited itself over every thread and pore on his body. Retching and coughing, he scrambled backward into the dark, fighting frantically for fresh air. Finding none, he crawled on, gradually stumbling to his feet, rapidly realizing that he would not outdistance the wretched odor. His eyes were burning, streaming with tears, and he was helplessly gagging.

He bumped into something, felt around a moment, and discovered it was Ben's old chopping stump. Either he was reeling or it was swaying to and fro. Roughly positioning his butt over the center of its revolution, he waited for the proper moment and let himself drop ponderously to anchor. What feeble cognizance he had of his surrounding was revolving in great, unending concentric circles, his stomach was heaving, threatening to turn like a catalpa worm, and his stinging nostrils ran in thick, ropy strings.

In the gloom of the night, the battle still raged. He could hear a pitiful cacophony of snorts, sneezes, scratches, and growls, and glimpse through teary eyes an occasional flurry in the loose beam of the grounded flashlight. The struggle appeared to totter furiously between setter and beast. He had no idea who was getting the better of the dispute, just who had gotten the worst, and at this point it probably didn't matter anyhow. Like Nugene and the wildcat, up the tree in Jerry Clower's old Mississippi 'coon hunting tale, "one of 'em needed some relief."

He was recovering from the initial impact. Beginning to breathe a bit again. Finding, as Clyde Wood always did, the humor of a thing. He was still sick as a bloated buzzard, two heaves shy of puking. But his wit was claiming the better of him.

It might have been easier, he contemplated whimsically, to simply have lain back and succumbed. He could imagine Darth's headline in the *Chronicle* once they found him: "Foul Play Leads to Death of Local Merchant."

God, but he stank!

It had finally happened. All his life to now he'd managed to associate with skunks, two-legged and four-legged, from a proper distance, and now in the short rows they had to get personal about it.

The musk abruptly overpowered him again. "Daaugghh," he heaved, jerking his head sideways and blowing mightily.

"God*dammit!*" he vented to nobody in particular.

Jenny meanwhile had outlasted the worst of the skunk's munitions and, finally seizing the exhausted varmint by the first piece of hide she could manage, was in the process of flapping it until the bones cracked. When she could feel nothing more of resistance in her jaws, she laid the fusty thing down to be sure, pawing it in a semicircle to see if anything moved. Nothing did. Unsatisfied, she grabbed it up and snapped it thrice over, then dropped it again and proceeded to wallow on it. Content at last that it was no longer a threat, she picked it proudly up in her jaws, pranced over, and delivered it to Clyde Wood's lap.

It was there before the old man realized, laid on his knees, eighteen inches from his already tortured nose, the very instrument of his misery — one very fragrant, chewed, and bedraggled black-and-white-striped polecat. At a similar distance stood the little setter, obvious eyes and happy tail, impatiently awaiting his praise.

Wood didn't revolt. He didn't even move. He simply rolled his eyes to the sky.

He knew . . . as long as he lived he'd know. Ben Willow had something to do with this.

Pushing himself up, he held the polecat at arm's length, lightly by the tail, and shuffled toward the scene of the battle. The flashlight still burned aimlessly along the ground. Arguing repossession rights, Jenny danced around and about, hampering his progress, threatening to topple him. Clyde submitted the objection that she'd done enough and to please get the hell out of the way.

He managed to right a garbage can with one hand while holding the defunct polecat at bay with the other. Centering the skunk over the maw of the container, he released his two-finger hold on its tail, and listened with considerable gratification as the carcass thumped against its tin bottom. A moment later he found the lid, and clapped it in place. Jenny watched the proceeding with great interest, unappreciative of the human idiosyncrasy that decreed it eminently necessary to be rid of something she had suffered so dearly to obtain.

Thirty minutes later one very odoriferous Buick pulled into the otherwise unoccupied parking lot of Clancy Garner's Quick Pic, the most remote and clandestine of the three convenience establishments available in Buckeye at such an hour, and remained curiously idle for more than five minutes as Clyde Wood pushed past the dread of presenting himself as a customer. When finally he clambered out and admonished the dog on the front seat to post guard, it was with both reluctance and inelegance that he advanced toward the front door and let himself in.

Clancy, behind the front counter, wrestling overhead to compel a new Red Man display onto a crowded shelf, did not hear Wood enter, but was within seconds aware of a certain and peculiar alteration to the normal character of his store. It had something to do with the air and his most immediate thought was that maybe Ruthy Simmons had left the grease to putrefy by the grill again or that he needed to go unstop the commode.

Clancy sniffed once, lightly, to test his hypothesis, and finding neither a match for the redolent agent at hand, inhaled more boldly. He urgently wished he hadn't. Whatever it was — and he was beginning to accept what seemed an improbable notion — was growing stronger. A moment later he had decided that it was of such imperative and odious proportions that it demanded his immediate attention.

Clyde, meanwhile, had slipped past, locating the canned goods and returning to the counter. He was hesitating there now, equally persuaded between departing and requesting service.

When Clancy turned to lock the cash register and smell out whatever was rotting Denmark, the undertaking was hardly difficult. Under his nose was a squat, balding, familiar, and very fragrant fellow merchant who looked like hair in hog grease. And yes, without further question, it was polecat!

For the briefest of moments, Garner stifled the smirk growing on his upper lip, only to choke on the guffaw bulging behind it. What erupted was something between a sneeze and a snicker.

"Damn you, Clancy Garner," Wood sputtered, "one word, tonight or any other, and Carrie'll know what else about the Blue Mist and Harietta Witherspoon."

Clancy held a finger to his lips, then sputtered into a fit of laughter, waving it off and shaking his head. Momentarily, he stifled it and pursed his lips.

"I need some tomato juice," Clyde ordered, "all you got."

"How 'bout some crackers to go with it," Clancy blurted instinctively.

"Dammit, Clancy!"

"All right, just wait," Garner tittered, vacating the counter and walking to the interior of the store. After what seemed an undue interval, he was back. Without to-do, he placed one large and one small can on the counter, shifting his eyes to Clyde.

"*Is this all there is?*" Clyde asked with dismay.

"Well, it ain't exactly somethin' we get a run on," Garner submitted in defense.

Clyde stood anxiously silent for a minute, stewing in his dilemma.

Clancy pulled a red bandanna from his hip pocket and wiped his runny nose. "How much longer you gonna stay?" he inquired.

Clyde shot him a sour look.

"I might have a case or two of Campbell's soup in the back," Clancy offered, trying to keep a straight face. "Just add water," he added, unable to control himself.

He looked earnestly at Wood for a moment longer, fighting himself, then snorted explosively through his nose and burst into another spasm of hilarity.

"Goddammit, Clancy . . ."

"You want it or not?" Clancy demanded mirthfully.

Surrendering, Wood nodded, glancing around to assure himself no one else was present.

"Just hurry up," he implored.

Exaggerating, Garner stuck another finger to his mouth. But only for an instant. He was laughing again as he left the counter and walked to the back of the market.

A flicker of car lamps swept the store. Nervously, Clyde glanced outside. Another vehicle — one he thought he recognized — had pulled in. A prim, middle-aged woman got out and started for the door. With a start and a groan, he realized it was Margie Wiggins.

He beat an instant retreat to the far corner of the store, his cane ticking a tattoo on the bare tile floor, seeking refuge between the candy rack and the paper goods display. Peeking over the top shelf, he saw Margie push open the door, hesitate a moment with her nose in the air, then proceed toward him. Directly toward him. He hastened to the next aisle. There, between the bread and the ice cream counter, seemed little better. He glanced anxiously around for an alternative. Next lane over was motor oil and the drink box. Something above the drink machine caught his eye.

A wire rack containing scattered packets of colorful foil. Squinting, he made out the small print on the marketing placard: ROUGH RIDER. Even in his present predicament, it registered humorously with him that it was the wit line for corrugated condoms.

Wanting to move, he hesitated. Margie was only two aisles over, fussing through the cosmetics. Intermittently, she raised her nose again, testing the air and squinching. He ducked. As she shifted his way, he sidled simultaneously and at opposite ends around the aisle she had left.

He still couldn't imagine what Margie Wiggins was doing in a place like this and at this hour. It wasn't her style.

He was glad he hadn't moved to the motor oil aisle. She was making her way there now.

She hesitated, looked quickly this way and that, then discretely sneaked a pack of Rough Riders off the rack and dropped it into her purse. Nonchalantly, she made her way toward the front counter.

Clyde forgot himself and grinned.

If she was going to a rodeo this time of night, it was a bet the cowboy wasn't Lester.

Unnoticed, Clancy had made his way back to the front. Clyde could hear him and Margie talking.

"When I pulled in, I coulda swore I saw Clyde Wood at the counter," she exclaimed.

"Nope, just me," Clancy lied. Maybe Clyde was joking about Harietta Witherspoon and maybe he wasn't. He'd give himself the benefit of the doubt. Margie looked at him doubtfully.

"That'll be four fifty-seven, Ms. Wiggins," Clancy announced. Clyde assumed that did not include the Rough Riders.

He peeped over the aisle, waiting until Margie had driven away, then crept back to the counter.

Clancy was ringing up the tab. Two obscurely marked boxes of Campell's tomato soup sat on the counter, along with a brown bag containing the juice.

There was an extended series of clicks, whirs, and clacks as Clancy tapped in the numbers and the machine attempted to digest them into a total.

"Damn," Clancy announced, and had to start all over again. Clyde rolled his eyes, fidgeted foot to foot, checking outside again. No other traffic, thank God. He could see the vague shape of Jenny through the front window of the car, fretting about the front seat. He'd have to sell the Buick for a goat hovel. He'd never get the stench out.

Finally, after another session of clicks and whirs, Clancy looked up. "Sixty-three ninety-two," he announced proudly, wiping again with the bandanna, then tying it around his head and tugging it up over his nose like a bandit. Behind it, he could grin with a degree of impunity.

Clyde glared at him anew.

"I knocked off seven-fifty 'cause you's buying bulk," he said importantly.

Wood dug out his billfold and threw down sixty-five dollars on the counter, ignoring Clancy's efforts at change, and reaching for the bag.

"Pleasure doin' business with ye, Mr. Wood," he gloated. "Why, let me help you with that," he proposed, a bit late and too politely.

Grabbing up the boxes of soup, Clancy rushed for the door, nudging it ajar before the old man with his toe. He did the same at the Buick, setting the soup on the trunk, swinging wide a rear door and relieving Clyde of his burden. In a moment, he had deposited the lot on the backseat. Jenny hung her forelegs over the seat back and stuck her nose down for an inquisition. Garner was glad he had tied on the handkerchief.

Wood labored himself into the driver's seat.

Clancy waited until the door was safely closed, then eased alongside the window.

"I'll have a special on cream o' mushroom next week," he announced as soberly as he could.

"Go to hell, Clancy," the old man muttered as he drove away.

Garner watched the funky Buick away, then lowered the bandanna to his neck and drew a long breath of fresh air. Chuckling again, he walked back to the store, found the stop, and propped the front door open. Without further hesitation he continued to the household goods shelf, gathering up a can of Lysol spray. He glanced at the label and frowned. "Mountain Air" scent, it said. He had that coming in the front door. He picked up another can: "Soft Powder," it claimed, "kills viruses, bacteria, mold, and mildew." Nothing about skunk. He stuck a couple more in his pocket, exhausting all three liberally about the store.

A few clicks and whirs later to debit in the Lysol and he still figured he was fifty-five dollars to the good.

"This is your fix I'm in," Clyde told the little setter once they were under way. He had all the windows down and the air was still so close he had to breathe in stages.

Jenny looked at him briefly and wagged her tail, perfectly satisfied with the situation.

"You know what's coming," he declared. If she did, she made scant allowance, absorbed with the catch of the headlights along the roadside. "A bath . . . you know, like 'wet' . . . and it ain't Saturday."

She turned her head just long enough for an impatient glance. There was light in her eyes, even in the darkness, recently born. He hoped it would last.

It was three-thirty in the morning when Clyde Wood finally poured his scoured, aching carcass into Ben Willow's bed. Without hesitation, he collapsed against the sheets and rolled the covers, and succumbed to utter exhaustion. Limp and drained, his body wilted luxuriously away, unattached to his senses, until only his mind lingered slothfully aware. He could hear the washer churning in the back room. The minute they had hit the house, he had peeled every stitch of his clothing and thrown it in the wash, along with Jenny's collar, setting the dial to SUPER WASH and tossing in a stiff ladle of Cheer. The skunk scoffed at the first cycle and continued generally unaffected by the second — forcing him to extremes for the third — and now the beleaguered Maytag had throttled down to agitate a stiff and troubled concoction of clothing, detergent, Pinesol disinfectant, lemon squeezings, degreasers, and stain removers, laboring in desperate measures to revive to "civil" what remnants would survive the final rinse.

Meanwhile he had opened fifty-three cans of tomato soup concentrate into the tub, drawn in enough steaming water to lightly dilute it, and soaked and scrubbed until his hide was raw. When some progress had been effected in his own condition, he had, stark naked and at length, searched the house before discovering Jenny secreted knowingly behind the settee.

Hauling her arduously back to the bathroom for equal treatment, he dumped her unceremoniously into the tub, resisting her clambering and clawing attempts at escape and dousing her with thick red tomato soup and apple vinegar, until, soaked and sopping, she looked pitifully like a rat in a pickle vat. Ignoring the doleful supplication of her eyes — "it's your doing," he told her ruefully — he had brushed and finger-scrubbed every inch of her.

Afterward, while she wallowed a sodden trail that wound from lavatory rug to the back door and all conveniences between, he had submitted himself again to similar measures, then drained the foul concoction into the septic system. As the last of the tainted pink suffusion had disappeared, he was left with the ultimate and profound reality of all polecat encounters: he had done the best he could; the rest would have to *wear* off.

Now, with Jenny twitching and snoring blissfully on a lap rug at the foot of the bed and the Maytag at work, he could, until morning at least, put the episode to rest. Conceding, he yielded to sleep.

For the next two days, Clyde Wood worked at a steady but leisurely pace at the household inventory. Then the contents of the outbuildings and grounds, until he was satisfied that he had accumulated the total of Ben Willow's humble estate. In the evenings, he reformed the details into a protocol that would muster acceptance by the court, checked in on Nettie, and tried as best he could to read himself sleepy the last hour before bed. But within the blunt silence and emptiness of the house he could not misplace his grief, nor the candor of how quickly and certainly a body can disappear from this earth. You get up one morning with the same dispatch you have on every other for eighty-nine years and then in hardly more time than it takes to pull your pants on, you're extinguished for all eternity. The world hurries behind to sweep up the bits and pieces, and time does its best to erase the traces. And what's left for how long to say how far a man had traveled, or to what ends? He wished old Ben could talk to him now . . . tell him. Was the procession of life and death a straight line, he wondered, or a circle?

Soon enough, he guessed, he would know.

However troubling the bouts of depression, it was Jenny who pushed him on. Slowly, she was finding herself again, and it was a wonderful thing to see. The light that had grown in her eyes with the skunk had not faded — nor the odor, unfortunately — but the careless shuffle of her feet had grown to a dance. Now she waited with budding impatience for him to tire of the tedium and offer her the door, anxious to explore the yard and pasture. On the third morning she had sight pointed a scatter of sparrows, and twice turned up missing on the fourth; when he called he was pleased to see her bounding lightly from the woods. As taken with the season as the dove that soared overhead in a courting flight, its spirit lofty with joy. All of West Virginia was singing the hallelujah chorus of spring, and it was impossible to ignore. There were butterflies and bees on the air, wrens at the nest, new leaves on the trees. Amid the abundance of life it was hard to place the presence of death. A bit at a time, more than he knew, he was recovering as well.

There were moments yet. On Thursday evening he became conscious of the setter's absence from the den rug, uncertain of how long she had been gone. Searching the house he had found her, after a time, lying in the dark behind the bedroom door on one of Ben's old coats. It had slipped off the peg and fallen to the floor and she had scratched it into a ball and curled tightly into its folds. She had lifted her head once, looked at him with lonely eyes, and did not leave it the rest of the night.

Friday morning he sat down to breakfast, worried that she might relapse. She had followed him from the bedroom, watching him as he put the coffee on and moved a jug of milk from the refrigerator to the table, showing only a casual interest in the proceedings. He hadn't felt like cooking. He had a vague recollection of Nettie sticking a box of cereal in a bag. He rummaged through the couple that were left and found the red-and-white carton. He pulled it out and looked at it. Kellogg's Special K. He sat the box on the table, half consciously turned it so he could see the picture of the shapely female jogger on the box front, then placed alongside a bowl and a spoon. Jenny was abruptly up and whining.

"Hungry of a sudden, huh?" he said mistakenly. "Well, I'm sorry . . . we're settin' a cold camp this mornin'."

Opening the Frigidaire again, he grabbed a quart of grape juice, filling a small glass and adding it to the table, returning the bottle and letting the door swing closed on its own. Settling into a chair, he dispensed a bowlful of flakes, poured on some milk until they floated, then sliced in a banana. Recalling some raisins in the pantry, he found the box and sprinkled out a few on top of the fruit.

Dancing on her toes, Jenny *wuffed* then nosed the cereal box.

Clyde blew slightly through his nose, feigning impatience, forcing himself up to locate another bowl. Actually, he was pleased at her enthusiasm.

"All right, but you ain't gonna like it."

The waxed paper crackled as he reopened the box of K and poured another helping of flakes. The little setter retreated, prancing on her front toes. "Hummph," the old man snorted. Setting the bowl on the floor, he laid a hand on his knee and helped himself back up. Sitting to the table again, he shoveled in a big spoonful of cereal and bananas, peering at the setter's reaction. Jenny nosed and sniffed the contents, then lifted her head and stared quizzically.

"Toldja," he mumbled as he chewed.

Her eyes burned a hole through him. Raising a foreleg, she pawed anxiously at the Kellogg's box. The tablecloth slipped, causing the box to tip and totter. She spun in a circle, whining.

He caught and steadied the box with a quick left hand. She looked disappointed.

"Jenny, what's the matter with you?" he questioned.

Her eyes were fixed on the cereal box. She had not touched the flakes in the bowl. Clyde was at a loss, now, at *what* she wanted.

"Damn, you're as quare as Ben," he muttered.

Her gaze had not once left the Special K box, locked like a cat on a mouse. Clyde shook his head, ladling in a mouthful of cereal and bananas.

In an exaggerated moment of amusement, he grabbed playfully at the cereal box.

The setter whined, stutter-stepping with anticipation, eyes afire.

The old man chuckled and spooned in another casual helping of cereal, chewing nonchalantly. After a moment, he threw a mischievous glance at the setter, feinted for the box a second time, jerked his hand abruptly away . . . and squarely backhanded his glass of grape juice.

Not then, not immediately, could even Clyde Wood locate the humor in the upended chaos that followed.

Cursing, the old man heaved with his off hand to stem the disaster, but managed only to contribute to it, missing the juice glass and grazing the open cereal box. Briefly, the jogger on the front walked the table edge like a drunk attempting a centerline, then toppled loudly to the floor. Meanwhile, unimpeded, the glass of grape juice had thumped soundly to doom, baptizing the tablecloth in the blood of the Lamb and shotgunning an open pattern onto Jenny, the floor, and the wallboard suggestive of mockingbirds on pokeberries. Onto the pooling juice was cast a crashing splatter of cereal flakes.

For Jenny, reincarnated with puppydom, waiting with bated breath, had pounced tooth and toenail in the same blinding instant the K box had hit the floor. She was now proceeding to shake the very stuffings out of it, banging and ripping it asunder in a horrendous clatter, and spraying a windmill of cereal across the expanse of the kitchen floor.

"Holy God," Wood croaked, as in almost the same instant he glanced down between his forearms and saw that a rich, thick rivulet of grape juice had reached, then trickled over the rim of the table. Immediately he thrust himself backward, fighting to free himself, only to add to the distinct chilly dampness already deposited in the hollow of his crotch the contents of his breakfast bowl.

It was then against the force of his efforts that his chair tumbled and he splattered butt-first into a growing pool of milk and bananas.

Then, and only then, amid the death clamor of the cereal bowl, as it rimrolled the last of a series of descending concentric circles at the center of the kitchen floor and clattered to a rest, with Jenny banging the remnants of Kellogg's best about his head and shoulders, did he imagine himself one trumpet shy of Gabriel and succumb to a lusty outburst of laughter.

He collapsed fully to the floor, unable to control himself, belly-heaving at the jollity of it all, until Jenny broke loose and stood atop him, panting into his face and lapping him exactly across the mouth with a great slaverry tongue.

"This your doin' or mine?" he asked her finally. She still stood over him, wagging her tail, trying to lap him again. There was happiness in her eyes and it was contagious.

He stared at the ceiling several seconds longer, and smiled, before he lugged himself upright again. He had caught, once more, for the briefest moment, a glimpse of Ben Willow there.

It was an hour and a half later, after he had scrubbed and mopped the floor, and suffered the bathtub for the third time in as many days, that he sat down again and redid breakfast.

"Jenny's healin'," he reported to Nettie that evening, "it was right to come."

And Nettie Wood listened gratefully to that, but not nearly so gladly as she did to the cheerfulness in her husband's voice.

But then Causey Saunders and his two boys, Jesse and Kermit, arrived Saturday noon to claim the cows. After some earlier, conciliatory palaver, then the customary bout of hemming and hawing, Clyde had painfully reduced the asking price to an austerity value, and Causey, resisting an unseeming flight of impetuosity, decided in due course that he could afford it. That was the fun of it, leaving a man to believe he'd bought indoor plumbing at a johnny-house rate, and Clyde prided himself on it. Always standing behind the product, naturally.

They came with two old stock trailers, one behind Causey's '71 Chevy pickup with the rusted-out rocker panels, and the other behind the boys' hot-rodded '73 Bronco, Granny Smith green with a pair of fluffy white dice dangling from the inside mirror. The Bronco idled like a bullfrog with a chest cold.

The thirteen cows loaded easily enough. Four heifers, seven steers, and a Charolois bull later they had rounded up the greater contents of Ben's dilapidated corral. There was only the one Hereford, a terrified white-faced yearling, that busted loose and escaped to the pasture and tried to make a run of it. The two boys quickly tricked it into a fence corner, threw a couple of loops over its neck, and dragged it back to the trailer. It fought and bawled pitifully the distance, and when its hooves clapped on the loading ramp and Jesse slapped it hard on the rump with the flat of an ax handle, it bounded fearfully into the trailer, fouling itself with slimy green manure. There was something crudely poignant in its resistance, and Clyde turned, wincing slightly when the door clanged shut.

Causey stuck his head out the window as they pulled away. "We thank ye," he clipped, spewing an odious stream of tobacco spittle onto the grass and wiping his mouth with his sleeve.

"Likewise," Wood had returned blankly. And that was the end of it.

Except that he was assaulted again by the burden of what he had done.

He watched them away until he could no longer hear the clatter of the trailer, then turned and took a last look at the pasture. It was forlorn and empty now, the gate standing open on droopy hinges, no longer useful. He dropped his head for a moment, his mind bogged in melancholy. Leaning onto his cane with one hand, he pulled off his hat and absently scratched his bald pate with the other, and looked away toward the mountain. Ben had loved his cows.

He ambled back to the house, let Jenny out. She bounded around the yard, then lined out along the old fence, caught the woods line at the foot of the hill. Tracing it to the break of the hollow, she disappeared boldly into the trees. Rapidly, she was regaining confidence. The burn growing in her eyes.

Following her, he shuffled down the path toward the spring run, inviting his mind to ease. But everywhere there were reminders. Ben and Libby's little garden spot, always before so perfectly kept, overrun and shaggy now with wild onions. The small cemetery beyond the orchard, which, save the plot at Shiloh, held the better part of Ben Willow's being. It was encircled by a three-foot wall of fieldstones, laid dry and meticulously set, and there were other stones, sixteen of them, each chosen and placed to mark a faint swell of the earth. All the dogs of all the years, given to dust. All the carefree and reckless days behind them—when no hill was too steep nor any hollow too deep, nor any destination hampered by its distance to home—gone to dust as well.

Old Ben's notion of Heaven was to be granted again the single, finest gunning day in the life of each of his dogs.

Maybe at last . . .

The sun was spilling through the soft green leaves in hazy yellow shafts, spackling the path ahead. From deep within the woodland shadows swelled the gushing trill of a thrush. He stopped to consider the tender green leaves of a stooping maple. With the mere tips of three fingers, he cradled a single leaf. So flawless and pulsing with life. Not a nick, not a blemish. Young and supple and free. Free of all the imperfections and infirmities a long, harsh summer would bring, oblivious to the brooding mortality that would bleed it crimson and bring it down in fall.

Such was the property of youth, and it was long beyond his reach. He strained, as his mood demanded, to find the resentment in that. But could not. It was as it should be. The greatest gift to youth was innocence. Without it, the world could never know idealism. And idealism was the stamina of perseverance.

Without the optimism stored in youth, no man could last his years.

He had not another friend like Ben. In a rush, the world was awfully close again, and he was painfully vulnerable.

Youth was long ago and far away, and yet he held the strength of its spirit at his fingertips. Another spring. The optimism for life and living.

Ben was gone, but there was Nettie. And Jenny. Jenny was the way ahead, the closure that would bring the serenity to continue completely his own life again, and lay Ben's properly to rest.

Reaching the fork of the path, he bore right, down the gentle grade that led to the ancient spring. Pausing there, he listened for her and heard nothing but the momentary hum of a passing bee and the slight rush of a breeze.

"Wupp." He spoke lightly, a casual summons.

A few seconds afterward came the patter of her feet, and then the pliant rustle of the leaves as she burst into the path in front of him.

" 'Ey, Jenny," he acknowledged.

She bounced on, tail at a merry click. Wood followed.

The path dipped slightly, leading into the shadows of a small depression at the foot of the rising hillside. The spring basin was just ahead.

Abruptly, the old man halted, a grab of excitement at his chest. He was almost certain that he heard the gusty departure of a grouse from the laurel. It could easily be, for they would love the greenery that prospered along the moist fringes of the spring run.

Now he was certain, for Jenny had heard it also and had stopped to honor the flight. She was intently rigid, a few yards ahead. She stood so stunningly that at first he thought she must be winding a second bird. He realized after a time that she was not; it was simply the quality of her character and training.

He'd seen his share of stylish dogs — many of them Ben Willow's. Even Tony. He'd seen Jenny in the woods before, hunted over her a few times with Ben. She'd slam your heart into your throat with every find. But it had been a while, and now again so sudden and dramatic was the impact of her brilliance that it was overwhelming. He'd forgotten . . . forgotten just how *very nice* she was. He stood mesmerized by the image before him, eclipsing all he could remember.

For the better part of a minute, he lingered as spellbound as if he himself were honoring her stand. The dog didn't even have scent in her nose and her air was astonishing. Easily he understood why she had been so formidable in cover trials.

Impatiently the little setter quivered and drooled, the extremity of her tail so taut it trembled at its tip with the kinetic convection of her hindquarters. In a collision of instinct and training, she had jacked high and tight the instant the bird blew out . . . her pose almost exaggerated, stropped razor keen by the painstaking artistry of Brian Castion. Expectantly now she awaited the shot and release. And still, for some reason, the old man stood waiting. She cut her eyes to him, just for a moment, as if the world might shatter if she lingered, and slowly back. Seconds later, chafing at his sloth, she shifted her weight — bringing up a trailing rear leg, squaring herself — every fiber within her screaming for relief.

In the measure of mere hundredths of a second, the flush of the grouse had triggered an avalanche of associations, and the fires smoldering at the heart of her had exploded into white-hot flames. She was burning to hunt now, boiling with the unquenchable passion that had been so extraordinarily gifted her at whelp: to search the breath of the telltale breezes until they whispered the lay of a hidden bird; to drink in at length the flavor of its warm and pulsating scent, fanned and freshened by fright.

At last the old man came to himself and remembered his part of the obligation. Without further hesitation, he shuffled over and tapped her on. She burst ahead, flashing up the path and cutting swiftly into the cover. Clyde could hear her chopping it up, quartering it out, reaching away.

It was thrilling and, oh God, so gratifying. She was back, or nearly so. He felt the warmth at his chest. He wished Ben could see this, be here, know what they had been through and share this now.

He could no longer hear her and a twinge of apprehension twisted his mind. He had never handled her before. She was a lot of dog. Great glory, he didn't want to lose her, after all else.

"Jenny!" he yelled overanxiously.

She bounced in from his deaf side, wound and happy, back to check by on her own.

"Hey, Jenny," he cautioned as she bounded away anew. She paused, looked at him, and came reluctantly back.

He eased a finger under her collar, caressed an ear, while she stood whining. "I know, girl," he said soothingly, "there'll be a time ag'in soon. With someone who can go the long and far with you. I promise."

Slipping the lead on her collar, he set her to heel and traipsed the few yards farther to the spring. It lay almost hidden at the foot of the hill, in a tiny cleft beneath a great outcropping of rock. The little hollow that encompassed it was sheltered by spruce, thick and bottle green, which muffled the bright sun until it lapsed to shadow. The air here was damp and cool, invigorating, fragrant with the fresh, clean breath of evergreen. The little circular pool itself stood as pure as crystal, almost perfectly a circle, neatly rocked a century before, and roofed more recently by a small shelter Ben had fashioned from white oak splits, silvered and splinted since, and splotched with gray-green whorls of lichen. Into one of the boards, Ben had fastened a wooden peg. On the peg a hollowed-out gourd hung by a pigging string.

Clyde lifted the gourd free, shook out a winter leaf or two, and knelt to the brim of the spring. In welcome, the little pool returned the reflection of his face, softened by the lucent surface of the water. It looked younger, fuller, some of the harsh reality of the years cleansed away by the abstraction of the likeness. Maybe the Fountain of Youth was no less, or more, a myth than the image he found there in the mirror of the spring. He lowered the lip of the gourd to the water, tilting it beneath the surface, so that the colorless liquid ran into the bowl. A faint scatter of ripples washed across his reflection. He raised the gourd to his lips, drank slowly. The water was cold and tasteless, so satisfying that he shut his eyes for a moment to savor it.

A moment more and he offered it to Jenny. She looked at it, smelled it, lapped it tentatively.

Again, Wood considered his reflection, then rested his cane over his arm, placed both hands on his knee, and pushed himself up. Then he hung the gourd back in place, begged Jenny to heel, and turned away. He stopped once more by the small silent cemetery, the idle little garden — for the last time he ever would — then slowly found his way back to the house.

It was midafternoon or later when they completed the circle, and he had napped on the den sofa until almost sunset. Jenny was still cranked up and had wandered the house for a time before giving in and settling at last to the rag throw rug.

Just before dusk he let her out again. She had been to the window a dozen times, rearing up on her hind legs and staring at something in the side yard. Before he could even get the door fully open, she wiggled her way brusquely through, nosed clear the porch screen, and flew off into the backyard.

"Dammit, Jenny . . . *Hey!*" he bellowed, too late. There was nothing to do but follow. Just as he grabbed his coat and cane the phone rang.

"Goddammit!" he fumed.

He started to ignore it, but he had asked Plunk Roberts to call about the house. Plunk moved more real estate than anyone else in the county and he had offered to handle Ben's transaction as a favor. But he was busy as a fly on manure and hard to get ahold of.

Wholly vexed, Clyde flung down his coat and cane and made for the den.

It was, indeed, Roberts, when he picked up the receiver. He limped his way to the window as he talked. He had banged his bad knee on a table edge in transit, and he stood now like a tipsy heron, lividly rubbing it, with his weight shifted to one leg. Meantime, he searched through the glass for the setter.

"Oh, I don't know," he told Plunk, craning his neck this way and that, "it's small. 'Bout sixteen hundred square feet, I think . . . Hang on a minute."

Clyde took a last worried look around the yard and crossed to Ben's chair. His knee burned like the mischief. Plopping heavily into the chair, he picked up the clipboard from the side table, flipping the papers open to Tom Cagle's appraisal specifics.

"Sixteen-fifty to be exact," he repeated.

He listened impatiently as Plunk reeled off a plethora of tedious inquiries about the state and fix of everything from roofing shingles to the toilet seat.

Antsier by the moment, Wood was seconds shy of inviting Roberts out to look for himself, but he never got the chance.

From the side yard arose an explosive commotion, and a sudden, hideous thud against the wallboarding that sounded like an accelerated confrontation with the broad side of a hog. Wood jumped like he'd been shot, dumping the clipboard from his lap in a banging clatter. As he clambered for footing, the rug slipped and he lost it, dropping the phone with a deadening clunk to the table and falling backward into the chair. He clung as the La-Z-Boy teetered in slow motion, then toppled, gathered velocity, and crashed to the floor.

Totally startled, he lay fighting for his wits.

He would not find them immediately. In the same instant the windowpane shattered to smithereens and a wild, cackling, and scantly airborne dishevel of polka-dotted feathers flapped frantically across the insufficiency of the sitting room airspace, struggled for altitude, and kamikazied with a resounding crash into the stovepipe. Knocked from its fittings, the tin chimney collapsed by consecutive sections in a clanging uproar, spinning across the floor and spouting an odious, smothering fog of coal black soot. Engulfed somewhere in the dusky midst of it, an old man sputtered a combustible confusion of blue English, a confounded voice clamored from an unattended telephone receiver, and a smutty heap of feathers, too drunk to fly, stumbled about the room in silly, wobbling circles.

Jenny Willow had roosted the guineas.

"Holy Jesus!" Wood finished, lying flat on his back in the fallen chair, trying to decide if he was hurt. Slowly he was collecting himself. He could hear Plunk resonating through the acoustics of the cherry tabletop.

It was dawning on him . . . what had happened. The worst, it seemed, was over.

Concluding he was in one piece, he braced against the chair, urging himself up. Twice in a week, he was telling himself.

Roberts was still screeching. Calmly, Clyde picked up the phone, pulling out his handkerchief and mopping the soot from his eyes.

"What'n the ass of Abraham is goin' on out there, Wood?" Plunk demanded.

"Housewarming," Wood quipped.

"Sounds like a house wrecking," Roberts objected. "Look," he continued, "can you assure me that ever'thing's in good enough shape to bring buyers around?"

Clyde took a long, doubtful look around the blackened room. "Ever'thing's perfect, Plunk . . . just perfect."

By Sunday suppertime, it was.

Nettie Wood was humming her way through house chores Monday morning when she heard the key rattle in the back door lock. She had on an old blue cotton dress, plain and faded, her hair was tied up loosely with a scarf, and her face was pale and unmade.

In a moment she heard the door open, and the rustle of paper bags being deposited to the kitchen table.

"Clyde," she called uncertainly.

"Yep," came the familiar reply. She caught the click of toenails and quickly Jenny came prancing in, her tail awag, the light dancing in her eyes. The setter came immediately to her, nosed and licked her hand.

"My, aren't we happy," Nettie returned, caressing her forehead. Something was curious, but she couldn't place it yet.

With a slight stir of air, her husband walked in. She felt the hair in her nose prickle. He stepped over and kissed her square on the mouth.

She almost gagged.

"What on God's earth is that awful smell?"

He guessed he had forgotten. The Buick was still pretty funky.

"Heaven's own perfume, woman," he blustered cheerfully.

Nettie grimaced. "If Heaven smells anything like that, Clyde Wood, I'm asking asylum in the other place. I don't know who smells worse, you or the dog."

She beat it for the closet, came back with a can of Glade.

"No need to bother," he ventured. "Won't touch skunk."

"Take off those clothes," she ordered, spraying the room liberally.

"Want me, huh?" he joshed.

"I want you in the tub, and take Jenny with you. The clothes go straight to the garbage."

"But that's my good coat, 'Ettie," he argued.

She glared at him without response. Reluctantly, Clyde shucked the jacket and handed it to her. She held it at arm's length.

"Now the pants," she dictated.

Meekly, he complied, sneaking aside his belt and knife. He knew better than to buck her.

"Didn't expect you till Wednesday," Nettie said.

"Jenny wanted to come home," he teased, his legs humorously scrawny under his underwear, sorting through the mail in his two hands.

Nettie was content, just not ready for her husband to know it yet. He was a different man, she could see, from the one who had left a week ago.

"And I suppose you're blaming this all on the dog," she suggested at last, a twinkle in her eye. "Or maybe Ben Willow."

Clyde winked at her. He knew he was home free then.

"Al'ays give credit where credit is due," he grinned.

· 23 ·

Therman Chadfield plucked another roofing nail from his pursed lips, set it in place atop the cap of a shingle, and raised the hammer to drive it home. He paused, glancing away to the murmur of the vehicle pulling into the yard, then returned, letting the hammer drop and slamming the nail home. He slapped two more in place before setting his hammer aside, mopping the sweat from his brow with his shirtsleeve, pulling his nail apron off, and tossing it alongside. It was mid-July, just nine-thirty in the morning, but already the sun was over the crest of Beech Pen Mountain and the heat devils danced the ridge of the barn.

He recognized the car now, Clyde Wood's old white Buick. Now Clyde was climbing out and Marcy was coming out of the house to greet him, exchanging a country greeting, wringing her hands dry on her apron as she went. He threw up a hand and got one in return. Easing himself to the eave, he reversed and crawfished his way over the edge, feeling with his toe for the first rung of the ladder. When he found it, he planted a foot, let his weight settle, and made his way off and down. He could see a white setter dog through the windshield as he neared the Buick, standing on the seat with a nose out the window, wagging a tail.

A terse supposition swept through his mind, something about the matter with Litton Thorne.

"Clyde," he pronounced emphatically, "whatcha know on ya'self?"

"Too bold to tell," Clyde grinned, shifting his weight to his cane and sticking out a hand to meet the one being offered.

Therman laughed, shook the old man's hand vigorously, gravitated to his wife's side.

"Why don't you ever let Marcy out of the house where a body can see her," Clyde jousted, "a gal this pretty hemmed up with an old billy goat like you?"

"'Fraid she might take up with that loathsome old fart at the farm store," Therman fenced, slapping Marcy playfully on the butt.

"Therman Chadfield!" she gasped, pulling away and casting him an untoward look.

Clyde was in his element, enjoying the show.

"Who's your girlfriend?" Therman inquired, stepping closer to the car window. He could tell by the softness of her face that the little tricolor setter in the car was a female. He offered her a hand and Jenny licked the tips of his fingers, her tail beating softly.

"This is Jenny Willow, Ben Willow's dog."

Chadfield turned to look at the old man. He had guessed so. "I'm sorry about Ben, Clyde . . . I am. I know you were close. I never knew him, but what I knew *of* him stood well. I've always heard he had some fine grouse dogs."

"He did," Clyde said, "the best. This is one of 'em, maybe *the* best."

"She's beautiful," Marcy declared.

"Actually, she's why I'm here," Clyde disclosed.

"Well, let's don't stand out here in the hot sun," Marcy interrupted cheerfully, "come on in. There's lemonade in the icebox and the cow's fresh, there's coffee and new cream, if you prefer that . . . and bring Jenny in with you. It's too hot for her out here in the car."

Clyde accepted the invitation, grateful particularly for the thought of Jenny. Already it was beginning to affirm his decision. He let the setter out of the Buick. She bounced around a minute, then accepted the open door into the kitchen.

Inside, the house was pleasantly cool, the air freshened by a gentle draft from the windows set ajar on either side. He could see the curtains wafting with the rise and fall of the morning breezes.

"Pull up a chair, Clyde," Marcy invited, motioning to the kitchen table. Clyde took one to the side. Therman sat down at the head.

"Lemonade?" Marcy inquired, her hand resting expectantly on the door of the refrigerator.

Clyde debated a moment, teetering this way and that. It was like choosing between blackberry cobbler and buttermilk pie.

"Coffee, I believe," he replied, "and a splash of that fresh cream."

Marcy smiled. "Good, I'll join you."

"Mr. Chadfield?" she queried whimsically, grinning at her husband.

"Lemonade," he requested, "I got to go back up on that roof."

Marcy started about the fixings.

"Where're the girls," Clyde asked her.

"Mama and Daddy's," she replied over her shoulder.

Jenny was wandering about the kitchen, sniffing one item to the next.

Clyde called her over and put her at "Stay." She stood beside him, eyes alert and watching Marcy's every move, wagging a lazy but hopeful solicitation with her tail.

"Tell me, Clyde," Therman proposed, a wry grin on his puss, "how do you like your new mayor?"

Clyde smiled. Calvin Hoover had defeated Lester Wiggins handily in the recent mayoral election, the best thing that had happened since the ink dried on the city charter, and everybody from the town clerk to the city council was ducking for cover.

"Well, you can bet your ass on one thing," Clyde drawled, "uh — 'scuse me, Marcy — there ain't gonna be no goldamn concrete statuary in the middle of his heifer run."

"Yeah, and Chief Clawin' Bear's likely to camp a while longer on the courthouse lawn," Therman added.

They laughed heartily, the three of them.

Marcy reached across the table and leveled a cup and saucer in front of him, of white china decorated with delicate blue lilacs, and slid a matching setting for herself onto the opposite side of the table. Crossing to the stove, she gathered up her apron hem and used it to foil the heat of the coffeepot handle as she transported the pot over and poured first his cup and then hers brim-full of steaming, black Maxwell House.

"How's Nettie," she asked.

"Shellin' peas last I noticed," Clyde replied. "She's fine."

"I need to call her," Marcy admitted, handing him a spoon and her husband a huge glass of lemonade, icy and sweating, the translucent liquid inside clouded with pearly shards of shredded lemon.

Clyde took a wistful look at the lemonade. If he'd known the glass was going to be that big . . . But then the cream boat arrived, white with blue lilacs too, and when he picked it up both the little handle and bowl of it were deliciously cool from the chill of the Frigidaire, and its contents rich and thick. He poured a liberal dollop into his coffee, watched it curdle and color, then stirred it in with the spoon until the mixture resembled hot chocolate without the bubbles.

Raising the cup to his lips, closing his eyes, he took the first gentle sip.

Meanwhile, to the center of the table, Marcy was setting a platter of yellow agate ware piled high with hot biscuits, little tendrils of steam climbing from its summit, and alongside a small crock of soft yellow butter. To this, she appended a fresh jar of sorghum molasses, and three extra serving dishes.

Outside he could hear the soft lowing of a cow and the liquid notes of a cardinal. He saw the curtains stir at the windows again and felt the mild caress of the newly born breeze as it arrived upon his face.

"Ben Willow had a daughter, I believe?" Therman mused.

"Andrea," Marcy avowed, delivering a molasses biscuit to Jenny before she sat down to join them. Jenny accepted it eagerly.

"Yes. She's in Germany," Clyde advised.

"We saw her at the memorial service," Marcy observed, "she looks a lot like Libby. Will she come home now?"

"It's not likely," Clyde responded, "maybe one more time for loose ends, but not permanently. Steve, her husband, has his work there, and there's not much of home left for her here now . . . nothing more than a memory."

Clyde helped himself to a biscuit. Therman was on his second. Jenny was nose-to-table, begging another.

"Jenny is, in fact, about all that's left," Clyde remarked.

"Andrea doesn't want her?" Marcy asked.

"She might, but it's not what Ben would want. It wouldn't be fair to Jenny."

There was a small space of silence, as Marcy considered his reply.

"You said earlier Jenny was the reason you came," Therman posed tentatively.

"Yes . . . she is," Clyde said. He paused a few moments and then framed a question to the man beside him.

"How much does Marcy mean to you, Therman?" he asked.

Taken by the bluntness of the inquiry, Therman started to react lightly, then read the gravity in the old man's face.

After a moment, looking at his wife, he replied, "Just about everything there is in this world." And when he finished, his eyes were glistening with emotion.

"That's just how much Jenny meant to Ben Willow," Clyde asserted.

"Before Ben died," he continued, "he made me promise, come whatever, to see after Jenny. Neither of us knew, then, what that would mean, and it wouldn't have mattered. Ben was the best friend I'll ever have.

"But it hasn't been easy—for me or Jenny."

"I heard . . . a little," Therman confided.

"It was worse," Clyde vowed, without addition, "but it happened and there's nothing I can do about it, and it's over now.

"Jenny's a grouse dog," he expanded. "She was born, bred, and trained for it. More than that, its in her blood, more than most. She lives and breathes it. She *burns* with it. And she's incredibly good at it.

"I can't hunt anymore. I'm too damn old and spent. She needs to be with somebody who can. Somebody who'll love it, and her, as much as life itself. Something like old Ben did. It's the only way Ben would have it, and its one of the last things I can do for him.

"I've watched Josh come up, Therman," he persisted. "He's made a fine boy. He's what—fourteen now?"

"Fourteen and a half," Marcy corrected.

"From what I can tell, he loves the woods and the water, loves to hunt and fish," Clyde solicited.

Therman chuckled. "What was it you said about living and breathing?"

"He loves it," Marcy affirmed, "has since his first breath."

Clyde paused, collecting his emotions, then gazed at them.

"I'd like for him to have Jenny," he explained, looking at the setter. "I'd like for them to have each other. I've got a little twenty-eight-gauge shotgun in the car; I want him to have that, too."

The little setter was looking on now, as if somehow she realized she had more than a casual interest in their conversation.

Therman and Marcy Chadfield sat in silence for several moments, solemnly absorbing the inference of the gift placed before them, and its responsibility. For that was the kind of people they were, and Clyde had known it before he came.

"He would be thrilled," Marcy said after a time. "You just can't imagine. He's wanted a dog somethin' awful. He brings in a grouse now and then on his own, prizes 'em above anything else in the woods, but Joel Clements took him one day last year — with his setters — and a dog's all he's talked about ever since."

"Good grouse dogs are steep, when you can find 'em," Therman observed. "We had thought about gettin' him a puppy, but I don't know much about trainin' a bird dog. I guess we could learn."

Therman Chadfield contemplated the proposition for a spell. No one spoke.

"It's a kind and caring offer, Clyde," he said finally, his eyes averting to Jenny, "more than generous. One we won't refuse . . . or forget."

Clyde Wood read the promise behind the man's eyes and knew that he understood, and that it was not tendered lightly. He had been right to come here. He would follow Jenny closely in the days to come, and the boy, but it was right and it was time. He could feel it in his soul.

"Thank you," he said.

"The thanks comes from this side of the table," Marcy answered, reaching over and laying a hand on his arm. There were tears on her cheeks.

"There is, however, a favor that must come with it," Clyde told them, "and it'll be Josh's task to do. I'll help him with it. But it is unusual — some folks, who don't matter, would say plain quare — but when I explain it to you, I believe you'll not find it out-of-the-way at all, but really rather fitting."

They waited, wondering, as the old man felt for words.

"Ben Willow was a passionate man. He lived that way, and he died that way. He had strong notions 'bout most everything, especially in his latter years, and most of all about eternity. Where he would spend it, and how he would get there. He agonized over it toward the end, and when he decided at last how it must be, he found himself torn unmercifully between the two greatest loves of his life.

"But I must say to you that Ben Willow cherished his wife, while not always selflessly, deeply and faithfully."

Clyde hesitated, his voice quivering.

"Beyond that," he struggled, "it is only necessary to understand that his dogs, the woods and wild things — these mountains — were the heart and soul of him."

And then he related to them as well as he was able, what had been, beyond Jenny, Ben Willow's most fervent request.

When he finished, Therman Chadfield was staring distantly past the window to the rolling blue ridges, and beside him Marcy was sobbing softly.

There were no words spent between them for several minutes. Finally, Clyde concluded it was his place to speak.

"I'd appreciate the pleasure of giving Jenny to Josh myself," the old man said.

"Now . . . today?" Therman asked.

"Yes . . . if possible."

"Well, he should be out behind the barn mendin' a fence," Therman replied, "if he hasn't slipped off. No guarantees. He wanted to be fishin', Saturday and all . . . I imagine the fish're happy," he added, more soberly than it deserved, "he's been awful hard on 'em lately on the Little Laurel. Want me to call him?"

"No, we'll go there," Clyde said instead, pushing himself up from the table and reaching for his hat and cane.

He was emotionally drained, but now he must see the boy.

"Thanks for the table vittles, Marcy," he remembered.

"Bring Nettie next trip," she said.

Jenny was fretting around him, whining, ready to be about. He started for the door, and she beat him there.

"Don't *you* go gallivantin' off," he admonished. "Somebody we have to meet."

The two of them followed him out the door, Jenny in the lead. The setter took a quick turn about the yard, squatting abruptly to pee.

Clyde opened the back door of the Buick, labored over and extracted a green canvas gun case. Laid it on top of the car. On the floorboard were two boxes of small-gauge Federal shells. Bracing with a hand on the back-seat, he picked them up, righted himself, and worked them into the right flap pocket of his old gray suit coat. It was a habit, the old coat, and the felt hat, even in summer. He paused, checking himself mentally for a moment, then patting his left breast pocket to be certain. There was a faint tinkle.

Satisfied, he slid the gun case off the roof and balanced it over his left arm. Tipping his hat to Marcy, he started along with the intermittent assistance of the cane.

"Sure you want to hoof it?" Therman called after him. "You're welcome to the mule," he offered, pointing toward the Deere.

The old man waved a "no thanks," continuing on.

Therman and Marcy watched him away, Jenny cutting broadening S's across the grounds.

Clyde saw her stop and eye the chickens in the barnyard.

"You know better," he cautioned. Thank God, there were no guineas in sight.

He ambled around the barn, through the pasture gate, and past the catch pen. Jenny fell in at heel. Before them three hundred acres of green grass pasture sprawled away, on a gentle, rolling dip-and-climb to the foot of Beech Pen Mountain. The mountain itself formed one of the lesser headlands of the Middle Mountains, near the center of the great Monongahela, between the Cheat and the Alleghenies. Rising on a friendly slope above the small, neighboring sink of the Stonewater Valley, it crested into a long, winding ridge stretching equally north and south from where he stood for the distance of more than three miles, from the Wolf Run to the Zinn. East and west of it coursed the Glady's and the East Fork, at the headwaters of the sparkling Greenbrier, and between them it was shot through with secluded little cold-water runs pooling with lithe native brookies, more colorful than a highland quilt, that looked like they'd been hand-painted by Grandma Moses with flecks of holly berries, bits of blue sky, and raindrops against the canvas of a delicate summer sunset.

A fine place for a boy to wander and wonder.

There were grouse here, too — Ben had told him so. Scattered about the mountain were the many old homeplaces yet, nothing more than rotting remnants of the days when hardy and willful folk scratched out a small clearing at the head of a hollow, laid an orchard by, and threw together a few logs to live in. Times when life beyond these necessities depended mostly on a few turnips and greens, a hog or two, and the larder of the wildwood. Years unfolded, travail overran temerity, and some moved away, back to the shelter of the little towns, like Buckeye, Spoketon, and Latchhaven. But most struggled on, pride over predicament, until the world had changed so much that no more would come like them, and they and their kind simply died away.

Though in their wake, the old apples survived — Greenings and Sweets and Pippins — on trees stooped and bent like arthritic old men, still bearing in summer and fall from the dimming memory of their rootstock the seed of their ancestry. Persevering, passing on at the core of their red and yellow fruit the entreatment of Eden, so that they might be perpetuated about the mountain by the cast and carry of wild things. From their birthright the seedlings sprang, singly or in small clusters along the slopes to bear as well, though not always truly. And to the apples each autumn, and the fox grapes, and the greens along the streambeds of the warmer, western flank of the mountain, the birds came.

He could see the boy at a distant corner of the pasture, working diligently over the wire fence. Mustering resolve, he shifted the gun case to his other arm and shuffled on.

Jenny drifted a few steps from his side and hesitated, gazing toward the mountain, expecting a caution. In its absence she seized the moment, breaking into a trot and then a headlong dash. Forced to a decision, Clyde gathered the summons in his throat, started to yell. There were broods about. But he let it die, let her go. She was almost back now, and with this he hoped — a boy, a gun, and a grouse woods — she would find herself completely again. As all dogs, she lived with the moment, and never with the past. And that would be her salvation.

He would back away, and let it be, and in the course of old Ben's affairs, there would be but the one last thing.

He watched the little setter fly; the happy clip of her travel, the merry click of her tail. In a few seconds she had grabbed the high edge of the pasture where it met the trees. Racing the woods line, she halted suddenly and wheeled, milled momentarily, then bored into the cover. He stopped, second-guessing the decision to let her go, waiting for her to reappear. If she turned up missing, he'd have to let the boy go looking. Moments later he sighed inaudibly as she popped out ahead, checking for him. Half running, half hunting, she pushed on, aware that it was less than the real thing, but lost to desire.

Clyde picked up his step again, bent to his mission. Sunlight spilled in pleasurably across the rambling expanse of the pasture. The grass stood lush and green from the cool, wet spring, thick against the travel of his feet. Behind him wound the distinctly silvered trace of his progress. He could see Angus cattle two hills over, black against the glistening luster of the grass, their noses stuck to the ground, grazing. Here and there clusters of red clover erupted richly, in big gray-green, tripetaled heads that favored the "clubs" symbols in a deck of playing cards, their stems crowned with the fluffy pink buttons of their flowers. A pair of buzzards languidly rode the thermals in a clear blue sky.

The boy was at some distance still, concentrating on his work, as yet unaware of their presence. From the body language, it appeared that he was struggling with a lever of sorts, trying to twist one more turn out of a stubborn turnbuckle probably.

The old man's eyes were pulled to the setter on the tree line. She had noticed the boy for the first time, and had stopped, studying him. Amused, he watched as she took a few curious steps in the youngster's direction, paused again, then committed fully. Breaking into a trot, she started off the hill toward him, pulling up only a few yards away, as Clyde saw the youngster turn and stiffen with surprise. He could see the boy relax then, sense the elation in the young man's face. Both boy and dog stood hesitantly introspective for several moments. Then Josh dropped to one knee, and Clyde could guess that he had spoken softly to her, for Jenny trotted the rest of the way to him and buried her head and shoulders in the fold of his arms, and her tail was beating happily. And then it all blurred in the old man's eyes.

He had anticipated this, hoped for this. That they might meet on their own, if only for a minute or so, before he intruded. He almost wished he could just turn away now and leave them to be as they would, for love grew from the tiniest seed, and would find a way of its own.

But he was old enough and needful enough to want the pleasure of passage with the boy, and there was the gun, and the need to tell him of the thing he must ask of him, which was not the chore of a boy, but the task of a man. So Clyde Wood rested on his cane a moment longer, and then gimped on.

The boy and the dog were still engaged as he drew closer. There was a small Massey Ferguson on standby, with a three-point posthole auger at the business end of its power drive, a few spent fence posts scattered around. A shovel and a tamping bar. A wire stretcher. Hammer and staples. Extrusions of fresh dirt around a series of newly drilled holes, which now held sound posts, and strands of bright new wire. But it was the fishing vest, hanging safely to one side, that most readily caught his eye. There was a fly rod propped against it, with an old Pflueger Medalist reel at its seat, and a small net hanging from the D-ring on the back of the shoulder yoke. It bulged with probably a set of stocking-foot waders, because beneath it rested a pair of wading boots.

Jenny heard the swish of the grass from Clyde's footsteps before the boy, pulled away to meet him, then rushed back to the young man's side, relishing the attention she was getting. Josh turned in the old man's direction, welcomed the setter back, then climbed to his feet. He was a sparse lad with cleanly cut features and gentle blue eyes, tall for his age and still growing into himself. He had his shirt off and wore a faded pair of Levis. Clyde noted enviously that there wasn't an ounce of fat on him, just the beginnings of a mustache over his lip. And none of the garish and sissified earrings he saw on the kids who hung out at the malls in Charlottesville.

The boy recognized the old storekeeper from the many times at the feed store. He had stood at length before the knife case on one occasion not long before, pining over a Barlow, and, noticing, Clyde had left the counter, walked over with the key and opened the case, and handed it to him. Charging nothing but a "thanks." It had not been the first time the man had favored him so and, of course, he had not forgotten. He stuck his hands loosely into his pockets, and shyly smiled a welcome. Jenny nosed at his hand through the cloth of his britches, her tail slowly working.

"Fine mornin', Josh," the old man supposed.

"Yessir," the boy said. He had retrieved a hand from a pocket and rested it once more on the setter's head.

"Fence-fixin', huh?" Clyde observed.

"Yessir," Josh explained, "the cows knocked the fence down—the posts had rotted—and got out. Daddy sent me out here to fix it," he finished, a hint of disappointment in his voice. He glanced again at the gun case over the old man's arm.

"But you'd rather be fishin'," Wood suggested, gesturing toward the fishing gear.

"Yessir," the boy grinned.

"Tell me," the storekeeper teased, shifting his weight to a fresh leg. "I'm gettin' too old to haul up there. But can a feller still catch a trout on the Laur'l these days?"

The boy smiled more broadly, warming now. He still caressed Jenny's ear.

"Yessir," he confirmed, "I caught twenty-three up there a week ago, one fourteen-incher!"

"Parachutes . . . ?" the old man asked, his eyes narrowing.

"Nosir, drakes," the boy replied, the triumph rising in his eyes. Clyde could remember when his own had burned as brightly.

"Be-dogged," he exclaimed with mock disbelief.

"Yessir," Josh declared. "But the biggest one got under a log and took the last one I had," he noted glumly, "and got away."

"But now he'll be there next time," Clyde promised.

The boy grinned, but said nothing.

"You'll find, boy, long before you git as ancient and decrepit as I am," the old man proposed, "it's *all* about lookin' for'ard to somethin'."

Josh grinned again, withdrawing self-consciously with the force of the philosophy. He was wondering why the old man was here; what a man with a gun and a dog was doing out here in summer. He looked down at the setter, stroked her ears again, and though he tried to avoid it so evidently, his eyes traveled the canvas gun case anew. Finally his curiosity bested him.

"Is this your dog?" he asked politely.

"For a little longer," Clyde replied. "Her name's Jenny."

"Jenny." The setter raised her eyes as the boy repeated her name.

"Does she hunt?" the young man asked.

"Yes," Wood understated.

"Birds?"

"Uh-huh."

Josh looked at the setter with greater respect, something that bordered awe.

"I'd like to have a dog," the boy said wistfully. "Mr. Clements has some setters," he followed immediately, his eyes brightening. "I went with him one day last fall."

"Yes, your mother told me," Clyde volunteered.

"We hunted grouse over by the Horn Rim," the boy continued, "the dogs'd stop when they smelled a bird. It was pretty. We didn't kill any, though. Mr. Clements thought he hit one, but we never found it."

"You like to grouse hunt?"

"Yessir, more than most anything. I try aroun' here, but I don't get close to many and I miss a lot."

"Well, that doesn't change much, I'm afraid," Wood observed, smiling.

"I don't care much for shootin' 'em in the roads," the boy noted.

"Good for you," the old man said, shifting his weight again, and shuffling the gun case to a fresh arm. The boy took keen notice.

There was a massive old stump nearby, scaly with white lichen, where once had stood a colossal walnut tree. It rested just within the shadow of the mountain.

The old man's underpinnings were giving out. "Let's sit a minute, Josh," he invited, motioning to the stump. The boy followed as Clyde tottered over, eased himself down with a exaggerated sigh of relief, and laid the gun case and cane alongside. Josh sat beside him, at the most respectful distance the stump would allow. He was still a little ill at ease. Never had he talked this much to a grown man before, other than his father, and rarely even then. But he was enjoying the old man's company, and certainly the setter's, even though the old man smelled funny. And already he had opened up more than he usually did. Nobody had ever taken interest in his hunting and fishing so easily before, nor so evenly, and it made him feel special.

Clyde glanced about, taking in the enormity of the old stump.

"This was a grand old tree," he observed.

"Yessir," the boy said. "Daddy wouldn't cut it, Mama said, when he cleared this side of the pasture. But then the lightnin' killed it and we sold it to Mr. Tetterlow down to the lumberyard."

"Shame," the old man acknowledged, pulling off his hat and wiping the inside of the crown with a faded blue bandanna.

"Yessir," the boy replied.

Clyde mopped his bald head as well, stuck the bandanna back into a coat pocket. From the corner of his eye, he noticed that Jenny had thrust her head into the boy's lap, and that Josh was studying the gun case again. Growing ever more impatient, no doubt, about why he was there.

The old man pulled a Baby Ruth bar from his coat, peeled away the wrapper, and broke it in two. Offered Josh the half he didn't keep. Shared a chunk of the one he kept with Jenny. They sat there quietly for a minute or so, the three of them, munching.

From somewhere above came the piercing scream of an eagle, wresting their eyes to the sky. Occasionally the birds would pass here. Moments later they found him. He was high, very high, cutting tight circles in the chaste, blue air. With only the camber of his wings and the telling glint of sunlight to give him away.

Jenny had heard it too, and left the boy, and was looking wishfully now toward the mountain. She strayed a few yards in its direction, restless suddenly, with the urge to go. Clyde could see the fire rising in her eyes. After a few more stuttering steps, she started away.

She needed to be here now, the old man thought.

"Jenny!" Clyde admonished lightly, arresting her departure as she hastened to a lope. The setter dropped back to a walk—hesitated—turned, then came trotting back. She stood at their feet, questioning his summons. In the absence of an explanation, she settled back, presently, onto her haunches, and eased herself to the ground.

All the while the boy sat in silence, gnawing the candy bar as an excuse. Waiting and wondering.

"Josh," the old man asked finally, returning the old felt hat to his head and turning to the boy, "did you know anything of Ben Willow?"

"Nosir," the boy said after a few seconds, "not much. My dad tol' me they found 'im dead not long ago, somewhere on the Seven Step."

"Yes," Clyde replied, "this past winter."

"We'd see him now and then . . . before, I mean," Josh resumed, "in an ol' blue In'ernational truck with a setter dog on the seat. Daddy said he was goin' huntin', likely, and had the best grouse dogs in the county."

"He did," the old man confirmed.

"Daddy always threw up a hand, but we could never tell he waved back," the boy remarked.

"Wad'n unusual," Clyde mused with a chuckle, "rarely waved at anybody, not even me, and I knew him forty years. Ben was never unneighborly exactly, just always had his mind off some'ers else.

"Got worse as he got older."

"Was he really a good grouse hunter?" the boy asked.

Clyde smiled.

"Somewhere near the best," the old man replied. "'Bout like you'll be thirty years from now," he said, clapping a hand to the boy's knee and squeezin' like a mule bites, winning a broad grin in return.

"That setter you saw with Ben Willow," Clyde said seriously, nodding to Jenny. She had solicited the boy's favor once more; his hand was at her ear. "This is the dog."

The boy's eyes widened, while gradually his face furrowed with confusion. "But you said she was yours," he protested politely.

"For a time," Clyde repeated.

The boy was no less puzzled.

"Sometime before Ben Willow died, Josh," the old man explained, "I promised that, come what may, I would see to Jenny.

"Do you know what it is to promise somethin' like that to someone?" he asked the boy.

"Yessir," Josh said, dropping his eyes to the setter and stroking her head more deliberately. "I *think* so."

"There was somethin' else I promised him, Josh," Clyde continued, "maybe even more important."

The old man's eyes leveled at the boy, and they were tight with emotion. "I need for you to understand," he said.

Josh could feel the beat of his heart. No one had ever spoken to him so earnestly before . . . as an equal. As a man. No one. And suddenly he realized he was afraid.

"It's the kind of thing one man does for another, come whatever," the old man said, "even though it's not always easy and he might rather not, because he knows — were things the other way — his friend would have done as well for him."

The boy was trembling. He could hear, almost absently, the clamor of the crows at the other end of the pasture.

"And that's pretty much what the years between two men sum up to," the old man vowed, his eyes catching and holding the boy's.

"Ben Willow asked me . . . when he was gone . . . to see him back to the mountain, Josh," he explained.

"And there's a particular way he asked me to do it.

"And it involves Jenny here . . . and you. 'Cause I'm too damn old and beat up to see it through."

The boy was bewildered. He looked at the old man, wanting to say something. There were things he *didn't* understand. But he was fighting tears back, too, and he didn't understand that either. So he had to turn away, and wait for the old man to continue.

"I have Ben Willow's ashes, Josh," Clyde said as gently as he could.

The boy looked at him once again, and his eyes were wet, both with fascination and fright. But there was strength and courage in his face as well.

"They belong on the mountain," the old man concluded.

"But how . . . " The boy finally found the words and then his voice broke, and the old man kindly interrupted.

"I can't go, Josh. I'm too far spent," he said as the boy's eyes searched his face.

"I'm askin' you to do it, Josh, for me and Ben, and I know it's a lot to ask, and there's only a little I have to offer in return. But if you do, I believe you'll find something more of yourself than you know."

The boy was struggling to speak. "But how . . . how will I . . . do it," he managed weakly.

"I'll help you," the old man promised.

Clyde looked at the setter, the bright questioning of her eyes, thinking of her and Ben. The vagaries of fate that had brought her to this point were as unpredictably perfect as the destiny that had seen them together at the onset. When Ben had decided how he wanted to be delivered the final three hundred yards to eternity, he had not known for certain it would be

Jenny. There was the strong chance, and likely he had contemplated as much. But any one of the dozen things that had happened in the last several months could have conspired against it.

"You would have thought well of Ben Willow, Josh," the old man declared, "and nothin' would have pleased him more than to show you the woods and a grouse dog. And I was workin' up to askin' him for you. But that won't happen now. Somehow Ben's gone, and it's left to me, and you, and Jenny.

"I want you to have Jenny, Josh," Clyde said, "I want the two of you to have each other. Ben would want it too."

The boy stared at the old man in disbelief.

"She's a fine grouse dog, Josh, maybe the best Ben Willow ever owned. And he had many a good'un. She needs somebody — now that Ben's gone — to care about, to trust again. She'll ask for nothin' more than your friendship, a bite to eat when she's hungry, and a dry place to sleep. Care about her, don't let her down. And most of all, take her huntin'. 'Cause that's what she lives for.

"In return, she'll give you nothin' less than her life and love, unconditionally . . . 'cause that's what dogs do. And nothin' on God's earth will come between you."

There were tears now, unabashedly on the boy's cheeks, and his eyes had met Jenny's, and he had his fingers buried in the silky ruff of her coat alongside her neck.

The old man fumbled for a moment inside the breast pocket of his old gray coat and extracted something. It was an old Acme Thunderer dog whistle dangling at the end of a blackened leather lanyard taut with age and weather. There were tooth marks in the Bakelite finish of the whistle — seventy years' worth — and light brown chips here and there, from decades of honest service.

Clyde held it in the palm of his hand for a short time. It was the only thing he had asked of Andrea. She had taken the guns back, including the old Parker, as should be. But he had asked her if he might have the old whistle, and she had placed it in his hands with tears in her eyes, and her kiss on his cheek.

It would have been hardly obvious to most, but, aside from the gun, the old whistle was Ben Willow's most cherished possession.

"Two things," Ben Willow had told him some thirty years before, as they sat atop a flat of granite at the eclipse of a ridge in the Tenfolds, in the chill of the swelling dusk, watching the fading sun collect the autumn colors from the high October hills. With their guns broken over their knees, and sagging game bags tugging agreeably at the small of their backs . . . and Pat and Gabe curled alongside, twitching and dreaming at the climax of a long day at the birds.

"Two things . . . ," Ben had said, between puffs at his pipe, as he shook the match dead he had used to light it, "carry beyond a man and his dogs — bind up all their days . . . and all the birds . . . and all these mountains while he was a part of 'em," he had added with a sweeping gesture of a hand and a swirl of smoke. He had paused, lowering his pipe to half-mast and pensively fingering this same whistle at the hollow of his chest. "A gun and a whistle," he had declared, "and you can round up every hymn book in the Alleghenies and throw in Heaven, and when the preachin' and the buryin's done, and folks think they've sent up his soul to the Almighty, St. Peter's gonna find it never got no further than the corner they stuck his gun and whistle in."

Clyde handed the battered old Thunderer to the boy. "This was Ben Willow's too," he told him, "he blew it over every dog he ever hunted, carried it every day he ever spent in the woods, to the last. It's yours now too."

The boy was overwhelmed, vacant for words. Over the dawning joy in his eyes, his forehead was furrowed with worry.

"I don't know much about bird dogs," he struggled to say.

"Oh yes," the old man remarked, snaking out a legal envelope stuffed with papers. He handed it to Josh. "These are Jenny's registration papers. They won't mean much to you now," he told the boy, "but one day you'll want to look back at them."

"I've never hunted with a dog before," Josh repeated uneasily, still clinging to Jenny, "I'm not sure about what to do. And I need to ask my folks."

"I already have, Josh," Clyde assured him, "it's fine . . . if it's okay with you. As far as Jenny goes, you just get to know her for a while, and be pals, then take her huntin' come September when the first frost cools the air and the leaves start coloring. You just go with her, and try not to get in the way. Just stay close. She'll do the rest. Then when the bird season comes in for real, you'll be ready."

He dug into his pocket again. There was a tinkle of Swiss brass.

"Put this bell on her collar so you can keep up with her. She's gonna hunt to your gun, and she's gonna point grouse. Your job's to get up there and kill her a bird. When it's done, you just cluck to her, or tap her on the ear lightly; she'll do the rest. Just watch her and follow your instincts. She'll teach you ever'thing you need to know."

The boy looked doubtful.

"You'll be fine. You're going to have a great time together."

Josh accepted the reassurance gracefully.

"Will she stop real pretty like Mr. Clements's dogs did?" he asked, his excitement growing.

"Wait and see," the old man said with a mischievous smile.

Jenny had stepped back and was watching them, her eyes brightly interested, her tail working.

"I know where there's a bunch of birds just the other side of that mountain," the boy motioned, his voice swelling with excitement, "where they cut the timber a few years ago and the thickets and the grapevines have grown up."

Clyde could feel the gratification ascending in his chest. He hoped old Ben was awake up there somewhere, listening.

"One last thing," Clyde declared. He reached around for the gun case, pulled it into his lap, slowly undid the zipper. As he did, the case parted sufficiently to reveal the toe of the gunstock, richly orange, the color of fresh pine resin, shot through with wispy whorls of burl that looked like purling wood smoke.

The boy watched hypnotically, as if the old man was revealing the very secret of life.

When the zipper had traveled its distance, Clyde slid a hand in, grasping the little gun at the receiver and pulling it free from the case in a single, fluid motion. It was a Diana Grade Superposed from the vintage years of the Belgium/Browning gun trade — a .28 — as petite as any ever crafted, and it was virtually flawless, from the smoke blue luster of the slender tubes to the graceful crescent of the butt plate.

Josh's eyes grew big and bright. He had seen but few shotguns in his short years, and none approaching this, not even the Ansley Fox .20 that Mr. Clements carried. Mostly, it had been his own little .410 Harrington & Richardson single-barrel that he got for Christmas when he was six, and the worn-white old 12-gauge Ithaca pump of his father's that he borrowed occasionally when he shot ducks on the river. But neither was an honest-to-goodness bird gun, like this one.

The old man held it up before him for a moment with cupped hands, studying it in profile. The spackled light of the sun through the leaves caught the luminance of the wood stock and played about the burl in carrot-colored highlights, continuing on to relieve the delicate engraving starkly from the face of the receiver.

There had been a day . . . and a time, he recalled wistfully.

"*This,*" he said, "was mine. It's as good a gun as a man ever pulled after a grouse. There was a time," he mused, "when I was pretty decent with it."

Clyde turned and held it out to the boy.

"You'd as well have it too, Josh," the old man said, "kinda ties up the package, I guess. I had planned to give it to you one day soon anyhow."

Josh accepted the little gun with trembling hands. It was lighter than he expected, and it felt different from any other that he had ever held, almost as if it had become a living, breathing part of him the moment he touched it. Mesmerized, he marveled at the travel of light through the hue and figure of the wood as he canted it slowly back and forth, and at the intricate perfection of the pheasants etched amid the leafy scroll beneath the barrels.

With the appearance of the gun, Jenny had become immediately interested also, and nudged her way between Josh's knees until she could properly inspect it of her own. She proofmarked it with a big wet noseprint just below the comb of the stock. Quickly, the boy wiped it clean with the underside of his forearm.

"Pull it to your shoulder," the old man suggested.

Josh complied, lifting the little gun from his knees and finding it almost suddenly at his cheek and shoulder, as if it had a matching energy that connected closely with his own.

"Pretend there's a bird, crossin' right to left," Clyde instructed. "Now!" The boy threw the gun up and pushed it through an awkward but purposeful swing, thrilling at the synergy. And then, abruptly, he was self-conscious, lowering it timidly back to his lap.

"It's beautiful," he said wondrously, turning it again in his hands.

The boy said nothing more for several seconds, then looked up and his eyes were full.

"Thank you, Mr. Wood," he said.

The words didn't seem nearly enough. The boy laid the gun down across his lap and returned a hand to Jenny's shoulder.

It all seemed a dream.

"For Jenny . . . for everything," he continued.

Still, it seemed too little.

"I'll take good care of Jenny . . . ," the boy struggled to add, tears rising, "and we'll hunt together, and I'll not let anythin' bad ever happen to her again."

The old man could feel the burn growing in his eyes and he turned away for a few moments to look beyond the pasture to the far blue ridges.

"And I'll not forget there's something more we have to do either," Josh said resolutely, "about Mr. Willow . . . and if you'll help me I'll be proud to do it."

Clyde's gaze swung back to the boy. And he looked at him for a moment like he knew him for the first time. He'd never had a boy. If he had, he would have wanted him to be like this one.

"This fall . . . when the time comes," Clyde said confidently. "I'll let you know."

"And tell me how?" the boy asked.

"Yes," Clyde assured him, "and tell you how."

Josh said nothing further, though Clyde could tell from the softness in the boy's eyes how desperately he wanted to.

The old man pushed himself up, braced himself on a knee, reached down and picked up the gun case where it had fallen by the stump. Brushing it off, he laid it alongside the boy. Digging into his coat pocket, he worked the two boxes of shells free, and set them on the stump also.

It was said and done. It was time to go.

He picked up his cane and reached into the old coat a final time, fishing out a check cord.

He handed it to Josh. "Put this on Jenny's collar," he cautioned. "She'll try to follow me."

Josh fastened the cord to the setter's collar, fumbling for a moment with the snap. Jenny, sensing something amiss, was growing fidgety.

Clyde looked into the boy's face one last time. He wanted to remember the glow, and the elation. The youth. But the anguish was still there, too, from gratitude left desperately unspoken. He laid a hand on the boy's shoulder.

"Just come tell me, boy," Clyde said softly, "come tell me when you and Jenny kill your first grouse . . . tell me every detail."

"Yessir, I will," Josh promised, in a voice taut with admiration.

"Jenny'll come with me," he could hear the boy pledging solemnly, as he turned and shuffled slowly away.

The old man paused once, near the brink of the hill, as he approached the barn. Looking back, he could see the boy standing only a few feet from where they had sat . . . small and solitary beneath the vast stretch of the mountain . . . watching. He still held the gun in one hand, and the end of the check cord with the other, and the setter was barking mournfully.

He considered them for a few seconds longer, dropped his eyes to the ground, and turned slowly away.

No matter the destination, there was pain in every passage.

Nettie Wood awoke gently, but did not move.

Her husband had rolled onto her side of the bed, nestling more snugly against the crescent of her body, and slipping an arm around her waist. She could feel herself sinking farther into the soft warm hollow created by the mutual weight of their bodies. For a moment she opened her eyes — considering the feeble gray light of dawn building in the windowpanes — then closed them again, relishing the man beside her and the gentle murmur of the rain on the roof. He had let his arm steal slowly up her side until he could cup the soft globe of her right breast gently into his hand. She could feel, ever so wonderfully, the slight swell of her nipple against the sensitive inner flesh of his palm. He did not allow his fingers to move, though she wanted them to. She savored the intimacy, the affirmation that he was hers and hers alone. She had loved him for a lifetime. She stirred, and the round, warm flesh of her breast, sagging and supple with sleep, melted more deliciously into his hand. Not so fully or elegantly as once it had, but hardly less thrillingly. She could sense the restlessness growing at the end of him, glad that he still retained the essence of his manhood. Once it would have throbbed for her. It happened more seldom now, and within the turmoil of recent times had not at all. She could feel his hand drifting cautiously downward, to the secret of her, feel him place one finger ever so gently upon the warm moist cleft of her. She waited anxiously for him to enter, but he resisted. Reluctant to wake her. She appeared to be sleeping so peacefully. She felt him relax, forcing himself to be content with her breast, allowing his body to flow vicariously into hers, and listening as well to the gentle patter of the rain on the shingles.

Until he felt the surprise of her hand, asking its way gently between them, the tips of her fingers working slowly and wonderfully down his belly, and embracing exquisitely his budding hardness.

They lingered in bed afterward, in the comfort of each other's arms, languishing in the afterglow. Listening to the lulling patter of the rain. Safe from the world.

Of their life together, these precious, mellow moments had always been her favorite. When they were truly one, and she could have him completely for herself, without distraction. When he would cling to her as if she were the center of his existence, and tenderly tell her so. And not let go. Until first he, and then she, fell asleep. And when later, they would awaken to talk at length of their years together, of both the triumphs and the tragedies, maybe even revisit a dream.

She could hear the deep and steady rhythm of his breathing now above the sound of the rain, feel the corresponding rise and fall of his chest. He was sleeping soundly. She slipped from beneath him, letting him roll to his back. Her arm was growing numb. He stirred slightly, but did not awaken. She snuggled herself against his side, resting her head easily upon his chest. After a moment she lifted her cheek, shook her hair softly aside, and returned it to the warm hollow between his pectoral muscles. She lay quietly then, letting herself drift as well, listening again to the whisper of the rain, and occasionally his heartbeat. Wondering that she had loved this man so deeply since she was barely a child of fifteen, remembering how he had felt inside her only a few minutes before. Remembering . . . until her eyelids closed . . . once, twice . . . and for a time.

Some while later she awakened to hear the clock chime boldly in the hallway. Her head still rested on her husband's chest. She could feel his hand lying upon her head. The rain had tapered to a casual drip. She stirred lazily.

"Awake, 'Ettie?" he asked quietly.

"Um-humn," she purred, stretching. She could feel the tips of his fingers now, teasing the wispy tresses at the base of her neck.

"I've been thinking about the store some, Nettie," he confided. "You know I've been there *forty-seven years!* That's a hell of a lot of horse feed. Maybe it's time to leave."

At first she did not take him seriously. Her eyes darted with surprise at even the suggestion. The store had been the axis of their universe for as long as she could remember. But she did not raise her head. She was relishing his caress.

"I'm old and tired, Nettie," he said acquiescently.

"Tired maybe," she replied, "not old. Old's how you feel."

"That's cliché," he argued.

"Still the truth," she countered, tracing circles in the unruly white hair of his chest with her fingertip.

"Tired then," he agreed.

"Maybe we ought to see a little of the world before it stops," he followed.

She snuggled her cheek more deeply into his chest. "Oh, I doubt it stops any moment soon," she said, still mellow with the moment.

"It did for Ben and Libby," he said bluntly, "it will for us."

Nettie grew rigid for a moment, holding her breath. Realizing at once that he was sincere.

She sat upright, gathering the sheets around her. Looking into his face, she quickly read the earnestness.

He was right. Soon, too soon, it would happen. If it happened to one of them it'd as well happen to both. Either way it would end the living.

"You're really serious, aren't you?" she said.

He pushed himself up against the bedpost and took her hand in his, rubbing lovingly at the splotches and veins with his shriveled old thumb, and then lifting his eyes.

"You remember how we talked about Vermont? How we always wanted to go?" he asked.

She felt the emotion surge to her eyes.

"Yes," she answered, smiling, as the first tear fell. "At Christmas . . . with snow, and frosted windowpanes, and sleigh bells and lap robes, and hot cider in front of a whispering fire."

"Why don't we do it," he entreated, "before it's too late."

Nettie Wood couldn't believe her ears.

"Why don't we," she spurted, crying and laughing together, "and then just keep going . . . right on up through New Hampshire, and Maine, and Quebec . . . go as long as the spirit moves us.

"There've got to be places up there where it's still real," she added, "little white chapels with steeples and horses pulling stacks of stovewood on a sled and blowing steam in the cold air and villages filled with little shops and people wearing red noses and a mackinaw. It can't all be just pictures somebody supposed."

"Surely there's some of it left," he declared, "we'll just up and go, by God, and see!"

Nettie Wood was brimming with joy, so happy it could not be contained. Her lifelong dream had been that one day they would leave the world behind and travel together . . . just he and she, here and there, and nowhere in particular.

And now, almost inconceivably, it was about to happen.

In her excitement, she had let the covers drop. She noticed now that his eyes had fallen to her naked breasts. She smiled, pleased that she could still turn his head.

He saw abruptly that she was aware.

"You're a foxy old biddy yet," he observed.

She laughed and threw herself on top of him.

"I love you, Clyde Wood," she declared, squeezing her eyes shut, and hugging him as hard as she could.

"Warts and all," he cautioned.

"Warts and all."

They lay in an embrace, silent for a time, enjoying each other.

"You know I could have left years ago, 'Ettie, and didn't," he reflected. "Now, suddenly, I don't understand why. It just dud'n seem as import'nt anymore.

"Maybe it never was.

"Maybe ol' Ben rubbed off on me more than I knew."

"You're your own man, Clyde," she said, "you've always been."

They had talked of Christmas, and Vermont, then, until they had transposed the dream roughly to a design, and, afterward, languished happily entwined until they had fallen asleep again. Now Clyde awoke once more with the glare of September sunlight in his eyes. The rain had ended while they slept and the sky had cleared, and the brilliant yellow light was streaming through the window. He squinted at the clock on the dresser. It was midmorning, of a sleepy Sunday. He could smell steeping coffee, hear Nettie humming brightly from the kitchen. Detect the pop and sizzle of bacon and eggs.

She would call him to breakfast soon.

He lay back with his hands behind his head and his elbow blocking the sun, savoring the reverie.

He'd go to work tomorrow and whack out a resignation notice for the board. They'd want a month's notice. He'd give them two weeks. Ray Satterwhite was up and coming. They needed to go ahead and let him.

He couldn't wait to see Lester's face.

Then he'd tell Christine. She wouldn't believe him at first, and then she'd cry, and then they'd laugh for a while over all the multifarious mischief they had managed in twenty-eight years. Most especially Darth Tysinger and the horse liniment.

And then he'd take the afternoon off, drive to Charleston, and buy the biggest damn RV their hope chest could afford.

His mind whirled 360. There was money in the bank. Likely more than enough. He'd put together some land years before in the southern end of the county, inherited some, bought some more. Who'd know they'd want to put a ski resort on it thirty winters later? He had made out handsomely. Invested a little here and there that had done well, too.

His thoughts spun again, like a free-spooling ratchet gear, and reengaged. Therman had brought Josh and Jenny by the week before. Jenny had been glad to see him, but already she doted on the boy. As he did her. They were going to the woods regularly, "mornin', noon, and night," Therman reported. Jenny had pointed another bird a day before, and Josh could not tell him enough of it. He could see that they were happy together. Ben would be pleased.

Things were good. Once again, life was spinning true.

There was but the one last task.

He roused himself, threw the covers aside, dropped his feet off the side of the bed, and sat up. Blinked like an owl two or three times, rubbed his chest, then struggled up. Went to the dresser and found a pair of clean shorts, then shuffled on to the bathroom and relieved himself. Washing his face in the sink with his hands, he toweled it dry, then took a look in the mirror and scowled. The hair over his ears, all he had left, looked as it had in the tenth grade the first time it had encountered a Vandegraph machine. He found his brush, wet it thoroughly, and ran it down both temples, then over the fuzz of his pate. He looked again, assenting with the mental equivalent of a shrug.

Struggling with his shorts, he inadvertently suffered the full effect of his profile in the door reflection. He turned to confront it, then wished he hadn't. His plump belly spilled over his shorts in a complete, copious circle, compressing his already unexceptional height to a stumpy illusion. Altogether, he resembled a channel buoy. He shook his head and fled back to the bedroom.

He sat on the edge of the bed again and pulled on his pants, one leg at a time. Went to the closet and found a shirt. Snugged everything in place with his belt.

When he made the kitchen Nettie was still humming a storm. Sounded like the "Tennessee Waltz," with the needle stuck.

He couldn't resist a modest surge of pride. There was nothing like a good roll in the covers to freshen a woman's constitution. Do the job well and invariably they surfaced like Scarlett O'Hara the morning after. In a pinch, it was a good thing for a man to remember.

She had her back to him, pouring a brace of glasses full of orange juice. He snuck up and kissed her lightly on the nape of the neck. She flinched, almost dumping the juice.

Turning, she kissed him back, full on the lips, balancing the orange juice carton precariously in her off hand.

"Good mornin'," she chirped sweetly.

"Mornin'," he returned, trying not to appear smug.

He could still tap the molasses barrel, he was telling himself.

"When we leavin'?" she inquired cheerfully.

"How quick can you pack?" he challenged.

She smiled again, and renewed the "Waltz."

It was around three in the afternoon, after a lingering breakfast and greater talk of New England, and the Sunday paper, and a short trip to the Dairy Queen with Nettie for a sundae, when his consciousness called him once again to the small, cedar-sided shop in the side yard. In but a few days, October would arrive. The time was near.

He twisted the key in the lock, pushed and left open the door, cracked the side windows to encourage a pleasant draft. Pulling off his old gray coat, he draped it across the peg at the back of the door, then turned to the three large, tin saltshakers lying on the yellowed old workbench. They were unexceptional, simply everyday table fare you could find almost anywhere. But they had been chosen methodically, for their sturdiness, and a single, essential distinction. By calculated volume, each would hold slightly in excess of seven ounces.

They rested there in curious company: a baking pan full of wood ash, a small drill, an ice pick, a dozen or so small wooden splits, some bradding studs and a small ball-peen hammer, a leather dog collar.

Idly, he studied the lay of the various pieces for a few moments, associating them mentally. He had figured to do things pretty much as Ben had suggested, and still saw no reason it shouldn't work, but there were nuances. He was working as yet to overcome them.

He picked up one of the shakers anew, held it horizontally, and shook it vigorously over the baking tin. Setting it aside, he tried another. The result was the same. Neither was satisfactory. In either case he had closed the container with rubber gasket sealant, then punched alternate holes in its underside, so that its contents would sift not from the cap, as normal, but ventrally. That was as had to be. But he had made the holes too large in the first and the flow was excessive. It would expend itself too quickly. And in the second, though the apertures were correct, their numbers had proved to be extreme, so that the same effect was achieved.

Now he turned to the third, examining it carefully before he started. Visualizing the outcome and the several steps necessary to achieve it. Removing the cap, he slipped the body of the shaker over the wooden mandrel in the vise, clamped it in place, and meticulously marked with a pencil and ruler the number and location of holes that by trial he had now determined to be appropriate. Patiently, with a center punch and a slight tap of the hammer, he affixed the beginning of each opening, so that the bit would not slip. Picking up the drill, he tried the trigger. The motor whined and the chuck spun.

When the holes were drilled and chamfered, he lifted the device for reinspection. It was tedious doings for old peepers. He removed his bifocals, pinched with two fingers the bridge of his nose, and rubbed his eyes. Replacing the glasses, he pushed them up in place on his nose, lifted his head, and tried again, peering down through the reading lens for several moments. Yes. It should work this time.

With a tablespoon, he ladled in wood ashes until the shaker was filled almost to the brim. Then returned the cap and twisted it down tight. Shaking it heartily up and down, he was rewarded with a pleasing puff of ashes each time. Until about the half-dozenth succession, when it balked, the ashes compacted around the holes so that they no longer sifted freely through.

He had anticipated this and next constructed a small, interlocking baffle of wood splits that could be inserted into the shaker to effectively loosen the ashes each time they were disturbed. When the baffle was installed, he again filled the tube and replaced the cap. This time it worked perfectly. With each disturbance of the shaker, for as long as he continued to simulate the anticipated cycle of motion, there was emitted a suitable modicum of ash. So that, by his notion, the shaker would be emptied in the approximate neighborhood of a quarter hour. That was an estimate, of course, and there was no need of being precise, except that it seemed a man's journey to eternity should lapse at least the space it took to read his obituary.

Pleased at his ingenuity, Clyde emptied the shaker one last time. Replacing it to the mandrel, he spun the body 180 degrees and carefully tapped in each of the two larger holes it would take to secure it.

All that was left now was to brad it properly to the dog collar.

When that was finished, he raised it aloft for a final assessment with the fingers of one hand.

For a few moments, once more, he considered its purpose.

"Well, Ben," he vowed solemnly beneath his breath, "it ain't much of a chariot, but I reckon with some dog power under it, it'll see you home."

He had never anticipated the old man's request that day. He had always surmised, as Andrea, that Ben would be buried beneath the maple at Shiloh Cemetery, beside Libby. They had been honeymoon close, for sixty-four years. Ben may have wandered relentlessly body and spirit, but never did he stray in his affection for Libby. Andrea had not taken it easily when she had discovered her father's wishes as a portion of his will. Immediately, she had attempted to dissuade him from the task as her father's executor.

"I promised, Andy," he had told her as compassionately as he knew how.

"You promised?" she had replied disdainfully. "And what of the promise my father made to my mother?"

He had no answer. He had tried to explain to her as Ben had explained to him that day, but he had not been successful. Womanhood was instilled with values of commitment and fidelity that remained fundamentally unaltered by arguments of passion.

Yet no one on earth, or who wandered the ether between here and eternity, himself included, knew Ben Willow better than Elizabeth Chandler Willow, and she would have been the first to understand. What was the old saying . . . of the greatest sacrifice of love . . . to set free that you most adore.

He had tried to place himself within a similar dilemma, should it have been he and Nettie, and had been unable to reconcile himself to a similar decision. But he was not Ben Willow.

All he knew was that his staunchest, oldest friend had asked of him a single, last assurance. And that was enough.

"When I'm gone," Ben Willow had said to him, "take me back to the mountain. Grind my old carcass up, put what's left on a hard-driving dog, and let him ramble. Hit the whistle and send 'im long and hard! Down a deep, deep hollow and across a high, ramblin' ridge.

"Ever'thing else of me'll already be up there," he said, "waitin' for what's left. I don't aim to disappoint it. It's the closest to life everlastin' I'll ever get," Ben Willow had vowed firmly, "and there ain't no chariot in Heaven could deliver me any finer."

"And what of Libby, Ben," Clyde had asked respectfully, after they had spoken of it for a time. "You're sure . . . this is the way you want it?"

"Do not make it," Ben Willow had said, "any harder than it has been."

· 25 ·

First light crept through the Alleghenies as softly as a wedding prayer. Growing onto the mountains. Settling over the foothills. Falling gently upon the meadows. Seeping silently into the vales.

Pausing in the keen yellow eyes of the bobcat on the bald, awakening the drowsy black bear within the copse of huckleberries in the foothills, reflecting in the watchful brown eyes of a deer by a stream. Stealing along the sleepy, slate gray travel of the Greenbrier with the delicate stir of dawn, surprising the sharp, cool breath of the hills, that rose from its tryst with the river in broken clouds of mist. Creeping about the forest, sweeping the brooding black shadows away, brushing aside the anonymity of the evening, chasing away the doubt of the darkness. Making way for the sun.

Andrea Willow Harding steered the wheels of the rented Cherokee into the familiar turn from 219 onto Traver's Creek Road, urging the motor back to speed.

She loved this first hour of a fresh new morning. When the world was washed clean behind the ears, and still lazy in bed, and had not decided how it would unfold for the day. When it was filled mostly with hope, only the least bit of sadness, and with nothing, yet, of regret.

Nothing of regret, even though she had departed Germany three days before, kissing her husband good-bye, and had followed her heart three thousand miles across the Atlantic to the hills of home.

It had not been easy. Steve had not wanted her to come.

But from the moment Clyde Wood had called, to tell her this would be the day, she had known that she must.

He had called of courtesy, of course, for he had known how she felt.

"I thought you might wish to be along," Clyde had said timorously.

"No," she had replied, "I've another thing to do."

Their conversation had diminished afterward, and when he had hung up, she had felt badly about treating him so bluntly. It wasn't Clyde's fault. He was merely trying to be what he had always been, a dear old friend.

Lord knows he, too, had suffered in the name of Ben Willow.

She had said nothing to him of her heartfelt obligation to return, though for a different reason, and he had no idea that she was there.

She had flown into Charleston the evening before, picked up the rental car, and settled into a Best Western. But the demons of her purpose had deprived her of peace, and finally in the small hours of the morning, unable to sleep, she had thrown her things back together, tossed them into the Jeep, and driven the rest of the night.

So now here she was, and only now was the magnitude of the undertaking sinking into her conscience. Not the physical dimensions of it, for she had traveled extensively before, across several worlds, and that was but a matter of logistics, but the emotive enormity of why she was compelled to come, which was far less uncomplicated. For what she truly sought to achieve, she was uncertain.

In the end, maybe nothing more, or less, than the peace of mind to go on living.

Off the right shoulder, against the gray light at the height of the ridge she could see the friendly silhouette of McCathern's Knob. She had lain in bed when she was only a girl, gazing at the rugged old promontory under the backdrop of a full moon, and easily imagining from the shape of it a grand black stallion upon whose back she would ride away one night to Sagittarius, which hung just over its withers, and Capricorn, which had loomed less distinctly beyond the flow of its billowing tail, and then on — and on and on — to all the magical places of the universe she had so wishfully marveled over in history books and encyclopedias, both genuine and mythical. And, yet, now that she had seen many of them, as grandly as she had imagined, there was still a feeling here that she could not replicate across the breadth of the continents.

It had to do with place and family, and blood ties, and the spiritual ob-ligation to the two people who had given you life and love that could never, no matter how diligently you tried, be repaid. And their obligation to one another, to be forever together, which seemed somehow both birth-right and heritage of a child born of their love, and that had always seemed so sacrosanct and inviolable. And now it had called to her and seen her home.

She had loved her father, her mother the more so.

She had loved him and admired him all her life, not the least his grit and tenacity, though she could not always tell him so in the way that she wished. She had known how intensely he had loved the woods, and the waters, the wildness. A dog and a gun. She had been with him, felt it with him, cherished it with him. She had loved him even through all the heart-ache and disappointment it had brought so many times, to her and her mother, when his restlessness carried him time and again beyond their reach, before perhaps the desperation of their yearning finally drew him back. She had known how deeply he had loved it. She had known!

She had known how deeply . . . but not, apparently, how completely.

And now, at the final parting, she could not escape, was haunted by, the thought of her mother lying there through the length of eternity, alone again.

She would honor his wishes, for she remembered how special wild-ness had been to him. She remembered also the words he had spoken to her not so very long before, on the mountain. "Live your own life, Andy, and let me live mine." She would do her best to think understandingly of his passage, and try as best she could to comprehend. Someday, somehow, she would even try to find the means to forgive him. But she would not abet it. At the moment of his exodus, it was her mother she would attend.

Now, nestled among the muted hills to her left, the small green pas-ture, the little white clapboard house — the charitable old mulberry tree that had housed the guineas each evening and held the tire she had swung in when she was six — appeared in their proper place between the dusky meander of Cloverlick Creek to the west and the stone stanchions of the moldering old homeplace, by the corner of the hay field to the east, that had slept away the better part of two centuries beneath a blanket of Vir-ginia creeper. With them came the memories, flooding back in eccentric arrangement. She could see in her mind's eye the tiny path that led from the back door of the house, down by the garden, to the spring hidden in the laurel at the base of Tattersall Mountain, where the salamanders resided. Remember the excitement of the swallowtails that frequented the lilac bush. The wrens that nested in the worn-out buckets they hung under the southern eaves of the outbuildings. Could still smell on chilled air the pungent beckoning of hams curing in the smokehouse and the waft of wood smoke from the kitchen stove before they had gotten electricity. The essence of nutmeg, and cinnamon, and peppermint, at Christmastime. Remember how, on rainy days, she loved to gather each new crop of setter pups into the hay shed, and frolic with them in the loose straw that had collected on the floor, and climb the stack of bales as if it were a mountain, while the pups clamored "no fair" at the foot of it, and mobbed her with wet tongues and little sharp teeth when she ventured down.

And always, on a cold morning in winter, when she could see the rime of white ice gathered on the windowpanes against the darkness of pre-dawn, how she would huddle close to the stove in her nightgown with her legs pulled up into her arms and revel in the cozy warmth of the little kitchen, and the sound of her mother humming softly — the gentle rustle of her clothing — as she stirred about the kitchen over breakfast. And watch her father — thrill at the strength and excitement of him — as he arranged the trappings of the day's hunt.

This day, of all others, she thought of the affection between them at those times, in the softness of a new morning. The tenderness of their chatter. The devotion in the kiss they shared as they lingered at the open door, and he readied to leave.

It was at once familiar and foreign, the whole of it now, felt the same and yet strangely, vacantly different. For it was no longer there, really, none of it. All that was left was diminished even more by the mute gray light of dawn, and broken memories. Under the old car shed where once the old International had stabled, there was a Suburban, another vehicle, a small car, parked to the side behind it. Something — a tractor shed, and a new woodpile — occurred off the side of the house where the kennels had been. In the front yard, by the lamppost, the third in the succession of old wooden wheelbarrows that had been the showplace for her mother's summer flowers was gone. Missing most profoundly was the feeling of belonging that makes a house a home.

She had debated about coming this way. Had thought not to. But, at the last, could not resist.

They were in the rearview mirror now, receding. The house, the mountain. Only in reminiscence would she ever retrieve them again.

She turned south onto the old Hillsboro Highway. It was a glorious morning. The underhills were yet purple with shadow, the long, cresting ridges gilded with molten gold, the sleepy pink and azure pastels of the dawning sky awakening alertly yellow-blue. It would be scarcely moments now, and she waited for it with childlike anticipation, and wished not to look away. Though a thin layer of frost was building on the windshield. She turned to the dash, flipped on the defroster, then the wipers. A minute or so afterward, when she could look back again, it was there — almost seizing her breath — the great burning crown of the sun. Climbing slowly into the clean autumn sky above the summit of the Sugartree, it grew and grew. Until it had escaped the constraints of the peak, spilling long nurturing fingers of soft yellow light across the foothills, appliquéing a mellow golden patina onto a pastoral canvas of scattered farmsteads and rolling hay fields, and the winter's worth of round bales gathered and curing about the tawny hillsides. To the east, between the near yellow ridges and hazy blue ripple of the far horizon, she could see a long, wandering ribbon of silver mist, billowing above what must be the Greenbrier. Westwardly, the sunlight was touching the lower slopes of the Bearwallows, setting to blaze the blood and honey colors of the maple and poplar, and fringing the gentle adjoining farmlands, where she had hunted quail with her father when she was nothing but a child and there were still a few small coveys nestled in these old hills. Everywhere she looked, the hand of God was upon an ancient and restless land.

It was too beautiful for her to bear, and she felt the tears grow in her eyes, and spill to her cheeks, and drop to her lap. She let them fall and did not wipe them away.

Almost mindlessly, she braked and turned onto Shandy Road. This had been an early trading path of the Tuscarora, her father had told her long ago. There, behind the church, along the stream, they had found shards of a native existence, once even some colored glass beads and the broken bowl of a trade pipe. He had first kissed her mother there, he had confided, before she was a product of their union. And it was there, now, that her mother lay buried, alone.

How could he do it? That he might think of it, yes, she could understand. Even the resounding dilemma of it, she could empathize. But in the end, when time was waning and he still had the presence to weigh the measure of their life together, how could he elect again to leave her?

The grade of the road banked sharply, then rose abruptly and the Cherokee climbed, and ahead on the hilltop she could see the little white steepled church. It, too, was bathed with sunlight, and about the bright whitewashed walls the glow in the tall, narrow windowpanes reflected so brilliantly that it seemed to emanate from within.

She allowed the gravity of the slope to repress the inertia of the Jeep as it reached the height of the grade, swinging onto the path that encircled the church. Pulling around back, she stopped, switched off the ignition, and sat for a time absorbing the grace of the little green prominence and the quaint country chapel. At long last, she was here, as her heart had willed her to be. Behind the little vestibule of woods lay the small burial ground and the grave site marked ELIZABETH CHANDLER WILLOW.

She stepped out of the car, snugged her scarf about her throat, made her way quietly down the tiny dirt path through the thin woodland to the base of McKever's Mountain. There the woods parted and opened to the little cemetery. How very beautiful it was, encompassed by a small gentle knoll that rose and fell before the mountain. She stood now at its threshold; around her the countryside dropped astoundingly away into the overpowering sprawl and wrap of the Brenadine Valley and, beyond the valley, ascended as breathtakingly through the endless procession of heaving ridges that stepped distantly to the horizon. And the whole of it was adorned with the multicolored cloak of autumn. Birds were singing and the dew sparkled like scattered diamonds on the grass, and she could feel the wonder of it all building within her throat.

Swallowing it away, she lapsed to the aura of the little cemetery itself. It was burnished with sunshine and embraced by the prim little picket fence, and about it the headstones stood in a simple symmetry. Some were old and silvered, and listing, nothing more than ancient fieldstones, their crudely fashioned messages to eternity already pitted to ambiguity; others were blue-green with moss and chalked by lichen; some had weathered to the shade of a precious memory, and a few, still, stood as starkly gray and fresh as a recent mourning. Sprinkled about the undulating ground at their feet were the bloodred leaves of a maple tree.

She made her way reverently through them, to the foot of the grand old tree itself. It still wore most of its leaves and the sun had caught and courted the color in them until they blushed brilliantly crimson, and it seemed that everything about her glowed with the warmth of their color. Occasionally a single red leaf sifted softly down, and then another, to gather on her mother's grave.

Andrea Willow felt the tears growing in her eyes and knelt by the gentle ground that lay beneath the marker, running her fingers softly over the letters that formed the words on the stone. It had been twelve years now since her passing. Not one day of her life, in that time, had been truly complete. Not one. No one of them ever could be again. They had been very close.

She was happy. There were days when the sum of special moments led to sheer bliss. And always, before they ended, maybe in the last minutes before sleep, other moments when the truth of the loneliness brought to reckoning the essential piece of her well-being that was forever gone.

Now her glistening eyes questioned the center of the stone. Yes. It had been done, as she had requested. At least there would be that.

She'd never forgive him, she thought. Not for this. Yet she had loved him, loved him so.

Her legs were cramping. She had to stand. She laid the single Cherish rose she had brought on the ground below her mother's name, among the maple leaves, said a small prayer, and urged herself up.

"As long as I'm alive, Mama," she spoke softly, "you'll never be alone."

She stood there for several minutes longer, lost in a bittersweet mix of memories, both pleasant and painful, and through them all came not only soft thoughts of her mother, but unavoidably, gentle reflections of her father.

Somewhere now, high on the step, she supposed, his life's journey was nearing its end also. Apart from them, as so often had been his way. And yet, try as she might, she could not brush aside the pang of his absence.

She dropped her gaze to the grave again, softly said good-bye, started to leave. Yet something held her. It was the voice of her mother. A gentle recollection, from years past, when with the ache of her disappointment at Ben Willow's departure upon some wishful occasion, her mother had cried. And Andrea had seen the tears, and her anger had risen, and she had spoken harshly of her father.

Her mother had been dismayed by the bitterness of her words, dabbed the tears quickly dry, pulled her close, and looked into her eyes.

"It's a small thing, Andrea," she had said, "just a water spot on a crystal cup."

Andrea lifted her eyes, looked across the spectacle of the valley, remembering that she had not been appeased, and had said still other things, unjust things, that had questioned the validity of her father's devotion to her mother.

"I could have married a lot of men, Andrea," her mother had asserted, "I had them at my door. Most of 'em would have waited on me hand and foot, and just generally got in the way. Your father was different. That careless wildness, the uncompromising passion for life and living. There's something very thrilling about that to a woman," Libby Willow had said.

"And very lonesome," she had countered.

"Oh, I knew I could never completely possess him," her mother had admitted. "But listen to me, child. Regardless of all the sass-shay otherwise, there's a timeless excitement with a thing you can never quite possess. It keeps life fresh. Because you never quit trying."

"Isn't it awfully painful," she had argued.

"Sometimes," her mother had confided after a moment of thought, smiling. "And so was having you. But look what I would have missed.

"We have loved, Andy," her mother had vowed finally, "with a passion few people ever manage."

The years had come full circle, and here they were again, and again she was questioning his devotion. How he could bring himself to abandon his wife. And once more her mother was telling her that love, as life, is made of mystery.

"Live your own life, Andy" — the words kept coming back — "let me live mine."

And now her eyes fell again to the grave, and the rose, and to the earth beneath the name BENJAMIN FRANKLIN WILLOW where there was no presence — would never be. A brier grew there, a single brier. She had noticed it the several months before, on the day of the memorial service, and had remembered. Had been amazed, and had left it undisturbed. It had flourished during the summer and had surrendered its height to bow in an arc over Libby Willow's grave.

From the moment she first saw it, even as she was struggling to comprehend the final wishes of her father, she had accepted what she must do.

There had been a song, an old Scottish ballad — "Barb'ry Allen," her mother's favorite. She would sing it softly from the porch rocker in the evenings, or hum the melody again and again in the kitchen as she worked. And of its several verses, there was the one in particular that symbolized their union as no other ever could.

Beneath and between their names, the words had been cut freshly into the stone:

And on her grave, there grew a rose,
on his, there grew a brier,
and they climbed and twined in a lover's knot,
And the rose grew . . . round . . . the brier.

As the tears rolled down her cheek, she tried to form the verse on her lips, but could not. She could only hum it slowly and sweetly, as it was meant to be, rolling out the last three words into a lingering refrain.

A few miles away a spanking-new, loaded-to-the gills, twenty-eight-foot Winnebago Brave also hummed earnestly, winding its way steadily northward on Route 19 from the small West Virginia burg of Buckeye, destination Peacham, Vermont. Behind the controls, a restless old storekeeper cackled like a triumphant rooster, tapped his left toes in time to the bluegrass breakdown climbing out of the stereo, and locked the cruise to a fearless fifty-five. Curious to custom, he was living the edge.

Across the plush, padded console, his wife reposed in the opulent splendor of the passenger cabin, reading a paperback, and fashioning a happy tune. Had you listened, above the whir of the engine, you could have placed the song as the "Tennessee Waltz." And could you have known her secretly, you might even have surmised the discretion of her involvement the evening before.

Clyde and Nettie Wood were living a dream, a dream that had arced across fifty-one years — push and pull, plod and plot, hash and hope — and had now, finally, plopped down ground-zero into stark reality.

Clyde reached up and grabbed a long blast from the air horn.

His wife jerked her head up from the book and looked about in alarm.

He scrinched up his face, and threw her a what-the-hell look.

"What say, 'Ettie?"

"Yes, well," she supposed brightly.

"The Sugarbush Inn," Clyde mused, "sounds kinda racy, huh, 'Etts."

"You've got a one-track mind these days, old man," she chided.

"Narrow gauge, maybe, but the train still runs," he replied.

She shook her head.

"Do you think it'll really be as we hope?" she asked. "It's waited so very long."

"Close enough," he assured her.

They talked of it a while longer, the arrangements ahead. His focus returned to driving, hers to her book.

Clyde looked out the window, glanced at his watch. All about him, as far as he could see, stretched the grand billowing splendor of the Appalachian highlands, the timeless majesty of the mountains.

In the large side-view mirrors, from the crest of an overlook, he studied the great network of interlocking ridges behind them — the hills of home. Despite his happiness, he could not throw aside a twinge of melancholy.

Ten minutes later he looked again at his watch.

Nine-thirty.

A slight tremor arose within his chest.

Josh and Jenny would be on the step now . . . maybe the top . . .

From a vantage ninety feet above the soaring, uppermost ridge of the Seven Step, among the bare, jagged limbs at the pinnacle of the silver-gray hulk of an ancient red spruce, the keen eye of the red-tailed hawk caught the tiny sketch of motion on the slope far below. Shifting its perch, the regal bird stretched its neck, cocking its head to increase its advantage, its freshly preened breast plumage gleaming under the glint of the sun. A moment later its sharp eyes found movement again. A momentary blur of contrasting color and form beneath the canopy of the trees. And then a second, more reliable, and closer, a trace of white flashing right and left. Approaching.

The great bird shifted upon its limb again, watching. The larger object below was more visible now, something big, and noisy. Its sensitive ears could easily detect the clatter of the leaves. Instinct and practice told it only one creature proceeded so ineptly, even when it attempted otherwise. The nearer intrusion was identifiable now, a dog, still crisscrossing the hill. The hawk could see it, flit-and-flat, in the intervals between the trees, at the fringes of the green thickets.

Growing wary, the redtail ruffled its plumage, let it drop again, shook its wings vigorously. In another minute or so the dog crossed beneath the massive dead spruce. The bird watched it by, refocusing its attention to the human presence climbing directly behind the dog. Less than a hundred yards away now. A moment more it sat, and then would wait no longer. The big bird squatted, stooped, spread its great wings, and glided away down the ridge. Screaming its shrill hunting cry upon the wind.

Josh Chadfield, fifteen years of age come Tuesday, topped the crest of the great ridge and paused under the spire of the old spruce, craning his neck upward toward the towering height of it, where only moments before the hawk had sat. It was just one more miracle of the mountain, and he lapsed in awe of it, his breath still heaving from the exertion and excitement of the ascent.

This was the day and his burden was growing. He felt for the object in the pocket of his game vest, reassuring himself for the dozenth time it was still there.

He had been twice upon the Step in the last three weeks, his father dropping him off each time at the ranger post on the second bench, where they were met by Casey Boyette, who kindly drove him the rest of the way, to the fifth step of the mountain, depositing him by a huge and blackened old chestnut log. It was there the old man had always parked, Casey told him. From the beginning, when he and his dad had made known their purpose, and Clyde Wood had called to explain in addition, Casey and the other rangers had been eager to attend his mission, clearing without hesitation his authorization upon the mountain, and facilitating his progress in any small way they could. To a man, they had known and admired Ben Willow.

A couple of them had even volunteered to accompany him up the mountain, but he had quickly refused. He would see this through. He alone.

Consenting to a radio, he carried it in the game bag of his vest. But barring life or death, he would never use it. These old mountains were home. He might be but fifteen, but he had been born and bred in these hills, was forever at ease in their keep. He harbored no fear of them. Had wandered them with his dad since he was six, alone with a rifle or a rod since he was ten. They were his friends. He had a compass but he used the sun. He carried his dinner, but he knew how to find his own. Had been alone out there, in the night, had felt the apprehension, but never the dread.

It was true he had not faced any challenge so formidable as the Step. He had lain awake many nights thinking about it, the many harrowing stories of the violent old mountain. But he would find the way. Whatever it required, he would do.

For Josh Chadfield had been raised charitably. If a man did you a good deed, you did him another, and a bit more. Clyde Wood and Ben Willow had done him a great deed, and he took its resolution seriously. It was the same reason his father stood proudly aside. A boy came to manhood quickly in these West Virginia hills. Long before and early on Therman Chadfield had taught his young son the highland paradigm of responsibility, and now it was time. The lesson had met the task.

Josh had prepared for it diligently. The old chestnut log at the fifth bench had become his benchmark, and each time he and Jenny had started there, watching Casey Boyette away and climbing higher and higher each trip, hunting as they went.

And each time he found no dread at all, only a deepening affinity, unlike any he had ever felt. For the very wildness of the mountain, the daunting roughness of it, the humbling, endless beauty of it. When, upon each occasion, he had reached home, his only thoughts were of a return.

Now he could hardly wait, one time to the next, relishing the excitement of the climb, the rush of exhilaration the closer he approached a summit. The incomparable feeling of life on high, the soaring of his spirit above the towns and the valleys below, the welding of his soul to the wilderness. The grand soaring independence wedded to the satisfying strength of self-reliance. The glorious trilogy of a dog, a gun, and a bird.

From the first trip, he could tell the setter had been there before. For she quickly caught the strike and rhythm of the slopes, the folds and buckles of the hollows, and he had little more to do than follow. At the brink of the sixth bench, he had killed his third grouse over her, a grand old cock that did its best to steal out the bottom of a laurel thicket. But he had watched carefully as Jenny had corrected, once, then twice, and had rushed ahead to place himself where the terrain suggested the bird would exit, and wonder of wonders, it had. It was airborne of a sudden, almost noiselessly. The little Superposed had jumped up in a trance and he had felt it trace past the flight of the bird, and abruptly go off, and somehow the bird had instantly lost its purchase on the air and tumbled to the ground. And a couple of minutes later Jenny was nudging the lovely russet splendor of it into his hand. And he had her around the ruff of the neck and they were down on the ground, the both of them, wallowing in reciprocal bliss, the bird drawn up between them.

Jenny was the first real dream of his life that had erupted to reality, and never again would one unfold more completely. He cherished her already, almost as deeply as he did his own mother and father, in some ways more. For they shared together the only thing that made them whole — the woods, the hills, the red-orange-golden days of autumn, a gun, and the evergreen mystery of the grouse.

The second trip they had taken a brace, a proud old cock, a clean little hen. He was learning. Jenny was showing him the way. In the past three months, he had read every pointing dog book he could find in the Randolph County Library, pored through every wingshooting magazine he could get his hands on. It had helped some. But in the end, it was like the old man had said.

"Just go with her. Watch. Don't get in the way. She'll show you what you need to know."

Now he lived, one time to the next, for her points — the lofty, statuesque quiver of the points — the spine-tingling hesitation at the heart of the hunt, when the bell ran silent, when he clamored toward the chance of it and found her there, pledged incredibly to style and instinct. Or even more wonderfully, when he was fortunate enough to share the privilege of the find itself, and see her stricken perfectly and instantly immobile by the moment of the scent. And the spine-chilling seconds that followed, while his mind fought for a method of approach and his heart thumped against his chest, when the tension was so tight that with the very next step he knew the world would explode. Best of all, it did! And there was left just the will of the gun, somehow bound with his, that fastened someway into the arc of the bird, and occasionally brought the wonder of the russet feathers so perfectly to rest upon the October leaves.

Already this morning they had taken a bird. Jenny had stood at the gentle bend of a hillside, at the sketchy fringes of an old orchard. Her head was thrown high and she was winding the bird from some ways back, had roaded in, stitching and weaving, until she was comfortable with its location. His heart had blocked his breath with the sheer beauty of it, and his lungs were heaving as he had approached. The setter was forward on her toes as he moved past her, leaning intensely against the scent, and it was all he could do to make his feet work. And the bird had held, within a thick copse of brier, until he had almost stepped on it. It roared up just beneath his feet, climbing fast and straightaway up the slope, and he had caught up with it on the second shot, tumbling it among the red leaves and green grass of the incline.

There had been a second bird. He had heard it up, higher on the hill, had dropped to his knees trying to catch it as it rose above the cover, but could not. And anyhow, his second barrel was spent, and Jenny was placing the sufficient loveliness of the first one softly into his lap.

Before the morning was done, there might be another.

Josh shifted his gun to his left hand, reached out, laid his right on the mammoth trunk of the old spruce. He could feel the surge of energy from the hard, coarse texture of the weathered, sun-kilned wood. Even in death, the huge old tree had tremendous authority. He could feel it running through him, the immensity of it, its overshadowing presence. Its equality with the wilderness.

He looked up again, to its pinnacle, embracing the thrill of it.

School the past week had dithered like a mopey Monday; the night before had seemed a deep sleepless eternity. But finally they were back. High and away. Back with the hunt, back among the birds, back within the irrepressible clutch of this grand, wild place. And not in any of the times before had it been so totally overwhelming.

The broad, blue ridges rolled on in every direction under the crystal sky. For the first time in his young life Josh grasped the meaning of infinity, time without end, distance without measure. It washed over him like a wave of absolution, and he could feel his spirit rushing to greet it, rejoicing with the clamor of emancipation.

He could see it all, it seemed, the vast, wandering height of the Monongahela, from the craggy spine of the Beaver Lick through the restless, rolling highlands of the Bear Pens to the gentle Breathed Hills of the Dolly Sods. It was high here. October was falling away. All around him, the great ridges were balding. There were a few sprinkles of color yet, droplets of orange and yellow and red strewn sparsely against the graying pate of the summits, like the spatter from a careless brush. But the days had shortened, and the nights had chilled, tripping the latchstring to November. Now the hues of autumn trickled in vibrant, spackling rivulets down the face of the slopes, around and through the bottle green veins of the evergreens, falling and gathering warmly about the shoulders of the underhills much as the drape and loft of one of his mother's vivid highland shawls.

Josh searched beneath the long blue ridges to the southwest, studied the wrinkles between them, straining to pick from the distant haze the rough approximation of home. Which of the many small headlands must be the Beech Pen, and where their tiny farm must lay. It all seemed so small.

They had not been this high before, and the boy realized at once that he stood now on the storied seventh bench of the mountain. Actually somewhat above it, at the very zenith of the rugged old monolith, for he remembered that Casey Boyette had told him the first day that the seventh bench did not entirely gird the mountain; it lay in a crescent about three sides of it. They had climbed up the opposite face. Below, falling to where the bench must be, he could see a deep, deep hollow.

Josh looked across the magnificence of Appalachia again. He had found here far more than he could realize. Deep inside, deeper than the welling of his consciousness, his heart was whispering to his soul . . . *never go back, stay here always, nothing below can ever be the same.*

This was the place, he thought suddenly, Mr. Wood had told him about. This was the place Ben Willow had loved most.

This was the place, and this was the day, and this was the time.

He could better understand now. He was but a boy, humble and small against the run of life and time. He lacked the perspective of the years, the measures of value and emotion that would come only with the passing decades, could not firmly grasp the precepts of death and eternity. But there were a few things he could empathize, even now. Already he loved his dog, the birds, and the mountain. From the clarity of this high hill, un-cluttered with the nearsightedness of the convention below, he could eas-ily believe, as his father had supposed, "that a man could have lived so completely in a place, he would wish no less than completely to give him-self back to it."

He felt for the object in the pocket of his game vest once again. It was still in place. In its very presence there was an oddness, a connection to another and stranger world. It was slightly unsettling, up here high and alone, and he would not allow himself to dwell on it, for he must see this thing done.

Jenny was returning now, to check on him, back from somewhere far ahead on the stretch of the long high ridge. He could hear the play of the bell, the beat of her paws upon the dry leaves. Heard both stop, as she lis-tened for him.

He could feel the tension mounting in his chest, the quiver of anxiety. With her return, the moment would be at hand.

"Here, Jenny."

She was in quickly, asking of his delay. She worried over him. The boy sat the little gun aside, gathered the thick ruff on either side of her neck, rolled it playfully.

"Hey, Jenn," he said.

She placed her nose close to his and looked him adoringly in the eyes. She was learning to love this boy, perhaps, one day, almost as much as she had loved the old man. He had returned to her no less than — her life.

Cause to trust again.

He was a little late getting up sometimes. Sometimes she had to wait a bit, and correct more than once to sustain a proper rapport with a bird. Often he was tentative on the flush — not slow, just bird-scared. She could sense it. When she was young, she could never have stood the pressure, would have helped. But she was long since practiced in patience, waiting for the old man.

She pushed through his arms, nosed the bird in the game bag.

"Still there," the boy declared.

"Find us another," he suggested.

The little setter was happy, got down and wallowed heartily in the leaves. Climbed up and shook herself. Looked at the boy anxiously, then away into the deep hollow, and back again.

For a moment he held her eyes with his own, acknowledging, but asking her indulgence.

The apprehension at his chest had grown to a queasy flutter. The moment had come. Something else was welling within him also, a thing he could not understand, so flooding him with emotion that his eyes welled. Some day later he would feel it again, and know then that it had to do with honor, and respect, and a grand, old circle.

He reached down and picked up his gun. The fire in the setter's eyes flamed and she bounced around him, whining impatiently, wanting to be off. The boy took a step toward her and she dug away.

"Whoa, Jenny!" Josh countered firmly.

The command hit the unsuspecting setter like the end of a check cord. It had been a long time. She skidded to a halt, spilling charismatically onto her toes, swelling slowly to a flawless, finished pose. Momentarily, upon the thin fold of skin at the make of her hindquarters, between leg and brisket, the effort of anticipation grew to a nervous quiver. In the split of an instant, one word had awakened the spirit of a warrior and conditioned every sinew within her. It might have been Kilkenny . . . Marienville . . . Dubois. The ingot at the core of her desire blazed with the intensity gifted to one dog of a hundred.

The boy was astounded. It was the first time he had used the word; he had only been told by Mr. Wood of its essential effect. Never had he expected this. It was exactly as if she was on point, so imposing he was almost afraid to approach.

Quietly, in awe, he moved to her. She turned her head slightly to him, stiffly back. Kneeling on one knee, trembling now himself, he reached inside the game bag of his vest, his hand closing on the cool round form of the table shaker, then the band of the leather collar to which it was attached. Gently he pulled it from his vest.

The old man had delivered it to him the night before. His instructions had been minimal. Whoa her, gently buckle on the collar.

He laid the gun aside again, was down on both knees now. Very carefully, he removed the two rubber bands that secured the turn of waxed paper around the barrel of the shaker. As he did, tiny bits of gray ash sifted into his palm. He stared at them for a moment, tried to comprehend and resolve that these were the flesh and bone remnants of a man. Unsure of what to do, he turned his hand to the ground. Some of the ash fell to the leaves; a bit remained. Finally, he wiped his hand gently across the front of his vest.

"Whoa, Jenny," he spoke softly, needlessly, again.

Cautiously, with both hands, he unbuckled the collar, lifted it to the setter's neck, closing and fastening it in place.

After a moment of being sure, he stood again, retrieving his gun.

He could feel the elevated rhythm of his breathing, the rise of his apprehension toward the climactic moment, the nervous beating of his heart.

Of one thing, the old man had been explicit. "Hit the whistle. Hit it hard!"

Josh fingered the whistle at the end of the ancient black lanyard, studied the faint old tooth marks for a moment, then raised it to his lips. Pulling hard against the bellows of his lungs, he packed his cheeks, and blew it just as loudly and shrilly as he could.

Not since the earliest days of her field trial training had Jenny Willow been thumped so soundly with the whistle. In the instant that followed, every fiber of her body contracted into an electrified rage of power that bunched the pistons of her haunches into steel springs and threw them violently free again in an earth-grabbing explosion of momentum. Only the clenching claws of her rear toes held the ground, as her forequarters and torso were jerked fiercely skyward. In the split second that followed, the whole of her body was airborne. The next time her hind feet hit the ground, she was scrambling for speed with every ounce of her faculty, and the bits of debris from her departure spattered waist high against the boy's vest. It was fifty yards to the break of the hollow. When she hit its brink, she was flying!

Josh stood transfixed, astounded at what he had unleashed. He could hear the urgent peal of the little bell, from deep within the hollow, fading away. He forced his feet forward, slowly at first, still straining to hear, but now there was nothing, and he started to run, throwing himself into the hollow.

Jenny was sewing one slashing cast into another now, racing the hollow, whipping starboard up the ridge. Digging, reaching, searching, catapulted by the insatiable furies that drive all great dogs.

Somewhere ahead, there is a bird. Somewhere ahead, in the secret of the cover, on the spoor of the wind, there is a bird. Ahead . . . the warm smiting scent of a bird . . . I will find it, somewhere ahead!

Josh was sliding, skipping, stumbling—down the slope of the long dark hollow—trying desperately to hang on to his gun, hoping frantically to maintain contact with the driving setter. He grabbed a stout limb, checked his momentum, halting abruptly . . . pumping . . . listening. There, the faint, in-and-out tinkle of the bell, two hundred yards left on the next hillside. He strained for it again, heard it once; Jenny was crossing again, below. He raced on, another hundred yards, stopped on the side of the hollow he had heard the bell. Then caught a flash of her, working the skirts of a laurel thicket halfway up the opposite ridge. She stopped, only briefly, to check back for him, maintaining a connection he couldn't— at the extremes. He pushed on, deeper into the hollow. The golden poplars were giving way to feathery green spruce. A small stream rose ahead, from the rocks, beading down the hollow. He followed it, rushing on.

He heard the bell again, ahead this time, breaking back to the right, quartering away once more to the shoulder of the next ridge. Jenny was soaring.

Josh stuttered on, halting—listening—running again. Following the little crystal stream, fighting the cover. The spruce was dense now, big green wispy fronds that shelved the stream. He heard the bell once more, lost it, then had it again, off to the right. His legs were growing leaden, his lungs burning with the searing abrasion of his breathing.

Almost abruptly ahead, the thick veil of spruce parted and he ran suddenly into the opening of a small green meadow, grown to saplings almost completely now, but a meadow yet. A meadow through which the chuckling little stream continued, a meadow that from the remnants of a few gray and ancient apple trees had once harbored an old homeplace, a meadow that had once been very beautiful. The ridges had mellowed around it, and he could see at the end of it that the ground gentled into a extensive plateau, over which the little ribbon of water poured. And the boy knew at once that he had found the seventh bench of the mountain.

He heard the bell again now, distinctly for a time, far to the left, stitching the hill. He ran again toward it, fighting aside the stemy overgrowth of the meadow.

He stopped again, could hear it clearly now, still above and left. And then it stopped — abruptly — dead still! For a few anxious moments longer, he listened . . . then hurried toward the silence.

The setter waited grandly on the hillside, above the cap of the meadow, her flanks heaving, her nostrils pulsating. Arrested by the scent of the bird. And for every step she had traveled in its quest, a tiny trace of ash had fallen.

Ashes to ashes, dust to dust, wish and will.

Ben Willow was back on the Mountain.